OF KERRY B. COLLISON'S OTHER BEST-SELLING NOVELS, REVIEWERS WROTE:

"If the international community had heeded Kerry's writings, it is possible that the present drama (in Indonesia) could have been better understood and dealt with." – Defense and Foreign Affairs Strategic Policy Journal, Washington.

"...it has reawakened a passion for discussion of what really did happen in the heady days that shaped modern Indonesia." – Lavonee Chea, Men's Review, Malaysia

"...inspired by his long experience...intriguing plot and vivid descriptions." – Sydney Morning Herald

"Vignettes will fascinate historians." –The Age

"Collison puts the Indonesian experience into perspective." – Sydney Telegraph

"Collison's knowledge of the region is unmistakeable." –The Cairns Post

"Authentically experienced and geographically recalled..." –The Canberra Times

'Kerry Collison demonstrates a keen observation of the forces which motivate the military and corporate elite.' – The West Australian

'...certainly a powerful thriller.' – Australian Book Review

'...written about Osama bin Laden and the Muslim militant/ terrorist presence in Indonesia three years before events of September 11th.' – Tracy Boyce, Men's Review, Malaysia.

Published by: Sid Harta Publishers
P.O. Box 1042
Hartwell Victoria Australia 3124
email: author@sidharta.com.au
Phone: +61 3 9650 9920
Fax: +61 3 9545 1742

First Published: 1 October, 2005
Copyright © 2005   Kerry B. Collison
Text: Kerry B. Collison
Cover design
& Typesetting: Chameleon Print Design
Printed by:

National Library of Australia Cataloguing in Publication (CiP):

Collison, Kerry B.
        Crescent moon rising.

        ISBN 1 921030 39 9.

        I. Title.

        A823.3

CRESCENT MOON RISING

© Kerry B. Collison

KERRY B. COLLISON

"Crescent Moon Rising" is partly a work of fiction, influenced by indisputable historical fact, tempered with not-so-imaginary characters created to enhance the story's delivery.

South East Asia

Mindanao

Philippines

Moro Liberation Front

Abu Sayaff bases

CELEBES SEA

• Menado

• Poso
• Tentena

Seram
Ambon

West Papua

Papua - New Guinea

Ombai-Wetar Straits

Timor

Darwin

Australia

PROLOGUE

DJAKARTA
31st March 1981
0325 hours

*G*rimfaced, General Benny Moerdani listened intently for the words he had waited so anxiously to hear.

'It's done,' the Indonesian Special Forces' commander reported.

'Casualties?'

'The pilot and one of our anti-terrorist team,' the officer's voice carried down the secure line from the Indonesian Military Attaché's offices in Bangkok.

'And Si Anu?' General Moerdani remained tense; he had personally briefed the Special Forces' officer. "Si Anu" referred to their undercover agent in the terrorist squad.

'He was killed fleeing the aircraft,' came the sombre reply, the commander's words signaling the success of Moerdani's covert operation, planned and executed to discredit the Komando Jihad, (Holy War Command) Islamic radical group.

'You've done well,' Moerdani offered, satisfied that the government agent would not come back to haunt him. 'Quarantine the team then get them back to Jakarta immediately.'

* * * *

Moerdani sat alone in his office smoking a Cuban Rey Del Mundo

1

Choix Supreme relishing in the success of the covert operation. The Garuda Indonesian Airlines DC-9 aircraft "Woyla", designated Flight 206, had been 'hijacked' by five members of the Komando Jihad when en route from Jakarta to Palembang and flown to Bangkok. Moerdani had spoken directly to the Thai armed forces chief and was granted authority to mount the rescue mission on Thai soil. Had this support not been forthcoming, the intelligence czar would have diverted the aircraft to a more receptive destination. Moerdani, Indonesia's Army Intelligence Chief and President Suharto's right-hand-man's ostensible purpose with this exercise was to demonstrate his troops' level of anti-terrorist skill and save passenger lives – his real goal, to destroy militant Islamic factions that threatened to destabilize the New Order.

The General blew a perfect coil of smoke through the stale office air, smiling at the irony of the situation. A decade before, with Indonesia experiencing an increase in radicalized Islam the Komando Jihad had been set up as a front organization by his predecessor, General Ali Moertopo with the aim of discrediting Islamic political groups perceived as a threat to the Suharto regime. Through the intelligence agency, BAKIN, Moertopo had recruited radicals from jails to work with the army, these extremists then forging the very network of militant Muslims that challenged the government of the day. The unintentional consequences of Ali Moertopo's Komando Jihad operation resulted in renewed and forged bonds amongst Islamic radicals across the archipelago.

Alarmed that the armed forces had lost control with the Komando Jihad metamorphosing into a number of even more dangerous organizations, General Moerdani was charged with the responsibility of destroying this product of the Indonesian armed forces' own creation. Government agents penetrated the pesantren, boarding school, Pondok Ngruki in Central Java. The founder, Abu Bakar Bashir was arrested

– his incarceration a precursor to a much wider operation to curtail the rise of anti-government sentiment.

The seeds had been sown – the dangerous stratagem of establishing unauthorized armed covert organizations to protect the Indonesian military's vested interests from the very people they were charged to protect, the genesis of the terror group, the Jemaah Islamiyah and what would become, the Laskar Jihad.

Satisfied that public outcry over the Garuda hijacking would provide a groundswell of local middle-class and international support for the government's imminent crackdown against outspoken clerics, General Benny Moerdani retired for the night – unaware that the American president, Ronald Reagan had just been shot, the assassination attempt displacing the Garuda 'hijack' from front pages, worldwide.

* * * *

BOOK ONE

CHAPTER ONE

JANUARY 1995
Caucasian Mountains – Georgia – Pankisi Gorge

Russian raiders were perilously close; Rusteli Uziyeva could hear them grunt and curse in determined pursuit; the Chechnyan guerrilla thankful that they were not hunting their quarry with dogs. Desperately weary he shifted the weight of the RPK-74 Kalashnikov strapped to his back and forged ahead. 'Pick up the pace – we're running out of light!' The enemy commander's voice carried through the forest, Rusteli quickening his step reminded that the Russians were not taking prisoners. In his haste he slipped then tumbled forward savagely cracking his head against the ground.

Suddenly the air ruptured with Russian automatic fire when soldiers randomly sprayed the heavily wooded slope in an attempt to flush him from hiding. Disorientated, the Chechnyan guerrilla rose groggily on uncertain feet only to trip over the spreading roots of a towering Beech – his body sliding uncontrollably down an icy ridge into a snow-filled hollow where he smashed against a half-buried metal container, incongruous in these surrounds. Dazed, Rusteli remained deathly still, his heart pumping wildly when the soldiers approached to within a few metres of where he lay – moments later washed with relief when their commander growled, 'Signal the men to regroup, we'll never find the dung-eating bastard now.'

The Chechnyan decided to remain in hiding until confident that the Russians had truly abandoned their search – his attention turning to the partially uncovered metal object. Curiosity aroused, he scraped ice away only to discover that there were two similar containers which, he concluded, had long been discarded and were therefore of no value – and, unable to lift the one-meter-long, four hundred kilo apparatus, he soon lost interest. With darkness rapidly descending over the mountainous Caucasian region he braced against the collapsing temperatures, and retraced his steps down the mountain to a hamlet on the flat, green valley floor.

He was forty kilometres south of the Chechnya-Georgia border.

The following morning Rusteli was already seriously ill with severe skin burns and internal organ damage. The Chechnyan was bundled together with some seventy other wounded guerrillas and taken to Amman for treatment in Jordan where sympathy and support for the Muslim rebels remained strong. Rusteli's condition rapidly deteriorated – he was destined to die. Before his death, the doctors were able to determine he had been exposed to some form of radiation and mentioned this unusual development to Omar Khattab, a key leader of the Chechen resistance, during one of the Arab's morale-boosting visits to the hospital. Omar questioned the dying Chechnyan who, until then, had not associated his illness with the discovery of the abandoned metal containers.

Within days of Omar Khattab's interrogation Rusteli Uziyeva died from his fatal dose of radiation, unaware that he had stumbled across Soviet-made RTGs, the radio thermal generators discarded some years before with the collapse of the Soviet

Union. The RTG's core, a flashlight-size capsule of strontium 90 had been encased in a thick protective layer of lead to absorb radiation.

Upon his return to the Pankisi Gorge, Khattab wasted little time in conducting a sweep of the forest area, sacrificing yet more of his followers in recovering the intact RTG unit, the real damage incurred when they too were exposed to the generator with the cracked shielding.

INDONESIA – JAKARTA

Gregory Young pounded the desk with enthusiasm, his lungs exploding as he shouted 'Yes!' – the senior staff holding options at P.T. Young & Budiono also pumped when the company's opening price leaped twenty percent in the first minutes of trading. Young, the senior shareholder and CEO watched the television monitor, hands clasped excitedly across his swelling chest, mentally calculating that his net worth had reached thirty million dollars. 'See if you can get Pak Agus on the line,' Young instructed his personal assistant, 'then get me Andy Graham.' He glanced up at the clock, back to the monitor, the words spilling sweetly off his lips, 'go baby, go!' the stock climbing another five points as he watched, the American near mesmerized by his construction company's debut on the Jakarta Stock Exchange.

The intoxicating financial mood in Jakarta was such that, seemingly, everything touched by those in the know, could only turn to gold, but only if one accepted that Midas was, in fact, a poor and distant relative of the Presidential Palace – and that the supreme finger belonged to the First Family. Obligatory tithes had to be paid – that was accepted – to do business in the resource rich archipelago which boasted more than two hundred million inhabitants came at a price – both for Indonesians and foreigners.

Over the past ten years the capital, Jakarta had become skyline alley, the fierce competition between the country's *nouveau riche* in constructing complexes incorporating shopping malls, office and apartment towers, stripping nearby mountains of material and driving the banking fraternity into an investment frenzy never before experienced in the multi-faceted society. Indonesian billionaires stoked the real estate markets in Europe, the United States and Australia acquiring hotel chains, rural land tracts and other investment properties – the once neglected Chinese, the nation's new czars. Jakarta's profile had lifted, the enormous growing tide of middle class wealth generated by galloping consumer demand, foreign investment and an 'it-will-never-end' mentality creating one of the most vibrant economies in Asia – disguising the avarice and greed which would, within two short years, bring the corruption-dependent, fragile economy to its knees.

'Mr. Graham is on line four,' Young's personal assistant announced from the open doorway. 'I have Pak Agus Sumarsono's secretary on hold, she said Pak Agus will meet you at the YPO luncheon.' Greg Young nodded, pausing before punching the button connecting him to Andy Graham.

The Jakarta chapter of the Young Presidents' Organization luncheon had momentarily slipped his mind. 'Tell her I'll catch up with Pak Agus there…' then, 'Hi Andy, got you on the speaker.' Young bounced around the desk unable to contain his excitement. 'Been watching the figures?'

A deep resonant drawl filled the room. 'Yep, the stock's doing much better than we thought.'

Young's eyes remained glued to the monitor. 'Seems to be stabilizing somewhat now?'

'Early profit takers,' the American advised. 'Could start to climb again in the afternoon session.'

Reminded of the midday appointment Young asked, 'Want me to swing by and pick you up on the way to lunch?'

'Mightn't be such a bad idea. Traffic's starting to snarl though. You might want to leave a little earlier.'

Young agreed. 'Fine. I'll be there around twelve.' He paused, his face serious. 'And Andy,' looking down at the speaker phone, 'thanks for a great job, my friend.'

Andrew Graham chuckled. 'Glad to be of service Greg. Besides, I took a substantial placement when the prospectus was issued – might even come out at the end of the day with enough change to upgrade the apartment.'

It was Greg Young's turn to smile as they disconnected. Graham's idea of change would run into the millions. The American had been building his own Asian-based empire for more than a decade, his group now a leader in public relations and the advertising industry.

Both men were members of the prestigious YPO, an organization founded in the USA by Ray Hickok and twenty others in 1950 with the simple concept of becoming better company presidents by learning from each other. The Young Presidents' Organization had grown into a global network of seven thousand young business leaders of the exclusive peer network spread across more than seventy nations. The power of the collective membership was such that world leaders including US presidents, royalty and even revolutionaries such as Fidel Castro, shared their time at private events offering their perspectives. Membership was zealously vetted, the criteria stringent for those who wished to join this elite club requiring that the applicant's age not exceed forty-four (members retired in their forty-ninth year); that their company's assets be in excess of US$ 10,000,000 with a staff of no less than fifty, and a gross minimum payroll of $1,000,000. Finally, the applicant's company needed an annual turnover of $160,000,000 if it was a financial institution to qualify for consideration, this figure dropping to a mere $8,000,000 for service and manufacturing corporations. The YPO produced an annual directory of its members, the reference tool containing members' names, family detail and private contact information. As for the Jakarta chapter, this read like a Who's Who in Indonesia and included a select number of expatriates who had managed to achieve success in this most competitive market.

Greg Young continued his vigil, watching the monitor, observing his company's stock ease even more before settling at a most respectful level just before noon. Then, during the short but agonizingly slow drive to Andrew Graham's office the stock rallied strongly, the company's CEO still grinning smugly when Agus Sumarsono, the Bimaton Corporation chairman interrupted his presentation during the luncheon, to acknowledge the debut of Young's company earlier that day.

*   *   *   *

Having extolled the virtues of doing business in Indonesia, Agus Sumarsono returned to his seat, his typically banal presentation attracting eager response as Agus represented one of the most influential conglomerates to emerge and survive, under the New Order regime. The Bimaton chairman cast a fleeting glance across the room satisfied that he had adequately acquitted himself, his eyes resting ever so briefly on the foreigner, Greg Young whose joint venture construction company had floated earlier in the day. At that moment the British expatriate happened to lock eyes, Agus immediately turning his head elsewhere, unguarded by the moment. Unbeknown to Young, Bimaton had taken a substantial stake in the public float through a number of nominees, Agus' position now of sufficient import he would be able to influence the construction company's direction.

Content with life and with every reason to feel so, Agus Sumarsono's family holdings exceeded two billion dollars. Although the company flagship was predominantly a property investment group, other assets Bimaton had acquired in less than thirty years of trading included shipping and warehousing, control of a major, turnkey infrastructure construction group and a string of joint ventures with other local entrepreneurs; some, attending the luncheon because that was expected of them.

An only child, Agus understood at an early age that he was heir to substantial wealth and power, his education at tertiary institutions in both the United States and Germany providing the grounding necessary for his future development. Agus had succeeded his ailing father as CEO. In five years he had taken Bimaton to even greater heights and, although cautioned by his father against an over commitment in the property sector, he plunged the company into projects converting vast tracks of land into satellite suburbs, his name now synonymous with the Indonesian boom.

With the luncheon program at an end Agus Sumarsono searched the room for Andrew Graham, raucous laughter pinpointing the American amongst others standing at the private bar. Agus did not consume alcohol although occasionally he carried a glass of fine red wine around just for show.

'Golfing tomorrow?' Graham had spotted Agus approaching.

'Yes, in fact I'm playing with the President's son.' Agus enjoyed the effect the statement had on the others.

'Have to keep the wheels greased,' someone suggested.

Agus raised an eyebrow. 'Yes, and aren't *you* the one to know!'

The light-hearted banter continued until Agus moved Andrew Graham aside. 'You did a great job on that float.'

'Just let me in on the ground floor if ever you decide to take Bimaton public.' Graham was outwardly pleased with the compliment but astute enough to know that Agus's hand had been in play when Greg Young's shares had commenced selling earlier in the day.

'Bimaton will never go public,' Agus responded, in no way offended. 'But there is something I wish to discuss with you, in private.'

'After the weekend?' Graham offered, his interest pricked by the suggestion.

'Yes. Let's make it Monday. We'll go out to the islands on my boat.' Agus paused, conspiratorially. 'Away from over-eager ears.'

*   *   *   *

Upon Agus' departure Andrew Graham rejoined the others and participated in the post-luncheon proceedings with typical panache, his anecdotes befitting the experienced raconteur. Greg Young remained shaking congratulatory hands, Andrew opting to withdraw from the proceedings now evolving into a celebratory event for Young's successful float. He left the hotel by taxi directing the driver to an address in South Jakarta, a private residence he maintained in an apartment tower, concealed from the scrutiny of business associates and close friends.

Captured by Jakarta's afternoon traffic congestion Andrew Graham remained introspective, mentally flipping the pages of his past, reflecting on his own successful enterprise – and the irony of how his achievements had created the perfect cover for another of his country's clandestine activities in S. E. Asia.

Andrew had served in the US Naval Reserve as an intelligence officer until the early 1980s subsequent to which, armed with a postsecondary degree in public relations, he joined the Department of State as a public affairs specialist. The following year Andrew attended the Defense Language Institute achieving reasonable fluency in both the Malay and Indonesian languages. Eager to travel Andrew abandoned his plans to remain in Washington pursuing a career in government, electing instead, to establish his own PR firm in Asia. When word of his intentions reached Langley he was approached – and became a willing recruit, seduced by the offer of financial support and a constant flow of government contracts. Six months later he had opened an office in Singapore, the first of a network which would service clients throughout the ASEAN region, the surprising speed of his success providing access to boardrooms regionally. The following year Andrew acquired a flourishing advertising entity and immediately amalgamated his interests. The powerful base created, provided significant cash flow for the relatively young entrepreneur, and a steady stream of commercial and political information to his demanding masters, in Virginia.

Now faced with his fortieth birthday Andrew was becoming increasingly disaffected with Langley's forever encroachments upon his personal life and, although he quietly enjoyed the subterfuge, he was constantly reminded of the penalty of discovery. Subversion carried the death penalty in this country.

Increasingly, these thoughts had led him to consider his options, the thought of liquidating his local assets frequently revisited his mind.

Quietly attracted to the idea of resettlement, or even retirement, he was considering testing the waters for potential investors who might provide him with an acceptable exit strategy. Whether he would leave Asia altogether was a question he would address when appropriate, the temptation to remain diminishing with opportunities being created by a revitalized Europe.

The normally dispassionate American closed his eyes and nestled with anticipation into the coarse canvas of his ride and, swept with images of the imminent rendezvous, squandered this moment of reflection as the former beauty queen-cum-actress danced tantalizingly across his mind.

* * * *

Angelina Panjaitan examined her image in the mirror. The pulchritudinous starlet tilted her head from one side to the other, gently dabbing her neck with *L'Air Du Temps*, the flowery, sandalwood fragrance lingering in the air-conditioned room. A hand brushed an out-of-place strand of hair into position and, satisfied that she was as ready as she would ever be, Angelina sat quietly in narcissistic repose, pondering her future with the wealthy American.

Introduced at a society wedding several months before, Angelina knew she had lucked out when, on the first date, Andrew Graham presented her with the most exquisite Versace bracelet. The following day when she had the gift valued Angelina became determined to do whatever it would take to maintain her latest beau's interest. She accepted Andrew's conditions concerning their relationship and became his mistress, willingly surrendering her body upon demand, accommodating his sexual preferences whenever they rendezvoused to play. Andrew had insisted that their assignations remain their secret; Angelina was forbidden from calling either his office or residence but was to remain at his beck and call. Resolute, she withdrew from her very public circle of friends hoping this would demonstrate the sincerity of her commitment, even when weeks often passed without word from Andrew – these periods of frustrating silence in no way improving her volatile temperament, this most severe of her character flaws carefully disguised whenever in her lover's company.

It was only a matter of time before Angelina's trysts came to the attention of a senior recruiter from BAKIN, *Badan Koordinasi Intelijen,* the Indonesian Intelligence Coordinating Body, the country's counterpart to the CIA. BAKIN'S recruitment of models and film stars of both persuasions was common to complement BAKIN's many covert operations designed to penetrate both the diplomatic corps and foreign commercial interests. Amongst its most recent accomplishments was the agency's successful compromise of a Jakarta-based, Australian assistant political attaché whose homosexual relationship with a local Foreign Affairs' officer facilitated access to the foreign mission. The substantial flow of sensitive information provided the Indonesian Government with a greater understanding of how the clandestine Australian Secret Service, ASIS operated, and the identity of its operatives in Indonesia.

When summoned by the agency Angelina's initial reaction had been to decline; photographs showing her naked *flagrante delicto* in a home movie convinced the actress that she should, indeed, do her part for her country. Unfortunately, the American never brought his business affairs to their rendezvous and rarely held any meaningful discussions over the phone. As the first months provided nothing of any real significance Angelina was suspected of holding back, the not-so-veiled threats exacerbating her dilemma. Pressed, she had pointedly inquired into Andrew's business activities and he had rewarded her inquisitiveness with a warning not to pry then left her hanging for more than two weeks. Relieved when he called earlier that day Angelina had hurried to the apartment, anxious to demonstrate to Andrew that she had learned her lesson, accepting that she may be obliged to fabricate information to keep BAKIN off her case.

Angelina sensed the maid's presence and turned.

'*Tuan* is on his way up,' the woman announced before disappearing into her quarters. Angelina rose and swept out into the lounge where she checked the curtains to ensure the fidgety servant had not altered the desired backdrop, then stood pensively, waiting for Andrew Graham to arrive.

When the front door opened she remained poised, with her classic Sumatran face half turned into the filtered sunlight, for maximum effect.

Andrew stepped into the lounge and paused, Angelina's captivating beauty momentarily stealing his breath away.

'Have you missed me?' he asked, extending open arms.

Angelina moved without hesitation. 'Every moment of every day,' she purred, moving into his embrace, the tantalizing effect of her body against his and the exotic, sandalwood fragrance stirring his loins.

'Then we should waste no time,' he whispered, leading Angelina into the bedroom.

Andrew discarded his clothes and rolled onto the bed watching his mistress slowly undress, her rehearsed movements provocatively erotic, his erection growing as she cat-walked naked around the bed on nine centimeter heels and stood at his side. Andrew's eyes drifted following her hand as she caressed firm breasts then trailed down to the mesmeric, minute mound of pubic hair and gently stroked her body. She released her pumps and crawled onto the bed with slow, sensuous, catlike movements. Lowering her head, Angelina cradled Andrew's testicles in one hand and licked softly. Then she inserted her tongue under the foreskin and circled around teasing the end of his uncircumcised penis with the warmth of her mouth.

Andrew's hand gently squeezed her nipples then wandered down to the soft, wet mound. Aroused by the stimulating strokes Angelina raised her head and body, mounting her partner, rocking against the length inside her, pushing down hard as his hands grasped and roughly kneaded her breasts.

'I'm coming,' he cried, hoarsely, pelvic thrusts increasing with climax now ineluctable, Angelina's cry of pleasure driving him to completion as her body was racked with recurring cycles of rhythmic contractions, the euphoric sensation plateauing as both achieved orgasmic spell.

An hour passed. Quietly motionless, pleasantly intoxicated by the exotic woman's sweet, musky fragrance as she lay naked by his side, Andrew Graham admitted, resignedly, that he would most likely persevere with the status quo, continuing to build wealth whilst accommodating Langley – at least, until he was presented with no other alternative but to graze, elsewhere.

* * * *

Mindanao

Philippines

Moro Liberation Front base

Abu Sayaff bases

CELEBES SEA

Menado

Balikpapan

BORNEO

Poso
Tentena

Seram

WEST PAPUA

Ambon

Ujung Pandan

Ombai-Wetar Straits

Bali

Timor

AUSTRALIA

Darwin

(West Papua)

EAST INDONESIA – SULAWESI (POSO)

John (Jack) McBride cried out loudly, his flailing arms entangled in the mosquito net as he struggled to flee the demons from his past – the imagery of a Somali militiaman standing over his body painfully vivid when he was jolted from the recurring nightmare. Outside a cock crowed. McBride lay motionless amidst tangled, sweat-saturated sheets, his nostrils assailed by the pervasive stench of vomit – the missionary silently castigating himself for having fallen off the wagon. Squinting through the gray morning light he fossicked for painkillers in a bedside drawer, fumbled the bottle open then swallowed two tablets, closing his eyes while waiting for the pounding between his temples to subside.

The village stirred. He rose gingerly then slowly attended to his morning ablutions, the former Special Forces soldier shaking his head admonishingly at the crumpled face staring back vacantly from the cracked mirror. His thoughts turned to the letter that had taken six weeks to arrive from Tennessee.

Raised in the Buckle of the Bible Belt by Methodist parents, Jack McBride was exposed to an environment of religious servitude, his attendance at the Vanderbilt University another accommodation of his strict father's wishes that he follow into the clergy. His own preference had been to study medicine however, due to his family's financial situation and his father's intervention Jack had attended the Vanderbilt University Divinity School on a full scholarship. Within that year his father suffered a stroke and passed away, his death bringing with it a sense of release. Jack abandoned his studies and enlisted in the army where he also underwent specialist medical training. He served with the U.S. Rangers for ten years, the career path he had chosen providing the independence and recognition he had so desperately sought from childhood.

During '*Operation Urgent Fury*' in 1983 when a Marxist coup resulted in the overthrow of the Grenada government, U.S. forces were ordered to the Caribbean island to seek the release of some 1,000 American medical students. Jack had been amongst those who had jumped with the 1st Battalion, 75th Ranger Regiment, securing the airstrip at Salines on the southern coast where Cuban paramilitary forces lay in wait – the young McBride earning the Silver Star for gallantry during the subsequent engagement. With the exception of a near miss whilst undergoing helicopter flight training Jack's military career over next ten years had been without incident. Then the United States became embroiled in the Somalia conflict.

He gazed back into the mirror, slowly ran a finger over the hairline scar, evidence of his near-death experience in Mogadishu just eighteen months before in October 1993.

The Rangers were part of the mission '*Operation Restore Hope*' – their task, to hunt down the Somali warlord, Mohamed Farah Aideed. Unbeknown to the Americans, Osama bin Laden's second-in-command, Egyptian-born Mohammed Atef had relocated to Khartoum from where they orchestrated an attack on U.S. forces. When it came, the lightning assault had turned into a prolonged and desperate battle for the U.S. soldiers to escape the hostile city. McBride had received a head wound when the al-Qaeda-trained troops attacked and killed eighteen of his fellow Rangers, leaving ninety wounded.

It was during his convalescence that Jack had succumbed to the bottle, his alcoholism resulting in hospital rehabilitation and, finally, a new career path when he was discharged from the army and returned home to Tennessee. With his mother's support he managed his drinking problem and was soon on the road to a full recovery. It was at this time, while rummaging through his father's papers that he happened across a newsletter which promoted 'vacations with a purpose', encouraging members of his congregation to consider stretching their personal and spiritual horizons by accepting short-term missions with the Church. The following month he volunteered to assist the Church establish a field medical clinic in Tentena, a small town near the northern tip of Lake Poso in Indonesia's Central Sulawesi – and he was now halfway through the two-year commitment.

Jack stared back into the mirror and rubbed a palm against the overnight stubble then commenced shaving – his thoughts returning to the family lawyer's letter advising that his mother had been diagnosed with an inoperative tumor, and pleading that he call. There was no phone connection to his quarters. Jack intended calling from the Church offices on the other side of town and, as it was only 0330 in Tennessee, he sat alone watching the clock anxiously, taunted by the possibility that his mother may have passed away in the weeks it had taken for the letter to arrive. An hour passed – then another, Jack's rekindled thirst drawing him to a bottle of locally produced *arak* that had remained sitting on the shelf unopened these past months, a gift from a grateful patient.

The first shot brought disappointment that he had broken his vow – the second, an air of resignation and surrender to a third. Within the hour he had consumed the entire bottle then collapsed into bed, missing his call.

Naked, Jack stepped into rubber thongs and entered the bathroom, confident that the footwear would protect him from the ever-present hookworm. A huge cockroach of prehistoric proportions took flight in his direction and he ducked, eyeing the creature as it crawled around the moss-stained ceiling out of reach. He dipped a plastic scoop into the concrete water tank then braced, paling cold water over his body until some semblance of his normal self was restored.

* * * *

McBride's assistant, Netty Tangali heard Jack splashing around in the *kamar mandi* and instructed the housemaid to commence cooking his breakfast, hopeful that *Bapak* Jack, the title restfully accorded the missionary, would be in higher spirits than that of the evening before. Netty had seen the postmark, aware that Nashville was his home town. She had waited eagerly for him to read the letter out loud as he had in the past – crushed when he had so brusquely dismissed her and retreated to his room.

Amongst her many attributes Netty Tangali was a trained nurse and fluent in English. When Jack first arrived in Poso it was Netty who had taught him *Bahasa Indonesia* and the essentials regarding local cultures. She had introduced Jack to the Saluopa waterfalls and the Pamona caves, journeyed with him to the Bada Valley where they examined the ancient and mysterious megaliths, and even sailed Lake Poso's enchanting setting together. 'Net', as Jack had come to call her, became his constant companion. Before their first year together as a team, Netty had become deeply attracted to the unsuspecting American.

* * * *

'Selamat pagi, Net,' Jack bade Netty good morning, glanced over at the housemaid then decided to speak English. 'Would you mind looking after the clinic by yourself, today?' he asked.

'Of course,' she responded, surprised, 'are you ill?'

Jack shook his head. 'No, Net. I just need some time to myself.' The housemaid placed a steaming bowl of *bubur* under his nose, Jack staring at the dish before waving the porridge away. 'I'll have something later.' Miffed, the maid raised her eyebrows at Netty.

The nurse noted his casual attire and frowned. 'Are you going out?'

Jack remained evasive. 'I have a few things to sort out. I'll be back before five.'

Concerned eyes followed as he strolled outside and unlocked a bicycle from its rack, then disappeared from view as he peddled across the Pamona Bridge to the Church's operational centre for Central Sulawesi. There he placed a call to his mother through the U.S. operator and, when the phone rang unanswered, he pleaded with the operator and was connected to the family lawyer's home.

'I'm sorry, Jack,' the foreboding words spilled down the line preparing him for the worst, 'your mother passed away more than a month ago.' Then, 'She was buried alongside your father.'

Jack struggled for words. 'Your letter arrived… only yesterday.'

'Don't blame yourself, Jack. There was nothing that you could have done – even if you'd returned in time.'

'I can arrange a flight and be back by the weekend?'

'That's up to you, Jack. There's no need to rush back unless you feel it necessary.'

'Have you attended to her will?' He was aware that his mother had appointed the law firm as executors.

'Yes. The estate is just about finalized. Apart from a number of personal items your mother bequeathed to you, her estate will pass to the Church.'

'I know,' he recalled the discussion, 'there wasn't much to leave.'

'We can store your mother's other personal effects if you wish, pending your return?'

Jack considered the offer. 'Thanks. I'd appreciate that.'

'Is there anything more we can do for you, Jack?' A weary note had crept into the lawyer's voice.

'No. Thanks. I'll write if something comes to mind.'

With the call completed Jack McBride walked his bicycle slowly back down the street to the bridge that connected the two parts of Tentena. There he stood, gazing over the four-hundred-metre-deep lake contemplating the news of his mother's death, pedestrian traffic passing him by, residents occasionally acknowledging the missionary with a knowing smile and a wave. Absent-mindedly, he turned to leave and stepped out onto the road, a Toyota pickup forced to swerve to avoid colliding into him. Jack whispered silent thanks, deciding then to ride up to his favorite site and spend some time alone, to reflect on his loss.

He peddled his way along the high road where Dutch-built bungalows dotted the mountain landscape overlooking the lake, the area surrounded by primary rainforest and lush plantations of coffee and cloves. He passed a farmer leading an *anoa* along the road, Jack steering a wide path around the dwarf buffalo as experience had taught that these animals were unusually aggressive and unpredictable. The indigenous fauna had fascinated the American from the outset. During an outing when Netty Tangali had taken him on a countryside excursion he had been fascinated with the unusual *babiroesa* deerpig, an animal with enormous, upturned corner teeth that pierced the skin as these curled towards the skull. The beast did not have split feet – Jack's interest growing when Netty explained that this odd mammal was considered *halal* by the local Muslims and could therefore be eaten.

Before entering the Church missionary program and accepting the assignment to Sulawesi Jack's appreciation of the delicate socio-religious intricacies of the region were all but nonexistent – the briefings he had attended back in the U.S., initially leaving him frustratingly short in facing the realities of what transpired in the field. He accepted that had it not been for Netty's dedicated and persevering nature, his knowledge of the local culture and language would have remained severely lacking.

Approaching his destination Jack began to tire and walked the bicycle the remaining distance up the slope, where a gigantic stone pillar had been placed to symbolize the Pamona ethnics' succession from East Toraja. Jack often visited the site where local folklore had it that at the top of this hill, heaven and earth were once connected by a rope, the myth, in some way providing him with a philosophical link of his own. He settled down on a grassy patch, head nestled upon knees, taking measure of his life, his decision to work in the field as a missionary and where it might lead.

*　*　*　*

Jack McBride's small but effective operation in the isolated and predominantly Christian township of Tentena was a ninety-minute drive from the district capital of Poso. The people were friendly and receptive to his presence and, apart from Nathan Glaskin, a cantankerous septuagenarian from Idaho who maintained authority over Jack's operation, life passed relatively smoothly in his domain. The fire-and brimstone minister had been ensconced at the regional headquarters for more than two decades, Jack's presence an obvious irritation to the ageing cleric.

Since arriving in the eastern Indonesian province, Jack had learned that medical missions were often considered to be an impediment to the indigenous church programs unless a clear distinction was made between a medical missionary practice and a general practice of medicine overseas. After a number of confrontations Jack accepted that the spiritual aspect of the ministry was to be left entirely to his fellow-American, Nathaniel Glaskin, *'As a missionary,'* Jack was often reminded, *'your purpose here is to raise the health standards of the local people, and meet their medical and surgical needs. I, however, am charged with caring for their spiritual needs, not you. And, as such, you should therefore refrain from referring to yourself as a medical missionary.'*

Jack had worked tirelessly with Netty to establish the now successful clinic which provided medical services not only to Christian, but also to Tentena's Muslim families. He understood that religious harmony prevailed throughout the district due to the wisdom of local authorities whose decision to implement power-sharing had removed the primary cause of most disputes. Strategic positions in district government were arranged informally so that a Christian appointee would be assisted by a Muslim deputy, and vice versa, the compromise bringing an appearance of social unanimity to the province. However, Jack's superior, Nathan Glaskin scoffed at the system, citing the growing influx of Muslims into the region, predicting that there would be a significant shift in the social structure with the many thousands of transmigrants arriving from Java and other over-populated Muslim islands. When Jack raised this most delicate of subjects with Netty, she had confirmed that the Christian hold on such key posts had diminished considerably over the past five years and that there was, indeed, a resurgence of animosity between the two groups.

As he lay contemplating the possibility of future conflict, Jack considered the genesis of the archipelago-wide conundrum.

When Indonesia achieved independence from the Dutch fifty years before, the new leadership successfully resisted calls for Indonesia to become an Islamic state, offering the people pluralism and affirming a diversity of religions which embraced Islam, Christianity, Hinduism and Buddhism. Jack had read that the Republic's founding fathers' wishes were later frustrated by President Suharto who, in an attempt to shore up his presidency courted Islamic radicals, understanding that this alliance would, undoubtedly, lead to an escalation in attacks on Christian communities. These were the seeds of discontent, planted for political gain, destined to rip the nation apart.

Jack lit a *kretek*, the familiar fragrance of the clove cigarette soothing the moment he inhaled, an image of his mother looking down critically, intruding on his thoughts. He visualized her standing there waving a disapproving finger. He looked skywards and smiled. It was time to bid her farewell.

Jack McBride offered a silent prayer to his mother, the people of Tentena and Sulawesi's fourteen million inhabitants. He cast his eyes across the horizon towards the east where the archipelagic province of Maluku accommodated a further two million Indonesian citizens, conscious that the majority were also Christian, their number spread across a thousand small islands covering a vast expanse of ocean. And, in that moment, he experienced the tug of history and vowed to visit the famous Spice Islands which had drawn Indian, Chinese, Arab and European traders to that destination.

EAST INDONESIA –
THE MOLUCCAN ISLANDS (AMBON)

Nuci recognized the modernized melody as one of the traditional Moluccan songs; the foot-tapping reggae beat lifting her
spirits as she went about the household chores. She paused, a
brief moment from childhood triggering images of her mother
singing in church, the memory momentarily distracting her
from the chore at hand.

Born into a Christian Ambonese family, Nuci had been
raised in an environment of want and despair following the
collapse of the Maluku independence movement in 1950, tales
of those events as related by her father, caught in the cobwebs
of her mind. Nuci recalled that both her parents had fought
for the Dutch-inspired autonomous state of 'East Indonesia",
the formation of the *RMS*, the short-lived Republic of South
Moluccas, and participated in the Christian-led revolt against
the Indonesian government.

As a child, Nuci had soon become aware that this close identification with the Dutch had stigmatized her people – branded
as traitors by Jakarta – punished, when the Sukarno-inspired
revolutionaries finally prevailed and the Moluccan Islands were
absorbed into the Republic. She knew that many Ambonese
Christians had either fled or were forcefully deported to the
Netherlands, whilst those who remained behind suffered the
ignominy of being treated as second-class citizens by their new
colonial masters, the Javanese. During her formative years she
became more aware that the Indonesian military had a very
long collective memory, treating most harshly those ethnic
minorities who had 'betrayed' the country during the War of
Independence against the Dutch.

Nuci's family had enjoyed the comforts accorded to civil service employees. She had attended a *Sekolah Menengah Atas*, her studies at the middle high school interrupted when her father was retrenched along with many others – replaced with Muslim workers transported from Java and Madura under the transmigration scheme. As Ambon's lucrative spice trade had diminished dramatically over the past century and, unable to find employment in what was rapidly becoming a Muslim-dominated provincial administration, Nuci's parents had relocated from the capital to Benteng Karang village. Her father had found work teaching at the local school; her mother retreating into a world filled with hymns and prayer. Nuci married early, withdrew into a life smothered by domesticity and reconciled herself to life in Benteng Karang village; her childhood dreams now mists from the past.

'Careful you don't burn my best shirt,' her husband, Lauren's voice jolted Nuci from her brief reverie. Ignoring the interruption, she placed the charcoal-fired iron to one side then placed the white shirt on a homemade wire hanger.

'I'd best get ready,' she murmured lethargically, her eyes dropping to the traditional meat dish she had spent the early hours preparing. 'We can have the *patita* before leaving.'

'Think I'll save my appetite for some more of Grace's *lalampa*,' Lauren said, immediately wishing he could retract the words.

Nuci's face clouded, piqued from the last visit to Grace Matuanakotta's home to finalize wedding plans between the two families. Nuci still smarted from Lauren's overly gracious servings of the steamed rice finger dish that Grace had prepared. Nuci flared, hands on hips, 'It's only migrant street-vendor food…and if you prefer that Minahasa woman's cooking to mine then why not just say so?' She stormed from the kitchen before her husband could defend himself, mumbling as she bustled down the hallway.

Nuci's mercurial mood swing had been triggered more by her husband's wish for their daughter to marry within the *Pela Gandung*, a centuries' old, Moluccan inter-village alliance social-bond structure that was based on an idiom of kinship, than Lauren's penchant for the banana-wrapped delicacy. *Pela* villagers exchanged mutually binding oaths and had been known to drink one another's blood at the conclusion of a pact. Before Javanese migrants had inundated the province, Moluccan Christians and Muslims had lived in relative harmony, the tranquility of interfaith relations protected by the *pela* alliance system. Under pela tradition, a village of one faith was "twinned" with a village of the other, with both charged to defend the others interests in the event of conflict.

Intermarriage between members of *Pela*-tied villages was taboo, Nuci's husband having successfully arranged for an exception arguing that Grace Matuanakotta had migrated into the area from Minahasa in the north, and her son could therefore be considered outside the *Pela* constraints. Although Nuci sympathized with her daughter, accepting that her choices were severely limited due to the increasing number of *pela* villages listed within their fold, Nuci was obstinately against the match – fearful that Grace's contumacious son Johanis, whose rebellious pursuits had placed him directly in the local authorities' sights, was destined for tragedy.

At first, the village elders had been unreceptive to Lauren's pleas on behalf of Lisa, arguing that it was a person's village affiliation that determined with whom a person is *pela*, as reckoned patrilineally. Eventually, because Grace was now widowed and the elders harbored a desire to see the end of her son's presence in their village the elders acquiesced, and the marriage plans moved forward – the meeting between the two families that day scheduled to finalize the wedding arrangements.

* * * *

Johanis Matuanakotta gazed indifferently at his fiancée's family. 'I still want the wedding to be held at the Marantha Church.'

Lisa tensed, her eyes fell from her mother's, dropping subserviently to her lap.

'We cannot afford such luxury,' Nuci argued. 'If you insist, then you will have to meet that expense yourself.'

Johanis smiled insolently. 'My *Coker* friends will contribute.' Then, with a contemptuous look at his in-laws-to-be, 'and we wouldn't want to disappoint the *Cokers*, would we?'

Intimidated by the not-so-masked innuendo, Nuci and Laurens exchanged anxious looks. The *Cokers*, the street name for the delinquent *Ambonese Cowok Kristen*, or Christian Boys, used the Marantha Protestant church as their headquarters. Rumor had it that they were closely associated with other Moluccan gangs in Jakarta where they dominated the shopping centers and gambling dens – and had access to the Palace. 'It's settled then,' Johanis announced with youthful arrogance, the decision now a *fait accompli*. He pushed a plate in Laurens' direction. 'Now, why don't you have some more of my mother's *lalampa?*'

MALAYSIA – KELANTAN

Mohamed Aziz Derashid looked out across the verdant *sawah*, the paddy fields stretching all the way across this northern Malaysian state of Kelantan to the southern Thai border, where towering cumulus clouds stacked the horizon. Sensing that weather conditions would imminently terminate the satellite conversation the Malaysian strained to capture Muhammed Atef's drifting words, Derashid's passive understanding of French exacerbating the problem.

'Hambali's visitor... from the Philippines... should be there... by now.' With the atmospheric interference the al-Qaeda military commander's voice sounded more strained than usual.

'Ramzi?' Mohamed Aziz Derashid was surprised.

'This is an open line,' Atef warned. Aware of foreign intelligence agencies' sophisticated monitoring systems, their conversation was deliberately ambiguous.

'No,' Osama's trusted lieutenant added, 'from... further south.' Derashid guessed that Atef was referring to the young *Abu Sayyaf* leader Abdurajak Janjalani who had recently established dialogue with al-Qaeda via Ramzi Yousef, in Manila.

'Then they're about to make their move?' Derashid was pleased that Atef was keeping him informed.

'Insha Allah,' came the reply.

Derashid replaced the receiver and beckoned to his personal assistant standing courteously out of earshot at the far end of the bungalow's veranda. 'Get the plane ready,' was all Derashid said; his PA disappearing as would a ghost in sunlight to ensure that the crew and aircraft were placed on standby. Alone, Derashid leaned back in the heavily cushioned rattan chair and absorbed the natural beauty of the terraced landscape below, the steep hillside contoured to accommodate never-ending fields of rice, shaped to enable the intricate irrigation system to flow harmoniously. The isolated country retreat was seven hours by car north of Kuala Lumpur's forest-fire-polluted atmosphere and he filled his lungs with country air and lay quietly, thinking, contemplating his relationship with those with whom he shared similar ideologies.

* * * *

Derashid was the son of a wealthy Malay *Datuk*, his father's title having been acquired through substantial donations to the local state government officials. The *Datuk* was a prominent player in developing the Malaysian economy, the entrepreneur's considerable holdings and wealth continuing to swell over the years, the consequence of the successful completion of a string of major infrastructure projects won through closed-door tenders. Bulan Sabit Holdings Sdn Bhd had then branched out into the resources sector, the group's subsidiaries growing exponentially with Malaysia's energy development boom.

An only child, Derashid had enjoyed an upbringing surrounded by wealth and envy, his ethnic heritage as a Malay *bumi putera* or indigene, a point of considerable pride.

Immersed at an early age in the teachings contained in the Koran, Derashid evolved into a devotee of Islam's more fundamentalist leanings, his commitment to the purist interpretations slowly creating an inner conflict and challenges he could not share with his father. Educated in England where he earned degrees in commerce and engineering, the Malaysian established strong personal links with a number of Saudi students. Upon graduation, he departed for Riyadh, already markedly resentful towards the British establishment and its not-so-disguised colonial distaste for those who dared to challenge the social divides. Derashid remained in Saudi Arabia for a year consolidating his relationships with his former fellow students and their families. He journeyed to Mecca on *Haj* – his outlook on life for a man still in his early years maturing immensely during this extended sojourn away from home.

Upon his return to Malaysia, Derashid announced that he was not ready to launch himself into the family's commercial activities; instead, he went in relentless pursuit of others who shared his opposition to the American presence in Saudi Arabia, and the West's growing influence in Asia.

One evening he was invited to attend an *usrah*, a religious discussion held in secret at the Kampung Sungai Manggis village in Banting, Selangor. It was there that Derashid first sighted the Indonesian speaker, Riduan Isamuddin. The meeting had been arranged for members of the *Kumpulan Militan Malaysia*, the Malaysian Militant Association grass roots' supporters of the Indonesian-founded militant group, Islamic Community, *Jemaah Islamiyah*. He had been moved by Riduan when the cleric addressed the meeting chronicling his exploits in Afghanistan, Derashid observing closely as others in attendance were seduced by Riduan's charismatic spell. The following month and much to the consternation of his parents Mohamed Aziz Derashid assumed another identity and disappeared from his homeland. When he returned the following year he was visibly changed, hardened by the time he had spent in Afghanistan, his sentiments now placing him on a road blighted by fanaticism which blurred the true Islamic way.

At the age of thirty and at the request of his ailing father Mohamed Aziz Derashid assumed the role of CEO of the family company, managing assets in excess of two hundred million Ringgit, further enhancing his attraction to the man identified by a select few as '*the Sheikh*', aka Osama bin Laden.

As of that time, only bin Laden and his inner circle were privy to Derashid's double identity, the relationship forged during his odyssey in Afghanistan later nurtured by Atef through frequent communication.

Derashid remained in contemplative mood considering how he might do even more to limit his exposure; his association with the terrorist group delicately concealed by a series of firewalls through his myriad of corporate entities held under his Malaysian flagship company, Bulan Sabit Holdings Sdn Bhd. The Malaysian was in no way involved in any operational aspect connected to al-Qaeda or its many loosely-knit offshoots, although Atef had sought Derashid's advice in establishing the front organizations through which funding for field operations would flow. Amongst these, Konsojaya Sdn Bhd, a corporate entity which the Kuala Lumpur companies' registry would list Hambali and Wali Khan Amin Shad as co-directors and shareholders.

Initially, Derashid had suggested that Atef veto Shad's involvement, citing the United States claim that he had been a principal instigator of the 1993 World Trade Centre bombing in New York. However when Atef reported that Mohammed Jamal Khalifa had insisted the company composition remain as originally contrived, Derashid refrained from further comment, pleased that he was in no way connected to the slow burning fuse.

MALAYSIA – PETALING JAYA

Riduan Isamuddin, better known by his *nom de guerre*, Hambali, sat silently also considering his relationship with Wali Khan Amin Shad and Ramzi Yousef, accepting that they were tied at the hip and would remain so, until death did them so part.

Hambali's given name at birth was Encep Nurjaman, and he was second in a peasant farming family of eleven children that had seen little of the world outside their mountainous

West Java village. A serious student from the outset, Hambali attended the *Al-I'annah* Islamic high school. It was at this time he became drawn to Abu Bakar Bashir, an Indonesian of Yemeni decent whom President Suharto had jailed for attempting to form an Islamic militia called *Komando Jihad*. Upon Bashir's release from prison in 1982 and facing further arrest for subversive activities, Bashir fled to Malaysia and Hambali followed. The pair became inseparable, Abu Bakar Bashir treating the younger man as if he were his own son.

It was during their self-imposed exile that the vision for a Pan-Islamic state was conceived; their dream to incorporate the ASEAN countries into one Islamic community group a concept that would predicate the re-birth of the *Jemaah Islamiyah*.

In 1987 Hambali traveled to Pakistan where he underwent arms training at the Sadar Camp. He was twenty-three years old. After entering Afghanistan as a volunteer *Mujahideen* he joined in the fight against the Soviet Union. There he met Ali Ghufron, a fellow Indonesian. Together, they fell under the influence of Osama bin Laden and, by 1990 when the billionaire Saudi considered Hambali ready for the mission, Hambali was charged with extending the al-Qaeda network into S.E. Asia and Australia, while Ghufron, who had adopted the name Mukhlas, concentrated on developing Indonesian cells.

Upon Hambali's return to Malaysia he secured residency and met a Sabah Chinese national, Noralwizah Lee Abdullah who was attending religious studies at the Luqmanul Hakiem School in Johor. By then Hambali had developed an affinity for wearing a *kopiah* – the white skull cap, bearded face and accompanying glasses providing Osama bin Laden's associate with the image of a religious figure – essential to his self-appointed position as a teacher. Assisted by his wife, Hambali ran religious classes that encouraged discussion relating to rebellion and holy war. With the growth in membership in the newly created *Jemaah Islamiyah*, Hambali's reach across ASEAN then stretched through Malaysia, into Indonesia and the southern areas of Thailand and the Philippines. Next, he planned to forge alliances in Australia.

His Malaysian company, Konsojaya Sdn Bhd, was a front import-export operation that provided financial and material support from Osama bin Laden, to many of the terrorist cells deeply ensconced throughout S. E. Asia. The company also provided funding and operational support to the *Abu Sayyaf* (Father of the Sword) Islamic separatist group through its Manila cell, The Benevolence International Corporation, an entity utilized to disguise their Philippines' operations.

Recently, Hambali had become increasingly dependent on Dr Azahari Husin. The Malaysian university lecturer had joined the *Jemaah Islamiyah* whilst engaged at the *Universiti Teknologi Malaysia* and had trained with Hambali in Afghanistan. He had been instrumental in establishing the first direct links with the *Abu Sayyaf* the year before, preparing the groundwork for al-Qaeda. Azahari, who held a doctorate in engineering from Reading University in the UK, had the necessary credentials to support his expertise as Hambali's chief explosives expert. As for Indonesia, Hambali had agreed to leave most of the network building to his close associate, Ali Ghufron who continued to enjoy the freedom of travel without raising suspicion.

A knock at the door interrupted his deliberations.

'Our guest has just cleared immigration,' his wife Noralwizah reminded from the other side of the door. She would not enter without being invited to do so.

'Have you checked the hall to ensure everything is in order?'

'Yes,' she confirmed, 'and security is already in place.'

'Good. I shall join you in a few minutes,' he said pompously then checked his appearance in the full length mirror attached to his side of the door. Satisfied, Hambali smiled, confident that the evening fund-raising event would be a success.

INDONESIA – JAKARTA

The Javanese twins ignored the fleeting, quizzical looks as they stood talking in the Sukarno-Hatta International airport concourse, the two Indonesian pilots identical in every way but for their uniforms. The Garuda officer smiled at his mirror image, Imam, and indicated the bars on his sibling's shoulder. 'So, now we are of equal rank?'

Imam Suprapto wrapped an arm around his older brother. 'The ranks may be the same but first lieutenant has a better ring to it than first officer,' he bantered.

'Maybe,' Anwar countered, 'but Garuda pays us better than you air force pilots.'

Imam laughed. 'True – and you get to pick and choose from the cabin crew as well.'

'How much time do we have?'

Imam checked his watch. 'I have to get back to Halim by 1300.'

Anwar steered his brother towards a coffee stall. 'How are you handling the Hercs?'

Imam shrugged. 'Surprised we manage to keep them operational. They're old, and spare parts continue to be a major issue.'

'How's that transfer request coming along?'

Imam cast a wistful look at an elegant tourist when she legged her way past and smiled. 'Haven't heard anything yet. If all else fails I'm going to take a shot at transferring to one of the outer squadrons, perhaps even get some time on those Broncos.'

Anwar sympathized with Imam. Neither had achieved their ambition to fly their aircraft of choice. Imam had yearned to fly the F16A fighters but fate had placed him in the cockpit of an ageing C-130 Hercules whilst Anwar was driving Garuda F-28s around the archipelago. His brother's suggestion that he might go down scale and spend some time flying the OV-10s did not come as a surprise.

Raised on the Madiun-Iswahjudi base within site of the grounded 'Badger' Soviet TU-16 bomber tactical strike wing, the Javanese brothers were destined to fly. Their father had piloted these long range bombers until they were grounded by British threats to destroy Jakarta and Surabaya with atomic warheads. As children they had listened, mesmerized, whilst their father had recounted his version of the brinkmanship displayed by the founding President, Sukarno in his quest for domination of the Malay and Singapore states. Even today both the Suprapto men could recall, verbatim, their father's revelations of how the Soviets had armed Indonesia to the hilt with the most sophisticated weaponry during the early *Sixties* which, in turn, emboldened Sukarno into declaring a war of 'Confrontation' against the Commonwealth states of Malaysia and Singapore. When their father had explained that his aircraft could carry 3,000 kilos of nuclear weapons a distance of 8,000 kilometers the youngsters were treated to a regional geography lesson pinpointing the Australian and Asian cities that lay within the TU-16s strike capacity – the twins' vivid recollection of Colonel Suprapto's rendition of how his flying career had ended and the confusion that had ensued, a constant reminder of the capricious world of aviation both had grown to embrace.

Anwar and Imam had often debated how the former President had folded to the British ultimatum and grounded the TU-16 squadron. They had not understood why the country's leadership had permitted the emasculation of their Indonesian Forces and, adding to the military's chagrin, why the Royal Air Force was not prevented from flying missions over Java's airfields. It would be decades before the pair would read Australian and British Cabinet papers released under the Thirty Year Rule revealing how British Vulcan bombers flew from Singapore to Darwin, the RAF crews carrying their deadly cargo low across Indonesian airstrips with bomb bay doors open, the threat significant as the Vulcan's were armed with atomic warheads. Anwar had scoffed at the reports of how ABRI, the Indonesian Armed Forces were then secretly subjected to an Australian-British blockade, the West alarmed when Moscow attempted to ship ballistic missiles to Jakarta. The Suprapto twins elected to believe their father's version of how the failed flow of spare parts had precipitated the squadron's demise, Colonel Suprapto amongst the many Indonesian pilots grounded in the absence of serviceable aircraft.

Imam again checked his wristwatch. 'Have to go.'

'We'll catch up again during *Hari Raya*?' Anwar asked. They had never missed returning home to celebrate the end of the *Ramadan* fasting month and the ensuing celebrations of *Idul Fitri*. Even though fasting would commence within that week neither would comply with the Islamic tradition as the strict restraints placed on their daily lives would impinge on their capacity to execute their flying duties effectively.

'You can count on it,' Imam assured.

'Keep me posted on that transfer,' Anwar insisted.

'Hopefully, I'll have some news regarding the OV-10s,' Imam responded, optimistically. Anwar punched his brother playfully on the shoulder, shook hands then went to join his Garuda crew to prepare for their shuttle flight to Medan, in the oil and gas-rich province of North Sumatra.

An hour passed since Anwar had farewelled Imam. Airborne, he stared out across the haze that covered Sumatra, the product of forest burn-off and the failure of corrupt officials to oversee the implementation of regulatory controls designed to prevent such environmental disasters. He looked out the starboard window across the Malacca Straits, his view impeded by the drifting smoke as far as the eye could see. The Javanese pilot slipped into sombre mood reminded that he might never be selected to crew international flights – the competition so fierce. An impatient sigh passed his lips.

With his mind revisiting what the future might hold Anwar Suprapto remained deep in thought, oblivious to events unfolding across the South China Sea and the machinations of the one solitary figure whose treachery would impact so disastrously on the Suprapto twins' lives.

CHAPTER TWO

THE PHILIPPINES – MANILA
THE DOÑA JOSEFA APARTMENTS

Ramzi Yousef gazed introspectively through a drawn lace curtain from suite 603's only window overlooking the well-lit path the Papal motorcade would take on 15th January – the day John Paul II would die. 'You are coming and we are ready for you,' he whispered, eyes narrowing as he envisaged the assassination scene and the carnage his team would wreak upon this predominantly Catholic nation.

Located in Manila's Malate district not 200 metres from the Embassy of the Vatican City in the Philippines, the Doña Josefa Apartments were perfectly positioned for the al-Qaeda terrorist cell's covert activities. Ramzi Yousef, aka Najy Awaita Haddad and his associates could come and go virtually unnoticed as locals had become accustomed to Middle Easterners residing in the nightclub district, satisfying their fantasies, drinking and whoring far from puritanical, condemnatory eyes. The Baluchistani-born Pakistani, Yousef, had rented the apartment in December as the headquarters for the implementation of *'Operation Bojinka'*, brazenly walking the capital's streets, thumbing his nose at the United States and the two-million-dollar bounty placed on his head for his role in the 1993 World Trade Center bombing.

A diabolical explosives and bomb technician, Yousef had attended college in England where he studied electrical engineering. But it was in the al-Qaeda training camps that he had learned to prepare explosives. Yousef turned to fellow accomplices.

'I want you to listen to the statement I have prepared for public dissemination once the first phase of *Bojinka* has been realized.'

Ahmed Saeed, aka Abdul Hakim Murad ceased what he was doing and glanced over at Wali Khan Amin Shah, the third conspirator in Yousef's terrorist cell, a stocky Afghani who was responsible for the financing of the operation. Shah had successfully established a network amongst bar girls whom he paid to launder funds from their indirect financier in Malaysia.

'We're all ears,' Saeed grinned. He had also been complicit in the World Trade Centre bombing and was on the US intelligence community's watch lists.

Yousef leaned over his Toshiba laptop and tapped the space bar bringing the screen to life. Although the manifesto's words were already deeply ensconced in his mind Yousef elected to read from the computer, the confidence in his voice testament to his commitment to their cause.

'Citizens of the United States and those who support that government will be our future targets for they are responsible for their government's actions and the USA's foreign policy' he declared. 'We will destroy all American nuclear targets and, should that government continue to support Israel, then we will continue to carry out operations inside and outside the United States to include...' A knock brought the room to silence as a maid attempted to unlock the double-bolted door. Yousef raised a finger to his lips and slowly shook his head.

'Mister Haddad, are you there?' the Filipino maid inquired, still challenging the lock as she was not expecting any response. 'May I change the linen today?'

Ahmed Saeed's eyes panicked their way around the room. Bundles of soaked cotton lay scattered around the single-bed bachelor apartment, a pungent odour permeating the scene. Various sized plastic, chemical containers with German and Pakistani stamps of origin lay scattered everywhere, the loops of electrical wiring and dozens of Casio wristwatches all conspicuous signs of the tenants' handicraft, obvious to even an amateur's passing observation. He moved anxiously, throwing soiled sheets over the explosive material, cursing his ill fortune when he inadvertently knocked an opened bottle of Chivas Regal against the bedside lamp sending both crashing to the floor.

'No!' Yousef shouted, immediately regretting the forcefulness of his reply. 'Leave the linen outside. I will change the bedding myself, later.' He waved furiously at the other two men to rectify the situation, shocked when smoke appeared from somewhere under the bed.

'I am sorry to have disturbed you, sir,' the maid apologized, 'my manager Miss Guerrera thought you had gone out.'

Ahmed fell to his knees to determine the seriousness of the accident and how quickly the alcohol-fueled fire was spreading.

'Put it out, now!' Wali Khan Amin Shah hissed, 'before she calls security.'

Outside in the hallway the maid stopped, tilted her head questioningly and sniffed the air, alarmed when smoke appeared from under the door. 'Mister Haddad, Mister Haddad,' the woman yelled, 'there's smoke coming from your room!' Suddenly she was afraid, recalling such fire traps as the Filipinas Hotel when flames engulfed the hotel trapping many of the guests, the huge death toll causing an even greater decline in the deteriorating number of tourist arrivals.

By now Yousef had filled the rubbish bucket with water from the bathroom and flushed the area directly under the bed. To their great relief, the flames died almost instantly, Yousef returning to the bathroom to refill the bucket.

'It's okay,' Ahmed looked up at Amin Shah, 'we have it under control.'

Again the maid called. 'Is there a fire in your room Mister Haddad?' now less concerned when she could see that the smoke had ceased.

'Just a cigarette burning in the waste paper basket.' Yousef assured as he emptied the second load onto the now saturated carpet. The fire appeared to have died. 'There's nothing for you to worry about.' Yousef pulled a hundred pesos from his pocket and unlocked the door, his frame hiding the view inside. 'I will clean up the mess. Here, let me have the fresh linen.' He smiled and passed the tip to the maid who surrendered the bedding, shrugged and went on her way.

Back inside the room Yousef and Ahmed examined the burnt carpet, all present sending a silent prayer that exposure had been avoided.

'I must leave. I agreed to meet with Khalid,' Amin Shah announced. 'We'll meet here again tomorrow, in the afternoon.'

Yousef smiled knowingly at Ahmed. The men accepted that Amin Shah would not be rendezvousing with Khalid Shaikh Mohammed but Arminda Costudio, a Filipino waitress who worked at the Manila Bay Club on Roxas Boulevard. Arminda had captured Shah's attention from the moment he had set eyes upon her.

With Amin safely out of the room Ahmed raised an eyebrow. 'Do you think he knows?'

Yousef snorted. 'That Arminda Costudio is also sleeping with my uncle?' He shook his head. 'Nothing to be gained in his knowing this.'

Ahmed refused to let it go. 'You don't think this Filipino whore could jeopardize the operation?'

Yousef's face clouded at the suggestion. 'Khalid is not one to cross. Leave it be.'

Khalid Shaikh Mohammed, the mastermind of the *Bojinka* operation who had been appointed by Osama bin Laden to command al-Qaeda's worldwide military operations and was number three in the terrorist hierarchy, was currently in residence just across the road. Ironically, Khalid's lavish apartment was juxtaposed to a dwelling occupied by a future Philippines president. Armed with an American education courtesy of the Baptist Chowan College in North Carolina and, later, the North Carolina Agriculture and Technical State University, Khalid had developed a most un-Islamic, Western disposition for go-go bars, karaoke clubs and hard alcohol. Khalid resolutely believed that everyone but him should faithfully observe the rigid tenets of Islam.

Whilst in the Philippines he traveled extensively visiting countries as distant as Brazil, his lavish lifestyle a cover for the Malaysian company he promoted, Konsojaya Sdn Bhd which covertly funded and trained militant Islamic groups such as the *Abu Sayyaf* and MILF in the country's restive, deep south. On occasions, the flamboyant Mohammed would arrange scuba diving excursions with Yousef, these merely a cover for journeys to isolated areas where they would meet with separatist groups to discuss strategies. Both Khalid and Yousef respected the *Abu Sayyaf* whose leaders had acquired their battle experience in the mountains and deserts of Afghanistan; courtesy of the CIA. Khalid and Yousef had listened to the camp-fire portrayals of how many of the eight hundred Filipino Muslim Mujahideen who been recruited, trained and paid by the CIA to fight the U.S. sponsored war in Afghanistan for a few dollars per day, fought against the finest of Russia's forces. Then, with the Soviet withdrawal how these guerrilla-trained Filipinos returned home bringing with them not only military expertise, but a deeply-ingrained appreciation of Islamic fundamentalism – Khalid surprised to learn that many now embraced the ultra-conservative Islamic ideology of *"Wahabi"* which was rapidly spreading across Malaysia, Indonesia and the southern Philippines.

The Malaysia companies' registry would show that Khalid owned half of Konsojaya Sdn Bhd's shares – his partner, Riduan Isamuddin, an Indonesian who lived in exile hiding from the clutches of President Suharto's regime.

Shah and Yousef had already tested their deadly explosives over the previous month. Shah had experimented by placing a bomb under a seat in the Greenbelt Theatre in Manila on 1st December to determine the result of such an explosion should a similar quantity be used under an airline seat. The detonation had left a number of injured. Then, on 11th December Yousef placed a device under his seat, 27F on Philippine Airlines Flight 434 before alighting from a flight into Cebu. This flight was scheduled to continue on to Manila and then Narita in Japan. He had set the timer to detonate hours ahead and, when this did eventuate, the bomb exploded over Minami Daito Island near Okinawa killing a Japanese businessman and injuring ten others. Incredibly, the Boeing 747 landed safely however, Yousef's experiment provided him with sufficient knowledge to develop the secondary phase in *Operation Bojinka*.

Ahmed checked the charred carpet again then rose to his feet and stretched. 'Let's get some fresh air. We can have a quick snack in the lobby.'

Yousef shook his head. 'What, and leave all this?'

'Hang the *Do Not Disturb* sign out. It's late; the maid won't be back. We won't be long. Come on, I'll buy you one of those Irish coffees in the bar around the corner you're always talking about.'

Yousef was adamant. 'Let's not take any risks. We're too close to screw it up now.' But he knew that Ahmed was jittery, spooked by the almost disastrous fire. Yousef closed the Toshiba laptop and placed it carefully in the top dresser drawer removing a bottle of Chivas Regal as he did so. Ahmed's eyes lit up and he smiled. He nodded affirmatively and fetched two tumblers.

An hour passed and, with the soporific effect of half a bottle of alcohol to assist, both men lay comatose, oblivious to the smoldering fire that burned slowly on the underside of the carpet. When fire alarms sent tenants scrambling from their rooms after the sixth floor had burst into flames brigade tenders sped to the scene. Emergency alarms also galvanized members of the nearby Manila Police Station No. 9, located five hundred metres down the street on Quirino Avenue.

With their room filled with suffocating smoke Yousef coughed awake to confused consciousness and stumbled from the shared, single bed.

'Ahmed! Ahmed,' he screamed as flames licked the walls. 'Get up, Ahmed!'

Moments later the men were seen fleeing along the corridor dragging their pants on as they fled.

* * * *

'Just some Arabs playing with firecrackers,' the doorman answered but the watch commander, a senior inspector from the No. 9, was not convinced.

'They let off firecrackers in their room?'

'That's about the gist of it.' The doorman had seen even more ridiculous situations.

'Where are they now?' Suspicions rising the inspector scanned the faces of pedestrians gathered outside on the street.

'Well, they scrambled down the fire stairs into reception and disappeared.' The doorman turned, his face becoming animated as he recognized Ahmed Saeed. 'That's one of them!' he pointed.

'Okay, let's see what he has to say. Bring him over here.'

Albeit risky, Ahmed accepted that he had no choice but to return to the apartment and recover whatever material and evidence may remain before the authorities uncovered the extent of their activities in the Philippines. He had not, however, envisaged being confronted so unexpectedly, his prepared explanation obviously not sufficiently convincing for the watch commander to let him return to apartment 603.

As Ahmed offered his version of events, explaining to the inspector that he was a commercial pilot and had been on his way to the precinct to explain what had happened earlier, the doorman tapped the officer on the shoulder.

'There's the other one,' he indicated Yousef standing outside, unaware that they were staring at Ramzi Yousef, a fugitive from United States for his role in the World Trade Center bombing nigh on two years before.

'Okay,' the inspector's gut feeling was making her nervous, 'grab that one outside and hold him with this man until we check their room.'

Ahmed whirled, managing to escape the clutches of the law as officers stood stunned by the foreigner's audacious move. They gave chase, Ahmed tripped over debris left by a recent typhoon, the police overwhelming the terrorist as he lay stunned.

Yousef took the opportunity to escape slipping away into the night.

Inside 603 the inspector's team discovered two remote-control pipe bombs, street maps of the capital indicating the forthcoming papal motorcade's route, the pontiff's photograph affixed to the bedside mirror along with a crucifix, rosary and Bible. With the recovery of a phone message from a tailor advising that the cassock Ahmed had ordered was ready for a final fitting the inspector knew without doubt, that the fire had delivered assassins into their hands, and prevented the assassination of John Paul II. Although at the commencement of the grueling interrogation conducted with 'extreme prejudice' Ahmed categorically denied such claims, at the conclusion of questioning he declared that there were 'two Satans that al-Qaeda would destroy – these being the Pope and the United States of America.'

*   *   *   *

Results of the white, Toshiba laptop's contents had revealed an even more sinister component of *Operation Bojinka* which, the four recovered diskettes disclosed, was designed not only to assassinate Pope John Paul II during his Holiness' impending visit to Manila, but also a commitment which called for a massive two-phased attack on American interests. This ambitious scheme proposed hijacking a commercial jet to be crashed into the Pentagon and for the placement of explosive devices on eleven aircraft bound for the USA – both operations the blueprint for a grim future.

Details of the militant group's suicide missions were passed to the United States Embassy, the ambitious plan treated with derision when examined by CIA specialists in Langley.

Both Yousef and Khalid Shaikh Mohammed managed to escape to Afghanistan. Information contained on the laptop also revealed that Wali Kahn Amin Shah used an address on Singalong Street as his safe house. He was arrested then mysteriously escaped, fleeing captivity seventy-two hours later to Malaysia from where, along with Hambali he would assist oversee the *Jemaah Islamiyah* spread its tentacles across S.E. Asia and into Australia.

*　　*　　*　　*

CHAPTER THREE

*"The Intelligence and security agencies are subject to the operation
of Australian law unless specifically exempted because of the nature
of their work." Australian Government Legislation.*

Peter Rigby waved the shared-intelligence report. 'How do they expect us to believe that so many nukes simply went missing?' he challenged rhetorically. The United States National Security Agency's document revealed that some thirty 'suitcase sized' nuclear weapons remained unaccounted for within Russia and Chechnya. The analyst crossed his arms and frowned at the damning report listing the former Soviet Union's nuclear armory that included 25,000 nuclear weapons, of which 12,000 were strategic warheads on ICBMs, submarine-launched ballistic missiles and bombers – and an inventory of a further 13,000 warheads for tactical nuclear weapons.

With deteriorating economic conditions and organized crime activities continuing to expand across the former Soviet states, Peter Rigby was convinced that it was inevitable for nuclear weapons to fall into the hands of terrorists. An ONA specialist analyst in nuclear weapons proliferation, Rigby's opinion regarding the veracity of reports suggesting separatist groups operating in S.E. Asia were in the market for highly mobile nuclear weaponry, foremost on the weekly briefing's agenda.

'Just how mobile are these weapons?' the Assistant Director for the S.E. Asian Branch of the ONA asked. The ONA was the government body charged with providing analyses covering international political, strategic and economic developments for the Prime Minister, Cabinet and government departments. ONA was one of the key agencies involved in the setting of intelligence tasking for the spy agency, the Australian Security Intelligence Service (ASIS).

'ADMs,' Rigby commenced then hesitated, his intelligence world pebbled with acronyms. Acknowledging the attendance of a Cabinet member Rigby accepted he would have to be more expansive in his delivery. 'That is, Atomic Demolition Munitions are significantly dangerous due to their mobility. An ADM can be transported and detonated, by a single individual. The result of a one-kiloton detonation could claim anything from 50,000 to 100,000 lives. Physically, the weapon is about the same size as a suitcase, doesn't require launch codes and can be prepared in less than half an hour.' He looked directly at the Secret Service deputy head, Andrew Grey. 'The Chechen rebels could place one under Boris Yeltsin's bed and none would be the wiser.'

Grey accepted the comment with an unnoticeable shrug. Without exception, Western intelligence agencies considered the inept Russian president's drunken guardianship, the premise explaining the disappearance of nuclear stockpiles. ASIS, Australia's most secret operational intelligence agency had reported from its Moscow station, local American agents' concerns of a thriving black market for such transportable weaponry in the former Soviet Republic's satellites. With the Chechen war entering its second year the country's mountainous borders offered a near-fail-safe exit for ADMs to weapons' dealers and fanatical fringe groups.

'The question is whether any of the separatists operating in the Philippines and Indonesia have access or the financial backing and infrastructure to successfully initiate such an attack?' He paused, cast his eyes around casually, then added, 'and our own analysts concur that those specific groups just don't have those resources.'

The ASIS deputy director droned on, Peter Rigby reminded of another report which had passed through his domain days before, the information contained in the US-shared information brief providing credence to intelligence claiming Osama bin Laden had recently visited Chechnya. An informant in Grozny had suggested that the purpose of bin Laden's visit was to consolidate his relationship with a prominent fundamentalist Muslim leader known as 'Hattab', a one-eyed Jordanian who had fought alongside bin Laden in Afghanistan before moving on to Chechnya.

'We might wish to consider Afghanistan as a potential depot?' Rigby suggested when Grey fell quiet. 'There's tracking evidence of movement from Malaysia that confirms a growing number of Islamic dissidents from Indonesia and the Philippines are attending military training camps in Pakistan and Afghanistan.'

'There is no intelligence to support that these are not more than simple dissidents escaping local regimes,' Andrew Grey waved a hand in the air, unaware of the fallout from the Doña Josefa Apartments' fire. The ASIS head of station in Manila had read the newspaper reports of the fire and, not privy to the report filed by the Philippine authorities with the Americans, summarily dismissed the incident. 'There has been no significant growth in militant Islamic movements in S.E. Asia that should be of concern to Australia.' The deputy director's face stretched into a knowing smile. He supported the pro-Jakarta lobby within the Defence Intelligence Organization. The DIO and ONA both came under considerable pressure from the Defence Department to produce pro-Indonesian assessments and tone down criticism of the Republic. 'Suharto and the other Asian heads of state have seen to that.'

With the exception of Peter Rigby, concurring heads nodded in assent as the first briefing for the New Year came to a close.

MALAYSIA – KUALA LUMPUR

Hambali's face remained crumpled with concern. The Indonesian cleric ceased pacing and turned to the al-Qaeda envoy. 'In view of these developments we must consider closing the company down.'

Wali Khan Amin Shah cast fiery eyes over *The Manila Times'* ominous headlines that signaled disaster for their cause. *'Operation Bojinka's'* potential to wreak havoc on the United States and its allies had been eclipsed by a Philippines crackdown bringing swift retribution to those involved.

Hambali could not contain his anger and disappointment, moving around the sparsely furnished surroundings, shaking his head in exasperation. 'We were so close…' He left the words hanging, flopped into a cushioned rattan chair and looked questioningly at his associate, seeking his concurrence to close down the umbrella company, Konsojaya Sdn Bhd which they had established only the year before.

Collectively, Konsojaya and its counterpart conspirators had developed the plan codenamed *'Operation Bojinka'*. Now, with the operation revealed and the Manila cells disrupted, Hambali knew that it would be only a matter of time before the international intelligent agencies would come after him, threatening disclosure of the newly created *Jemaah Islamiyah* cells in the region.

* * * *

The events of the past twenty-four hours had all but destroyed what would have been Hambali, Ramli Yousef and Osama's finest hour – the *Bojinka* plan.

Hambali considered the consequences of abandoning the corporate structure Konsojaya Sdn Bhd and whether existing linkages might lead the authorities to their door. He frowned. It was crucial that the trail end there, in Kuala Lumpur, and that no connection be established between the front organization and their covert activities elsewhere.

Although the *Bojinka* disaster in Manila represented a major setback in their timetable, Hambali remained determined that, one way or another, his network would be restored and continue to grow until delivering the near half a billion ASEAN population to the *Jemaah Islamiyah* at whatever the cost. He turned to Wali Khan Amin Shah. 'We must close the company down – then wait. It would not be wise for you to come here again. Until we know the extent of the investigation we should not communicate. I will wait for when you send word from the 'Sheikh'. Do not lose heart – time will repair what has been done. The Americans and their allies will pay – that, I promise as surely as Allah is the one and only true God.'

JAKARTA – THE THOUSAND ISLANDS

Andrew Graham followed Agus Sumarsono forward of the engine room on the lower deck into the owner's stateroom, quietly envious of the entrepreneur's twenty-five metre, Italian built Tecnomarine 80 series executive launch.

'This is Anita,' Agus smiled at a bikini-clad beauty adorning one of the two settees watching a video. The stunning Menadonese girl smiled coyly and waved. 'She brought a few friends,' Agus added, 'you'll find them down the passageway.'

Andrew mentally inventoried the cabin's layout and lavish furnishings... 'You might have difficulty convincing me to leave when we return.'

'The ship's only recently been refurbished,' Agus proudly explained, 'there are five guest cabins, all with private en suite facilities and spa.' He was enjoying the moment. 'Even the four-man-crew's quarters below deck are air-conditioned.'

Andrew had met the expatriate captain when he boarded. 'How often to you get to take it out?' he asked.

Agus shrugged. 'Whenever the opportunity arises,' he answered, not evasively. 'Come, let's go up top and enjoy the view.'

Andrew filled his lungs with sea air, leaned forward and gripped the railing, scanning the line of scattered islands reaching out to the horizon. He had frequented the tropical setting on many an occasion over the years, mooring his ageing Grand Banks cruiser off one of the virgin, uninhabited islands and spending the weekend diving amongst the multicolored corals. As powerful twin-engine 750 horsepower GM diesels drove them deeper into the one-hundred-and-twenty-island cluster away from the more popular day-tripper resorts of Pulau

Ayer and Bidadari, Andrew relaxed, the pressures of Jakarta life dissipating as the capital's skyscrapers slipped from view. He turned to his host. 'Where are we headed?'

Agus grinned. 'Did I tell you I bought a place out past Pulau Putri?'

Andrew raised a brow; surprised that Agus had managed to keep such an acquisition secret from the city's plethora of rumor mongers. 'When?'

'Oh, about a year ago.' Andrew could see that Agus was pleased with this revelation and raised his glass in salute.

'Good for you, Agus,' he leaned over and patted the other man's shoulder, 'and thank you for sharing this confidence.'

'I had a team of Singaporeans come down with materials and build the bungalow so I could keep the venture under wraps,' he confided.

Andrew could not resist laughing. 'My God, Agus, I am impressed!'

They arrived at their destination mid morning, Andrew whistling his approval at the idyllic setting, the bungalow's architecture blending with the island's natural ambience. Surrounded by the whitest sand, the atoll remained covered with lush vegetation, coconut palms swaying lazily under an azure sky, the pristine waters so clear he could see fish swimming idly, metres below the surface. Agus issued instructions for the mini-harem to remain on board. Andrew was then given a tour of the five-hectare island, the pair strolling along a narrow path that meandered through the flora to a clearing on the far side of the atoll.

Andrew lifted his face to the sun. 'Must remember to make more time for moments like this.'

Agus removed his sandals and waded into the shallow water

then turned, shielding his eyes from the brilliant sun. The men could no longer hear the monotonous thumping emanating from the resort's generator, both now conscious of the island's rhythm as wind ruffled palms, and an occasional surge from the wake of some passing freighter spilled imperceptibly onto the sand.

'One thing that has always frustrated me in being Javanese,' Agus opened, Andrew recognizing that he was about to learn the purpose of their outing. '…and that is having to be so damn circuitous when attempting to establish a point.'

Andrew smiled inwardly. Agus was already heading down that tortuous, cultural path.

'Before I continue, I need your assurance that if we don't arrive at an agreement today, whatever transpires remains here.'

Andrew considered the request before responding. He felt reasonably confident that whatever Agus had in mind there would be sufficient enticement to ensure the response he expected. 'You have that undertaking.'

'Good,' Agus waded from the lukewarm sea and strolled the few metres to a copse of coconut palms seeking refuge from the sun. He looked up into the trees and, satisfied that none of the fruit would strike in the event one fell, sat on his haunches in relaxed Indonesian pose. Andrew remained standing soaking up the rays; his curiosity building as to the direction their conversation might lead.

Agus picked up a shell and threw it aimlessly. 'Would you mind telling me what stock you hold in Greg Young's new float?'

Andrew was caught by surprise. 'My group was not registered as a buyer,' he parried.

Agus crowed. 'My sources inform me that you are holding around ten percent.'

'And you want to know because…?'

The Javanese entrepreneur looked the American directly in the eye. 'I am holding you to your promise. What is said here stays here…okay?'

Andrew nodded. 'Okay.'

'I want to buy your stock,' he hesitated, before adding, 'off market.'

'Why don't you just go out into the market and buy another ten percent?'

'Come on, Andy,' Agus opened his hands as if helpless, 'once the word spread that I was interested the stock would rocket.'

Andrew accepted this comment. 'Then why didn't you take a position when the prospectus first went out?'

'I did,' Agus resisted a sneer, 'but the nominees' allocations were cut back due to the flood of applications. Greg Young had instructed the brokers to widen the spread of shareholders.'

'Why the interest in Young & Budiono, won't it directly compete with Bimaton?'

Agus dropped his chin and looked over his sunglasses at Andrew. 'There is a closed tender coming up. There will be only two contenders.'

Andrew understood immediately. 'Must be some tender…' he left his thoughts hanging.

'I'd be receptive to paying you a premium of, say, twenty percent on today's closing price.'

Andrew calculated quickly. The company's market cap had reached around $100,000,000. He held ten percent and should he accept Agus' offer, he would increase his profit by a further $2,000,000. 'I'm interested. If I were to proceed I'd need to have the deal done offshore as I wouldn't be interested in paying tax penalties.'

'The deal would be done off market. We can arrange the transfer to avoid the taxes.'

'When do you want my decision?' He had already decided to accept the offer.

Agus forced a smile. 'Today.'

Andrew was amused. 'How about we have lunch, gather up the ladies and you give me a couple of hours on the way back to sleep on it?'

It was Agus' turn to laugh. 'And by sleeping on it you mean...?'

The men shook hands.

The following week control of Greg Young's publicly listed company passed covertly to Agus Sumarsono. Before the end of that year Young & Budiono would become the darling of the Jakarta Stock Exchange, having secured two major infrastructure projects by what virtually amounted to government proclamation.

TENGGULUN VILLAGE – EAST JAVA

Sweat trickled into Amrozi's eyes as he worked away in the galvanized-iron-roofed shed repairing his Yamaha motorcycle. A loud speaker crackled shattering the air, the mid-morning call summoning the faithful to prayer. Immediately, he downed tools, wiped grease from his hands and ventured outside the makeshift workshop where he observed other villagers gravitating towards the muezzin's call. A dilapidated bus sounded its horn as it competed with an ox-drawn cart for dominance over the broken macadam. He wrinkled, then picked his nose, inspected the three-centimeter fingernail on his left hand then flicked the hardened mucus into the dust.

A group of girls caught his attention as they walked purposely in the direction of the mosque, seemingly oblivious to the lung-parching heat. He frowned disapprovingly, observing that although their heads were covered with the traditional, white *hijab* scarf, the girls all wore jeans. There had been a time, he admitted silently, when he would have coaxed them inside and tempted them to play. But now, having learned to act in a manner more appropriate to his family's standing in the local community, Amrozi's delinquent ways had changed, the pious metamorphosis directly attributed to the reverence he held for his older brother, Ali Ghufron.

Amrozi's sleepy and dirt-poor village of two thousand inhabitants lay in a dry and unkind environment, a few miles inland from the East Java coast, and two hundred kilometres from Surabaya. As a child it had been Ghufron who had watched over Amrozi, singling him out from amidst the other twelve siblings and providing him with special attention, taking Amrozi's side whenever the younger brother's frequent escapades earned their father, Nur Hasyim's ire. When three of his brothers, Ghufron, Imron and Jabir left Tenggulun and traveled to Ngruki in Central Java to study at a school established by Abu Bakar Bashir, Amrosi's delinquency had flared.

The greater majority of Tenggulun followed the more moderate thirty-five-million-strong Nahdlatul Ulama, an Indonesian Muslim society founded with the purpose of maintaining and developing, *Ahlussunnah-wal-Jamaah* Islamic teachings. Their members represented the majority of Indonesian Muslim traditionalists who, for generations, blended the rich cultural mix of local beliefs with Islamic doctrine, and tended to be bearably tolerant of other religions. There were very few Christians in this poverty-stricken community – the remaining inhabitants, followers of a strict form of Muslim fundamentalism known as *Wahhabi* which emphasized ties to the Arab world and 'legitimate' Islam, dismissing traditional practices as superstitious and archaic. Craving attention, Amrozi torched the sacred tomb of the town's patron saint, Sinori, the action creating a village feud between the Nahdlatul Ulama and local adherents of Wahhabism. Tombs were regarded as having special mystical powers by the Nahdlatul Ulama. However, to the opposing Wahhabis and their unforgiving interpretation of Islam, these beliefs were primitive and blasphemous and, in consequence, Amrozi had done no wrong.

Overnight, he became a village celebrity to supporters aligned with Abu Bakar Bashir.

When Ghufron graduated from the *pesantren* in Ngruki and followed Bashir into self-proclaimed exile disappearing into Afghanistan to join the Mujahideen, all communications ceased; the void created by Amrozi's brother's absence, unbearable. Four years passed before Amrozi heard that Ghufron had returned to Malaysia and was teaching at a Wahhabi-based religious school founded by Abdullah Sungkar and Bashir. Amrozi successfully traced his brother to a small *Madrasah* off Sungei Tiram where Ghufron taught. Initially, he was embarrassed to attempt a reunion, concerned that his lack of piety would displease Ghufron.

It was at this time he learned that two of his other brothers had also opened their own school in Tenggulun to teach Wahhabism, he became determined to mend his ways, and become a better Muslim and, in so doing, became ensnared by the militant extremist organization Ghufron helped build. He supported himself working as a mechanic, attended prayer five times daily and, at night, studiously read the Koran.

He stole from his father and made his way to Ulu Tiram in Malaysia's southern state of Johor, unaware that his destination was, in fact, a *Jemaah Islamiyah* recruiting station and a transit point for S.E. Asian Muslims on their way to fight in Afghanistan. There he sought his brother's blessing, Ghufron welcoming Amrozi with open arms. Amrozi then became even more fanatical in his emulation of his older brother, undertaking training at a newly-established *JI* camp where he learned a number of skills and developed a competency for building explosive devices.

As his respect grew for Ghufrom who was then known by his adopted name, Mukhlas, so did his admiration for Riduan Isamuddin, the *JI* operations commander whom he was instructed to refer to as 'Hambali'. Mukhlas worked closely with Hambali and there were times that Amrozi envied their relationship. When his brother founded a second Islamic boarding school in Johor, Amrozi was included in the new network, developing strong ties with one of the religious teachers, Abdul Aziz, aka Imam Samudra.

With the Malaysian government making it increasingly difficult for foreign laborers to obtain work, the brothers returned to Tenggulun to find their seventy-five-year old father bedridden and their tiny, ageing mother Haji Tariyem unable to cope. By now, his sisters had all married and the remaining brothers preoccupied with their own lives.

Although a changed man in many ways Amrozi was still not considered sufficiently dedicated to join his brother Imron teaching at the village *Pesantren*. Instead, he eked a minimal existence from repairing motorbikes and the occasional car or bus, devoting his free time to caring for his father who now spent his final days wrapped in a sarong, lying listlessly on a concrete floor.

Seeking action, Amrozi led a demonstration to topple the village head. When this failed, he became disillusioned, slipping back into the mundane life he had previously escaped, his waking hours filled with a desperation for recognition which he brooded, might never be achieved.

Again, the muezzin's call fell upon his ears. Reminded that he was running late for the noontime prayers Amrozi moped his way to the mosque, arriving minutes before the sun reached its zenith.

IPIL – MINDANAO ISLAND
THE PHILIPPINES
3rd April

Panicked, women and children ran screaming through the small southern town as *Abu Sayyaf* "Bearer of the Sword" guerrillas literally shredded the town center's buildings with automatic fire. The founder and the leader, Abduragak Abubakar Janjalani, a veteran of the Afghanistan war strutted into the local police headquarters knowing he would find not find any resistance there. The *Abu Sayyaf* enjoyed a most unusual de facto relationship with those who held power in Manila, which not only assured Janjalani of advance intelligence assisting his force elude capture, but also provided for financial and material support.

Since he had orchestrated to split from the Moro Liberation Front in 1991, Janjalani had almost exclusively operated in the southern parts of the archipelago, developing close ties with other Islamic radical groups. Afghanistan had provided him the opportunity to establish a direct link with al-Qaeda and when Ramzi Yousef and Mohammed Jamal Khalifa had ventured into the Philippines, it was the *Abu Sayyaf* that had been the beneficiaries of their material and financial support.

Janjalani trained his recruits well, specializing in assassinations, kidnappings and extortion, the first of which bringing his splinter organization to the attention of the CIA in 1991 when a grenade attack killed two foreign women. Bathing in the success of this action he consistently targeted foreigners, enjoying the notoriety the media provided, taking his activities to new levels in 1993 with the kidnapping of three Spanish nuns and their priest.

With Ramzi Yousef's much publicized capture in Pakistan the month before and his appearance before New York judge to respond to an outstanding indictment over the World Trade Centre bombing, al-Qaeda funding had all but ceased. Janjalani realized that he needed to raise his organization's profile if he were to expect further funding from the Sheikh.

Satisfied that the Ipil township attack would make headlines in the Manila Times and assist in someway restoring the severed lines of monetary flow from Hambali's nerve centre in Malaysia, Janjalani had the town set ablaze, then called for his troops to withdraw.

In the aftermath of the botched *Bojinka Operation* the CIA increased its presence in the Philippines sweeping the city and countryside, recruiting informants and identifying anti-U.S. militants. And, with Ramzi Yousef's voluminous revelations regarding his connection to the *Abu Sayyaf,* its leader, Abduragak Abubakar Janjalani's life was suddenly destined for an abrupt end.

MANILA – THE PHILIPPINES
4th May

Sprung with a fake passport Omar al-Faruq had been arrested whilst unsuccessfully attempting to enter flight school, later admitting that he had intended using commercial aircraft in a proposed terrorist attack. After being subjected to three months of brutal interrogation at the hands of his Filipino captors, twenty-four-year old Kuwaiti-born Omar al-Faruq broke down and confessed to his association with al-Qaeda, revealing all to the American observers.

The Kuwaiti admitted to having spent three years at an al-Qaeda training camp in Khaldan, Afghanistan where he became close to the camp's leader, al-Mughira al Gaza'iri and an upper echelon bin Laden associate, Abu Zubaydah. It had been on Zubaydah's instruction that he traveled to the Philippines and ensconced himself at Camp Abubakar, the Moro Islamic Liberation Front's terrorist-training facility. At that time Afghani veterans had become the trainers of a new generation of *Mujahideen* based in Mindanao. Working with the Moro Islamic Liberation Front (MILF) in a reciprocal arrangement recruits were trained in everything from scuba diving for seaborne terror attacks and the use of explosives to blow up ships, bridges, power plants and even the occasional assassination attempt.

The Americans were jubilant with their catch. Following months of coercive re-indoctrination al-Faruq was turned. He became a willing CIA 'sleeper' within Philippines separatist and Islamic movements, al-Faruq's deep-cover role then known only to the most senior officers within the CIA.

* * * *

Chapter Four

Petaling Jaya – Malaysia
1st January 1999

Azahari Husin listened while Hambali articulated his reasoning for their involvement in the imminent action in Indonesia's eastern Christian provinces. They had driven from Shah Alam to Klang where Hambali maintained a one-bedroom unit for transients associated with their cause. The city was an appropriate location, just thirty kilometres from Kuala Lumpur and only eight kilometres from the port.

'Why start with Ambon?' Azahari wished to understand Hambali's logic.

'There are five main provincial areas which have non-Muslim majorities. These are West Papua, Indonesian Borneo, Sulawesi and Bali through the string of islands to the east known as Nusa Tenggarra. In the Moluccas, the demographics have changed substantially with the forced transmigration processes and now we outnumber the Christian population by a narrow margin. However, Ambon still supports a Christian majority and, if we are to subjugate the non-Christian provinces then we must reverse the trend in Ambon and bring all the Moluccas under Islamic domination.'

Azahari suppressed a yawn. The streets were deserted but

for the occasional itinerant strolling aimlessly around, lost in the post-celebratory haze of the New Year. Azahari and his passenger had both risen before dawn – *Ramadan* had commenced ten days before and both men continued to fast during daylight hours. 'How much support do you expect from our cells in Java?' he asked.

Hambali shook his head. 'Nothing of any great significance,' he said, thoughtfully, 'at least, not yet. They'll follow once we demonstrate what we are capable of achieving in the Christian areas.'

'And the military?'

Hambali's lip curled. 'We have the backing of General Sumantri and his *Kopassus* clique.'

It was Azahari's turn to smile. 'From antagonist to benefactor?'

'Why not use the opportunity? At this point in time we share some common interests.'

'How is it going to play out?'

'Sumantri's people started the ball rolling last year; to stir the pot, they had Deddy Hamdan, one of the pro-democracy activists, disappear. Word on the street is that elements of the *Kopassus* Special Forces carried out the kidnapping, which shouldn't come as any surprise. Then Sumantri orchestrated a turf war between Christian and Muslim Ambonese gangs in Jakarta back in November by spreading rumors that Ambonese Christians had burned a local mosque. A couple of hundred of the *Cokers* were then repatriated when…'

'*Cokers?*' Azahari interrupted.

'An abbreviation for *Cowok Kristen*, the Christian Boys,' Hambali clarified, 'they operate in Ambon as well as Jakarta. As I was saying, when the street fighting broke out in Jakarta there were half a dozen or so *Cokers* killed. More than twenty churches were torched. When they were forcibly repatriated the *Cokers* raised hell upon arrival in Ambon. Won't take much to light their fuse when we're ready, especially if we can stir the Moluccan Muslim Student Movement.'

'These Ambonese – are they well armed?'

'I don't expect they'll put up much of a fight. Besides, Sumantri will see to it that the military look the other way when we strike.'

'How will your troops be able to differentiate between the Muslims and Christians?' Azahari was curious to know.

'The disruptions will commence during the *Idulfitri* celebrations. We'll spread the word for Muslims to wear white armbands to distinguish them from the others. We expect to mobilize support from the Leihitu Peninsula area and from Ternate in the north.'

'And you are confident that we won't be compromised in any way?'

'Yes,' Hambali responded, assuredly, 'with Suharto gone we have forged our own niche with the new powers-to-be. They see us as an opportunity to do their dirty work for them.' He moved to reassure his serious-faced companion. 'Don't worry. This action is just the beginning. The *Jemaah Islamiyah* is about to make its mark in Indonesia.'

Azahari considered Hambali's comment. 'Might be an ideal opportunity for our friends in the Philippines to mount a simultaneous campaign?'

'The MILF is too fragmented to be effective,' Hambali complained. 'Also, their objectives are more of a domestic nature.'

'But, they're close enough to lend material support to the operations planned for Sulawesi and the Moluccas?'

"They'd be reluctant to offer weapons.'

'What about the North Korean shipments?' Azahari was aware that Pyongyang had sold the Moro Islamic Liberation Front more than ten thousand U.S. M16 rifles, grenades and other arms over the past year. The secret, two-million dollar deal had been negotiated on Malaysian soil at Sandakan, which had become the main logistics airport for arms supply into the Philippines, with Ghazali Jaafar, the MILF vice chairman for political affairs in attendance. His sources had also revealed that the MILF had expressed interest in purchasing a North Korean mini-submarine which, to Azahari, demonstrated the Filipino separatist group's sound financial strength. He knew that they financed their guerrilla activities by trading drugs produced in Mindanao, and frequently received funds from al-Qaeda sources in support of their quest for an Islamic state in southern Philippines. Also, there was considerable cross-pollination between the *Jemaah Islamiyah* and its Philippines counterpart with Indonesian and Malaysian recruits frequently undergoing training in the Mindanao camps. Equipped with sophisticated computerized satellite communications, the well-armed MILF force of ten thousand represented a formidable challenge to the government and its armed forces. Azahari knew that more than one hundred and twenty thousand Filipinos from both sides had died in the conflict during the past thirty years.

'When I last visited Camp Abu Bakar in Mindanao they'd already received most of the M16s,' Hambali reported. The camp was the principal MILF stronghold located in heavily forested, mountainous terrain and oversaw a further sixty military pods spread throughout the provinces which bordered Indonesia's Kalimantan and Sulawesi. The MILF and al-Qaeda had established strong ties over the past decade and discussions regarding the establishment of an al-Qaeda training post under the MILF umbrella were well advanced. 'But, again, I don't believe they'll give up any of their armory. Also,' Hambali added, 'we have to remember that they are currently still operating under a ceasefire with the government. Would strengthening our relationship with the *Abu Sayyaf* be the best way to go?'

The militant Islamic *Abu Sayyaf* had recreated itself over the past four years since making headlines with the attack on Ipil. Both Hambali and his deputy were aware that only within the al-Qaeda-linked hierarchy was it known that the *Abu Sayyaf* had played an important role in placing the bomb on the Philippines Airlines flight to Tokyo in December 1994. Although the flow of arms and munitions from Afghanistan had slowed to a trickle following the *Bojinka* disaster *Abu Sayyaf* remained a reliable source for the *Jemaah Islamiyah* whenever explosive material was required, as the organization maintained close ties with the Philippines armed forces, and their U.S. supplied armories.

Azahari agreed with Hambali's suggestion. 'Will you make arrangements for the funds?'

JAKARTA
BAKIN (Indonesian State Intelligence Coordinating Agency)

General Hadi Suharman's granite expression signaled his determination. 'No excuses, Colonel, we should already have assets on the ground. I want the situation rectified immediately. And,' he glared at the two officers present, the air sticky with testosterone, '…the balls of whoever was responsible for this screw up.'

Colonel Sutrisno moved to damage control. It was his department that had missed the significance of the intelligence that had raised the General's ire. He indicated the Special Forces officer on temporary assignment to BAKIN. 'The Major has offered to oversee the operation personally.' BAKIN, Indonesia's State Intelligence Coordinating Agency was the central intelligence-gathering body which scrutinized both domestic, and foreign intelligence gathered by its own agents, as well as that collected by the army and police. BAKIN was directly under the President's control and maintained its own communications network outside the civilian and military administrations. Army officers were regularly seconded to BAKIN for special duties – whereas BIA, the Armed Forces Intelligence Agency was charged with the collection of information relating to external defence and internal security, processing and operational functions.

General Suharman challenged the Major. 'You are familiar with this piece of shit, Isamuddin?'

In no way intimidated by his corpulent superior Major Tony Supadi responded confidently. 'Riduan Isamuddin, aka Hambali.' He paused, drawing upon information from files he had studied, 'returned to Indonesia last week, intelligence suggesting that he may be in Ambon training others in explosives applications.' The Major was careful not to reveal more than the BAKIN files contained.

Suharman's eyes narrowed. Although the young officer had the necessary skills to carry out the assignment he had yet to be tested. 'You are to remove Isamuddin and his supporters from the scene. Is that clear?'

Supadi glanced over at Colonel Sutrisno who remained expressionless. 'Yes General.'

'Then get your team together immediately and report back to me.'

Colonel Sutrisno intervened. 'With *Ramadan* well under way it might be tricky.' The 'Dirty Ops' departmental head was not overly keen to commence the covert operation during the fasting period. 'Sending a 'housekeeping' team at this time might not go down too well.' To peaceful, devout Muslims, *Ramadan* was a time of prayer and reflection.

Suharman's lips barely moved. 'I remind you that *Nabi Mohammed* fought to retake Mecca at the Battle of Badr during *Ramadan*. You are to act during the festival of *Lailat al-Qadr*, to achieve the most effective results.'

The Colonel shuffled his feet nervously, always uneasy when the General used references to the Koran to support his own distorted views. The festival marked the night Allah first revealed the Koran to the Prophet Mohammed and was celebrated during the final ten days of *Ramadan*. Nominating *Lailat al-Qadr*, the 'Nights of Power'— a time that many extremists believed themselves to be empowered with super-normal capabilities, when martyrs are fearless, for to die as such sacrifice, would guarantee purification and acceptance to heaven— worried the officer as it would be his responsibility to lead the covert action in Ambon. 'But General, *Lailat al-Qadr* is less than two weeks away! That doesn't give us adequate time to prepare.'

General Suharman waved a hand dismissively. 'Then I suggest you get to it. There will be no further delay.'

* * * *

Alone and deep in thought General Suharman considered the consequences of the unlikely event his clandestine operation being exposed. With President Suharto's shock resignation in May the year before creating the worst leadership vacuum the country had seen since the 1966 *coup d'etat,* Suharman and a number of other generals had gathered, determined to protect their vested interests.

When Suharto's regime came to its abrupt and violent end the long-standing ideological divisions that had festered unnoticed under the former president's iron rule suddenly flared, revealing the depth of factional rivalry within Indonesia's armed forces. Faced with the disgrace associated with Suharto's resignation, General Suharman and his fellow loyalist officers moved to consolidate their positions against their younger opponents, preparing for exigencies that would undoubtedly occur during the looming power struggle.

General Suharman's old guard, referred to as the *'Merah-Putih'* officers whose loyalty was symbolized by the red and white colors of the Indonesian flag, had prevented the *'Hijau'* (Green), reformist officers' attempted *coup d'etat* against Suharto's nominated successor, Habibie, within days of his ascent to power. Suharman despised the *'Hijau'* group of officers, so named because of their identification with modernist Islamic teachings, for it was these traitors who had provided information and logistical support for students back in May, precipitating Suharto's fall, and the collapse of the *New Order.*

Suharman knew that most of the *'Hijau'* members were military academy graduates from the years 1973-1974. He had learned that these officers were integral to the inner-circle, known widely as the *"Kelompok 20"*, 'The Group of Twenty'. During the past nine months when *Reformasi* had suddenly became the new, all-embracing, catchword, many ambitious senior military officers, in line with the country's evolving mood, commenced looking for alternative leadership further exacerbating existing factional rivalries within the powerful military machine. This group of twenty generals and influential reformists with their radical reformist ideas were considered an abomination by the old guard.

With widespread disappointment growing amongst Indonesian intellectuals, both civilian and military, General Suharman and his *'Merah Putih'* loyalists refused to wait quietly in the wings, their impatience growing as their positions continued to be marginalized, this loss of power impacting heavily on revenues generated by the complex foundations under their control.

But the obese general knew that significant funds would be needed to meet the threat from within. Faced with international condemnation relating to human rights offenses, Suharman's TNI, Indonesian Armed Forces' associates were suffering the consequences of partial weapons' embargoes – and the 'commission well' was rapidly drying up. That half the nation's F16s were no longer operational and the air force C130s were grounded due to the lack of spare parts, weighed heavily on his mind. That morning he had read, with dismay, that even the British Hawk aircraft were no longer fully operational.

During Suharto's reign arms contracts generated lucrative commissions for the military machine. However, although some U.S. defence contractors had managed to circumvent their Congress' ban, these multinationals were extremely difficult to deal with. Suharman unhappily accepted that it was now most unlikely his group would benefit from the Lockheed Martin and Boeing's collective $54 million in contracts, President Clinton's Administration had recently approved.

Faced with the revenue loss Suharman's fellow generals had taken alternative measures to shore up their incomes, targeting foreign companies which they then proceeded to squeeze. Mining giant Freeport's West Papua management succumbed when TNI elements incited unrest which, in turn, jeopardized the mining operations, the U.S. based miner then forfeiting an additional $35 million to the military to ensure that the 'rebellious elements' were removed from the mine's environment.

With President Habibie's diminishing popularity both internationally and domestically rumors suggesting a possible coup attempt were rife – and another major concern to the loyalists was the country had no Vice President and, according to the Constitution, the Ministers for Foreign Affairs, Defense and Internal Affairs would assume joint, temporary leadership in the event the President were to fall.

When the 'Merah Putih' loyalists learned that the 'Hijau' reformists were mounting a major operation in the country's eastern provinces, Suharman had become alarmed upon discovering that he had been deliberately left out of the intelligence loop. It would seem that the 'Group of Twenty' were making their move – and Suharman was determined to disrupt their plans.

CIJANTUNG – EAST JAKARTA
KOPASSUS Special Forces HQ

Following his BAKIN briefing Major Tony Supadi went directly to the outer Jakarta suburb of Cijantung, driving past the heavy machine-gun post and entering the marble-fronted *Kopassus* HQ. There he informed other members of the Special Forces of his meeting with General Suharman; the consensus amongst these officers loyal to the 'Hijau' reform movement was that swift action was imperative to unseat the Suharto loyalists – even if this conspiracy resulted in thousands of their fellow countrymen losing their lives. Special Ops teams were covertly created and charged with destabilizing sensitive areas; their aim to prepare the Indonesian people for a revitalized TNI's return to power when the country's experiment with democracy, as predicted, failed. Plans for secret paramilitary forces were only months away from realization, the first training camp already under construction in the mountainous terrain two hours south of Jakarta. This paramilitary arm would be designated the *Laskar Jihad* or Islamic Holy Warriors, its rank and file to be drawn from Islamic student groups, and armed by the Indonesian Special Forces.

Major Supadi was a highly skilled officer, trained in intelligence gathering, sabotage and special operations' techniques. He had already achieved the rank of captain when Prabowo Subianto, the President's son-in-law assumed leadership of *Kopassus* in December 1995. When the command was reorganized in the following year Supadi was promoted to major and Prabowo became the country's youngest, two-star general, overseeing the elite corps of red berets' growth to 6,000. And, they had powerful friends for within two years, three of the most senior positions at TNI headquarters would be dominated, for the first time in Indonesia's military's history, by *Kopassus* Special Forces officers.

An opportunist, Supadi had never hesitated in volunteering for missions that would raise his profile within the corps. Beginning in late 1998 with rumors that President Habibie was considering a referendum in East Timor, Supadi led *Kopassus* elements in the systematic liquidation of Timorese associated with the struggling resistance movement, this action forcing thousands to flee into the jungles. The Major's involvement in East Timor would continue, in parallel with his additional responsibilities in the Moluccas, both theatres in Indonesia's

Christian-dominated eastern provinces.

As a pragmatist, when the lines had been drawn between the loyalist and reformist officers Supadi had considered the long-term ramifications of identifying with either group. Believing that both factions were fundamentally flawed and in no way influenced by the conflicting ideologies, Supadi had made his choice based solely on career considerations, secretly committing to the *'Hijau'* movement.

Confident that the old guard would soon be swept from the TNI halls of power the Major was determined to make his mark, assisting the 'Group of Twenty' set about stealing control by instigating conflict aimed at destabilizing the nation – and thus inspire people to seek their leadership. He would turn General Suharman's *Lailat al-Qadr* mission into the perfect opportunity to demonstrate his skills to his superiors. Riduan Isamuddin would not be harmed. The Maluku region would become the vanguard for the reformists' military cabal's endeavors to destabilize the country by provoking religious violence in the eastern provinces – its success assured with al-Qaeda's S.E. Asian operations commander, Hambali already on the ground, preparing for the Special Forces arrival.

JAKARTA
The Bimaton Group

'I have Pak Suwanto on line,' Agus Sumarsono's secretary called.

Agus scowled at the phone, the knot in his stomach tightening as he lifted the receiver. *'Pagi, Mas.'*

'Good morning, Agus,' the banker reciprocated.

Agus's jaw tightened. They were not on a first name basis, Suwanto's signaling the role reversal from a time when the haughty, Bimaton president was accorded the respect his position in the community demanded.

'I have good news; at least, it's good news for Bimaton. The creditors have agreed to reschedule the meeting until next month,' Suwanto advised, not un-patronizingly. 'I trust that you will be able to present your restructuring options at that time?'

Agus seethed, detecting the supercilious tone in the other's voice. 'I'll be ready,' he countered. Agus was cognizant of the banker's envy, the man's poignant criticism of debtors maintaining luxury cars and boats whilst reluctant to repay loans still fresh in his mind.

'Well, the creditors *will* be pleased to learn that you will resolve the debt issues, finally.'

The sarcasm was not lost on Agus. 'Bimaton will pay its debts,' was all he could muster before terminating the call.

His mind polluted with a myriad of issues Agus cleared his thoughts to address the problem of the next creditors' meeting. Although he had secured limited backing from a number of government bank officials by pledging payments for their support, once the restructure had been approved, the Bimaton president was conscious of a growing dispathy within monetary circles towards his group. Agus understood the urgency of his determining a more efficacious method to dissuade the financial scavengers from forcing an asset fire sale, as he sincerely believed that the conglomerate's cash-flow predicament could be resolved, given the benefit of time.

When the Asian currency crisis had struck it gave the corrupt, over-inflated Indonesian economy the enema it so infinitely deserved. Preoccupied with amassing wealth Asia's elite had failed to recognize the economic and financial indicators that portended the currency collapse. CEO and heir apparent to the distressed Indonesian conglomerate, the Bimaton Group, Agus Sumarsono had seen his family's wealth wither in the aftermath of the financial crisis, the Bimaton conglomerate's book value having collapsed to less than twenty cents in the dollar.

The Bimaton Group, as with so many of its contemporaries, had been founded in the early Seventies under the protective umbrella of Suharto's New Order. Commencing with a simple coastal trading operation the fledging company had grown to prominence during Suharto's thirty years in power. Then the Asian currency crisis of 1997 precipitated the collapse of the country's economy, an outcome that even the International Monetary Fund's twenty-three-billion dollar multilateral financial package injection could not prevent.

In the twilight years of the Suharto dictatorship corrupt bank officers approved loans amounting to tens of billions of dollars that fueled massive growth in all sectors of the economy. Now the debt-ridden companies were unable, or refused to repay these loans. In a country with no functioning bankruptcy system the conglomerates simply stopped servicing their creditors. Terrified bank customers withdrew their deposits, placing most banks on the verge of collapse, further roiling the market. The government bailed them out with aid donor funds and taxpayers' dollars and the banks surrendered their bad loans to the government which, in turn, brought about the creation of the bank restructuring agency, IBRA, ostensibly to force the debtors to meet their obligations.

However, in an environment where corruption was so endemic, the situation could only deteriorate – and it did. Company accounts had already been guttered by directors, the funds mysteriously disappearing into overseas numbered accounts in destinations such as Singapore, and property investments across the globe.

Indonesia was in chaos – the leadership was most likely to again change hands, the currency had imploded leaving land based assets near worthless – and, to further aggravate the rapidly diminishing foreign investment flow, the country was in danger of losing East Timor. The possibility of a successful referendum and defiant mood was a potential stimuli for other separatist movements.

Agus accepted that in this bittersweet transitional period from despotic rule to the promise of some semblance of democracy, he and others of his ilk would remain in financial jeopardy. Indonesia had flipped from being an international destination for fund managers, to that of pariah, the flood of investment funds exiting the republic fueling the crisis.

And now, the Brobdingnagian Bimaton conglomerate was, incredibly, perilously close to collapse. A two-billion-dollar satellite city development now valued at five-hundred million due to the Rupiah's collapse had been the primary cause – Agus Sumarsono's personal guarantees now threatening his core wealth.

Faced with the disconsolate economic landscape Agus recognized that his salvation would depend on frustrating the creditors until he could successfully restructure his conglomerate in such a manner as to attract further investment funds. Amongst the group assets that remained viable was his indirectly controlled construction company P.T.Young & Budiono which, due to its turnkey-oil and gas activities, continued to pump desperately needed cash flow into the Bimaton Group.

In ruminative mood Agus considered the expatriate, Greg Young, whose management skills and single-mindedness had guided the construction arm through the economic downturn. Young had remained at the Y & B company helm since going public and Agus would not have it any other way. The London-born engineer had proven an invaluable asset and, although Agus had seriously strained their relationship with demands on Y & B's cash flow, he expected that Young would continue to toe the line.

Encumbered with the mounting pressures of the moment Agus gazed out through the office tower's double-glazed windows, the city's panorama impaired by haze. Even the majestic peaks of Gunung Salak and Gunung Gede mountains were hidden from view, the momentary sense of isolation adding to his dispiritedness. Agus exhaled slowly; he had never felt so alone. He leaned over and touched an intercom button. 'Call Greg Young and Andrew Graham and ask them to meet me at the club. Have the driver bring the Rolls to the front of the building then ring the course manager and tell him to book my foursome for a one o'clock tee-off.'

* * * *

Andrew Graham arrived half an hour before the others, eager to limber up on the driving range before the game – and to ensure that his customary caddy was available. Reminded of Agus Sumarsono's competitive nature Andrew relied heavily on the bare-footed Sundanese caddy to compensate for Agus' natural swing. The caddy had saved the day on many an occasion with his enormous, splayed feet by simply picking Andrew's golf ball from any impossible rest, and repositioning the customized Wilson unseen, in a more favorable lie.

Sitting, sipping an iced tea observing other golfers going about their game, Andrew recognized David Shaw, an Australian diplomat who had only recently taken up the post of

First Secretary, Political Affairs. Andrew knew from his own masters that this man headed the Australian Secret Service ops throughout Indonesia, the American's interest growing when he identified General Suharman waddling off the eighteenth green with Shaw. Minutes later Greg Young arrived.

'Getting in some practice?' Young asked.

Andrew chuckled. 'And I have my usual caddy.'

Greg waved at a waiter then sat down, lowering his voice as his face became serious. 'What's up?'

Andrew sighed heavily. 'Who knows with Agus? Maybe he's just looking for some consolation in the company of those who can't break his balls.' Then, 'Is he still bleeding your group's cash flow to keep the rest of Bimaton afloat?'

Young shifted uneasily in the rattan chair. 'Y & B can't keep on going like this, Andy.' A fleeting look around confirmed that none were within earshot. 'We might not be in a position to post a performance bond for the next project.'

Although *au courant* with the kind of chicanery Agus Sumarsono practiced, Andrew's brow corrugated with surprise. 'I'm really sorry to hear that, Greg,' he empathized, 'I didn't realize your situation was *that* tight.' Andrew spotted Agus strutting into the clubhouse. 'What are you going to do?'

'Can't do much, unfortunately. I'm locked in. I'm still holding most of my original stock.' Young shook his head despondently. 'Fuck it!' he cussed bitterly, 'If I'd bailed out three, four years back I could have walked away with thirty million. Now, with the Asian markets deflated as they are, my holding isn't worth shit; especially with Agus continuously milking the company's coffers.' He flicked an ant that had courageously ventured onto the glass-topped table. 'Besides, with the stench of corporate Indonesia's death driving would-be-investors even further a field, who in their right mind would even consider throwing capital into the country at this time?' He leaned back tilting the chair, crossed his arms and slowly filled his lungs. 'And, as if we didn't have enough to worry about, there's rumor that before the end of the month Habibie's going to cave to international pressure and permit a referendum in East Timor!' Anger rising, he leaned forward and clenched fists under the table. 'That should see an end to all offshore negotiations until the outcome is known.'

Andrew knew there was little of any consequence that his companion could do to prevent Agus from siphoning funds. 'What will you do?'

The British engineer cum entrepreneur straightened his back. 'Not much choice but stay in for the long run and just hope that he doesn't suck the well completely dry.'

Andrew threw Greg a warning look. 'Speak of the devil.' Then, 'isn't that Mulyadi from the Bank of Asia?'

Greg swung his head around. 'Surely is,' he confirmed, *sotto voce*, '*the* senior creditor in person.' Disguising his concerns he winked at Andrew. 'Lay you fifty to one Agus has him in his pocket by the end of the game.'

Andrew's mouth curled at the corners. 'If he hasn't already...'

BOGOR – INDONESIA

Al-Faruq shuffled down through the sleepy village of Cijeruk with his wife Mira Agustina at his side. Arriving at the intersection he bid Mira farewell, reminding her of their pact, that if for whatever reason he did not return she was not to go searching for him. Armed with his recently-acquired ID card stating he was an

Indonesian citizen and resident of Ambon, he hailed a minibus, offered his blessing to those already on board then, because of his limited *Bahasa Indonesia* lay back and closed his eyes pretending to sleep to avoid being drawn into conversation.

Following his exploits in the Philippines the CIA sleeper had been ordered to Indonesia where he covertly established his credentials with local militant groups. Al-Faruq had blended in well by keeping a low profile, marrying locally, attending the mosque, and generally maintaining the appearance of a reserved, ungregarious person – his fellow villagers incognizant that there was an American spy in their midst. The former Kuwaiti terrorist's long-term brief was to exploit his connections with al-Qaeda and infiltrate Indonesia's emerging, militant Islamic organizations at every opportunity. And more recently, as a result of the 1998 bombings of U.S. embassies in Africa, he was also directed to gather intelligence regarding Saudi charities, such as the Al-Haramain Islamic Foundation, suspected of operating in Indonesia through fronts to disguise al-Qaeda's inwards capital flow.

As the minibus continued on its way to Jakarta al-Faruq appeared outwardly calm, his demeanor belying the bizarre situation in which he now found himself, actively participating as a terrorist in order that the United States remain informed. At times, his role playing became all too real, such as when along with an Indonesian trader by the name of Agus Dwikarna, he secretly co-founded a paramilitary group called *Laskar Jundullah,* the 'Fighters of God'. Al-Faruq deliberated upon the discombobulated outcome his relationship with the Americans had generated and the absurdity of it all; that the United States was now providing him with the very means to further the terrorist cause – his activities totally devoid of any moral dimension.

Arriving on the outskirts of the capital al-Faruq then changed his mode of transport and made his way to Agus Dwikarna's home. There, with fellow *Laskar Jundullah* conspirators he would engage in the final preparations for the assassination of Megawati Sukarnoputri, then report his activities to his CIA masters via an established letter drop procedure, before returning home.

CHAPTER FIVE

MOLUCCAN ISLANDS– AMBON
19th January 1999

Muslim youths boarded the targeted bus and demanded money from the driver. When he refused the man was savagely beaten, his assailants yelling anti-Christian slogans as they then kicked and punched, dragging him feet-first down the steel steps and onto the street where they emptied his pockets. Fuelled by Muslim extremists this single criminal act sparked immediate reprisals from the Christian sector, Hambali's teams of provocateurs well prepared for their enemies' response. During the first days more than one hundred died on Ambon's streets, the police and army electing to remain on the sidelines as the lawlessness intensified, spreading through the city unabated.

Hambali's agitators took the fight from the town centre to the harbour where they attacked a karaoke bar, dragged two young women outside and hacked the Christian girls to death before throwing their mutilated bodies into the sea. The Christians retaliated; their bloody trail leaving decapitated bodies along footpaths wherever Muslim storekeepers took a stand. Then the carnage spilled from Ambon City into surrounding hamlets where the villagers were caught, unprepared, the slaughter intensifying with Hambali's teams destabilising the countryside.

* * * *

Nuci carried Anna, her granddaughter on her hip as she strolled down the street, her curiosity aroused as to the markings that had appeared overnight on the walls of the village dwellings. An intelligent woman, Nuci recognized that the small number of Muslim homes had different symbols to that of the Christians. Approaching her house Nuci was startled by a group of approaching men, chanting as they made their way along the main street. Suddenly, there was a scream, Nuci's heart leaping when she realized that the mob had turned violent. Without hesitation she lifted the child from her hip and broke into a half-run, stumbling with the weight of the infant in her arms. She heard someone shout – Nuci looked back over her shoulder as several men ran towards them waving short-bladed swords, severing the head of an elderly woman caught in the bloody melee as she stood frozen in her tracks in the middle of the street.

Nuci's husband had watched, terrified from inside their home. He half opened the door to call her inside, overwhelmed when he witnessed men running amok wielding their razor-sharp *goloks* at anyone in their path.

The mob had swept down from the neighbouring Muslim village of Hitu seeking revenge for an earlier attack, the spontaneous wave of reprisals sweeping Ambon Island decimating entire village communities. Overnight, the *pela* tradition was invoked, Muslim and Christian villages united along sectarian lines.

Nuci made it to the safety of her home where she gripped her husband's arm and shook him, terrified for her family. 'The children…' the words choked in her throat, 'what… about the children?'

Lauren's face was grim. 'They should be safe at the school.'

Not convinced, Nuci's face remained a sea of concern. 'What are we going to do?'

'I don't know!' He cried, 'why are they attacking us?'

Lauren's voice echoed her own anguish and she looked to her husband for comfort. 'Will we be safe, here?' At that moment she detected smoke in the air. Ashen-faced, she shook her husband wildly. 'Lauren, you've got to get us out of here!'

'How?' he groaned, wringing his hands, 'it would be suicidal to leave the house!'

'Can't you smell the smoke? They're burning the village. We'll die if we don't flee!'

Nuci opened a window shutter and peered cautiously outside. Across the street she identified a number of security personnel embracing the raiders.

Unbeknownst to the Nuci's fellow villagers' Muslim scouts had slipped into the village to disperse residents and place distinguishing marks on buildings differentiating Christian from Muslim homes. A second group then arrived after, for the kill. Finally, a third group followed and looted whatever had not been burned. Indonesian police and army allowed Muslim rioters to pass through checkpoints unchallenged during the riots.

* * * *

In the neighbouring village of Telaga Kodok, Nuci's daughter Lisa screamed in horror as she was dragged from her dwelling and forced to the ground.

'Torch it!' one of the raiders demanded, and a soldier dressed in civilian attire stepped forward and threw kerosene into the home Johanis Matuanakotta's mother had bequeathed to the couple. Lisa had been alone when Telaga Kodok had come under attack, her husband, somewhere between Benteng Karang and their home having dropped their daughter off at her parents' for a few days.

'Kill her!' the group leader shouted, 'we don't have time to mess around with these Christian sluts.'

Lisa's assailant placed a knee on her chest and lifted her dress exposing her thighs. 'Don't! Please, I beg you, don't!' she pleaded, her eyes opening wide in fear as her attacker flashed a knife and grinned lewdly.

'Get on with it!' she heard someone snap and her panties were torn away. The raider applied greater pressure with his knee – Lisa struggling helplessly with the soldier's foul breath hot upon her face. When he leaned down and whispered 'Say hello to Jesus' in her ear she felt the cold steel against the soft flesh of her thigh and she sobbed, uncontrollably, with the real-ization that death was imminent.

Lisa's terrifying scream with the shock of his knife being driven up between her legs and deep into her womb brought only laughter from those gathered around.

'Finish it!' the soldier was ordered – but Lisa heard nothing above her pain when he twisted the knife as he extracted the weapon, then swiftly dragged the blade across her throat.

* * * *

The following morning Nuci and Laurens, together with their granddaughter found their way to temporary refuge at Hunuth village, their own hamlet now nothing more than a ghost town strewn with dead. They sought protection from *KOSTRAD*, the army strategic command's 733 Unit, however the officer in charge simply ignored their plight and abandoned the area.

Fearing that Hunuth would also come under attack, Nuci

and her family boarded a boat and sailed out to sea accompanied by a number of other villagers. With the army having deserted the settlement Hunuth then fell to the Muslim raiders wearing white bandanas to distinguish their own from those they would murder. When word reached outlying villages, mosques, churches and government buildings were all burned to the ground, the escalation in violence bolstered by elements of Hambali's army-trained assassins.

* * * *

Johanis Matuanakotta remained dry-eyed throughout the mass burial proceedings. A week had passed since his wife Lisa died in the slaughter. Armed *Cokers* now lined the streets providing the necessary security when surrounding villages pooled their resources and came to bury the dead.

A visiting church elder from Ambon's Marantha Protestant church placed a hand on Matuanakotta's shoulder. 'This is the work of extremists, my son. I know your heart is heavy with your loss but I must urge you not to join with the others in seeking revenge.'

The young man shrunk from the *pendeta's* comforting hand, then turned and stared the minister down. 'I will do what has to be done.'

* * * *

Efforts to provide support to the Christians had been severely hampered by confusion amongst the Indonesian military commanders who had arrived to resolve the conflict. The overall military commander was surprised when Strategic Command, *KOSTRAD* troops under the influence of Islamist officers poured in from Makassar as Buginese/Makassarese were also involved in hostilities on their own front. Upon their arrival fighting had erupted between *KOSTRAD* troops, *BRIMOB*,

93

the elite police force, the Marines and the air force's *PASKA-SHAS* units which remained under the control of nationalist officers.

Confusion reigned; Hambali and his murderous thugs were on a roll.

U.S. DEPARTMENT OF STATE -WASHINGTON
13th June 1999

The strategic meeting was coming to a close when James Bolting, Deputy Undersecretary for Arms Control, S.E. Asia threw the question back at the team of State Department analysts. 'With Suharto gone is the interim president, Habibie, strong enough to send the Indonesian military back to their barracks?' Bolting's responsibilities included directing and coordinating arms control policy, nonproliferation policy, military assistance for the State Department and foreign assistance programs. In the post-Suharto climate, due to the earlier Asian currency collapse that had led to massive unemployment, food shortages, a rapid rise in crime and a general social breakdown, Indonesia's 450,000-member armed forces, which included 175,000 police, moved brutally to maintain internal security and stability. Growing international displeasure with the Indonesian military's human rights violations had generated sufficient pressure for President Clinton to consider an embargo on all military cooperation with the *Tentara Nasional Indonesia*, the TNI. 'And how will the generals respond to his imminent announcement of a referendum in East Timor?'

One of Bolting's senior analysts fielded the question. 'Habibie won't go the distance. He doesn't have a military background. While Indonesia grapples with the question of East

Timor's status our relationship with the TNI remains crucial for the United States in view of Indonesia's geostrategic position and regional influence. Our trade with S.E. Asia is nearing half a trillion dollars annually and this accounts for some three million American jobs.'

'Guess we should consider ourselves fortunate that a blockade against U.S. product could never be effective,' Bolting mused.

The senior analyst grabbed the moment. 'A blockade would cripple S. E. Asia and impact dangerously on China's foreign oil dependency. The United States must maintain a cooperative bilateral defense relationship with the country. Its vast span over thousands of islands not only form a three-thousand mile gateway between the Pacific and Indian Oceans, but straddles some of the world's most critical sea lines of communication.'

'We have to come up with something to justify ongoing military support.' Bolting appealed to one of the older departmental hands, a senior analyst with the National Security Agency who had remained uncharacteristically silent. 'What do you have, Pete?'

Peter Cook uncrossed his legs and leaned forward. 'Well, Jim, you know that I've always supported the view that stronger U.S. ties with the Indonesian military is the only way to transform the TNI. Our International Military and Education Training program has provided a generation of TNI offices with human rights education, and an opportunity to develop long-term relationships between both countries' future military leadership.'

The senior analyst intervened. 'And if the U.S. refuses to meet their military equipment needs there is always the danger of the Ruskies moving back into play.'

Bolting considered the career officer's point. The State Department had turned a blind eye to the blatant circumvention of standing legislation that had severely curtailed the flow of weaponry to nations with a history of human rights violations. The Deputy Undersecretary had still been in high school when the pro-West General Suharto grabbed power in 1966 and paved the way for the United States to displace the Soviets as the largest supplier of weapons and military training to Indonesia. Then in November 1991 when Indonesian troops armed with American M16s fired on a funeral procession in the Santa Cruz cemetery in East Timor, killing 271 the U.S. Congress had cut off Indonesia's (IMET) International Military Education and Training aid. The legislation had become law in 1993 and the Foreign Operations Appropriations Act was re-enacted 1994 and 1995. In 1996, the Pentagon facilitated Indonesia military training without congressional notification or consent throughout that year causing Congress to limit all future appropriations.

In March 1998, the East Timor Action Network released Pentagon documents showing that U.S. Army and Marine personnel had trained Indonesian soldiers under the Joint Combined Exchange Training program every few months since 1992. Indonesia's notorious *Kopassus* Special Forces had undergone U.S. training in air assault, urban warfare, and psychological operations between 1992 and 1997, without congressional knowledge or approval. While this training was technically legal, many in Congress felt as though the Pentagon had evaded the clear intention of the IMET prohibition. It was only in the past year that, in response to Congressional pressure, the Pentagon suspended the program for Indonesia. However, Bolting knew that even after Congress had closed many of the loopholes exploited by the Pentagon, the

CIA, Justice and Customs Departments, the Drug Enforcement Agency, the FBI and U.S. Marshals all continued to train Indonesians. He addressed the senior analyst. 'Where are we at with current training programs?'

'Not much on the agenda at the moment; we've expended around a million dollars on training over the past twelve months.'

'And where do we stand with hardware? If Habibie does announce a referendum we can be assured that the TNI will increase its presence on the ground.'

Confident that Peter Cook could deliver the information, verbatim, the senior analyst nodded in the older man's direction and Cook assumed the floor. 'As you know, Jim, we have exported over a billion dollars in U.S. arms sales to Indonesia since 1975, the year Indonesia first occupied East Timor. These weapon sales range from M16s to F16 fighter aircraft.' Cook glanced over at an attentive White House aide monitoring the meeting. 'Even under President Clinton's Administration our arms export policy to Indonesia has been…' Peter Cook hesitated, searching for a less offensive definition, 'let's say, supportive. Although not huge in relation to what we have given other nations, the critics are bound to raise comment that the Administration has supplied over one-hundred and fifty million in weapons and ammunition to Indonesia, which includes an increase of twelve million last year – plus another couple of million in manufacturing licenses and technical assistance to make U.S. designed weapons.'

The White House aide moved to influence the meeting's outcome. 'The Council on Foreign Relations and the U.S. – ASEAN Business Council are both of the consensus that the TNI is central to Indonesia's stability.'

James Bolting's expression did not reveal his annoyance. U.S. multinationals had, in his opinion, far too great an influence over the State Department's policy decisions and were notorious for their funding of TNI's vested interest groups. Bolting's files revealed that as much as eighty percent of the TNI's budget originated from illegal activities and security arrangements, with corporations such as ExxonMobil's Indonesian activities, and Freeport's Grassburg copper and gold mining operation in West Papua. 'It won't be the Business Council the American people will penalize at next year's presidential elections should the referendum go contrary to expectations, and the Indonesian military get out of hand again.'

'The Pentagon supports Jakarta and Australia's position that the referendum will not result in any dramatic change to Dili's status quo,' the aide offered. 'After two decades of Indonesian occupation the East Timorese won't invite further reprisal. They'll vote to remain within the Indonesian Republic – of that we're certain.'

'Well, let's just pray that we won't see TNI soldiers carrying American-made M16s on the front cover of Time Magazine before it's all over.'

* * * *

With the meeting concluded Bolting indicated to Peter Cook that he sought a few words in private.

'Nasty business, this Australian guy, Jenkins topping himself,' the Deputy Undersecretary led Cook to a quiet corner. 'Why did he do it?'

The NSA officer glanced around to ensure they could not be overheard. 'His death won't impact on State in any way,' Cook understood that would be his old friend's primary concern. 'Seems Langley was really squeezing this guys gonads for more material than the Aussies were prepared to give.'

'Just wanted to know in case any shit started to flow our way,' Bolting said, observing the White House aide reappearing and heading in their direction. 'Thanks for coming over today,' he placed a hand on Cook's shoulder as he indicated the approaching aide and whispered, 'Don't know where the White House finds some of these idiots.'

AUSTRALIAN EMBASSY

The First Secretary remained deep in thought as he entered the embassy, Merv Jenkins' death foremost on his mind. Word had spread quickly through the closely-knit diplomatic community that morning, the ASIS chief amongst those who were aware of the machinations that had led to the senior intelligence officer's apparent suicide.

Canberra's politicians, acting against the advice of their intelligence chiefs had decided to conceal the depth of Jakarta's involvement in the East Timor massacres, taking the position that the Indonesian military was not involved, misleading the Americans by blaming the militia violence on rogue elements within the TNI.

Jenkins had been under close scrutiny by his own intelligence agencies for having leaked highly sensitive material relating to the activities of Indonesian militias and troops in East Timor. This included detailed information intercepted by the Shoal Bay station near Darwin. He had been severely reprimanded. However the damage had been done with the CIA then aware that the Australians had been withholding intelligence from the United States. The screws tightened, and Jenkins became the object of bitter recriminations from within

Australian intelligence circles with some suggesting terminating his highly-questionable activities with extreme prejudice. When an investigation had been launched Jenkins had crumbled, offering to return to Canberra in August to account for his actions. Then, in contradiction, Jenkins had hung himself outside his residence in Arlington.

The diplomat remained introspective as he caught the lift up to the quarantine floor where ASIS maintained its offices, curious that Jenkins had elected to end his life earlier that morning, on his forty-eight birthday.

*   *   *   *

Across the Potomac in Virginia, senior CIA analysts remained disgruntled with Australia's failure to divulge specific intelligence to its closest ally; this perceived betrayal the very genesis of constraints being placed on future information flow, resulting in the most internecine of quid pro quos in modern history.

SHOAL BAY – DARWIN
DEFENCE SIGNALS DIRECTORATE STATION
June 1999

Nick Dennison stomped the gas pedal hard to the floor as he wrestled with the 4WD, correcting the vehicle's dangerous slide along the road's shoulder. Back on the macadam he checked the Oyster chronometer strapped to his heavily tanned wrist, squinting in the harbor city's direction – Darwin but a shimmer in the distance ahead. The senior communications analyst glanced at the rear vision mirror, evidence of the ultra-secret listening post with its nine satellite tracking dishes locked into regional communications satellites, now lost with distance as he drove the fifty kilometers to his meeting at his favorite drinking hole, Rourke's Drift.

Dennison was looking forward to that first schooner of beer away from the high-pressure environment in which he worked, the isolated location in the country's "Top End" irreverently dubbed by the 1,400 Defence Signals Directorate employees as 'Australia's Siberia'. The past few days at the communications station had been extremely demanding, with operators working additional shifts listening to high-band radio frequency traffic between Jakarta and Timor. Transcripts of digitally recorded conversations between Brigadier General Mahidin Simbolon, the Chief of Staff of the *Udayana* regional command based in Bali and Eurico Gutteres, the head of the Jakarta-sponsored militias in East Timor, had gravely concerned Canberra.

With an advance party of Australian troops preparing to embark, the government intensified its monitoring activities of Indonesian units, the current flow of information supporting claims that the murderous militia squads were receiving substantial support from Jakarta.

As he hurried towards his destination, Dennison considered the rising risk of a direct confrontation with Indonesia, and the significant role DSD played in maintaining the high level of intelligence reporting over S.E. Asia, through its ring of powerful satellite and radio intercept ground stations. DSD used state-of-the-art sophisticated electronic spying techniques to intercept phone and radio calls across the Asia-Pacific region, Dennison's station beaming the information gathered to Russell Offices' Defence Headquarters in Canberra where it was processed and analyzed.

It was not Dennison's concerns over Indonesia's provocative position in East Timor that occupied his mind as he drove into Darwin, but the intrusive nature of the American government which had, in his mind, threatened to compromise the integrity of the Shoal Bay operation. Until recently, the signals intelligence or SIGINT flow collected by the station had been for Australian Eyes Only and excluded both the United States and the British, a matter of some contention as Australia was a signatory to the UKUSA agreement. The U.S. National Security Agency along with its British, Canadian, New Zealand and Australian counterpart, DSD, had joined forces to operate a giant network of highly automated tracking stations around the globe. These stations targeted commercial satellites and downloaded all computer data messages and every fax, telex, email and telephone calls that were transmitted. Dennison's secretly objected to the American and British moves to force the Australians to provide even greater access to the Shoal Bay station intercepts.

Dennison was incensed that Australia's primary listening post was scheduled to become part of the UKUSA chain, which would provide for the United States to spy on Australian citizens, at home. And, as the greater part of all information gathered was forwarded directly to the CIA and NSA bypassing Australia's own intelligence apparatus he believed it his duty to reveal this intrusion to the general public. Having secured an undertaking that his identity would be protected, the analyst made arrangements to meet with Eddy Kwang, a Singapore-based journalist, the purpose of his meeting that afternoon.

* * * *

'Wait!' the journalist raised a hand, 'have to change the tape.'

Dennison waited patiently, eager to tell all. He had steadied himself with two drinks at Rourke's Drift then strolled slowly down to the corner of Mitchell and McLachlan Streets, where he cased the Poinciana Inn's poolside for familiar faces. Satisfied that he would not be recognized, he then ventured up to the journalist's room.

'Okay, it's rolling.' Kwang, the defence specialist writer then remained silent, permitting Dennison to continue his one-sided dialogue.

'As I was saying, 'Echelon', is a global spy system established and controlled by the NSA with its headquarters in Menwith Hill on the English moors where some two thousand American and British Ministry of Defence staff manage the site. Other intercept stations are located around the world and maintained by the U.S., Australia, England, Canada and New Zealand, all bound together in a still-secret agreement called UKUSA, this vast network of electronic spy stations designed to spy on each other's citizens by intercepting and gathering electronic signals. That is the problem I have with what's happening with our Australian stations. The system captures and analyzes virtually every electronic communication that passes through the airwaves, recording all phone calls, Internet emails, facsimile transmissions and telex messages across the globe.'

Dennison rose and helped himself to a whiskey from the mini bar before continuing, the journalist taking advantage of the pause. 'And you're saying that the Shoal Bay station hasn't been part of the Echelon system until now?'

Dennison's voice was dripping with contempt. 'The Brits and the Yanks have their own analysts staffing the Pine Gap and Kojarena stations.'

'Kojarena, where's that?' Eddie Kwang pretended not to know.

'Near Geraldton in Western Australia. It was built a few years back to monitor Indian and Pacific Ocean satellites. You can't miss the bloody thing,' he added sarcastically, 'the station has four huge satellite tracking dishes wrapped inside radomes, those golf ball-like structures often shown in aerial shots of

Pine Gap. These stations are on Australian soil yet some eighty percent of all messages intercepted at the Kojarena installation are automatically forwarded to the Americans with us having to beg for access to the information.'

'Are you willing to reveal what specific targets Kojarena covers?'

The analyst nodded. 'Kojarena mainly targets our more northerly neighbors, from Japan across to Pakistan.'

'And the S.E. Asian countries?'

'Not as a rule,' Dennison replied. 'That's mainly our bailiwick here at Shoal Bay. Our facility is a much larger station but not as technologically advanced as Kojarena. If you were able to fly over the location you would see that we have nine tacking dishes. What you wouldn't be able to determine is that these are locked into regional communication satellites such as the Indonesian Palapa birds, in their geostationary orbits above the equator.'

'Security must be very tight?' the journalist probed.

'Not as great as it should be,' Dennison smiled sardonically. 'The Kiwis also have an interception site at a place called Waihopai on the South Island. It's about half the size of Kojarena but mainly just monitors a couple of Pac rim comsats.' He paused again and looked over wistfully at the refrigerator.

'Help yourself, Nick,' the journalist offered, waving at the mini-bar. He was already aware of the New Zealand installation as its existence had been all over the newspapers several years before.

'Thanks.' Dennison did so then returned to his seat alongside the recorder. 'Is it still on?'

'Yes…you were saying something about the Kiwi operation?'

The analyst shook his head. 'You'd think that with so much

at stake they'd at least put a decent security system into place.'

'Meaning?'

'Echelon stations…and I should mention here that in Oz we don't use that terminology to deflect the claims that we are, in fact, doing what the Brits and Yanks want us to. The facilities are protected by electrified fences, and state-of-the-art detectors on the assumption that these will suffice.'

'And you don't think so?'

'No,' Dennison swirled the swizzle stick in his glass, 'in my opinion it's only a matter of time before one of the installations is seriously compromised. Those New Zealand reporters who broke into Waihopai a couple of years back is proof of that.'

The journalist leaned forward to check the recorder's counter. 'Let's get back to the Australian stations. What other installations contribute to the spy network?'

'Well, apart from Kojarena and Shoal Bay the most important facility to the Yanks would be Pine Gap. That's where they have their Air Force's seismic nuclear detection system but, more importantly, Pine Gap is where they control the CIA's *Rhyolite, Magnum* and *Aquacade* electronic listening satellites. Then there's our own defence communication posts such as Cabarlah in Toowoomba and other Aussie defence units around the continent which Mister Public knows all about anyway, and that's about it except for the new station at Wagga Wagga.' He sighed heavily and finished the whiskey. 'Look, mate, I don't have any problem with what we do for ourselves…even with sharing our intelligence. But, what really gives me the shits is how we are giving the Yanks what amounts virtually to carte blanche over our intelligence apparatus. There is a much more sinister side to what is happening here. At DSD we monitor communication traffic only outside Australia…or, that's how it's supposed to be. Our domestic spooks, ASIO have control over all internal eavesdropping.' He looked the interviewer directly in the eye. 'Did you know that, just two years back the Feds forced our telecom carriers to incorporate an intercept capability into all domestic networks? Only a fool would think there's any such thing as privacy, anymore.'

'Yeah, I'd had a piece that I was going to run but the story was squashed.'

'Well, what do you think will happen once we give the Yanks a similar access to Shoal Bay as they currently enjoy in the other so-called, joint facilities? There, they just filter out information from those stations before disseminating intelligence scraps back to us. Under their control, Shoal Bay would suffer similarly. Let's face it, we have a very limited defense capability and will always be dependent on the Americans. If they want Shoal Bay then Canberra will most likely give it to them. And, when that happens, we can all kiss our privacy goodbye.'

'Then why do *you* think we're considering going down that path?'

Dennison shrugged. 'Beats me…I can only speculate that it's got something to do with that Star Wars crap the Republicans came up with. Australia's position geographically would be essential to establishing any such preemptive satellite strike capability.' The analyst's shoulders slumped. 'I don't really care about all that. As far as I'm concerned I just want Canberra to rethink its position and keep intercept facilities on Australian soil, under our own control.' A thought crossed Dennison's mind. 'For instance…' he hesitated and frowned, unaware that his words were a touch slurred. 'Look, what I'm about to reveal must remain off the record. Okay?'

The journalist nodded then checked the recorder again.

'Let's assume that the Darwin facility was already under

U.S. control. Over the past days we have been monitoring a shitload of activity relating to the militias in East Timor and a build up of Special Forces activity across the country's east. You don't believe that the Americans wouldn't sanitize *that* intelligence if they were in the driver's seat before passing it onto us? Shit, it's U.S. weaponry the bastards are using!'

The journalist raised is eyebrows. 'You have intercepts substantiating Jakarta's involvement in what's been happening in Dili?'

Dennison flashed an annoying look across the table. 'Not just Dili, but in Aceh and Ambon. All hell's gonna break loose in the Moluccas…and *that's* off the record.'

'Okay, but I'd like to hear more.'

The analyst shuffled his feet uneasily. 'They'd hang me out by the balls to dry if you use it.'

'I won't…trust me.'

Dennis tried to read the other man's eyes. 'If you do, they'll be able to identify me as a possible source.'

'You have my word.' The Singaporean leaned across and turned the tape recorder off, slipped a hand into his trousers' pocket and activated the backup he carried. Placated, Dennison then revealed the names of the Indonesian officers whose conversations directing militia elements in East Timor had been intercepted —amongst these, a *Kopassus* Special Forces Major by the name of Supadi whose name was listed on file as a member of Group 5, more commonly known as Detachment 81, the TNI's 'dirty tricks' center.

Within two hours transcripts of both tapes would be on the Director of Security and Intelligence Department (SID)'s desk in Singapore.

Four months later when the story broke in the press,

American spy agencies decided unanimously to be far more circumspect in any future dealings with the Aussies. The U.S. dominated intercept station at Kojarena in Western Australia was instructed to broaden its brief to include the Indonesian Palapa satellites. Information gleaned from communications between the militant Islamic groups, the Philippine *Abu Sayyaf* and the Moro Liberation Front, the *Jemaah Islamiyah* in Java and Malaysia was monitored and sent directly to the U.S. National Security Agency.

Emphasis at the Shoal Bay installation remained concentrated more on Indonesian military interception – and the flow of information relating to the alarming rise in communications between militant Muslim extremist groups across S.E. Asia was channeled to Washington. ASIO and ASIS's preoccupation with the approaching East Timor referendum and the Indonesian presidential elections continued to blind Canberra's intelligence eye, permitting Abu Bakar Bashir and Hambali to pass through immigration channels undetected, during their frequent visits into Australia.

JAKARTA

General Suharman ground his teeth when he came to the end of the report, intensely annoyed that Major Supadi's teams had still been unable to locate and remove Riduan Isamuddin from the Moluccan scene. He glared at Colonel Sutrisno, the BAKIN 'Dirty Ops' departmental head. 'What do you make of this?' he demanded, 'are we supposed to believe that even the *Kopassus* can't find this piece of shit?'

The Colonel stood uneasily. It was his 'housekeeping' team that had failed the General. 'Hambali has proven to be most elusive,'

'Elusive?' Suharman's chuffy cheeks filling with blood as he prepared to explode, 'I don't want to hear, *elusive*, Colonel,' he pointed at the report, his hand shaking angrily. 'And they are now referring to him as a field commander?' He stabbed at Hambali's photo staring back up at him. 'He's nothing but dog's vomit,' he scoffed; his voice then becoming menacing, 'just get me his head!'

* * * *

CHAPTER SIX

JUNE 1999
The Netherlands – Amsterdam

Volkert van Leeuwen signaled his associate to commence filming the demonstrators gathered in Dam Square outside the Grand Hotel Krasnapolsky, chanting in opposition to the presence of an Indonesian general who stood accused of atrocities against humanity. Van Leeuwen's team were members of the *Binnenlandse Veiligheidsdienst* or BVD, the Dutch Internal Security Service, charged with the responsibility for maintaining surveillance over members of the Dutch chapter of the Indonesian outlawed Southern Maluku Republic (RMS). As the BVD agent panned the five-hundred-strong throng, the high profile RMS leader in exile raised his arms, collapsing the crowd into silence.

'The brutal reign of the so-called New Order in Indonesia is nearing collapse due to the undying resolve of those who continue to support the popular student-led movement to bring equality and justice to their country. I say 'commenced its collapse' because Suharto's repressive, militaristic and anti-democracy regime remains desperately clinging to power. It is imperative that we are reminded of our Christian friends and relatives in the Moluccas who at this very time are being subjected to the ...'

The speaker's voice drifted as agent Rima Passelima lifted her head and squinted against the early summer, midday sun, her eyes roaming the buildings surrounding the square, alert to the possibility of this demonstration turning ugly. A Dutch Internal Security Service operative, Rima had successfully penetrated the RMS the year before and, with intelligence reports suggesting the possibility of confrontation with non-Christian Indonesian students studying in Holland, she remained vigilant.

Born to Evalina de Rooij and Johannes Passelima, Rima enjoyed the richness of the Dutch-Ambonese mix, her head-turning Eurasian features catching the eye of a BVD recruitment officer on campus during her final year at university. Although her parents had been enthusiastic at the time and supported Rima's desire to join the government agency, Rima recalled that her father had expressed concern when learning that his daughter would be required to participate in field operations; somewhat bemused when she posed as an active member of the RMS in Amsterdam.

In 1950 her father had been amongst the many thousands of Ambonese who had been granted asylum in Holland, when a bloody attempt to secede from the fledgling Indonesian Republic failed. With the Japanese defeat in 1945 Indonesian nationalists had seized the opportunity to declare the country's independence, sparking a war with their former colonial masters that would continue until 1949. The Dutch sponsored the formation of the Republic of the United States of Indonesia to counter the nationalist movement. As the southern Moluccans were predominantly loyal to the Dutch, many of whom having devoted their lives to their colonial masters and achieved both administrative and military skills, they were urged to declare their independence when the RUSI movement crumbled.

The Dutch manipulated the Moluccans in order to maintain a foothold in the archipelago, particularly during the period Holland and Indonesia fought over the sovereignty of what would become West Papua. In 1949 when Indonesian independence was acknowledged the Netherlands ceded what had been a separate colony to be incorporated into the new Republic of Indonesia – and tens of thousands of Moluccans were transported from the Spice Islands to Holland where they remained hostile towards Jakarta and the Islamic community, never abandoning their dream of a free and independent Moluccan state.

Rima recognized Volkert van Leeuwen moving surreptitiously across her peripheral vision, the senior agent's presence comforting the young operative. She scoured the curtained windows above again, curious that her section chief had taken an active role in the day's operation. As the RMS leader appealed for support in the ongoing cause against the military suppression of Ambon, East Timor, Aceh and West Papua, Rima caught the momentary sparkle of the sun's reflection from a second storey window. Alarmed, she turned to see if the other BVD agents had identified the imminent danger. Realizing they had not she focused on the open window and knew, instinctively, there would be no opportunity to disarm the shooter. Without hesitation, she launched forward, elbowing her way to the front of the crowd, the surprised would-be-assassin hesitating, sending the silenced projectile wide, creasing Rima's head and rendering her unconscious.

Concluding that the young woman had slipped on the pavement in the crush, concerned hands lifted the unconscious agent and carried her out of harm's way, one of the demonstrators hailing a white-topped, yellow taxi that transported her to the hospital.

The demonstration then continued without further incident, none present other than the Indonesian assassin dematerializing from the scene, aware of the passing danger.

*   *   *   *

CHAPTER SEVEN

DECEMBER 1999
Ambon

Snipers were evident everywhere. No one was safe. Even the Chief of Police was shot as he drove through the strife-torn city filled with armored vehicles and grenade-carrying children. As nigh on three thousand had been massacred since the beginning of the month Ambon was now unmistakably a war zone. With Christmas again falling during the month of *Ramadan* the volatile mix of Muslims fasting and Christians vocal in their own preparations, continuing to fill the streets with dead.

Untold numbers of Christians lay buried in mass graves while hundreds of thousands of displaced persons filled hastily erected refugee camps on adjacent islands. Muslim mobs streaming through Christian-dominated areas chanting 'God is great!' leaving bodies in their wake had become an all-too familiar sight. Soldiers from various army, police and marine units disobeyed their superiors taking sides and joining the carnage, the Christian troops pitted against their Muslim brothers further inflaming the crisis. As the religious-ethnic conflict spiraled, the violence entered a new phase with Muslim radical groups endeavoring to burn down all Christian quarters before *Ramadan* came to a close at the end of the first week in January.

Six hundred kilometers to the south the Catholic capital of Dili in East Timor had suffered similar consequences. It would seem that the scholars and clerics of the Indonesian Council of Ulamas supported the view that the declaration of a holy war against Christians in the provinces was justified, citing attacks against Muslims and their places of prayer.

Ambon was divided into two clearly definable areas – the airport and parts of the city controlled by Christians and the harbor, now occupied by the Muslims. Military units guarded the unofficial boundaries segregating the two as houses, churches, mosques and schools were burned to the ground. A group of soldiers from the elite strategic reserve, *Kostrad* broke into the Immanuel Church and dragged twenty-four parishioners outside where they doused their victims with kerosene and set them alight. In the Roman Catholic area of Ahuru, well-armed Muslim gangs supported by military elements terrorized the inhabitants, driving them away from their homes. They then looted the dwellings before setting fire to the buildings, fleeing the area in army trucks. Armed with homemade handguns the Christians were no match against the Muslim gangs that had been equipped with automatic weapons, grenades and even teargas. Silo Church, the main Protestant Church situated some one hundred metres from the grand Al-Fatah Mosque, was destroyed by fire. Thirty-nine Christians were shot when the building came under attack by soldiers in armored vehicles.

In a statement issued in Jakarta the Indonesian Communion of Churches (PGI) called for international peacekeepers to be placed in the riot-torn province fearing that the Muslims planned on taking over all of Ambon before the *Idulfitri* celebrations which marked the end of the *Ramadan* fasting month.

> *"The massive attacks against Christian congregations is a direct consequence of the lack of transparency in the handling of the conflict in Maluku by the Indonesian Military (TNI) and the Police Force. If accountability is not undertaken, then, taking into consideration the continuing violence and heeding the people's strong feelings, it would be best if the Indonesian army and police forces were pulled out of Maluku and replaced with international peacekeepers. We consider this conflict, which has been given a religious label, as an extermination of the indigenous Maluku people along with their social institutions to be replaced by another society whose form cannot yet be ascertained."*

The statement was signed by the PGI Chairman, and General Secretary.

In all, seventy-five churches, mosques and other places of worship were destroyed in December. Then, the holy war was taken to the streets of Jakarta, with eighty-thousand demonstrating outside the Indonesian Parliament clamoring for more troops to be sent to deal with the Christian problem in the country's eastern provinces.

* * * *

Caught in a wedge movement Johanis Matuanakotta remained deathly still viewing the *Laskar Jihad* column of heavily armed men approaching the village. As the militia stormed the hamlet screaming *"Allahu Akbar"* he could see that most carried automatic weapons, their intentions frighteningly clear as they humped cans of gasoline into the square and prepared to light homemade torches.

Shots shattered the air when a stray teenager was spotted

fleeing the scene, Johanis shrinking lower into the underbrush as bullets traced the youngster across the square, delivering the young man dead at Johanis' feet. Suddenly, the air crackled with flames dancing from thatched roofs into overhanging coconut palms, the running-crown fire sucking the surrounding air dry, enveloping the entire village within minutes. Johanis rose cautiously seeking an opportunity to run only to be struck with the butt of an M16 from behind, Johanis already unconscious when his attacker drove a bamboo bayonet deep into his side.

The day passed, the evening delivering a tropical storm. Drenched with rain Johanis regained some semblance of consciousness. Aware of the serious nature of his wound he dragged his body into the charred remains of the nearest structure then fell asleep, savagely awakened the following morning with a probing kick from a TNI regular.

'This one's still alive,' the soldier called out, aiming his rifle at Johanis' head.

'Well just shoot him, you idiot!' the platoon commander snapped, stepping forward to see for himself. The solider raised his weapon, Johanis' eyes locked with those of his executioner. Suddenly, the sergeant stepped forward. 'Wait!' he ordered, brushing the rifle aside with one hand when he recognized the *Coker* gang member he had seen loitering around the Marantha Church in Ambon. 'We'll take him back for interrogation.'

JAKARTA
Presidential Palace

The presidential aide hovered in attendance observing with a critical eye while the Palace household staff busied themselves dusting and polishing Abdurrahman Wahid's spacious office.

'Clean around these,' the aide pointed to the stack of Beethoven CDs strewn across a massive desk, positioned in accordance with the principles of Feng Shui. A crooked painting offended the aide's eye. He danced across the room to rectify the problem then stood overseeing the domestics complete their chores before President Wahid, whom they all referred to by his honorific childhood name, Gus Dur, returned for another of his crisis meetings. 'Finish up now,' the aide urged, ushering the staff from the spacious office when his opposite number, the household political aide signaled through the doorway. He nodded in approval and slipped out of sight, unnoticed, as the powerful military commander arrived for his appointment with the President. The aide positioned himself in readiness to serve when summoned, remaining in thoughtful silence ruminating, considering the President's first two stormy months in office.

With the media portraying the President as unpredictable, ambiguous and impetuous, the torrent of optimism following Wahid's election had quickly subsided. The economy remained sluggish; religious and ethnic violence had flared and his efforts to promote dialogue with secessionist forces had failed to harvest support from the armed forces. In Aceh, the separatist Free Aceh Movement (GAM)'s five-thousand-strong guerrilla force had effectively gained control of much of the northern province, the TNI incensed when Wahid rejected their demands to impose martial law. Then, in the past week when sectarian fighting had broken out in the Moluccas, the conflict had provoked street demonstrations in Jakarta with Muslims calling for a holy war against Christians. In Kalimantan, Indonesian Borneo, ethnic clashes between the indigenous Dayaks and Madura transmigrants had again erupted, the bloody toll clearly demonstrating that elements within the Indonesian military were complicit in the turmoil.

Undermined by military hardliners, business and political vested groups and while Vice President Megawati Sukarnoputri waited impatiently in the wings, the Wahid Administration had already started to crumble.

The aide considered the flurry of most recent Palace rumors. Although gossip had it that General Wiranto, the pro-Suharto military commander would be replaced for resisting the President's conciliatory approach towards secessionist leaders, the aide knew from conversations he had overheard of deep concerns that Wiranto was being encouraged to challenge the nation's leadership. With ownership of the media predominantly in the hands of Wahid's political opponents and ambitious Muslim leaders such as the fundamentalist, Amien Rais biting at his heels, the atmosphere within the Palace had, in a matter of weeks, switched from one of euphoria to that of fear for survival.

*　　*　　*　　*

An angry exchange reverberated along the Palace corridors startling the staff. Suddenly, the door to the President's office was flung open and the General stormed out leaving an empty, foreboding silence to descend upon them all.

AMBON
Laskar Jihad HQ

Johanis Matuanakotta coughed and spluttered his way to consciousness, his interrogator removing the soggy pillow case that had been tied over his head to inhibit the flow of air into his lungs. Blindfolded and handcuffed to a chair he could but listen, identifying what his captors had planned for him next when someone attached a metal clasp to his testicles. His sphincter muscles tightened, the shock of the electric charge choking the rising scream in his throat.

Major Tony Supadi observed the interrogation dispassionately as the prisoner jerked wildly then slumped forward, unconscious. A guard stepped forward and pulled Matuanakotta's head back by the hair and poured water over the prisoner's head.

'You'll get nothing out of this one,' Hambali's bearded figure moved to the center of the concrete chamber. 'If he had anything he would have given it up by now.'

Supadi was relieved. He had happened to be at Hambali's quarters when the TNI regulars had passed Matuanakotta to the *Laskar Jihad.* Supadi had insisted on being present during the interrogation, prepared to personally intervene and execute the *Coker* should he incriminate *Kopassus* over their covert support for the Christians. Fortunately for Supadi, the prisoner was rank and file and had not yielded anything of any significance during his incarceration. 'Bury him with the others,' he ordered.

Matuanakotta's body was dragged from the room leaving the Major alone with the *Jemaah Islamiyah* operations commander.

* * * *

Hambali's elements, masquerading as soldiers had successfully raised the level of the conflict over the past months by arbitrarily shooting Christians on Ambon's streets. The Christians had responded accordingly, the sectarian violence spreading across the Moluccan Islands into Sulawesi, the rising death toll in both provinces dwarfed by events in the former Indonesian province of East Timor as Australian troops were confronted with the horrors of Jakarta's scorched earth policy and militia reprisals.

'You still plan on leaving tomorrow?' Hambali heard Supadi ask.

'*Insha Allah,*' he replied in his typical, succinct style. Deliberately vague, he did not feel the necessity to elaborate for the *Kopassus* officer's benefit. There was much for him to do; to prepare. As for Ambon, for the time being, his work was done and he needed to be elsewhere – in Malaysia, to reaffirm his position as the *Jemaah Islamiyah* number two following the movement's co-founder, Abdullah Sungkar's death. Also, Hambali wished to facilitate the arrival of some one hundred and fifty hardened Afghani *Mujahideen* soldiers who would be deployed to Ambon.

Once these matters were settled he would visit Mukhlas and his family in Java, to provide spiritual and material support the embryonic cell that had been established there – and Mukhlas, who would one day, assume operational control of the *JI*.

* * * *

Johanis Matuanakotta struggled to breathe under the suffocating weight as he fought to maintain consciousness in the shallow trench, the sickening smell of rotting flesh from earlier executions assailing his nose. Slowly, painfully, he freed an arm and pushed past the body directly above, his hand clawing through the thin layer of mud covering the hastily prepared grave revealing a trickle of sunlight.

He blinked through one eye, the alarming realization that he had been buried alive spurring him into frenzied action, his bloodied fingers scraping a hole to freedom.

JAKARTA

'*Bangsat Australia semua!*' General Suharman cursed all Australians, the outburst reflecting his fellow-officers' feelings. Three months had passed since the East Timorese voted overwhelmingly for independence from Indonesia.

When the interim Indonesian President, Habibie had announced that the annexed province would be given the opportunity to vote on whether to remain as part of the Republic or become an independent state, Jakarta, Washington and Canberra believed the outcome to be a *fait accompli*. The people of East Timor had been subjected to the most brutal occupation since the Indonesian invasion of 1975, and the United Nations-sponsored referendum was expected to favor Jakarta. History again repeated itself with the Indonesian military increasing its intimidating presence throughout the former Portuguese outpost to ensure a pro-Jakarta outcome. However, when the brave Timorese came down from their mountain hideaways through the early morning mists and cast their vote against their oppressors, the Indonesians were stung and formally withdrew from their Security Treaty with Australia.

It was now only weeks since the Australian-led multinational force, INTERFET had began landing troops in Dili, their presence a smart slap at Indonesian pride, the Indonesians humiliated, as the Australian-led force was the first time a foreign army had occupied their sovereign territory since Dutch Colonial forces agreed to withdraw from the archipelago in 1949.

Australian Collins Class submarines had sailed into Indonesian waters undetected, gathering information on shipping and activity around naval bases from periscope depth while RAAF EP-3 Orion maritime aircraft carried out 'black' surveillance flights over the archipelago, monitoring both military and civilian movement. Missions were also carried out with the reconnaissance version of the F111 bomber, the RF111C which were equipped with long-range imaging pods enabling the crew to record signals and sounds over great distances.

With foreign aircraft wandering wide of established air corridors Indonesian F16s intercepted a RAAF Boeing 707 air tanker and four F/A18s in its airspace whilst another came within metres of engaging an Australian Hornet.

'It's not all over yet,' General Sumantri served with army intelligence. 'If the current level of instability continues we would be justified in maintaining our military presence,' his lip curled into a sneer, 'to restore peace,' the statement sending the room into speculative silence.

General Suharman disliked Sumantri; they were on opposing, philosophical sides. Sumantri's 'Greens' had made substantial inroads within the military leadership since Suharto had stepped down; Suharman annoyed that his own position was constantly being challenged by the younger officers.

There were seven senior officers present; the meeting called to put aside differences between the 'Red & Whites' and the 'Greens' to determine what action would be taken to resolve the military's dilemma concerning the embarrassing loss of East Timor – and to discuss the TNI's future with the election of President Abdurrahman Wahid and his VP, Megawati. All present recognized the dangerous precedent of losing a province at a time when separatist movements threatened the Republic's unity. Secretly, additional troops had been deployed to Aceh, West Papua, West Timor, Sulawesi, Kalimantan and more recently, Ambon to extinguish the growing tide of anti-Javanese resentment. Now, with the loss of East Timor a potential catalyst for other separatist movements to attract international attention, the country was faced with its own domino collapse.

Although the generals in attendance were engaged in their own power struggle, all clearly understood the consequences of losing another province and the disastrous consequences such an event would bring for the Javanese people. The country's population had grown beyond two hundred million; half of that number occupied Java, the conundrum being that the wealth lay outside the island, most in those provinces now under pressure from separatist movements. The consensus amongst those present was that the military must be returned to power; and at whatever cost.

As for the relationship between the new president and the TNI, both groups present accepted that on that front, they should remain united. During the presidential election run-up more than one hundred and sixty generals had attended Megawati Sukarnoputri's Indonesian Democratic Party congress to offer their support, believing that due to her inexperience she would become increasingly dependent on the military. When the near-blind cleric, Wahid stole her thunder, a tremor of concern shook the military establishment. Wahid had a reputation as a moderate, tolerant religious leader, dangerous to the military because of his support for the democratization of the Indonesian Republic. Wahid had been elected with the support of Islamic and Muslim-based parties and, although those in attendance all followed the Islamic faith, they were determined that there would be no power-sharing with those to whom the new president was indebted.

'I spoke to the Americans and they confirm that no U.S. troops will be sent into Timor,' General Sumarlin broke the silence.

'But that won't prevent the Australians from sticking their noses in where they're not wanted,' Suharman responded.

'Well,' Sumarlin glanced around the room, 'why don't we just bloody that nose a little?' Heartened by supportive nods he continued. 'The Australian public didn't support their involvement in Vietnam. If there are heavy casualties, the Australian voters will insist that their troops are withdrawn.'

'Surely you're not suggesting our engaging the Australians?' a recently promoted Brigadier challenged. He had participated in a number of training programs under the Defence Cooperation Agreement and had attended the jungle warfare training course at the Kanungra base in Southern Queensland.

Suharman looked at the young 'Greens' officer with disdain. 'You don't think that our soldiers are a match for the Australians?'

General Sumantri came to his colleague's defence. 'I believe that most of us would be more comfortable having the militia elements involved. If it became apparent that Indonesian troops were ordered to engage the Australians then we would be tantamount to inviting the British and the Americans to the party. How long do you think our hardware can survive without spare parts and other technical support? As it is, with President Clinton's suspension of military ties and the U.S. Congress moving to suspend all military and economic assistance we are already grounding aircraft.' He paused, gathering his thoughts. 'Why not just increase our support for the militia and see where that takes us first?'

'I agree with *Pak* 'Mantri,' the Brigadier jumped back in. 'The militias have proven their value and we should continue to support them.'

'I'm not convinced that they have the numbers to do the job.'

'They will, providing they have our support all the way.'

Subsequent to former president, Habibie, offering the opportunity for the East Timor autonomy vote the TNI revived old militia groups such as the *Gada Paksi* (Young Guard for the establishment of Integration), a unit that had been formed from young recruits who were trained by the *Kopassus* Special Forces in 1994-1995. Eurice Gueterres, the leader of the *Aitarak* militia was a prominent participant in the *Gada Paksi*. The revamped militia groups would then become the main component of the Integration Fighting Force under the command of such infamous names as Joao Tavares, Eurico Gueterres and Costa da Silva. Even the former head of the TNI, General Wiranto recognized the role the pro-integration militia would play when preparing his Combat Contingency Plan.

The well-armed militia totaled some eleven hundred men with an additional support base of twelve thousand spread through organizations such as *Besi Merah Putih, Aitarak, Guntur Kailak, Halilintar Junior* and the Red Dragon. Apart from the weapons left behind by the departing Portuguese twenty-five years before, the militias were supplied with SKS carbines, M16s, Mausers, grenades and pistols.

In the weeks following the referendum, Jakarta-sponsored East Timorese militias had gone on a murderous rampage across the province killing more than a thousand, forcing locals from their homes and into the mountains. All but a few buildings had been destroyed, the international community watching the carnage on live television as Indonesian paramilitaries armed with American-M16s carried out their slaughter.

'There are already calls for an independent West Papuan state in Irian Jaya and there is growing support from Australian church groups for the Ambonese RMS separatists. Our failure to respond will ensure a domino effect in demands for independence.' General Suharman remained belligerent towards the Australians. 'If we don't send the Australians a very clear signal of our displeasure then we are only putting off the inevitable. Mark my words,' he warned, 'one day our troops *will* fight the Australians over Indonesian soil. Believe me, East Timor is just their litmus test to challenge our resolve.'

* * * *

General Sumantri smiled inwardly as he threw a fleeting glance at the blubberous Suharman. Although this meeting between the 'Greens' and the 'Red & Whites' represented a step towards reconciliation, any real rapprochement would be dependent upon Suharman's faction surrendering some of their power – or, alternatively, having the new president replace the Suharto loyalists, severing their culturally ingrained obligations with the past when it became apparent that they had lost control over the nation's security.

Sumantri's 'Greens' had conceived a most diabolical plan to bring about such an unstable environment. Secretly, they had supported the formation of a paramilitary, Islamic guard to be known as the *Laskar Jihad*. Although training camps had been operational in the mountains south of Jakarta for most of that year, the formal announcement regarding the *Laskar Jihad's* existence was not scheduled until early in the New Year. The communiqué would establish that the paramilitary force had been established in response to the deliberate persecution of Muslims in the eastern Indonesian provinces. Furthermore, the press release would provide evidence that Protestant churches were planning to form a breakaway Christian state which would incorporate the Moluccan Islands, West Papua and Northern Sulawesi. Charges would be made that remnants of the RMS, the Republic of the South Moluccas elements based in the Netherlands, were providing material support for this movement which would wage war on Muslims and drive them from those provinces.

The *Laskar Jihad* would be used to create an environment of fear and instability, and undermine those positions held by the Suharto loyalists whose lingering presence remained an obstacle to the 'Greens' ascendancy.

AMSTERDAM
Dutch Internal Security Service BVD Headquarters
(Binnenlandse Veiligheidsdienst)

'You were extremely lucky.'

Rima Passelima nodded at Volkert van Leeuwen, conscious that her hand had moved to the scar where once she might have considered parting her fine, brown hair.

'Lucky,' the Assistant Director continued, 'and exceptionally brave.'

Rima shifted uncomfortably in her chair with the unexpected accolade. 'Thank you, sir,' was all she could manage, apprehensive that this interview might lead to her being permanently deskbound.

Four months in convalescence and rehabilitation following her release from hospital had provided Rima with ample opportunity to reflect on how perilously close she had been to death. Now the possibility that she might be forever precluded from further field operations as a result of her injury continued to play heavily on her mind.

Van Leeuwen's brow wrinkled as he closed her file, Rima tensing in anticipation of unfavorable news. 'Your medical report indicates that you are fully recovered.'

'Both physically and mentally,' she answered confidently, 'I believe I am...'

'Be that what it may,' van Leeuwen interrupted, with a wave of a palm, and Rima's heart sank. This was it; she was going to be deskbound for the remainder of her career. The BVD director's eyes narrowed as he considered the young agent before him. 'But are you ready for a field assignment?'

Rima's heart leaped. 'Yes sir,' she responded emphatically. 'I am as fit as I was before…'

Again the director waved her down. 'It's an overseas assignment,' she heard him say. '…and would require that you be permanently based in S.E. Asia, reporting directly to me.'

'Overseas?' she cocked her head quizzically, 'where in Asia?'

'Indonesia,' van Leeuwen revealed.

'You mentioned permanently?'

'Yes. The assignment is to establish a deep cover presence. We would need to be confident that whoever we select to fill this post accepts that they will be isolated from the Service… and expected to remain in situ for as long as required.'

'There are others being interviewed for the position?' Rima asked anxiously.

'Yes,' van Leeuwen lied, now with a twinkle in his eyes, 'but your name is at the top of our list.'

'The BVD director rose from his desk and nonchalantly flicked open a stainless steel Zippo lighter. Rima watched impatiently as her director slowly went through the routine of lighting his favorite meerschaum-lined briar, the room's silence deafening to her ears. Van Leeuwen leaned his tall frame against the desk, flourishing the curled pipe in the air.

'Back in Seventy-Five, seven South Moluccans hijacked a train at Wijster Drente. The hijacking ended with three killed – the subsequent internal inquiry determining that, although the BVD had maintained surveillance over members of the Dutch chapter of the Indonesian-outlawed Southern Maluku Republic, we failed to identify the resurgence of the RMS and its threat to national security. Third generation Moluccans had assimilated into the Dutch environment in every way…even to the point where they were more accustomed to thinking and verbalizing their emotions in Dutch rather than in their fathers' and grandfathers' native tongue.' Van Leeuwen paused to draw on his pipe before continuing. 'Then, around five years back when we dismantled the Foreign Intelligence Service, the BVD suddenly found itself without an appropriate information flow from external sources.' The director smiled knowingly at Rima. 'One of the reasons we intensified our watch and infiltration over the RMS during the past two years is because of concern that they may be linking with some of the more militant organizations which have developed a predilection for using Holland to launch their European operations.'

'Ayman al-Zawahiri?' Rima wanted to demonstrate that she remained acquainted with current BVD 'watch' lists of foreign nationals.

It had recently come to light that Al-Zawahiri, the Egyptian co-founder of the al-Qaeda had spent time in Holland during the previous year, in possession of a forged Dutch passport. The CIA had alerted the BVD of the Taliban presence, the Dutch Security Service amazed when they discovered the extent of the network which had established cells in Amsterdam, Eindhoven and Rotterdam.

'Yes, al-Zawahiri,' van Leeuwen replied. 'We had missed him completely during our investigations into the Saudi-funded al-Muwaffaq Foundation in Breda which, as you know, is considered a front organization for Bin Laden.'

'How is the RMS connected,' Rima asked, 'seems that they would make strange bedfellows considering their opposing religious leanings?'

'Our concern is that the Islamic extremist groups have become far more sophisticated in their penetration of other organizations. In the past, these extremists operated predominantly through mosques and Islamic foundations, even schools. Since Chechnya became unstable they have supported separatist groups there, as they have in Afghanistan. There's even a website run out of The Hague calling upon Muslims here to support the Chechnya jihad movement. If you visit the site you'll see that local Muslims are directed to join the Dutch army to take advantage of the training offered.'

'And the connection with the RMS?' Rima reminded.

'With the massive flow of Muslim immigrants over the past twenty years, we have seen international organized crime playing a key role in facilitating the illegal entry of many of these illegals across the badly-guarded Schengen borders. The BVD's position is that this migration poses a substantial security risk. Because we enjoy a reputation of tolerance towards political and religious refugees, terrorists and other subversive elements have increasingly been establishing their presence in this country under the pretext of asylum. So, in answer to your question, the BVD believes that the RMS has been infiltrated by extremist, Indonesian elements impersonating Moluccan sympathizers connected either directly with Saudi terrorist groups, or any of the growing number of S.E. Asian cells.'

'Unfortunately, I didn't have enough time to check out the local membership.' Rima unconsciously touched the scar on her head again, reminded of her near-death experience. 'So, the assignment I'm being considered for is connected?'

'Yes, but we'll leave that until a decision has been made as to whom the successful candidate might be.'

'If I *were* to be chosen,' she pressed, 'would I remain in the employ of the BVD?'

Van Leeuwen placed the pipe at one side of his mouth. 'Most likely you have heard the scuttle bug about the BVD undergoing a shake up?'

'Yes sir,' Rima replied, 'It would be safe to say that we've all been following the proposed changes since legislation was submitted to the Lower House last year.'

'Well, I can reveal something of what we can expect.' The director returned to his chair. 'The Service will be restructured and renamed with a new function being added.' His face became more serious. 'If you are selected for the assignment you will be part of the new section charged with external operations.'

Rima showed her surprise. 'International Ops?'

'Yes. The BVD will become the General Intelligence and Security Service, the AIVD. Although operations will basically be related to non-military matters there will be times when the new organization's activities will overlap with other departments.'

'When will the restructure take place?'

'It's imminent. We're ready to move, just waiting for the legislation to be passed. Mind you,' van Leeuwen stared directly at Rima, 'all of this remains here in this room.' The director tried to smile. 'Wouldn't want to jeopardize our chances with that posting, would we?'

Rima nodded affirmatively. 'I appreciate your taking me into your confidence, sir.'

Van Leeuwen stoked his pipe with the end of a paper clip as he ended the interview. 'Well, let's keep our fingers crossed that we'll have some good news for you within the month.'

Dismissed, Rima headed directly for the files registry to

brush up on information connecting the RMS and any al-Qaeda related activity.

* * * *

Assistant Director van Leeuwen sat contemplating his choice of Rima Passelima for the deep cover assignment which would take her to Indonesia, and the Moluccan Islands. He flipped open the personnel file and gazed admiringly at her photograph, the Dutch-Ambonese features captivating, even without a smile. Rima would be required to assume the new persona created for her, one which would place her in a position where she could build trust with elements associated with the RMS in Indonesia.

Having whetted her appetite van Leeuwen in no way doubted that she would accept the conditions of the assignment. Officially, Rima's employment with the BVD would be terminated due to mental health considerations, a tragic result of her having been shot during the June demonstrations.

The creation of a community-based organization had been van Leeuwen's idea, enthusiastically supported by the BVD director, suggesting that if the project proved to be successful, the idea may well become a model for establishing intelligence gathering networks elsewhere. Van Leeuwen's Non-Governmental Organization, or NGO, would be so structured as to enable the placement of an officer on the ground in Indonesia, ostensibly to oversee the establishment of a promotional training enterprise to lift the level of technical expertise amongst the target community. Rima's role would be to assist with the placement of Ambonese with commercial, government and non-profit organizations, wherever these opportunities arose.

Hopefully, the NGO would also provide Rima with the opportunity to develop lines of communication into Indonesian government agencies and departments, further enhancing the viability of the long-term intelligence gathering station. Van Leeuwen would run this operation directly. And, until such times as Parliament cleared the BVD to conduct such clandestine activities, only he and the Director would be aware of Rima's covert assignment.

Van Leeuwen ruminated upon the BVD slosh fund allocation the director had approved to finance the NGO operation. Such an arrangement would have been impossible under previous administrations when finance was so tight the United States CIA financed the BVD to prevent its collapse. And, it was not until the success of "Project Mongol", that the Treasury finally loosened its purse strings to oil the intelligence gathering machine.

In ponderous mood, van Leeuwen looked back upon the sting operation that had resulted in his rapid rise within the BVD ranks and considered running a similar operation again, to ensnare some of the militant Islamic groups. The BVD had created its own clandestine operation code-named 'Project Mongol', by establishing what appeared to be a Maoist front organization called the 'Marxist-Leninist Party of the Netherlands'. The intention was to determine what influence Mainland China exerted on Maoist groups in Europe, the results staggeringly successful. Beijing chose the MLPN as the 'best' among the different Maoist fractions in the Netherlands and honored its 'chairman' accordingly. They even gave financial support to the 'party'.

The Assistant Director's eyes again fell to the black and white photograph. He placed a finger to his lips then to Rima's and sighed wistfully, opening his trousers and stroking his crotch thoughtfully, conjuring up an image of her lying naked before him.

JAKARTA – MENTENG

Lt. Colonel Tony Supadi was ushered through the renovated colonial residence with its teak-paneled walls and other appurtenances reflecting the Dutch era. Entering General Sumantri's inner sanctum he saluted the new *Badan Intelijen Strategis,* (BAIS) Strategic Intelligence Agency chief. General Sumantri reported to TNI Headquarters…usually directly to the Commander-in-Chief. Whether he passed the sensitive information on to the President was his call, under the restructured arrangements.

'I thought it more appropriate that we meet here in my home,' Sumantri waved the recently-promoted officer to an ornately carved teak chair, 'where the walls don't have ears.'

The Colonel remained silent, his eyes surveying the setting with drooped regimental flags and two decades of military memorabilia. A row of wall plaques arranged chronologically evidenced some of Sumantri's career highlights, including stints at Fort Benning and Fort Leavenworth, in the United States.

'Your work in Ambon appears to have achieved the desired effect,' the General offered, approvingly, lowering his gaunt frame to sit opposite the younger man.

'If only the same could be said for *Tim-Tim,*' the Colonel countered, referring to the former province by the more familiar acronym for Timor-Timur.

Sumantri nodded solemnly. 'Yes,' he paused, reflectively, 'who would have thought…?'

General Sumantri leaned back and to one side favoring an injured hip sustained during a training drop earlier in his career. He peered over rimless spectacles. 'No doubt you are aware of the calls for an international tribunal to be established?'

Colonel Supadi shifted uncomfortably. 'I had heard the rumor.'

'I don't believe it's going to amount to anything serious,' the General commented, the absence of conviction in his tone, unsettling.

'The President only has to say no,' Supadi proposed, hopefully.

'Perhaps he'll throw *Pak* Wiranto to the wolves and that'll be sufficient to satisfy the activists?' Sumantri suggested, contempt dripping from his voice. 'Even the Americans have abandoned the General.'

Lieutenant Colonel Supadi believed there was substance to the rumor that the U.S. Commander-in-Chief of the Pacific, Admiral Denis Blair had been ordered to deliver a message to General Wiranto at the height of the violence in East Timor, condemning Indonesia's handling of the crisis. Word had it that Blair not only failed to deliver the message but actually signaled Wiranto that he still enjoyed the Admiral's support. 'But surely President Wahid realizes he would disaffect many in the military if he sacked *Pak* Wiranto?'

'Not all,' Sumantri intimated, referring to the 'Greens' within the military, 'there are those amongst us who would prefer to see the old guard replaced with those more receptive to reformist ideals.'

'I understand, General,' was all Supadi could say.

Although now an integral part of the 'Greens' movement the Colonel still secretly harbored the greatest respect for the former Armed Forces Commander and Defence Minister who had served both the Suharto and Habibie presidencies with distinction.

Less than two months before, Abdurrahman Wahid had

appointed Wiranto as Coordinating Minister for Politics and Security. Now, it would seem, Wahid was moving to sweep the powerful general into oblivion along with others from his camp. Lt.Colonel Supadi accepted that General Wiranto was ultimately responsible for everything that his soldiers did in East Timor. He knew from his own involvement with *Kopassus* that Wiranto had become the 'fall guy' and was now expected to fall upon his sword primarily because he backed the interim President, Habibie in granting East Timor the UN-sponsored referendum.

The Colonel was also cognizant that the outcome had been determined at the outset by the 'Greens' through the *Kopassus*-dominated, parallel command that operated within the military's overall structure. Although General Wiranto was, in fact, Commander of the Armed Forces, *Kopassus* Special Forces' commanders followed their own course, operating with impunity. How many fellow officers would follow Wiranto was yet to be seen, with speculation suggesting that Lieutenant General Susilo Bambang Yudhoyono's appointment may also be precarious as he served under Wiranto as Chief of Territorial Affairs at TNI Headquarters, a position that coordinated all territorial commands including those which covered East Timor during the conflict.

'I've called you here to finalize our liaison protocols,' General Sumantri interrupted the Colonel's thoughts. 'To support our operations in Ambon and Sulawesi,' the General eyed his subordinate. 'And other destinations as these arise.'

Supadi had expected as much. 'Does this involve the *Laskar Jihad*?'

'In every sense,' the General replied, 'the first intake will complete their training within the month. I want you to spend time at the camp prior to their departure for Ambon. 'You will be their only link to my office.'

'And Hambali, will he be involved?'

'Not directly. Again, you will be his conduit directly to me.'

Supadi understood the necessity for the BAIS intelligence general to avoid any dissemination of information via BAKIN as both agencies were under the control of opposing camps within the military structure. BAIS operatives were usually recruited from the Armed Forces Intelligence School at Ciomas near Bogor in West Java, his selection from outside this chain of command a further firewall to protect anonymity. What made BIA officers such as Sumantri, powerful, was the fact that they enjoyed influential positions elsewhere, their rivalry with BAKIN counterparts a constant source of resentment between the two intelligence groups.

'Will my activities be funded in the same manner as before?'

General Sumantri's face creased with a smile. 'Of course.'

Although unhappy with this response the Colonel held his tongue. Initially, the East Timor Black Ops had been funded by using clandestine slush funds obtained from BULOG, the state-operated logistics bureau until the military intelligence agency, BAKIN authorized a counterfeit money operation to fund the militias.

'When do I leave?'

'Immediately,' the General rose slowly to his feet. 'You realize of course that we are coming under greater scrutiny as a result of East Timor. And this requires that you are far more circumspect in selecting those you trust.' Sumantri stepped closer to the Colonel and whispered as if the walls could hear. 'Be extremely careful. This is a dangerous game that we play.'

He extended a hand. '...and Colonel...'

'General?'

Sumantri squeezed Supadi's hand firmly. 'I don't need to remind you of the consequences if you lead any unwanted guests to my door.'

* * * *

In the solitude of his temporary accommodations Lt Colonel Supadi considered the General's not-so-veiled threat and was reminded of the precarious nature of the sinister world through which he moved. The success of his previous year's activities confirmed his credentials as a competent field operative, the discreet accolades and his recent promotion evidence of his superior's trust. However, Supadi knew that, should he fail in the execution of this mission, he would become immediately expendable – as had so many others who had fallen from grace during Indonesia's turbulent past.

Supadi mulled over General Sumantri's comments concerning the establishment of an international tribunal, re-examining his own activities to determine whether he had left any loose ends that might incriminate. When he had been seconded to BAKIN from the *Kopassus* Joint Intelligence Unit (SGI) and ordered to Ambon, Supadi had been placed in the perilous position of not only serving two masters, but carrying out missions in separate areas of conflict, the Moluccas and East Timor. He had journeyed to Dili from Ambon regularly, monitoring both theatres and reporting sanitized versions of what he had encountered to BAKIN'S General Suharman, whilst actively engaged in *Kopassus* field operations. He had been instrumental in the training of the East Timorese militias whose teams then terrorized their own people to discourage them from supporting the independence vote.

An attack against Dili's inhabitants resulted in the execution of more than two hundred, their bodies left outside homes sending a wave of panic and fear throughout the provincial capital. The operation had been a huge success for the Special Forces and, as these killings went unpunished, the militias turned their attention to the homes of Bishops, the seminaries and schools. The Archdiocese of Dili's curia was torched, burning twenty-five alive, this action alone sending more than one hundred thousand fleeing into the mountains. Supadi's teams had then turned their attention to the town of Suai where they executed four nuns and three priests, eye-witness reports of this action now of most concern to the Lt. Colonel with the U.N. exercising control over East Timor.

Supadi's thoughts turned to the hard-nosed Hambali who had returned to his base in Malaysia, having played a major role in raising the level of sectarian violence in the Moluccas – the officer slipping into a state of brooding disquietude about the cleric's extrinsic relationship with *Kopassus* and General Sumantri. In Ambon, he had listened with tongue in cheek when Hambali expounded the tenets of the *Jemaah Islamiyah* philosophy to create a Pan-Asian Islamic State, Supadi unaware that this man known to many only as Riduan Isamuddin, the teacher, was responsible for extending al-Qaeda's reach into Asia.

Although it was clear that Hambali's growing network provided the Special Forces with ample opportunity to expand their clandestine operations throughout Indonesia, Supadi remained mistrustful of the ambitious cleric's motives and the growing influence of the *Jemaah Islamiyah* within Indonesia's fragmented military, and political circles. Whatever role the *JI* operations commander would play in future Black Ops had yet to be determined, however Supadi expected that Riduan's participation would be significant, in furthering the 'Greens' cause.

With the loss of East Timor both sides of the Indonesian military spectrum agreed at least on one major issue – that the unitary state must be protected from further fracture, at whatever the cost. Lt. Colonel Supadi's mission to support Islamic paramilitary groups across the Republic was designed to further exacerbate domestic instability – and return power to the military once the flirtation with democracy failed. Instead, the classic Indonesian-Machiavellian plot would turn the country into a pariah state, identifying the archipelago as fertile ground for international terrorists.

EAST JAVA – TENGGULUN

Amrozi waved solemnly as Hambali was spirited away in a Toyota minibus, the heavily tinted windows concealing the occupants from view. He turned to his brothers as they dispersed. 'The entire time he was here, he hardly spoke to me,' Amrozi complained.

'He didn't come to see you,' Mukhlas chided.

'He should have come for the wedding,' Amrozi rattled on. In March of that year he had married Khoiriyanah Khususiyati, a one-time neighbor to Fathur Rohman Al-Ghozi, the *JI* bomb making expert.

'Be satisfied that he remembered your name,' his younger brother, Imron called back over his shoulder as Amrozi sulked away.

*   *   *   *

Hambali remained deep in thought as the van sped through the parched Javanese countryside. With the Wet Season still months away, apparent from the dry and untended fields, the

land's caretakers remained absent, the fortunate few now itinerant workers in city slums.

The *JI* operations commander contemplated the possibility
of succession should something happen to him and Mukhlas'
face again came to mind. Although Hambali considered the
man a potential challenger to his authority, he accepted that
Mukhlas would be the most appropriate choice to assume
operational control in the event of his own demise. Although
privately annoyed by Mukhlas' claim that he had been visited
by the prophet Mohammed in a dream encouraging him to
join in the holy war in Afghanistan soon after his induction
into the *JI*, Hambali admired the man's commitment to their
cause. Mukhlas had spent two years fighting the Soviets and it
was at this time, when Jori had come under attack, that he met
with the resistance leader, Osama bin Laden. It was there that
Hambali and Mukhlas had first came into contact, the new
comrades-in-arms subsequently returning together to Johor
in Malaysia where, at the suggestion of the *JI* leader, Sungkar,
Mukhlas established the Lukman nul Hakim religious school
– their front for recruiting followers who shared their militant
beliefs.

A sinister smile crossed Hambali's lips as he recalled drawing
upon selected students from the al-Mukmin Islamic boarding
school at Ngruki in Central Java, and moulding these youngsters into the anti-American fanatics they had become. Mukhlas
and his plethora of hard-line brothers had been instrumental
in maintaining the flow of Javanese dissidents into Malaysia,
where they received both religious instruction in the Wahhabi,
and tactical training in the preparation of explosives.

Operational cells dividing the region into commands
called *Mantiqis,* were created, with Hambali anointing himself

as chairman of *Mantiqi 1,* which covered southern Thailand, Malaysia and Singapore; *Mantiqi II* was allocated specific control over most of Indonesia whilst *Mantiqi III* covered all of Sabah and East Kalimantan, Sulawesi and to the north, South Philippines. Indonesian New Guinea, Irian Jaya and Australia fell under the authority of *Mantiqi IV.*

With the *JI*'s founder, Sungkar's passing Hambali believed that Abu Bakar Bashir would be endorsed as the organization's new spiritual leader. However, since Bashir had returned to Indonesia to establish the Indonesian *Mujahideen* Council Hambali continued to operate as the *JI*'s *de facto,* supreme commander – sustaining the organization's vision for the creation of a S. E. Asian Islamic state – and nurturing affiliations with like-minded militant groups and throughout the region.

The van continued on its journey to the airport of Semarang where Hambali boarded a Garuda flight and returned to Malaysia, the operations commander unaware that his visit had been monitored, the report detailing his activities passed directly to General Sumantri at army intelligence in Jakarta the following day.

A copy would then be sent to the CIA chief at the U.S. Embassy in Jakarta.

*   *   *   *

CHAPTER EIGHT

5TH JANUARY 2000
U.S. Embassy Kuala Lumpur

Pointing Agent Daniel Pedersen to a chair as he entered, the CIA station chief continued his phone conversation with the Malaysian official on the other end of the line. 'The U.S. Government appreciates your cooperation. Yes, we understand. No, our agents will not interfere,' he lied, 'we're leaving the surveillance entirely in your capable hands.' The room fell silent momentarily as the station chief listened to the Malaysian secret service head lay down the ground rules governing the operation, Pedersen remaining strait-faced when the station chief shook his head and rolled his eyes. 'Of course, we'll keep you posted once the targets leave the country.'

With the conversation over the station chief rose and moved around his desk to stretch. 'Are you ready to roll?' he asked Pedersen.

'Yeah, I have Davis standing by. We're leaving for the airport in fifteen minutes. Their flight's not due for another two hours.'

The station chief glanced at his wristwatch. 'That should give you plenty of time.' Kuala Lumpur's recently opened international airport was located sixty kilometers from the capital, the freeway frequently congested with traffic from the burgeoning Pudu Raya information technology city, Malaysia's answer to Silicon Valley. With more than half the country's population embracing Islam, traffic had lessened considerably during the *Ramadan* month, due to the general lethargy that always prevailed during the fasting month.

The CIA chief leaned over his desk and retrieved a number of photographs he had been examining before the interruption. 'These just came in,' he said, passing the black and whites to Pedersen. 'Agents took these as the targets boarded their flights.'

Pedersen accepted the photos and checked them one by one. 'Who's this?' he raised an eyebrow and held the picture for his superior to see.

'That's Nawaf Alhazmi. That photo was taken when he left his safe-house in Yemen. We've been tracking Alhazmi and his cohorts through eight CIA offices and a similar number of friendly foreign intelligence services in the hope that he will lead us to bigger fish. It's only in the last couple of hours that we've learned he's heading our way. We already have a copy of his latest passport. The bastard's somehow managed to get a multiple entry visa to the States.'

'He's on our list?' Pedersen referred to the U.S. Bureau of Intelligence and Research's TIPOFF program, an all-source database which contained biographic and derogatory information associated with more than 50,000 entities suspected of terrorist activities.

'No, not yet,' the chief replied, 'but he's sure as hell gonna make it this time round.'

Despite the officer's confidence Nawaf Alhazmi would fly into the United States under his own name, passing through customs and immigration at Los Angeles airport, remaining off the radar due to an oversight which failed to report Nawaf's existence and intentions to visit the USA, to the FBI.

JAKARTA
7th January

With the end of the *Ramadan* fast period rapidly closing, tempers were tested, the city's mood precariously approaching flashpoint. An air of volatility permeated the scene below as Special Forces' sharpshooters scanned for rogue elements amongst the one-hundred-thousand strong gathering rallying around the National Monument, on Merdeka Square.

'…and we shall resolve the 'Christian separatists' problem by force and cleanse the country of disbelievers.' The crowd roared their approval. 'Do we want what happened in East Timor to be the catalyst for the disintegration of the Indonesian unitary state?'

'No!' the crowd exploded.

'Shall we deal with this Christian conspiracy…' the speaker had to pause as others on the towering obelisk's steps waved their supporters into silence. '…a conspiracy funded by separatist Ambonese who abandoned their country to live in Holland?'

Again, the crowd screamed in unison then fell into thunderous chant, the speaker coaxing his followers into near frenzy as he screamed into a megaphone, 'Shall we rise up and take action before these subversive elements amputate yet another of our provinces?'

Across the square on Jalan Merdeka Selatan, U.S. Marines guards remained tense at their posts, prepared should the rally deteriorate into another anti-American demonstration. Above, American agents videotaped the event from behind bullet-proof, double-glazed windows. Inside the embassy, Defense Attaches, State Department analysts and intelligence section chiefs attended an ad hoc briefing to discuss the most recent developments in Indonesia's ongoing political crisis.

'Perhaps it might be best if someone could bring us up to speed on who this new group…' the Deputy Head of Mission paused to refer to notes, 'the *Laskar Jihad* are, and what they're all about?'

The Political Counselor took the lead, remaining seated as he addressed the meeting. 'If you would just bear with me for a few minutes, I'll give you some relevant background before moving onto the current situation.' The counselor continued without waiting for a response. 'The *Laskar Jihad* which loosely translates into 'Holy War Warriors' is a paramilitary organization founded by militant Indonesian Muslims to wage *Jihad* against Christians in the country's eastern provinces. Its members subscribe to the Wahhabi creed of Islam. It's headed by one Ja'far Umar Thalib. Among the group's aims is to introduce Muslim Sharia law.' The counselor glanced around the room. 'You'll find reference material appendixed to the briefing notes.'

'Have they issued any manifesto?' the Deputy Head of Mission asked.

The counselor shook his head. 'No, just some rather ambiguous mission statement. Basically, the *LJ* claim that they are not an anti-Christian movement per se, but an organization founded to prevent the collapse of the unitary state.'

'Might be a little too late for that,' the CIA station chief quipped.

'The *LJ* have announced that they will intervene in the Moluccas on the grounds that they intend combating the RMS secessionist movement.'

'RMS?' the Deputy Chief of Mission inquired as he checked his notes.

'It's an Ambonese-based group of secessionists that date back to the 1950s. The Dutch report a resurgence of the RMS in Holland over the past months and, as it's a Christian organization, its existence was bound to become a factor in the *Laskar Jihad's* attempts to garner support from Indonesia's more militant elements.' He tapped the clipboard nestled in the crook of his arm. *JI* argues that East Timor's independence is part of a Christian conspiracy to sever areas under their control and steer these towards independence. They claim that Christian fighters have been receiving arms and funds from the Netherlands.'

'They're not the first to suggest it,' the embassy's Public Affairs head remarked.

The counselor ignored the comment and continued. 'It's obvious that they selected the eastern provinces to establish their operations as government control has chronically broken down in these Christian populated areas. This group has substantial political and military backing. Our observers...' he pointed a thumb outside, 'suggest that Hamazh Haz and Amien Rais are amongst the speakers supporting the rally. Some of Jakarta's more prominent profiles are also present, including Bimaton Group's Agus Sumarsono.'

'Strange bedfellows,' the Public Affairs head suggested, 'although one shouldn't be surprised to see Rais hustling for support to shore up his own political party.' The official frowned thoughtfully. 'He was practically wiped out in the elections. Seems that modernist Muslims want a foot in both camps.

Bit surprised that Hamzah has attended though, considering his position with the United Development Party. As for Agus Sumarsono showing his face, considering his current financial imbroglio with the banks, he's likely to appear anywhere there's the smell of money.'

The CIA chief made a mental note to set up a meeting with Andrew Graham and see if he could pump Agus Sumarsono for more detail.

'Why Ambon?' the ambassador's deputy persisted, 'why not other Christian areas such as Sulawesi?'

'Because sectarian violence has already broken out in Ambon and the *LJ* would most likely plan to draw other Muslims into the fight. *Jihad'* is a powerful call...and the conflict could easily escalate and spread across the archipelago.'

Annoyed with the interruptions, the counselor dragged the briefing back on course.

'Conservative modernist Muslims were severely impacted when Suharto stepped down and then by the democratic elections six months ago. The hardliners amongst them feel threatened by the system as they remain in the minority. Over the past year since the Moluccas collapsed into violence they have worked to channel outrage at the government over their apparent impotence in dealing with the Christian militia over there. With the most recent of attacks in northern islands in the Halmahera group leaving five hundred Muslims dead, the hardliners' calls for *jihad* are receiving significant support from all levels of the country's Muslim majority.'

'We have evidence that the *Laskar Jihad* receives financial support from the al-Qaeda,' the CIA chief reported. 'Their leader, Thalib, served in the anti-Soviet *Mujahideen* in Afghanistan. He claims to have met bin Laden. Our Indonesian counterparts have him under constant surveillance.'

Privy to most secrets contained within the embassy walls, the counselor briefly locked eyes with the Langley officer. The CIA had yet to penetrate the *Laskar Jihad* as it had with other Indonesian paramilitary groups.

'Who's arming them?' the Deputy Chief asked.

'The TNI – the Indonesian military,' the Defense Attaché responded, matter-of-factly.

'American weapons?' the diplomat challenged, 'are they using U.S. weapons?'

'Yes,' the attaché confirmed. 'But there's not much we can do about that.'

'How strong a force *are* they?'

'Well,' the attaché replied with a touch of indifference, 'intelligence suggests anything from three, to ten thousand. It's difficult to determine with any accuracy as we have reason to believe that most are current serving members of the TNI.

'What is Wahid doing about them?' the Deputy directed this to the counselor.

'The President most likely considers what's happening in the Moluccas as having a low priority. He has his own problems to contend with right now. The province is far from the country's political centre-stage and with less than one per cent of the Indonesian population, historically, Jakarta has always ignored the outlying islands. Wahid would most likely be pleased to have the *Laskar Jihad* out of his hair here in Java, taking whatever unpleasantness they plan as far away as possible.'

'Risky,' the Public Affairs head interrupted again, 'considering what's happening in Aceh.'

The counselor cast an impatient look in his direction. 'It's not the same,' he countered, 'the hostilities in the Ambon area don't represent a serious threat to the country's territorial integrity whereas in Aceh, the population is almost entirely Muslim and represents a collective movement fighting for independence. When Jakarta sends troops to Aceh it results in Muslims killing Muslims. No, the Moluccan conflict cannot be compared to what is happening in Aceh.'

'But you agree that the conflict could spread to other provinces?'

'Yes, but the *LJ's* activities will mostly be confined to non-Muslim areas such as Sulawesi, the Moluccas, perhaps West Papua and even Bali.'

'But, aren't you saying that the *Laskar Jihad* is basically a strategic ploy by conservative Muslims to regain some of the influence they lost in the elections?'

'Yes, with the support of marginalized TNI officers. The *LJ* leader, Umar Thalib would not have demanded the President's resignation without their backing.'

'Then we're looking at a prolonged period of conflict?' the Deputy suggested.

'Yes,' the counselor agreed, 'the conflict serves as a reminder to all Indonesians that the country's stability is directed related to how much control the TNI can exert over political security and more importantly, economic policies – which, we've learned from the Suharto era, can generate billions in revenue for such vested interest groups.

* * * *

When learning of the *LJ* declaration to send a vanguard for the Moluccas to engage the Christians in holy war, President Abdurahman Wahid explicitly ordered them not to go. However, the Indonesian armed forces stationed at the Tanjung Perak port of Surabaya in East Java ignored the order, permitting the *LJ* contingent to board ships and sail unhindered, to the restive province.

With their embarkation, the *Laskar Jihad's* prominence and membership grew quickly, with recruits signing up from all levels of the Islamic community. Within a month the violence would spread from Ambon to the adjacent provinces across Sulawesi where agent provocateurs would lay the foundations for the arrival of a four-thousand strong, Muslim paramilitary force and embroil the American Jack McBride, in their mission. These would be the *Laskar Jundullah*, the militant wing of the Committee for the Enforcement of Islamic Law (*Komite Penegakan Syariat Islam*, KPSI). The KPSI embraced a broad program of special autonomy for the Sulawesi province, including formal implementation of Islamic law and governance under the ultimate control of an unelected group of religious scholars, a Council of Ulamas. The *Laskar Jundullah* would be led by Agus Dwikarna, a member of presidential-hopeful, Amien Rais' National Trust Party, PAN which advocated decentralizing power and giving more regional autonomy.

Militant Islam was on the move with vested interest groups standing back permitting the country's slide towards anarchy.

KUALA LUMPUR
8th January

'Where the hell has Yazid Sufaat disappeared to?' the Indian-Malay agent leading the stakeout wobbled his head irritably and mumbled to himself. The businessman's condominium in the Kuala Lumpur Hotel had been under Malaysian intelligence surveillance since Echelon intercepts confirmed the departure of the al-Qaeda-linked Saudis for the Malaysian capital. Khalid al-Mindhar's dozens of calls to Yemen during which he discussed travel arrangements to Kuala Lumpur had initiated the interest.

Working through Malaysian authorities U.S. teams had also documented the arrival of Ramzi Binalshibh, Nawaf al-Hazmi, Tawfiq bin Attash and Abu Bara, without identifying who these participants might be.

'That's him!' his partner captured the former army captain on camera as he accompanied another man out of the building.

'Who's that with him?' the agent craned his neck.

'It's Khalid' the agent identified Khalid al Mihdhar, unaware that on CIA files he was listed as a known bin Laden associate. Khalid's bio data revealed that he was second in the al-Qaeda chain of command after bin Laden, and the mastermind behind the 1998 truck bomb attacks on U.S. embassies across Africa which killed more than two hundred and left four thousand injured.

The agent lifted his shoulders then let them slump. 'If only we'd been able to get the bastard's condo bugged in time.'

*   *   *   *

Dressed in flowing Arab dress and trademark *kopiah,* skull cap atop his head to impress, Hambali's spirits soared. Although *Operation Bojinka* had been compromised some years earlier, with the arrival of Khalid and the others, the revised operation was now on track.

Khalid had entered Malaysia from Yemen whilst Abu Bara, Hazmi and Khallad had all flown in via Karachi en route to the United States, where they would take their *jihad* to the American people. Hambali's chest swelled with pride – the four operatives who had all volunteered for the suicide mission were there, under his command.

153

He had suggested that Kuala Lumpur be used as the staging point for the Saudis as citizens of Saudi Arabia or other Gulf States were automatically granted visas upon arrival in Malaysia. There had been a substantial flow of *Mujahideen* wounded requiring treatment at the city's Endolite clinic, their identities and the origins of their injuries easily concealed in Malaysia's lax security environment. When this mini-summit was called, Hambali had arranged for the group to be accommodated at Yazid Sufaat's condominium; his fellow *Jemaah Islamiyah* co-conspirator instrumental in providing documents for this group to enable the Saudis to obtain visas into the USA.

The Saudis conversed in their own tongue, a language not entirely unfamiliar to the Indonesian cleric. Hambali listened intently as they completed their arrangements for deployment to the United States, his excitement growing with the enormity of the Sheikh's audacious plan – grateful that the foreign intelligence agencies had not pursued the information that had fallen into their hands during the Manila debacle five years earlier, almost to the day.

It was during these discussions that specific targets were debated, amongst these the *USS Cole,* the Pentagon, and the World Trade Center's Twin Towers. As it became apparent that resources and logistics would not permit simultaneous hijacked-aircraft attacks both in Asia and the United States, the group sought guidance from the Sheikh. When a communication arrived instructing the group to abandon the Asian targets and prioritize mainland U.S.A., Hambali appealed directly to bin Laden who, in turn, supported the Indonesian's idea to mount more conventional attacks on U.S. interests throughout S.E. Asia.

Over the past year Hambali's reputation had grown immensely – as did his following. With tales of his exploits fighting against the Russians in Afghanistan, the Christians in Ambon and the southern Philippines, and his determination in furthering the *Jemaah Islamiyah* cause, the Indonesian cleric was awash with young admirers. Amongst these, Nik Adli Nik Aziz, the son of Kelantan's most senior government minister and others from the PAS, Malaysia's Islamic Party.

Hambali's network outside the al-Qaeda links now included not only the militant *Kumpulan Militan Malaysia*, but also the Moro Islamic Liberation Front (MILF), the *Rohingya* Solidarity Organisation, the *Patani* United Liberation Organisation (Pulo), the *Arakanese Rohingya* Nationalist Organisation, the *Gerakan Aceh Merdeka* and the *Laskar Jundullah* – all operating under the myopic vision of the West's intelligence apparatus.

The *Jemaah Islamiyah's* tentacles now reached across S.E. Asia and into Australia. His work now done in facilitating the Saudi connection through Kuala Lumpur, Hambali intensified his efforts in the preparation for war against the West, and Christianity, assembling teams that would strike Asia's capital and demonstrate the depth of the *JI's* commitment to a Pan Islamic State.

He called his own summit with the *JI's* inner circle in attendance, and during the meetings was appointed Secretary General for the secret Asian *Mujahideen* Assembly. His territory, all of S.E. Asia, Australia, New Zealand and Japan – his first task to orchestrate a series of bombings that would bring the Indonesian capital, Jakarta, to its knees.

* * * *

By the end of day three the summit came to a close as Muslims worldwide observed *Idulfitri* by holding mass prayers in mosques and public squares to celebrate the end of *Ramadan* and the fast – a time of hospitality when one visited relatives and sought forgiveness.

The Saudis remained under constant surveillance until all departed within the following week. They were followed and photographed wherever they ventured; whether on a shopping expedition, visiting restaurants or attending the summit meetings in the condominium complex. Upon their departure the information collected was collated and examined and, for the most part, then passed to the CIA agents at the U.S. embassy.

The CIA had failed to fully brief the Malaysian secret service as what to look for from those attending the summit; or the import of the assembly. The CIA also failed to ensure that electronic eavesdropping devices were in place. Although the Malaysian secret service videotaped the movements of Khalid Alminhdhar, Khalid Shaikh Mohammed and another dozen individuals whose profiles fitted the intelligence brief, many local Malaysian and Indonesian 'hosts' who served as drivers to the Saudi contingent were permitted to participate in the meetings without being monitored.

The CIA and FBI would miss many opportunities to arrest Hambali, Almindhar and Shaikh Mohammed whose activities had been recorded as far back as 1995 in relation to *Operation Bojinka* in the Philippines – the CIA's failure to neutralize these terrorists whilst they plotted together in Kuala Lumpur hatching future schemes against the West, was to prove devastating.

* * * *

JAKARTA
17th January

The tropical downpour paused momentarily leaving humid, tropical evening air dripping with the scent of jasmine. Waiters juggling trays of *hors d'oeuvres* and cocktails glided silently amongst the chattering guests who had spilled out into the marquee-covered garden setting – Andrew Graham's networking skills apparent as he mingled, addressing each by name, pausing to flatter the ladies and exchange knowing smiles with the men.

'Delighted you could make it, Yashwant,' Andrew joined India's ambassador and his loquacious wife, Nilima.

'Almost didn't,' the diplomat replied, 'what with half the city's roads underwater.'

'Yes, this Wet Season has been absolutely dreadful,' Yashwant's wife complained, placing her hand on Andrew's arm to secure his attention.

'This would be a first for Jakarta?' India's ambassador suggested, 'I don't believe that I have ever attended a function celebrating Martin Luther King's birthday.'

'What a clever idea,' the ambassador's wife lauded, hands clasping her fourth cocktail, 'especially with the dearth of social activity following the *Idulfitri* celebrations. I don't know how you managed to cope with…'

'Please excuse me, Nilima,' Andrew waved when Greg Young made his entrance, taking advantage of the opportunity to extricate himself from the garrulous woman's presence.

As he moved forward to greet Young, the Dutch *chargé d'affaires* stepped into his path. 'Andrew, you were preoccupied with your other guests when we arrived.' He turned to his companion. 'Rima, Andrew Graham, our host.' The embassy official buried a smile as he observed Andrew's reaction to the young woman. 'And, Andrew, this is Rima Passelima. Rima is a new arrival.'

'I hope you don't mind my crashing your party?'

'Not at all,' Andrew beamed, gently squeezing her extended

hand. 'You're with the embassy?'

'No, I am with N.I.C.D.'

'And that would be…?'

'It's a Non Governmental Organization,' Rima explained, confidently, 'an NGO. N.I.C.D. stands for the Nusantara Integrated Community Development Organization.'

'I'm sorry,' Andrew apologized, captivated by the Eurasian beauty, 'not one that I'm familiar with.'

'That's okay,' Rima replied, 'the N.I.C.D. is still very much embryonic. It's a Belgium-based non-profit organization.'

'Belgium based?' Andrew jokingly challenged the *charge* who opted to ignore the innuendo.

It was common knowledge that many NGOs had been covertly established by governments for the specific purpose of furthering commercial and political interests. NGOs were not legally recognized international entities and did not exist in any legal sense at the international level, often relying on the pretext of '*de facto*' recognition to facilitate their operations.

'Our NGO is a grassroots initiative.' Defensive, Rima repeated her well-rehearsed lines, '…established to facilitate community development in Indonesia's eastern provinces.'

'Well then, you'll have your hands full considering the current conflict. Where will you be based?'

'I'll spend most of the time in Ambon. Have you been there?'

'Not recently,' Andrew turned to greet Greg Young. 'Wasn't sure you were going to make it.'

'Bloody roads are still swamped,' Young pointed out lightheartedly, 'might have to swim back if we get another deluge like this afternoon.' He acknowledged the Dutch envoy with a nod then turned his attention on Rima. 'Hi, I'm Greg Young.'

Andrew completed the introductions, winking mischievously

at Rima. 'Greg's company operates in the Ambon area. Who knows, he might even be able to point you in the right direction in helping you get established over there?'

'What does your company do?' she asked innocently as Andrew slipped away.

The Dutch diplomat interposed. 'What does his company *not* do would be more appropriate!'

Rima looked at the entrepreneur questioningly. 'Should I be impressed?'

Young smiled politely. 'I'm just the CEO.' He spotted Agus Sumarsono talking tête-à-tête with the governor of the Central Bank, across the lawned setting. 'But we do have commercial operations in Ambon if we can be of assistance in helping you get established.'

'Thank you,' Rima gently touched Young's forearm, 'I hope you will remember me when I call?'

Young chuckled. 'You can be assured I won't forget.'

At that moment Andrew Graham reappeared and took Young by the elbow. 'Greg, there's someone I'd like you to meet inside.' The host apologized to his Dutch guests. 'Sorry, have to take him away for a few minutes. Promise to bring him back.'

The *chargé d'affaires* waited until the men were out of earshot. As temporary Head of Mission he was privy to the highly-classified directive relating to the young BVD agent's presence 'in-country'. The invitation to attend the Martin Luther King birthday celebrations had provided an ideal opportunity to introduce her to some of Jakarta's influential players.

'Both Graham and Young are contacts worthwhile cultivating,' he whispered into Rima's ear. 'Don't be misled by Greg Young's beguiling modesty.' The diplomat looked casually in

Agus Sumarsono's direction. 'Young is about as tough as they get. He built the construction giant that was taken over by the Bimaton Group controlled by Agus Sumarsono, over there.' He paused, thoughtfully. 'Might be an idea if I make my apologies and leave you to your own resources?'

Rima nodded. 'I'll be fine.'

Andrew Graham was taken aback with the Australian First Secretary, Political Affairs' choice of partners for the evening. When Angelina had appeared on the intelligence officer's arm his initial reaction had been one of resentment. Then, as he fleetingly visualized his former lover's warmth of embrace his sentiments softened, the hostility he had experienced was displaced by curiosity for her new-found relationship.

Aware that the Indonesian intelligence agencies frequently employed local talent to penetrate foreign missions Andrew found himself wondering if Angelina had been operating under such instructions when they had first met, the possibility that BAKIN had identified him as a potential source of information somewhat alarming.

As midnight approached all but the resilient had abandoned Andrew Graham's official residence. With typical panache Greg Young, believing he had finessed his way into the BVD agent's confidence whisked her away from the cocktail party to the salubrious surrounds of BATS, an up market New York-style bar in the Shangri-La Hotel. The following morning Greg Young awoke to the joyous sight of a naked Rima Passelima lying alongside.

Within the week, when the Dutch-Ambonese beauty arrived in the restive Moluccan province she had an operational office at her disposal.

* * * *

19th January

General Sumantri read the *Jakarta Post* story, folded the influential English language newspaper and sat quietly contemplating the repercussions of that morning's leading article linking former President Suharto and General Wiranto, to the sectarian violence in the country's eastern provinces. With the Wahid presidency vacillating on all major issues Sumantri believed that the country's brief experiment with democracy would come to an abrupt end – providing the Clinton Administration ceased issuing warnings that the United States would continue to support the new president regardless of the consequences.

Sumantri's face clouded; the U.S. Secretary of State, Madeleine Albright had again publicly stated that Washington clearly frowned upon any suggestion of a military coup.

As American support for the indecisive president could impede his own faction's plans to move, whilst Wahid remained in crisis with members of his Cabinet, the General decided that the capital required another form of distraction. He would slip across the Straits to Malaysia and confer with Hambali as how best to achieve this aim.

CANBERRA
OFFICE OF NATIONAL ASSESSMENTS
Tuesday 15th February

Andrew Grey responded to the ONA Director's introduction to address the extraordinary meeting, called as a result of the most recent developments in Indonesia. His eyes swept the room filled with grave faces, registering the attendance of those responsible for each of the Australian intelligence services; the Prime Minister's office in its role overseeing the ONA; the Foreign Affairs Ministry for the Australian Secret Intelligence Service (ASIS); the Attorney-General as head of the Australian Security Intelligence Organization and the Ministry for Defence which was responsible for the Defence Signals Directorate (DSD), the Defence Intelligence Organization (DIO) and the DIGO, the Defence Imagery & Geospatial Organization.

'Although it would appear that, for the time being at least, the probability of a military coup in Indonesia has diminished,' the ASIS deputy head commenced, 'Major General Sudradjat's statement of last month suggesting that the armed forces, the TNI, would assume power if government policies failed to resolve the communal violence in the Moluccan province and end the secessionist movement in Aceh, demonstrates the TNI's resolve to maintain influence over the Wahid administration.'

'Who is this general?' a politician asked.

'Sudradjat is spokesman for the Indonesian military. He was the one who warned of a military coup if President Wahid went down the path Habibie took on East Timor, and agreed to a referendum in Aceh.'

'If the TNI still maintains such a position of power in government how is it that Wahid managed to remove General Wiranto?' the PM's departmental head inquired.

'Well, the announcement caught us all by surprise. Until now, most considered Wiranto untouchable having survived Suharto's fall from grace and the ensuing confrontation with Suharto's son-in-law, General Prabowo Subianto. Even international opinion with respect to the military's role in East Timor failed to damage his position.'

'Your last assessment had Wahid on the ropes, not the General. Wasn't the TNI backing Wiranto's demands for the declaration of a state of emergency in Aceh and the Moluccan Islands?'

'Yes,' Grey admitted, 'but that was prior to the release of the National Human Rights Commission report implicating Wiranto in the East Timor violence. Upon its release Wahid called on the General to step down but the former armed-forces chief refused, resulting in a long-distance standoff until last Sunday when, upon his return, the president called Wiranto to a meeting with his VP, Megawati and the Attorney-General, Marzuki. Apparently, the General insisted on remaining in Cabinet, citing the commission's report as being nothing more than a political attack without legal basis.'

'I was told on Sunday evening that after the meeting Wahid announced that Wiranto would retain his post,' the Foreign Affairs representative interrupted. 'What happened between then and Monday morning?'

'Wahid summoned his VP again, later in the day.' Grey smiled when referring to his notes. 'Rumor has it that Megawati was out dining at the time and left for the meeting with her staff carrying doggy-bags.'

The comment fell flat and the Secret Service deputy continued. 'The result of their meeting sealed Wiranto's fate. They decided to suspend him from Cabinet until a final decision regarding his role in East Timor became public. When the announcement was made everyone was taken by surprise.'

'Would have thought that his dismissal would have brought tanks onto the streets?' the officer persisted.

'It's early days but our intelligence indicates that Wiranto has taken the announcement in his stride. The Indonesian public seems to agree with their president's decision as the stock market remains calm and there's no indication that we should expect street demonstrations in support of Wiranto.'

'The Americans have come out rather strongly?'

'They've not pulled any punches,' Grey acknowledged, 'Richard Holbrooke, the US Ambassador to the United Nations, issued a very clear warning suggesting that a military coup would do Indonesia's economy immense damage, which Jakarta should interpret as a trade embargo in the event the TNI overturns the newly elected, democratic Wahid administration. President Clinton has sent a personal message of support to Wahid and the U.S. Treasury Secretary, Lawrence Summers and Assistant Secretary of State for East Asia and Pacific Affairs, Stanley Roth will visit Jakarta over the next several days. Apart from trade and military sanctions the U.S. can also threaten Indonesia through its dominance of the IMF by withholding loans which, at this time, amount to something like $42 billion as part of the country's restructuring package.'

'And the TNI hardliners,' the PM's representative asked, 'they'll keep their troops in the barracks?'

'Some of the hard-line elements have signaled Wahid that they are annoyed with the loss of face but that line of TNI rhetoric is to be expected.'

'Have to admit, Wahid's sense of timing was quite clever,' the comment came from the Foreign Affairs representative, 'what with the U.N. Secretary-General Kofi Annan arriving virtually on the heels of the announcement.'

'I don't believe we should misconstrue that meaning Wiranto's suspension is only temporary,' Peter Rigby, the senior ONA specialist warned. 'There is formidable opposition to Wiranto from within the TNI rank and file,' he elaborated, 'and that comes from his association with the old guard.' The analyst continued. 'The growing split between the two TNI camps known as the 'Greens' and the 'Red & Whites' will most likely see an end to the careers of a number of former Suharto loyalists over the coming months. And that internal bickering will guarantee heightened tensions across Indonesia as elements within the TNI jockey for control, exploiting the separatist issues and flaming existing sectarian violence to further their aims.'

'I'll take it from here if I may, Peter?' the Assistant Director for S.E. Asian Branch of the ONA, took the helm. 'Ongoing armed engagement between Muslims and Christians throughout the Moluccan Islands continues to fuel religious conflict in other parts of Indonesia. Last month's rally in Jakarta that drew around a hundred thousand was clearly designed to incite the Muslim population. We have photographic coverage of banners demanding the slaughter of Christians and a recorded speech by Husain Umair, the Muslim Committee for World Solidarity chairman, in which he called for three million Muslims to be sent to the Moluccas to participate in a holy war against Christians. Even Hamzah Haz, the leader of the Islamic United Development Party called for a military emergency to be declared under a united Muslim front. Then we have the Indonesian chairman of the Parliamentary Assembly, Amien Rais who is also the head of the National Mandate Party. He spoke at the rally accusing the Human Rights Commission of ignoring what was happening in the Moluccas but some analysts suggest that his position is politically motivated at garnishing TNI support for his party. He blamed the Commission for serving foreign interests by conducting its investigation into the armed forces in relation to their role in East Timor. At the end of the day, the problem is that the Indonesian President is now under considerable pressure to find a solution with the death toll now into the thousands, and property damage recorded at close to ten thousand buildings. Estimates suggest that ten percent of the population of two million have either fled the area or are now displaced.'

'And do we have concrete evidence that the TNI is behind the violence?' the AG's office queried.

'Field reports forwarded by a number of Christian organizations including the Council of Churches state categorically that the TNI have been actively engaged in killing sprees. This fits with Peter's assessment that the country's military leadership is fuelling the violence in an attempt to strengthen their position within the government. It's something more like a 'creeping coup'. They have some six to seven thousand troops on the ground yet appear to be unable to put an end to the conflict. Even regional media reports have identified the correlation between the sharp rise in violence in the Moluccas and the power struggle within Wahid's government. One would have cause to agree, considering the capture of French-manufactured assault rifles and grenades from militant extremists, weapons that could only have been provided by the Indonesian army. Apart from the divisive actions by the 'Greens' and the 'Red & Whites' reported in earlier briefings, now we have both acting independently to distract both the navy and the marines who openly support the President, by broadening the Moluccan conflict. In so doing, the army would increase its control over the capital and, of course, Java.'

'Why hasn't Wahid done more to diffuse the situation?' another of the politicians present, asked.

'Wahid presides over a shaky coalition of parties which includes the military and former president Suharto's Golkar party, and Megawati's PDI-P, obviously the main reason there is so little rapport within the new Cabinet. He's preoccupied with maintaining his own power base and is most likely content to have the distraction so far to the capital's east. Quite cunningly, Wahid charged his Vice President, Megawati with the responsibility of resolving the Moluccan crisis, no doubt expecting her failure to tarnish her image. Mega remains a threat and is expected to win in the next election.'

'Is there any possibility of U.N. intervention?' the politician pressed.

'Not at this time,' the Foreign Affairs representative fielded the question, 'although there has been some support from the Dutch for an international force to be stationed in Ambon. I guess we can all understand the Indonesian response to *that* suggestion?'

Knowing smiles and shaking heads acknowledged the comment at the unlikelihood of a Dutch-led U.N sponsored force returning the original colonizers to their former outpost.

'Do we have anyone on the ground?' the Defence chief asked.

'No,' Andrew Grey explained, 'since travel to the area is now restricted we have been unable to place any assets in Ambon. Also, Jakarta is determined to keep a media lid on the conflict although they have not been successful to date.'

'Our station in Shoal Bay continues to monitor all communications to the area,' the Defence chief advised, 'and will continue to do so, on a twenty-four-seven basis.'

*　*　*　*

With the conclusion of the meeting extraordinaire Wiranto's dismissal and the inevitability of a prolonged conflict in East Indonesia was accepted as being of no great significance to Australia's interests in the immediate region.

The following week three hundred men wearing white robes and armed with machine guns and grenades leveled a Christian village located on one of the Moluccan islands, the slaughter failing to gain the attention of the Australian press.

* * * *

TALIPAO – SULU ISLAND – SOUTHERN PHILIPPINES
30TH APRIL 2000

Summoned by Khaddafy Janjalani, Aldam Tildao crossed the jungle clearing and entered the *Abu Sayyaf* leader's hut. The young Filipino was in high spirits.

'They've agreed to pay the ransom,' he announced, 'and I believe that we have you to thank for that.'

The egotistical Tildao, who preferred the name Abu Sabaya which translated into "thief of women", accepted the praise diplomatically. 'It was your idea to go on air.'

'Sure, but without your media contacts we mightn't have been given the opportunity.'

Abu Sabaya knew this to be true. Abandoned by Muslim parents at a very early age he had been raised by Christians and attended Claret College. He had studied engineering and worked part-time at Zamboanga's popular radio station, RMN Radio in Mindanao before recanting and taking up the sword, disappearing to the Middle East for several years. 'The Malaysians will make the payment?'

'No,' Janjalani slapped his thigh, 'my namesake, Libya's Muammar Khaddafy of all people!'

'Your namesake is to make the payment?' Sabaya disguised the disappointment in his voice. Acting on Hambali's advice Sabaya had gone on radio offering to exchange the hostages for one million dollars each, and demanding the Americans release Ramzi Yousef.

'That will mean that Ramzi will not be released!'

'It doesn't matter,' Janjalani was already planning how he would spend the ransom, 'what is important now is for you to arrange the exchange with Manila.'

'You're not going?' Sabaya was surprised.

'No,' the *Abu Sayyaf* leader started to stroll outside, 'not with the bounty the Americans had offered for our capture.'

Together they inspected the prisoners they had kidnapped from the Malaysian resort on Sipadan Island during a lightning raid the week before.

'It was a good move hitting the resort,' Janjalani eyed the group which consisted mainly of Europeans. He observed one of the women defecating in the open and leered. 'Don't tell them they're to be released just yet.'

Sabaya understood. Then, 'Will we have to share the proceeds with Hambali?' he asked.

Janjalani considered the question. The *JI* operations commander was also the unofficial financial conduit for channeling funds from Riyadh, having dealt directly with the *Abu Sayyaf* following Ramzi Yousef's departure in 1995. 'Hambali won't expect to share in the ransom. But, be assured he will call upon us when the need arises.'

* * * *

CHAPTER NINE

BALI
May 2000

C oconut palms swayed casually accommodating the morning breezes, the timeless trees standing in twisted majesty over broken footpaths where intricately adorned poles with palm leaf ornaments, offerings of rice and fruit for the gods, lined the broken macadam flow. Fiona Barnes stretched her neck out the minivan window, desperate for air – her concerned Balinese driver urging the woman to alight before she fouled his vehicle. With great difficulty, she dragged the sliding door open and, confronted by a scavenging dog staring up at her, smiled in stupid confusion. Mistaking the traffic-scarred animal from some childhood memory, a sickly smile dripped from her face and she tried to engage the animal in conversation. Instead, she threw up, the effects of the hallucinogenic mushroom confounding her brain and gripping her stomach in bowel-twisting cramp. When she fell headfirst into the street, vendors hurried to her aide – one local recognizing the Australian from the evening before. Some minutes passed and, with assistance, she struggled groggily to her feet and staggered towards the *losmen* complex where the journalist was ushered into a room, woefully resembling the most basic of backpacker accommodations.

The morning passed. Awakened to the sounds of village children playing outside Fiona lay on the bed gathering her thoughts; annoyed that she had not exercised more caution when ordering the mushroom omelet at breakfast. Charily, she raised herself on one arm, lit a cigarette and remained deep in thought contemplating her options.

Fiona Barnes was a 'stringer' journalist and, as such, operated as an independent reporter without the financial support of any specific media group. When news broke in relation to the militant *Laskar Jihad* forces arriving in Ambon Fiona gambled that international attention would be drawn to the event. She flew to Bali, the hub for all east Indonesian air travel, hoping to circumvent the government's visa travel ban on foreign media wishing to visit the province.

When Fiona discovered that travel passes could only be issued outside the country, and that Indonesian embassies were unlikely to process such permits for the Western media, she decided on another approach. After checking with a local tour company and identifying the Sanur Aerowisata Beach as the hotel where the Garuda crews stayed, she moved into a *losmen* a kilometre down the beach. Then she commenced her search for a captain who would be receptive to her request – determined to employ whatever aggressively sexual tactics necessary to achieve the required result. 'Sleeping for the story' is how she often explained her mediocre successes to close friends, her reputation for dropping knickers for even the most meager results, often the subject of many a bar conversation amongst her peers back in Sydney.

Having spent days hovering poolside engaging a number of cabin crew in conversation, Fiona understood that flights destined for Ambon originated from Jakarta and remained in Bali until the early morning hours, before continuing onto the eastern province. A copy of the airline's schedule flights into Ambon lay on the bedside table. Aware that the next crew would be arriving within the hour she showered and dressed, selecting the undersized tank top and denim shorts purchased specifically for the mission, then made her way along the broken beachfront path to the Aerowisata Beach Hotel.

* * * *

Wailing tires announced the ageing Boeing's arrival at Ngurah Rai Airport, gateway to the Island of Gods, the aircraft's unorthodox impact with the runway, spilling stowed baggage from overhead compartments, further startling the Garuda passengers. Agus Sumarsono raised protective hands, recovered his demeanor and again glanced at the brushed steel bezel Piaget on his wrist. Then he glared at the partition separating first class from the cockpit as if willing his eyes to drill through the paneling and punish the pilot for his ineptitude…and their late arrival.

Although the delay had infuriated, Sumarsono's face remained a mask of Javanese propriety. Disembarking, he smiled thinly at the petite and apologetic Garuda attendant manning the forward exit – the incident reaffirming the entrepreneur's commitment to acquire his own private jet once financial stability had been restored to his family's corporate structure.

The high profile executive was ushered down the aircraft's steps to a limousine, windows heavily tinted for privacy, security protocols having been abandoned to accommodate the influential visitor. He nestled into the Mercedes' comfort, isolated from the desperation of those strung along the streets outside his immediate realm, his mood reflective as the vehicle made its way from the airport.

Agus Sumarsono was on a mission to shore up the company structure before the newly created government agency IBRA could sell the group's assets at heavily discounted values – as they had with other debt-ridden enterprises. The image of the Indonesian Bank Restructuring Agency offering the Bimaton Bank to his competitors tempered his resolve to do whatever was necessary to protect his family's interests.

In this atmosphere of financial and political destabilization the few survivors, including Bimaton, were cash strapped and desperate for any major capital injection. The family empire teetered dangerously close to the edge of financial collapse, the reason for Agus Sumarsono's mission to Bali. He had scheduled a meet with Johnny Salem, one of Indonesia's more successful money merchants whose reputation had grown out of the demise of Jakarta's failed tycoons. Salem had a track record of successfully negotiating the reacquisition of seized assets, ensuring that original ownership remained, albeit indirectly, intact – and Sumarsono was there to seek his help, the meeting to remain covert at Sumarsono's request.

DENPASAR
Udayana Military Command HQ

Colonel Hidajat stood deep in thought observing the two *Kopassus* officers being driven away to the airport. A Hercules aircraft would transport his old friend Colonel Tony Supadi and a group of hand-selected Senior NCOs to Ambon and Jayapura, two emerging hotspots in the archipelago's restive eastern provinces now threatened by separatist and anti-Jakarta movements. The Special Forces contingent had been recalled from Dili where, in the aftermath of the referendum militias that had previously fallen under their command, they had continued their wave of terror. The Colonel was not concerned at the extent of the carnage in the former province as, along with his military peers, he shared the bitterness of East Timor's unexpected exit from the Republic.

The Colonel was Commanding Officer of the covert, tactical control teams within the 9th Military Regional Command *(KODAM IX/Udayana)* which exercised control from Bali, across a thousand kilometres of scattered islands, to the east. Prior to the previous month's international, political intervention East Timor had fallen under the *Udayana* Command which had enjoyed overall charge of the troops in Timor. His responsibilities included the financing, training and equipping of the militias that had attracted world wide condemnation for their genocidal behavior both prior, and subsequent to, the referendum.

Militia leaders such as Eurico Gueterres, Cancio de Cavalho and Joao Tavares had all been beneficiaries of the Udayana Command's attention.

Colonel Hidajat had ordered the *Kopassus* contingent to Ambon where they would organize the redirection of military hardware from East Timor. Over the past six months the Colonel had overseen the build-up of a three-thousand-strong *Laskar Jihad* presence in the Moluccan Islands – the extremist militant group, trained by the Indonesian army in a camp at Munjul, a village near Bogor in Java, and transported to the Moluccas to wage their *Jihad* against Christians in the eastern provinces.

Hidajat brooded over Australia's growing involvement in East Timor, stung with the announcement that the once close ally had lobbied to lead United Nation's forces into the emerging nation – an act that would be certain to have a most malodorous effect on the countries' future political and security relationships. And now, with growing support for the West Papuan independence leader, Theys Hiyo Eluay, Australia's recent meddling had aroused Jakarta's concerns of a future confrontation over West Papua. The Papuans had called for a second "Great Meeting" to voice their independence aspirations and the Colonel was determined to undermine the Second Papuan Congress scheduled for that month. In consequence, Hidajat had dispatched teams to work hand in hand with elements of *KODAM VIII*, the *Trikora* regional military command, to establish a *Laskar Jihad* presence in the far-flung province.

Bitter with the lingering taste of Australia's interference in Indonesian affairs, Colonel Hidajat approved of the level of anti-Australian sentiment that existed amongst his fellow officers, and fanned this prejudice with every given opportunity – convinced that in time, Indonesia would have its day – the prayer constantly on his lips that he would be there to savor the sweetness of revenge when the moment arrived.

SANUR BEACH

Garuda captain, Anwar Suprapto strutted through the Sanur Aerowisata Beach Hotel lobby, nodded perfunctorily at the bored reception clerk, gave the registration form a cursory examination and signed his name with a flourish. He then turned and inappropriately, publicly admonished his crew for their earlier tardiness.

'I won't tolerate any more delays. There will not be a repeat of what happened today. You have embarrassed us all. Be on time tomorrow.' And, with jutted chin, an affectation acquired immediately following his recent promotion he warned, 'with the current cutbacks, you might do well to remember that retrenchment is a real possibility for those who don't meet the standards of our airline.'

Responding with all too familiar assurances the disheartened crew dispersed to their allocated rooms leaving the captain to his own preoccupations – the Javanese pilot unaware that he was being closely observed.

Fiona Barnes focused on the pilot across the lobby contemplating how best to approach the captain, subconsciously chewing at the inside of her lower lip, wincing when a thin strip of flesh tore away. She sighed resignedly, pulled her shoulders back and strode purposefully in Anwar Suprapto's direction, hoping that Garuda pilot would not be too difficult a seduction – and her ticket to the restive Moluccan province.

* * * *

LEGIAN BEACH

Agus Sumarsono shifted uneasily in the rattan chair, considering Johnny Salem's last remark. The Malaysian investor proposed as Bimaton's savior would insist on placing a number of their own members on the failing conglomerate's board.

'We would not be interested in giving up Board control,' Sumarsono insisted.

'The Datuk's group would most likely be content to have two operational positions including that of the CFO,' Salem suggested, aware from his discussions with the Malaysians, that they considered this to be a condition-precedent to their entry as a major shareholder in Bimaton.

Sumarsono frowned – Greg Young currently held the

position of Chief Financial Officer– there would be considerable resistance from his bankers as well. 'I'm not confident that I can convince my group to offer that position to the Malays.'

Salem's eyes did not betray. He knew that the near broken man before him had little choice. 'If they are not receptive then the Datuk's investors may very well baulk at the deal.'

Sumarsono shoulders visibly fell as he accepted the reality of the Bimaton group's predicament. Time was running out and officials from IBRA were already banging on his doors. He stood and extended a hand. 'I will take the offer to the Board.'

* * * *

Knees on pillow, Fiona Barnes knelt before the standing pilot and gently caressed his inner thighs. Then, she slowly guided her lips over the tip of his shaft, coordinating her movements as both hand and mouth moved tantalizing in unison. When she applied pressure to his perineum Anwar Suprapto moaned, pleading with Fiona to continue but she ignored his cry. Removing him from the warmth of her mouth she guided the pilot backwards onto the bed, lowered her body onto his and began rocking her hips until he called out, shuddering in climax, spilling himself into her womb.

An hour later the Australian journalist repeated the less than satisfying engagement at Suprapto's request, having received his undertaking that she would accompany him on the early morning flight.

At 0630 when the Boeing 737 lifted into the skies above Bali on route to Ambon, Fiona Barnes sat in the jump seat smugly behind her temporary lover, who would, until confronted by the challenge, remain oblivious to the enduring gift that their tryst had bestowed upon him.

* * * *

SABAH – EAST MALAYSIA
SANDAKAN AIRFIELD
8th June

Hambali held his breath as the Fokker powered along the two-thousand-metre-long runway, sighing in relief when his precious and cramped cargo of one hundred and sixteen hardened Afghani *Taliban Mujahideen* fighters climbed into the early morning sky.

The Afghanis were a gift from Osama, sent to train *Jemaah Islamiyah* and *Laskar Jihad* forces in the Sulawesi and Moluccan theaters. Incredibly, Hambali had successfully finessed the Malaysian authorities by declaring the group as transit passengers, arranging for their arrival and departure through less frequently used airports.

He remained observing the aircraft until it disappeared from sight, then used his hand phone to connect to the air traffic control centers that would track the charter flight, confident that no record would be entered at any of these locations, regarding the incidence of this non-scheduled aircraft.

AMBON – THE MOLUCCAS
NGO – Nusantara Integrated Community Development Organization

Rima Passelima winced in pain as she straightened, wishing she had listened to Nuci's advice and waited for Johanis' return.

'*Non, jangan angkat lagi,*' Nuci pleaded, warning of the consequences to her mistress' back, '*nanti punggunnya sakit!*'

With six months in-country experience now under her belt Rima could comfortably hold a conversation in *Bahasa*

Indonesia. She ignored the advice then stubbornly put her hip against the desk and gave it another push. Then, she stepped back gauging the distance between the wall and where she would sit. Satisfied, she then wheeled into place, the restored antique Dutch, bobbin-turned-teak chair she had found in the local market.

'*Sudah dulu,* – that should do it,' she announced, then stood back to admire her new office setting.

Having found the temporary offices in the Bimaton Group compound intolerably restrictive Rima had moved the NGO presence into her own premises, away from the constant scrutiny of the company's suspicious, local management.

Nuci had come to her through word of mouth and occupied the servants' quarters to the rear of the bungalow. Rima had learned that Nuci's husband, Laurens remained with their granddaughter Anna and other offspring in a resettlement camp, the meagre wages paid to the Ambonese woman sent to supplement the family income.

When Nuci had brought her recalcitrant son-in-law Johanis Matuanakotta to the office and pleaded his case for employment, Rima had initially declined – the moody young man's demeanor signaling trouble – her decision revisited when Nuci tearfully related the events leading to her daughter's death and the reason for her son-in-law's residual anger at the unfairness of life's blow. Reluctantly, she engaged Johanis as a general roustabout – Rima surprised when he demonstrated an unexpected depth of intelligence which, in turn, led her to reconsider his position of employment. She moved Johanis into the NGO office where he quickly acquired the basic fundamentals of administration. However, when it became apparent that his skills were more mechanical in nature Rima placed his name on her list of those for whom she would seek scholarships under one of the schemes being promoted by quasi-government agencies in support of her NGO. Their ages were similar and, in Johanis, Rima identified a kindred spirit, enjoying his company in a brotherly way. Their relationship evolved, Johanis now more of a companion than employee.

'*Kopi, Nona?*' Rima nodded, accepting the Arabic blend Nuci now knew to serve. She sipped the boiling coffee under Nuci's watchful eyes, smiling inwardly at the woman's concern, Rima refusing to drink the brew, lukewarm, as the locals insisted. Cup in hand, Rima strolled to the front windows and peered outside, her view restricted to whatever was evident through the iron-bar gate standing between two-metre-high plastered brick walls, topped with strands of barb wire.

As she sipped the coffee her thoughts centered on the difficulties she had encountered in laying the foundations for her cover, and the time consuming demands of operating an actual NGO. Her mind wandered as she watched a group of street urchins playing on the broken footpath, their harsh life on the streets a new phenomenon in the Ambonese environment, the orphaned children driven onto the street as a result of the sectarian tumult.

Settling into the alien environment had been difficult from the outset, her activities severely curtailed by the ongoing civil unrest. Although her arrival had coincided with a decrease in violence resulting from a curfew imposed by the security forces, rumors circulating suggesting that the conflict was a Java-inspired attempt to inundate the Christian population with Muslim transmigrants, causing confrontations to flare in the mini-archipelago's outlying districts. Mutually destructive fighting escalated in the northern areas following the visit by Vice President Megawati Soekarnoputri. Then, when it appeared that Ambon's warring factions might be receptive to peace negotiations, boats carrying three thousand members of the militant *Laskar Jihad* arrived, and the city was again plunged into darkness.

Fighting then erupted across the three Moluccan provinces, Rima now clearly understanding that the violence was flamed by political, economic, ethnic and religious agendas. She witnessed, firsthand, the expansion in the number of sophisticated weapons used by both Christian and Muslim groups, mortified that the government ignored the growing intensity of the level of violence. Mosques, churches, schools and in many instances entire towns had been leveled, the death toll now counted by the thousands.

Even outlying island villages were not spared. During the past five months Christian and Muslim gangs, each supported by their own militias attacked isolated communities, these killing sprees accounting for the swelling numbers of displaced fleeing to already overcrowded relocation centers. Rima accepted the danger – her life having been threatened on more than one occasion when violence had erupted on the streets – her Eurasian features attracting unwanted attention from the fearsome *Laskar Jihad* elements that continued to roam the city and countryside – another sound reason for her to keep Johanis by her side.

* * * *

Johanis Matuanakotta glared fiercely at the urchins loitering around the office entrance and threatened to flog them with the fictitious cane he kept inside. He waited until the untidy children drifted away before wheeling the company Honda into the front yard where he chained the motorcycle to the building.

Seven months had passed since his torturous interrogation and miraculous escape from death; his all-consuming hate for the Javanese and, more recently, Ambonese Muslims in no way diminished by his good fortune in meeting Rima Passelima. Lisa's murder and his incarceration at the hands of the Jakarta-inspired militants had left an indelible mark – revenge now the highest of priorities amongst the desiderata that monopolized his mind.

PATTIMURA AIRPORT – AMBON

'Your passport will be returned once you have boarded in Bali,' the immigration official informed Fiona Barnes as she was escorted to a holding room to wait for the flight which would return her to Bali, pending deportation to Australia. She had been arrested photographing a contingent of *Laskar Jihad* troops disembarking from the ship which had carried them from the eastern Javanese capital of Surabaya; her truculent response to the soldiers' seizure of her equipment landing her in jail. Disappointed to the core at having her notes and photographic record of the provincial city under siege, destroyed, she sat silently in custodial care brooding, colligating the events which had inspired her journey to Ambon.

When the Indonesian government had arrested the head of *Laskar Jihad*, Jafar Uman Thailib, and charged him with murder, Fiona correctly assessed that the move would not augur well for Ambon's Christians. She had managed to survive in the Moluccas for three days before being challenged by the authorities, the crackdown resulting in her arrest directly associated with the attack on a *Laskar Jihad* post which had killed twenty-two Muslims.

The immigration official reappeared. 'They want you to board now. Come on, let's go.'

Fiona crossed her arms and strode belligerently past the post where members of the *Laskar Jihad* maintained a "welcome desk" for their foreign supporters, amongst these, hardened Afghani *Mujahideen* soldiers who had been flown into the area aboard charter flights originating from Malaysian airfields.

CENTRAL SULAWESI – POSO CITY
July

Withering tropical heat beat down on the Christian militants draped listlessly across motorbikes as they observed Jack McBride inspect the carnage. The American's grim features remained hidden behind a handkerchief as he walked through the grotesque mise-en-scene along the line of fly-covered bodies, some decapitated, most blooded beyond recognition. Further up the street machine-gun posts monitored movement while troops armed with assault rifles checked pedestrians' papers.

McBride had raced to the scene when word of the Christian attack had reached his clinic, the missionary expecting such a response since the fighting had erupted over Easter, destroying eight hundred homes, shops and many of the local churches. No one had been arrested; the Christian community, incensed at the injustice and the TNI's failure to punish those responsible then taking the initiative, retaliated, dispensing the same kind of justice the militant extremists had inflicted so mercilessly. The ensuing confrontation resulted in fifty thousand from both sides of the sectarian divide fleeing their homes, the conflict then attracting the attention of the *Laskar Jihad* leadership back in Java, now determined to seek retribution for recent arrests.

McBride was aware that prominent members of local communities had written directly to, Kofi Annan, urging the U.N. Secretary-General to pressure Jakarta into considering a U.N. peace-keeping force to resolve the present crisis. President Wahid had rejected the plea. However, faced with international condemnation over his reluctance to act he declared a state of civil emergency across the troubled, eastern provinces. Amazingly, the Justice Minister, Jusril Mahendra then openly defended the *Laskar Jihad* by supporting the militants' right to travel freely to the volatile areas. Jack McBride was becoming increasingly concerned as the emergency decree gave the police and military wide powers, the information flow reporting the crisis, now but a trickle, through to the international arena.

Nathan Glaskin, the elderly administrator had finally retired and was yet to be replaced, this vacancy providing Jack with greater freedom of movement than he had enjoyed in the past. He maintained regular contact with other posts his mission supported, and received regular updates on events as they continued to unfold in the adjacent Moluccan Island group – the most recent development, the destruction of the University of Pattimura.

Rumors were of course rife, but Jack had no doubts that the military would fulfill their commitment to send the proposed *Yon Gab* Joint Battalion into the region, a force that would be comprised of elements from other parts of Indonesia, in the hope that these troops would not take sides in the conflict.

When he learned that the U.S. Navy and Marines and the Indonesian Navy would engage in the Combined Afloat

Readiness and Training (CARAT) Exercises he mistakenly identified this announcement as a move by his government to position assets in the archipelago in support of the democratic movement and to save President Wahid's administration from collapse – surprised when the Voice of America reported that some four thousand U.S. sailors and marines would participate in a number of aid projects in East Timor as part of the overall exercise.

He completed his inspection of the row of corpses. Sliding into the depths of depression at the inhumanity he had witnessed, Jack McBride cycled slowly back to the safety of his clinic where he locked himself in his quarters and demolished the greater part of a cask of altar wine – appropriated from the Nathan Glaskin's rooms, prior to the aged missionary's departure.

JAKARTA
1st August 2000

Fathur Rohman Al-Ghozi gave an impatient grunt when he checked the Seiko on his wrist then glanced over at his accomplice, Abdul Jabar. It was 12.25 p.m. and the ambassador's car was running late. He shifted his weight on the motorcycle then scanned the pedestrian traffic crawling through Jakarta's affluent suburb Menteng, where many government officials and diplomats were located. Al-Ghozi was the *Jemaah Islamiyah's* most skilled bomb maker. The target he and his associates Abdul Jabar and Dulmatin had selected for this day was the Philippines Ambassador to Indonesia.

Cautiously, he leaned forward for a clearer view of the red Suzuki van they had parked outside the residence, his heart pumping hard when a patrol car slowed, then accelerated away when the ambassador's approaching vehicle's lights flashed, signaling for the police to clear the access driveway. Al-Ghozi hand tensed, gripping the remote inside his jacket as the diplomat's Mercedes swung into the official residence's driveway, then he activated the twenty-kilo TNT bomb gunning his motorcycle and fleeing the scene before his presence could be noted.

*　*　*　*

Amazingly, Ambassador Leonides Caday survived the attack which would leave him crippled for life. The bombing killed three, seriously injured another eighteen bystanders, and destroyed buildings, homes and some thirty vehicles within the attack zone.

The *JI* operation was a precursor to a string of devastating Christmas bombings across the archipelago targeting churches, whilst in the Philippines, Al-Ghozi's attack on a Manila passenger train would leave twenty-two dead, and more than one hundred injured. Although it was Al-Ghozi who would build the massive, twenty-one tonnes of explosives cache in the southern Philippines city of General Santos for actions aimed at Singapore and other parts of S.E. Asia, it would be Amrozi who, having earned his reputation for providing the explosives used in the Hambali-funded attack on Ambassador Caday, who would play a leading role in Indonesia's dark future.

Jakarta
13th September 2000

The chief judge read the announcement. '…and with the greatest respect to Bapak Suharto who is unable to attend these proceedings due to continuing ill health, the trial shall be post-poned indefinitely.'

Former President Suharto had been placed under house arrest three months earlier, in May, and charged with corruption. As his lawyers hurried to advise their client of the welcome outcome in another part of the city along the capital's main thoroughfare, Jalan Jenderal Sudirman, Greg Young alighted from his BMW and entered the thirty-six storey building housing the Jakarta Stock Exchange and the World Bank. His driver took the vehicle directly to the underground car park situated on the second basement level.

The time was minutes past 3 p.m., with less than an hour left before trading on the markets would cease for the day.

Greg caught the lift to the twenty-seventh floor to consult with his insurance broker as a *Kostrad*, Strategic Forces Corporal, Ibrahim Hasan and his co-conspirators, *Kopassus* Special Forces Sergeants, Irwan Ibrahim and Abdul Manaf Wahab left the building. They had just set the timer attached to the RDX explosives they had planted in an abandoned vehicle across from where Young's driver was seated, enjoying a snack at the driver's food stall.

The bomb detonated fifteen minutes later achieving maximum effect with traders packing the Exchange floor, the result catastrophic, as secondary explosions followed when parked cars, engulfed by fire, erupted throughout the basement car park driving more than one thousand people from the building. For hours smoke billowed from the structure's bowels as fire fighters fought the inferno into retreat, recovering the bodies of fifteen whilst ambulances attended to the seriously injured.

Across the city General Sumantri waved dismissively at the Special Forces' messenger who had relayed the most recent update of the blast, Sumantri then sitting alone considering the multiplicity of his most recent destabilization ploy, smiling quietly with the expectation that the blame would be placed elsewhere.

THE PHILIPPINES
16th September

As spokesman for the *Abu Sayyaf*, Abu Sapara had left little doubt in the radio listeners' minds how the leadership would respond to the United States 're-colonization of the Philippines by stealth'. Previously, the U.S. had maintained air and naval bases in the country until public sentiment resulted in U.S. stations being closed in 1992. Then, in 1998 Washington had pressured Manila into accepting the proposed 'Visiting Forces Agreement', paving the way for American troops to return. Now, for the first time in four years U.S. Navy ships had sailed into the Philippines within the framework of the "Cooperation Afloat Readiness and Training" military exercises.

The separatists were livid.

Although the country's whorehouse owners were overjoyed with the return of sailors and other military personnel to their establishments, there was considerable resentment elsewhere. Alarmed that the U.S. was using the CARAT exercises to secretly deploy further American troops into the country to seek out and destroy the separatists, Janjalani and Sapara had decided to demonstrate their opposition by taking direct action.

The *Abu Sayyaf* leader, Janjalani sensed betrayal by his country's military with the about face permitting U.S. troops on Philippines soil. In January, the Moro Islamic Liberation

Front's *Camp Abubakar* had been overrun by government forces signaling an increase in support from Washington. Most of the Indonesians who had been training there managed to escape through Mindanao's porous backdoors, however at Fathur Rohman Al-Ghozi's urging, a number of *Jemaah Islamiyah* foot soldiers remained and shifted their allegiance to the *Abu Sayyaf.*

Fathur Rohman Al-Ghozi, a senior member of the *Jemaah Islamiyah* and leading explosives expert had established a joint operational arm within the *Abu Sayyaf's* Mindanao structure. With funding from Hambali's cell in Kuala Lumpur, the Indonesian had managed to accumulate a substantial cache of arms and explosives at the camp, through illegal purchases from elements of the Philippines Armed Forces. Al-Ghozi could no longer travel freely without fear of arrest; his request for assistance in sending detonators to Indonesia coinciding with Janjalani's shift in operational tactics, and his search for a soft target to attack.

The idea and the target was presented to them with the conclusion of the Indonesian-U.S. Navy CARAT exercises only weeks before when the United Nations suspended its operations in West Timor when an American and other U.N. workers had been brutally murdered. The office of the U.N. High Commissioner for Refugees was reported to have relocated operations to Bali and, in consequence, had been identified as another potential *Abu Sayyaf* target.

Abu Sapara had Hernandes Oscar Mercado go over his orders.

'Our people at Ninoy Aquino International will ensure that I'm not hassled. I'll fly Garuda to Jakarta where Fathur's people will meet and assist with customs and immigration. I give them the box of detonators and they provide me with the material for my mission.'

Al-Ghozi had explained that chemicals used in bomb preparation were in abundance in Indonesia, only detonators being difficult to acquire.

'And your local ID papers will show that you are traveling to Dili, if asked, as an employee of the National Cooperative Business Association.'The forged papers had been copied from documents found in a stolen wallet lifted from a traveler working with the coffee farmers' cooperative in East Timor.

'Then I'll continue on to Bali where I'm to assemble the material and identify the hotel where the U.N. personnel are staying.'

The briefing continued until Abu Sapara was satisfied that Mercado would get it right, the Filipino bomber then departing by air for Bali the same day.

JAKARTA
19th September

Andrew Graham passed the article he had clipped from the *Indonesian Observer* to Greg Young. 'Have you read this?'

Greg leaned over the coffee table and examined the report as staff in the Mercantile Club's "Shutters Bar" hovered as he read the article from the English language daily relating to the arrest of a Filipino, one Hernandes Oscar Mercado, caught upon arrival at the Ngurah Rai International Airport in Bali.

'That's a shitload of explosives to be carrying on an aircraft,' Andrew pointed to the story. The police had discovered twenty kilograms of explosives in Mercado's luggage.

'Typical,' Greg scoffed, 'the police claim they thought it was narcotics. He might have got away with it if he'd given them a few bucks.'

'Says he admitted that he was going to bomb one of the five-star hotels in Nusa Dua,' Andrew annoyingly ran his finger down the page.

'Must be one of those nuts from the Philippines' south,' Greg mused. 'What are they called...Maro, Motto...?'

'Moro Liberation Front,' Andrew offered, 'or to be precise, the Moro *Islamic* Liberation Front.'

'What the hell are they doing in Bali?'

'Soft target,' Andrew guessed, 'that and the presence of U.S. troops might have been the attraction.'

'There aren't any American troops based in Bali,' Greg challenged.

'In a matter of speaking, they may as well be,' the American argued, 'what with the joint military exercises and half the god dam Seventh Fleet hanging around just over the horizon rotating troops on R & R into Kuta, we may as well plant the Stars and Stripes in the ground down there.'

'Yeah, why not,' Greg sassed, 'you've stuck your bloody flag just about everywhere else.'

Andrew Graham laughed, leaned across the table and lowered his voice conspiratorially. 'Wasn't it the Brits that claimed the sun would never set on their empire?'

'Careful, or the next time we send our fleet across to the Falklands we might just sweep by the old colony on the return voyage and reclaim it.'

Andrew Graham raised his drink in camaraderie. 'Here's to creeping colonialism.'

Greg Young responded with a toast of his own. 'Here's to the gutsy President Abdurrahman Wahid who has had the balls to take the Suhartos on, regardless of the consequences.'

'I'll drink to that,' Andrew acknowledged before adding, 'but they're not going to go down without some resistance.'

'You mean Tommy Suharto?' Greg asked.

'Now there's a real piece of work,' Andrew became more serious, 'and the fact that yesterday, Wahid had to sack his own national police chief, General Rusdiharjo for failing to carry out the arrest demonstrates just how much power the former First Family still holds.'

'That won't endear him with the pro-Suharto elements that remain in the military.'

'No, it won't. Rusdiharjo's dismissal is quite a slap in the face for the TNI. They're not accustomed to being treated in this manner.'

'I had a call on the way over that Wahid's ordered Suharto's bodyguards to disarm.'

'Yes, I heard that too,' Andrew confirmed. 'Wahid's raising the stakes in light of Suharto's lawyers' apparent success in having the case against Pak Harto dismissed on medical grounds.'

'Do you think he'll go the distance?'

'Gus Dur?' Andrew used the name by which the President was more affectionately known. 'Would be great if the military backed his reforms but I don't think that's going to happen.' He paused. 'An Indonesia President not under the heavy hand of the TNI? No, I don't think so...at least, not in our lifetime.'

'He's not making many friends amongst the military.'

'True,' Andrew agreed, 'and we're all paying for that.' Suddenly he appeared glum. 'You know, the bastards could have hit almost any other building in Jakarta and the business community would've taken it in their stride.' His face became even more serious. 'But to hit the bloody Stock Exchange...?'

'Don't expect investor confidence could fall much further. Have to tell you, Andy, I was really shaken.'

'Wasn't your driver injured?'

'Some superficial wounds; it was the smoke inhalation that got him. He's okay now. I sent him back to the *kampung* for a month.' Greg then appeared distracted. 'My car was a write-off, of course.'

'I was across the road in the Hilton.' Andrew fiddled with a coaster as he recalled the explosion. 'You know the police have already made some arrests?'

Greg Young gave a contemptuous snort. 'Of course they have…but don't expect anything to come of it.'

'Not sure,' the American countered, 'word is they've picked up a number of *Kopassus* soldiers and you know what that means!'

'The Special Forces will claim they'd acted by themselves… renegades of sort.'

'Sure, but it's a sure sign that the military is going to give Wahid a run for his money.'

'Damn,' Greg complained, 'this place is becoming worse than Beirut!' He nodded with the waiter's inquiring look, and placed his empty glass down. 'And God knows where it's all going to end.'

KUALA LUMPUR
October 2000

'It's settled then,' Hambali rose, bringing the meeting to a close. 'May Allah watch over you and bless this enterprise.' One by one the members of the *Jemaah Islamiyah* conspiracy filed out of the company offices, each charged with specific targets to be attacked on the rapidly-approaching Christmas Eve.

Hambali had elected to retain responsibility for Jakarta and other Java targets, Imam Samudra (as Abdul Aziz came to be known), the island of Batam, and Enjang Bastaman aka Jabir, the West Java provincial capital of Bandung. The *JI* Malaysian leader, Yazid Sufaat would lead the attacks on Medan's Christian minority – the detonators supplied by the arrested Filipino, Hernandes Oscar Mercado whilst en route to Bali, delivering the required effect.

INDONESIA
December 2000

Prior to the wave of Christmas bombings Hambali frequented Pondok Ngruki in Solo to meet with Abu Bakar Bashir and his secretary, Zulkifi Marzuki. He also met secretly with General Sumantri at his home in Jakarta where he explained, in detail, where the attacks would take place. As overall coordinator for the Java attacks Hambali relied heavily on his close friend, Jabir, a fellow Afghanistan-theatre veteran. However, due to an oversight on Jabir's part, not all would go according to what would otherwise have been a meticulous execution of their bombing strategy.

In the West Java town of Ciamis a Chinese-owned hotel was targeted, the two inexperienced bombers victims of their own intent when their bomb detonated prematurely, killing one and injuring the other, the latter later captured by the police – only to "escape" custody.

In the university city of Bandung, Hambali's associate Jabir would meet his *ajal,* the perceived predestined moment of death. He had rigged a number of devices to be detonated remotely, utilizing GSM cellular phones which had interchangeable cards, providing the opportunity to change the phone's number as required. Inadvertently, Jabir had used his own phone in one of the bombs and, at 4 p.m. in the afternoon of Christmas Eve someone called this number, the resulting explosion killing both Jabir and his companion.

As unsuspecting Christians across the country flocked to their place of worship Hambali's heinous enterprise entered its final phase, and the country ruptured.

* * * *

The Christmas Eve bombings of December 2000 dumbfounded the nation. Thirty-eight bombs were set and wired to detonate simultaneously, the devastating attacks impacting on churches and congregations in eleven cities across six provinces in Indonesia.

Investigations into the archipelago-wide attacks would be hampered by vested interest groups. The TNI would remain stigmatized by the innuendo associating military elements with the professional manner in which the action was executed. In Bandung and Medan evidence linking the military to the atrocities would be traced back to senior, serving officers. However these claims were repudiated by the Department of Defence, those discrediting the TNI for their involvement, ultimately condemned.

METRO MANILA
31 December 2000

Six days following the Indonesian church bombings, five explosions wreaked havoc across the Philippines capital of Manila killing twenty-two and leaving more than one hundred seriously injured. The bombings were executed by Hambali's chief of Philippines' ops, Fathur Rohman Al-Ghozi, supported by the MILF's Special Operations Group in retaliation for the Philippine Army's attacks on over forty MILF training camps, including *Camp Abu Bakar*.

The loss was devastating to the *Jemaah Islamiyah* and al-Qaeda as both had operated their own training schools within the camp.

At noon on New Year's Eve, four of the bombs were detonated simultaneously. One exploded in the forward coach of a Light Rail Transit train when it came to rest at Blumentritt Station. Eleven died and sixty were injured as another device exploded on a passenger bus as it was arriving at the Quezon City passenger terminal. A third bomb exploded in the Plaza Ferguson in front of the U.S. Embassy and the fourth device at the cargo terminal of the Ninoy Aquino International Airport. Several hours later a package was discovered at the Dusit Hotel in Makati City. Security guards removing the parcel accidentally triggered the device, the explosion killing a police officer and injuring another.

Militant Islam's crescent moon continued its ascendancy.

*   *   *   *

Chapter Ten

Georgia – Pankisi Gorge
February – 2001

O mar Ibn al Khattab held the field glasses steady, observing a Russian truck wind its way through a herd of grazing cows, towards the building where his Chechen rebels waited in ambush. Khattab scanned the sky then returned to the unfolding scene, the sound of gunfire reaching his ears from across the snow-covered field as soldiers poured from the truck moments before the vehicle erupted in a massive explosion.

'Let's go!' he snapped, climbing into the front of a GTS-M his men had captured during the 1994-1996 war with Moscow. They broke from the forest and crossed the field, Khattab in high spirits as they approached the burning wreckage.

Within minutes the skirmish was over, the winter landscape strewn with Russian dead, his men forcing two of their captives to their knees. Khattab climbed down from the light utility carrier and schlepped around the ankle-deep snow checking bodies, removing the 9mm Gurza handgun holstered at his side as he approached the prisoners.

The soldiers looked up at Khattab's huge frame and shaggy features and trembled on their knees. Khattab held his weapon at arm's length and fired point blank, the sound of the weapon discharging puncturing the air as the first soldier's lifeless body collapsed slowly to the ground. Then Khattab signaled one of his men. When the rebel stepped forward brandishing a blade the soldier sobbed, words spilling from his mouth as he begged for his life – rebel laughter accompanying his execution when the Russian's head toppled to the snow and lay face upwards, in shocked surprise.

Khattab re-holstered his Gurza, the weapon taken from the body of a Russian Federal Security Service agent days before. With his name listed high on Moscow's most-wanted list the FSB had been hot on his trail since the restart of the Chechen war in 1999.

Moscow had already claimed to have killed him several times before, the bearded Khattab smiling as he tugged at unruly growth covering his face. During interrogation the agent revealed plans of imminent raids on local Kisti elders' country properties suspected of harboring rebel fugitives, the information accelerating the late Muhammed Atef's plans already in place, to find a new guardian for the precious cache.

The Russians had recommended aerial bombing of targets in Georgia and the Pankisi Gorge along the Chechnya-Georgia border. Home to seven thousand Chechen refugees the lawless gorge was infamous throughout Eurasi and Russia as an area that harbored Islamic Chechen militants, al-Qaeda mercenaries and criminal warlords. It would seem that, with pressure from both Moscow and the West, the safe haven was nearing its end.

When the Georgian President, Shevardnadze visited Washington two months earlier the U.S. President, George W. Bush had assured Shevardnadze of substantial material and financial assistance in dealing with Pankisi's rebels. Khattab's contacts in Grozny had warned that, as a result of President's visit, the United States would soon announce the deployment of American soldiers to train more than a thousand Georgians to help fight the war against terrorism. At first, Khattab had scoffed at the suggestion of U.S. troops being sent into the region. However, when the U.S. Secretary of Defense, Donald Rumsfeld had visited Tbilisi to finalize the American military assistance package, Khattab accepted it might be time to reconsider his position, now believing that the disguised American putsch would result in Chechen rebels losing their Pankisi stronghold and, ultimately, seal their fate

'Load the equipment!' he ordered, leading the way into the farmhouse where his four-hundred-kilo Radio Thermal Generator had been secreted for the past six years. It was time to relocate the RTG to a safer depository – one outside Georgia, a place where engineers could fully realize the potential the RTG's core offered with its capsule of strontium 90 still intact.

The vehicle was loaded, and its precious contents transported to another safe house where the RTG was disguised amongst a timber shipment and carried across the embattled Caucasian state until reaching its first destination, a warehouse in the Black Sea port of Sokhumi.

Atef's deadly cargo was on its way.

* * * *

HAT YAI – THAILAND
March

Mohamed Aziz Derashid replaced the SIM card in his hand phone with the prepaid card he had received in the mail, then stood in semi-darkness surveying the pedestrian world below, his view of the Kim Yong Market partially blocked by the Novotel Central Sukhontha on Sanehanusorn Road. The sun blinked then disappeared, transforming the tropical setting from dusky grey, the Malaysian entrepreneur amusing himself whiling time counting the number of hotel room lights across the way as each came to life. With his tally complete Derashid lost interest and abandoned the scene, returning to the reclusive world of his apartment while he waited patiently for the *Sheikh's* contact to call.

Another hour passed, Derashid falling into cogitative mood as he analyzed the events of the past seven years, grateful that Malaysia, under Dr Mohamed Mahathir's leadership, had been relatively insulated from the aftermath of the Asian financial and economic crisis.

Following the failure of their *Bojinka* operations in Manila, Mohhamed Atef had kept Derashid informed as Hambali's operations appeared to unravel, with the al-Qaeda Malaysian front company's closure sending Hambali scurrying temporarily to ground – Derashid subsequently even more cautious than before when communicating with Atef after Hambali's co-conspirator in the Philippines operation, Wali Khan Amin Shah had been arrested in Malaysia's Langkawi.

Derashid considered the role played by Hambali's mentor, Abu Bakar Bashir – the coincidence of Bashir and Osama both being of Yemeni descent, interpreted as a prophetic sign. Although Derashid had never met Bashir in person he was, nevertheless, well informed as to the cleric's activities both in Malaysia, and abroad, including the *Jemaah Islamiyah* spiritual leader's visits to Australia. He knew that Hambali, Bashir and Sungkar had slipped in and out of the country on more than eleven occasions without raising any alarms, their visits arranged within the framework of extending the *JI's* presence across the Australian continent.

With growing interest Derashid had followed Bashir's further exploits when the cleric returned to Indonesia, where he ensconced himself at the *pesantren* he and Sungkar had co-founded near Solo in Central Java. Derashid considered Bashir's timing propitious as the nation's more established Muslim organizations were splintering, and it appeared that he intended to seek leadership of the Indonesian *Mujahideen* Council – the MMI an umbrella group for like-minded organizations that wished to make Indonesia an Islamic state.

Derashid's thoughts turned to the string of houses and apartments he had acquired over the past five years. Situated in the Ahai province of Songkla, the Hat Yai city apartment was one of a number of safe houses Derashid had purchased through Malaysia's offshore financial centre in Labuan – the Offshore Companies Act of 1990 providing the wealthy entrepreneur with adequate firewalls disguising his beneficial interests in the acquisitions. He had selected this location as the southern Thai city was but one hundred kilometres across the border from his Kelantan country hideaway in northern Malaysia – and Songkla, along with its four neighboring provinces was predominantly Muslim.

Derashid understood that Hambali's hand had played a significant role in the recent resurgence of separatist fervor in Thailand's southern provinces, channeling funds from Saudi supporters into *ponohs*, the local independent Muslim schools. Now, with many *ponohs* teaching the extremist *Wahabi* interpretation of Islam as practiced across Pakistan, the schools had become recruitment centers for *Jemaah Islamiyah*. Those selected trained in bomb construction at *JI's* secret military border camps, under the watchful eyes of Hambali, Dr Azahari Husin and Afghan *Taliban* instructors.

Derashid's hand phone rang twice then stopped. Minutes later the device sprang to life again and the Malaysian responded, uttering his two-word identification code before disconnecting the call. He then inserted a third replacement chip into the hand phone and waited, the hand phone springing to life, Derashid immediately recognizing the Egyptian's voice as he placed the phone to his ear.

'April Sixteen, *"Cosco Qingdao"*, Port Klang,' was all Osama bin Laden's military operations' commander said before the line went dead.

Derashid appreciated the necessity for the complicated precautions. Telephone contact remained the most expedient method of communications. However, as an additional precaution and out of respect for the West's advanced eavesdropping technology, conversations were always kept brief, and enigmatic. The Malaysian made a mental note of the incoming shipment's arrival then destroyed the chips used to facilitate the contact with Mohhamed Atef.

When the al-Qaeda military commander had informed Derashid of the Sheikh's request Derashid had reluctantly accepted the responsibility of 'key holder' for Osama's proposed S.E. Asian sensitive weapons depository.

Derashid remained deep in thought as he drove back across the Thai-Malaysian border to his isolated villa in Kelantan, the journey providing the opportunity to excogitate a way to conceal the insidious cargo once it had been cleared through Port Klang, and transported to the countryside.

ENGLAND – NORTH YORKSHIRE
U.S. NATIONAL SECURITY AGENCY
ELECTRONIC SPY STATION
Menwith Hill

The U.S. National Security Agency (NSA) analyst handed the morning intercept report to his British counterpart. 'We checked the Lloyd's Ship Register. The *"Qingdao"* is one of COSCO's container fleet. She sails under a Panamanian flag.'

The British defence expert shook his head in frustration. 'What's the connection?'

The American opened another file and extracted a photograph of Mohammed Jamal Khalifa. 'Remember him?'

'He's back in Saudi?' the Brit was surprised but could not resist the dig, 'bet you guys wish you'd never released him.'

The NSA analyst acknowledged the comment. 'Yeah, we screwed up, big time back in '94.' He looked up at his colleague. 'Do you know that, at the time of his arrest the goddamn INS and the FBI found training manuals in Arabic covering all aspects of terrorist training from bomb-making to assassination tactics? Now this prick's brother-in-law, bin Laden is on the FBI's most-wanted list with a twenty-five-million dollar tag on his head over last year's bombings of our embassies across Africa.'

The British analyst recalled that more than two hundred had died in the 1998 Nariobi, Kenya and Dar-es-Salaam attacks, another reason that Khalifa's name had been introduced into the Echelon database as a 'trigger' that would activate intense surveillance procedures whenever he picked up a phone.

Major domestic fiber-optic telephone trunk lines were wired through Menwith Hill providing the capability to monitor up to one hundred thousand calls simultaneously. Once captured, the signals were fed through super-computers that were programmed to identify keywords from the Echelon "dictionaries", Khalifa and the eremitic *Sheikh*, Osama bin Laden's names but two of the many millions of keywords that triggered further action whenever their voices were identified as being online. Surveillance satellites scooped up the electronic communications and transmitted these back to the primary downlink facilities at Menwith Hill and Pine Gap in the Australian Outback, whilst other satellites orbited as high as two hundred miles above the earth's surface, enabling the downlink stations to produce twelve-centimetre resolution photographs of any designated target.

Just months before, when intelligence had determined that bin Laden was in the Zahawar Killi camp in Afghanistan, (which, in another time he had built for the CIA) the Echelon system provided the targeting information that led to the U.S. launching sixty Tomahawk missiles at the site.

With the alarming prospect of the West's number one enemy having acquired portable nuclear devices, weapons, which one person alone could detonate and kill more than one hundred thousand, Echelon's highest priority had been raised as a result of intelligence reporting bin Laden's presence in Chechnya. The report had been given even more credence when 'in-country, on-the-ground' MI6 assets confirmed that Osama had paid the Chechens thirty million dollars in cash along with two thousand kilograms of Afghan heroin, to sweeten the deal. This coupled with testimony given by the former Russian security chief, Alexander Lebed when addressing the U.S. House of Representatives that some forty-three nuclear 'suitcase' weapons had vanished from the former Soviet Union arsenal, galvanized the

Americans and British intelligence forces into action.

Now the most recent intercepts indicated that al-Qaeda had an operation afoot in Malaysia. The British analyst took a copy of the report. "I'll flag this for the SIS lads over at Vauxhall Cross,' he said, referring to the British Secret Intelligence Service, MI6. They'll no doubt insist that the Malaysians provide a copy of the ship's crew and cargo manifests when it docks.'

MALAYSIA – PETALING JAYA
1st April

Hambali's usual disposition had collapsed into a mood of self-recrimination with the news of Jabarah's arrest in Oman. Although the information relating to the incident had been sketchy, Hambali prepared for the worst, resigned to the probability that his prime fund raiser would end up in American hands temporarily severing his financial links with the Saudis.

He called Wan Min bin Wan Mat. 'Have you already given Ghufron those funds?' he asked.

'Yes,' the Malay businessman who acted as the *Jemaah Islamiyah* treasurer confirmed. 'I gave him thirty-thousand, five-hundred American.'

'Better let him know that there won't be anything more for a few months.'

'Problems?' Wan Min pried.

'It's serious...' Hambali hesitated, 'I'll fill you in later but not on the phone.'

Hambali then returned to deliberate on the matter of Jabarah's arrest. Deeply concerned that Jabarah would reveal his whereabouts the *JI* commander decided he would relocate, and commenced making arrangements, notifying Ali Ghufron who was now in Java, that he had provisional command of all *JI* operations.

MALACCA STRAITS OFF MALAYSIA
17th April

The men moved stealthily under cover of night, offloading the crate into a smaller vessel which had been motoring alongside. The cargo swung precariously as it was lowered from the container ship, those paid to smuggle the shipment ashore suspecting that weapons were involved. With the transfer complete, Omar Ibn al Khattab's internuncio paid the Chinese captain and returned to the solitude of his cabin, leaving the cargo to disappear into the night.

The following day when the *"Cosco Qingdao"* docked at Port Klang the vessel was subjected to the most intense search by Malaysian and Interpol officers. At the end of the day the bewildered investigators apologized to the ship's captain and abandon their inspection, concluding that their intelligence had been incorrect.

U.S. EMBASSY – JAKARTA
July

The CIA station chief's shoulders sagged. 'They let them leave, just like *that*?'

'We had no warning,' the Political Counselor replied. 'Why weren't they kept under surveillance?'

'They were, but when the government vehicles picked them up and drove them away our surveillance team assumed that the group were being taken into custody and didn't follow.'

The counselor shook his head at the blunder. 'And we have no idea whatsoever where they might be?'

'We've put out an alert across all Asian airports but they've had far too much lead time for that to be effective.'

'If this is any indication of how Megawati will run things in the future then relationships with the new President are going to be bumpy.'

'Could it be that she didn't give it enough consideration, after all, she's been President less than three days?'

The counselor considered the question. The Indonesian political scene was still fluid having been subjected to the vacuum created subsequent to Suharto falling, Wahid failing and Megawati ascending to the throne. 'The new President certainly doesn't have much experience to bring to the leadership. She doesn't appear to have much political savvy as we could see from the manner Wahid manipulated her out of the running before. Looking at her profile one can only hope that she will surround herself with those who can bring some understanding of how the economy works as she's not very well educated.'

'The TNI seems to have taken the change quietly, in stride.'

'And why wouldn't they?' the counselor retorted, 'the generals know that the international arena is watching to see if they'll interfere in the democratic processes. My guess is that they'll continue to mark time until Megawati's tenure has passed and then make their move. We shouldn't misinterpret their mood as one of ambivalence towards terrorism, in spite of the apparent lack of enthusiasm we've witnessed in their rounding up those responsible for the Christmas bombings.'

'Has to be the old guard,' the chief claimed, 'they're the ones with the money and clout.'

'Pity about Wahid departing the scene so quickly,' the

counselor grumbled, 'he wouldn't have screwed us around like this.'

'I still can't believe they let those bastards go,' the CIA chief complained, 'we were so damn close...'

The counselor inhaled deeply. U.S. efforts to round up five members from the al-Qaeda network who had arrived in Indonesia from Yemen earlier in the month had been thwarted by the President's refusal to have the men arrested. U.S. intelligence sources had tracked the team to Jakarta and, from satellite intercepts had corroborating evidence that the Yemenis planned to attack the U.S. embassy there. The counselor appreciated that Megawati, only days after being appointed President, would have found it difficult being caught between Washington upon whom Indonesia was dependent for aid, and Indonesian-Muslims' anti-U.S. hostility over Afghanistan.

'Her lack of support doesn't bode well for the future,' the exasperated Langley chief repined.

KUALA LUMPUR
August

For one brief moment Agus Sumarsono's hand hesitated as he held the gold Conway Stewart fountain pen in the air. Then, with a flourish disguising his air of despair, he commenced signing the contracts which, effectively, consummated their arrangements and passed control of the Bimaton Corporation to Mohamed Aziz Derashid's Malaysian conglomerate: Bulan Sabit Holdings Sdn Bhd.

'Congratulations, Aziz,' Agus extended his hand, the moment captured by staff photographers.

'To the marriage of our two great enterprises,' Derashid

offered diplomatically.

'And a mutually rewarding relationship,' Agus responded, the sense of decrepitude and failure having surrendered his family interests, burning deep into the pit of his insides.

* * * *

Derashid bid Agus farewell following the celebratory luncheon then returned to his residence where he remained alone in the privacy of his penthouse overlooking Kuala Lumpur's hazy skyline. His successful acquisition of the Bimaton Group would not only greatly enhance his commercial reach across S.E. Asia, but would also provide the Malaysian billionaire with the political clout necessary for his secret quest to mould the region's socio-religious structure, in pursuit of a Pan-Islamic state.

JAKARTA
September

Greg Young appreciated how difficult surrendering control must have been for Agus Sumarsono and felt saddened by the outcome, pleased that at least Agus would retain the chairmanship of the Bimaton Group.

With his replacement as Chief Financial Officer, Young was tempted to sell his holdings and bail out all together. However, although the acquisition had only marginally lifted the value of his stock the company's shares were no longer traded on the open market and therefore difficult to offload. And, even had the company been re-listed, he doubted that their potential would have been recognized by the traders in the current mood of economic and political crises.

The bitter power struggle between rival factions of Indonesia's ruling elite had ended, with the Peoples' Consultative Assembly's nine-month campaign to oust Abdurrahman Wahid succeeding in replacing the President with his deputy, Megawati Sukarnoputri. However, Greg Young doubted that the inexperienced daughter of Indonesia's founding President Sukarno would be capable of finding a solution to the country's deep economic and social crises. During Wahid's tenure the population had experienced an unconscionable deterioration in living standards and increased instability, the combination of which had spilled more than fifty million into an environment where they were obliged to live below the poverty line. Since the currency crisis of two years before, more, than eight million workers had joined the huge pool of thirty-five million unemployed.

Young knew that his credentials in the construction industry were sufficiently strong for him to break away and re-establish his own operations. Nevertheless, as his stock holdings remained significant he decided to remain with the restructured Bimaton, hopeful that past demands upon construction revenues would cease with the injection of new capital from the Malaysian investors, permitting the profitable arm to grow. Notwithstanding the deplorable state of the domestic non-oil and gas construction industry Young remained confident of the construction arm's prospects and, consequently, would swallow his pride and call Agus to accept the new board's offer of Director of Operations, Construction and Property Development (Indonesia).

With construction cranes idly adorning partially-completed, grandiose shopping malls and office towers Young accepted that he would need to redirect the construction group's energies more towards the oil and gas sector, where profits could still be made – and the income stream was guaranteed in dollars. Security issues would remain of concern he knew, recalling the recent

Exxon-Mobil shut down of their Arun, LNG operations in North Aceh where fighting between separatist guerrillas and government troops continually threatened the stability of the province.

Young expected with Megawati's ascension to the presidency, that the TNI would move swiftly and crack down even more brutally on secessionist movements, than they had under Wahid. He also counted on Indonesia's ruling class ensuring that the outlying resource-rich provinces of Aceh which produced one-third of the country's exports, and West Papua, the sixth-largest contributor to Indonesia's national income, would remain within the fold.

Greg Young accepted also that it was axiomatic in such a politically corrupt environment, that business would continue as usual and Megawati's Presidency would result in few, if any, changes for Indonesia's neglected masses. Understanding that the country faced growing anti-Javanese dissent, the depletion of oil reserves, the destruction of forests and an increase in religious militancy, the Republic would come under increased pressure and ultimately fracture with the exit of Aceh, or West Papua from the unitary state. And, in view of these long term expectations, Young recognized that he would be faced with a most difficult road ahead.

He checked the time before making the call to Agus. It was 2048 hours on 11th September 2001 – morning, in New York where the first pictures of the burning World Trade Center were being broadcast live to television viewers across the globe.

KABUL – AFGHANISTAN
November 2001

An eight-metre long *Predator* streaked through the sky twenty-thousand feet above the earth, beaming a continuous live video feed to the operator sitting at his console hundreds of kilometres away. Equipped with missiles directed via a laser-targeting system, the *Predator's* belly-mounted video camera scanned the terrain, recording, searching for its target, launching its Hellfire missiles upon receiving the operator's command.

On the ground an unsuspecting gathering of al-Qaeda leadership was incinerated in a flash when the Rockwell warhead struck, amongst the eight killed Osama bin Laden's designated successor Muhammed Atef.

The list of names of those who knew Mohammed Aziz Derashid's connection to al-Qaeda had suddenly been reduced to four.

CENTRAL SULAWESI – POSO
December 2001

Jack McBride was far too distracted to appreciate Poso's Dutch-inspired churches and government buildings as he made his way down to the harbor, stopping repeatedly to bend down and scratch where scrub mites had attacked, the maddening itch around his sandaled feet driving him to despair.

Concerned with the further escalation in sectarian violence Jack traveled to the city to ensure Netty's safety when she arrived from Gorontalo. It was evident that the *Laskar Jihad* had now divided their attention between neighboring Moluccas and Sulawesi, the death toll in Ambon and its surrounding islands now exceeding nine thousand. Over the past week thousands of homes, schools and churches had been destroyed across Sulawesi when the *Jemaah Islamiyah*, the *Laskar Jihad* and the more-recently formed *Laksar Jundullah*, armed with machine guns, rocket launchers and bulldozers swept through the provinces pillaging and burning Christian villages. Even Poso's largest church had not been spared, bombed then burned during the onslaught.

In the aftermath of the September, al-Qaeda attacks on the United States, Indonesia's militant groups had become more determined, raising the level of conflict between Muslims and Christians across the archipelago in an attempt to garner greater popular support within the country.

Jack had caught a minibus from Tentena – now partially under siege, the journey delayed when demonstrators blocked the main arterial roads entering the city and forced passengers to alight. Angered by the inconvenience he had continued on foot, his apprehension growing when it became apparent that Poso was now under the control of the seven-thousand strong, TNI-backed *Laskar Jihad* – and the *Laskar Mujahideen,* the *Jemaah Islamiyah's* armed forces which totaled some two thousand men. The *Laskar Mujahideen,* although smaller in numbers than the *Laskar Jihad,* were significantly better trained, the two armed groups often clashing.

The Christian community's conspiracy claim that the recent cycles of recrimination and revenge were the handiwork of outside provocateurs, had been substantiated with evidence of Afghani hardened *Taliban* soldiers arriving to train local Muslim militants at a newly created al-Qaeda training center.

When a group of six Afghan and Pakistani 'observers' were caught during an attack on the Christian village of Pendolo, then surrendered to the TNI only to be released without being interrogated, the reports mysteriously disappeared within the military's bureaucracy. McBride concluded that Jakarta's apparent indifference to their presence was a direct result of pressure from the country's fundamentalist Islamic parties which had played a major role in keeping former President Wahid in power, before switching their alliance to Megawati. The new President's failure to act, foreshadowing an ominous future for the eastern provinces as the *Laskar Jihad* continued to engage Christians with its policy of religious cleansing.

Jack McBride accepted that the violence was not all one-sided with reports of Muslim women and children being stripped naked and their genitals inspected, and Christian vigilantes supported by their 'Black Bat', so-called ninja raiders perpetrating some of the province's worst violence. Earlier, when he had journeyed towards Poso he had passed a mosque, the site of one of the Christians' killing grounds. A charred, headless body lay outside in the eerily quiet of the day; the blood-spattered walls a sinister reminder of the depth of hostilities that flowed through here.

McBride knew that being American brought considerable risk. Walking slowly into Poso he felt the chill of the *Jihad* militants' hate-filled glares, the missionary careful not to provoke confrontation with eye contact – aware that any perceived aggression on his part would undoubtedly bring swift reprisal.

He reached the city's center, his attention drawn momentarily to a sign advertising Internet services and he recalled that the *Laskar Jihad* now maintained its own website which enunciated claims of Christians forcibly converting Muslims with others being subjected to rape, torture and kidnap for use as sex slaves – these accusations loading Muslim minds with suspicion and hatred towards the Christian community. On the Internet café's walls were posters of Osama bin Laden with writing proclaiming '*This is our Leader*', the armed TNI soldiers lounging around outside apathetic to the locals' woes.

* * * *

Shielding his eyes against the midday sun he waved at the incoming ferry, pushed through a throng of persistent hawkers, taking Netty by the hand when she disembarked.

'I hadn't expected to see you here,' Netty gushed, genuinely relieved.

'Thought you might be safer with me by your side.'

Netty squeezed his arm. 'Thank you, Jack. To tell you the truth, I was really concerned about what to expect.'

'What's the situation in Gorontalo?' he probed.

'Recovering, as I left.' She fought back tears. 'I just can't believe what is happening!'

Jack raised his leg and scratched furiously, the relief immediate. He removed Netty's overnight bag from her shoulder then took her by the arm. 'Poso is becoming more volatile by the hour. Best we don't dally. I had trouble getting into the city so it might be an idea if we walk over to one of the hotels and grab a taxi.'

'It'll be expensive,' she warned, picking up the pace to match Jack's long strides.

Jack negotiated the fare and they drove out of the city slowly, the sense of dread remaining as they headed back to Tentena, the journey taking three hours due to the number of check points scattered along the way. The smouldering remains of the mosque passed by, Netty slipping her hand into his as she looked away from the charred remains still lying alongside the road, the corpse now under attack from a pack of village dogs.

'The country's going to implode,' Jack whispered forebodingly 'if this senseless slaughter across the country's eastern provinces isn't stopped.'

'Jakarta is to blame,' Netty implied, 'they could bring this to an end if they really wanted to.'

'I know,' Jack agreed, 'but when is it all going to end?'

'Only the generals can answer that,' she responded cynically.

'The other day I did a tally on the number of churches attacked over the past twelve months.' He looked over at his companion. 'The figures are outrageous. There have been more than one hundred bombing incidents in less than one year, and these don't include non-sectarian attacks such as the Atrium Mall bombings in Jakarta.'

'Aren't the authorities claiming that some Malaysian group was behind that? Netty asked.

'Don't believe that Jakarta really wants to know,' Jack replied, irritably. 'What we need is more international attention.'

'We live in the shadows out here, Jack,' Netty said, resignedly, 'most of the outside world doesn't even know we exist.'

'An unfortunate fact of life,' he muttered. 'Even Theys' death in West Papua doesn't seem to have attracted the attention it deserves.'

Netty considered the lack of international comment relating to the suspicious circumstances surrounding the death of the popular West Papuan independence leader. 'Why do you think there's so little interest in what's taking place in Indonesia?' she asked.

Jack had already considered this issue. 'What's happening here has been eclipsed by the attack on America. I guess that in the aftermath of September Eleven priorities have changed…and that is understandable. Let's face it, most Westerners couldn't find Jakarta or even Bali on a map let alone Poso and Ambon.'

Netty remained silent, sickened that without international pressure on Jakarta and the TNI, the slaughter would continue.

SINGAPORE
Security and Intelligence Department (SID)

SID's Deputy Director read down the list of proposed targets mentioned in the interrogation reports, hesitating when arriving at the Australian High Commission. He muttered something disrespectful before continuing, the senior public servant still resentful over the ABC TV's 'Lateline' program which suggested widespread espionage by Singaporean agents in Australia.

At the time, there were grave concerns that the report might influence the Australian Treasurer's deliberations over whether to permit the sale of the country's second largest communications carrier, Optus, to Singapore's Telecoms. Before the Australian government would approve the sale, Singapore had been required to sign separate agreements with Australia's Defence and intelligence organizations. Although the acquisition had proceeded, Telecoms shares had fallen sharply and that, in turn, had affected the health of the country's sacrosanct superannuation fund.

The Security and Intelligence Department (SID) was charged with gathering and assessing information relating to external threats to Singapore and remained a highly secretive unit known only to the most senior military and government officers. The SID maintained at least one agent at the Republic's embassies and consulates, these officers selected from all branches of the civil service and most with extensive military experience. The identity of SID officers was a closely guarded secret, many maintaining secondary workplace entities with government ministries and agencies such as Foreign Affairs, Defence, Singapore Airlines and the Tourism Board to enable them to operate undetected.

The Deputy considered the successful operation which had resulted in the arrest of fifteen Muslim militants from a relatively obscure group, the *Jemaah Islamiyah*.

When a field operative, Eddie Kwang had alerted his superiors to information he had received whilst interviewing students at a Malaysian *madrasah*, the SID had passed the intelligence to the Internal Security Department. The ISD's operational charter confined the department's activities to matters affecting Singapore's internal security and was not empowered to operate overseas. ISD officers had moved quickly, detaining the group before they could implement their plans to bomb foreign assets in Singapore.

The Deputy scribbled a comment alongside the reference made to the group's leader, Hambali, asking for further information regarding the detainees' statements suggesting that their organization was funded by the al-Qaeda. When he read further and discovered that Hambali had stockpiled enough ammonium nitrate to build seven truck bombs to be used in the Singapore attacks, the Deputy Director's jaw fell measurably, envisaging the flow-on effects to the Singaporean economy should the attacks be successful.

Without hesitation the SID director instructed operatives attached to Singapore's embassy in Jakarta and the High Commission in Kuala Lumpur, to determine whatever links existed between the *Jemaah Islamiyah,* and other known militant organizations operating across the country's borders.

* * * *

BOOK TWO

2002

CHAPTER ELEVEN

JAKARTA
January – 2002

Captain Imam Suprapto joined the other air force officers observing the Gulfstream V jet parked out on the Halim Perdanakusumah apron, under lights.

'What's up?' he asked, unaware that the aircraft belonged to Premier Executive Transport Services Inc, a CIA-owned shelf company whose office bearers were as fictitious as their Social Security numbers listed on federal and commercial records.

'Foreign registration,' a fellow-flyer remarked, pointing to the aircraft's tail number N379P. The Gulfstream had landed shortly after dusk and taxied away from the main military terminal building, the jet immediately placed under the U.S. Embassy Marine guard watch.

Suddenly, there was a flurry of activity, Imam Suprapto and his fellow officers then witnessing what the CIA referred to as "rendition" ops where U.S. government agents slipped into friendly countries and secretly whisked detainees away under a still-classified directive signed by President Bush within days of the Sept. 11, 2001. An unmarked van had been driven alongside the Gulfstream and a prisoner dragged from inside. CIA agents wearing hoods covering their faces stepped down from the aircraft and assumed custody of the man.

'They're Americans!' Iman exclaimed.

'What in the hell...?' another slammed his fist against the heavy-duty glass. 'Who's *that* they're taking?'

Flabbergasted, Imam could only watch as American agents bundled their captive into the Gulfstream V.

'They'd have to be operating with our government's approval,' he muttered, annoyed with what was taking place. 'Wonder who their prisoner is?'

The group continued to monitor the activity below, ignorant of the identity of Muhammad Saad Iqbal Madni, an Egyptian traveling on a Pakistani passport who had been kidnapped by U.S. agents in Indonesia and was now on his way to Cairo. There, he would be subjected to coercive interrogation techniques during months of brutal treatment.

What Imam Suprapto and his fellow flyers had just witnessed was the Bush Administration's secret program of transferring suspected terrorists to friendly countries for interrogation, in action. The Indonesian pilot was not aware, however, that the action was in total contradiction to the *"Convention Against Torture"* – the international agreement that bars signatories from engaging in extreme interrogation techniques.

Imam's attention remained locked on the operation as it came to a close with the Gulfstream tearing down the runway and lifting into the evening air. The excitement over, he then returned to his bachelor quarters to catch up on outstanding correspondence.

Imam Suprapto had not been successful with his many transfer requests over the years, relegated to more of an observer status with the Hercules squadron due to the diminished number of serviceable aircraft. The U.S. unofficial embargo on spare parts had all but crippled the squadron. Even with the growing exodus of pilots leaving the military for more lucrative positions in the private sector, the opportunity to fly was infrequent and the morale amongst the crews now at an all time low.

The Captain ceased writing and switched on his TV set connected around the barracks to a communal TVRO that permitted access to free-to-air broadcasts. For a while he watched CNN, the monotonous news repeats causing his mind to wander, Imam drifting into sleep with the imagery of the Egyptian captive being forced into the Gulfstream, buried deep within his mind.

BALI
February 2002

Dressed inconspicuously in civilian attire Colonel Agus Supadi stood at the back of the Benoa Harbour meeting hall and listened intently, as the fishermen voiced their disapproval over the presence of U.S. Navy ships, in their domain.

'It happens every year when they visit,' their spokesman complained, 'they come into Bali as if they own our waters, establishing security perimeters that make it impossible for our fishing fleet to set to sea.' A chorus of support reverberated through the meeting.

'Our fishing fleets are not safe when they venture out. Just last week an American aircraft carrier ploughed through our waters sinking a number of our boats.' The mood was turning ugly. 'We are putting you on notice,' he directed his warning to the local member of Parliament, 'that we intend claiming compensation for our losses.' The statement was greeted by an affirmative roar and with fisherman waving fists in the air. 'We are not intimidated by the American ships and demand that our government moves their moorings somewhere that does not interfere with our traditional livelihood.'

'We will ask the harbor authorities to consider your request,' Ida Bagus Budiharma promised.

'We have been given the same undertaken for the past four years,' the spokesman assumed the floor again, 'going back to when *the U.S.S. Bellawood* spewed its three thousand sailors and marines onto our shores.'

With the mention of the aircraft carrier the fishermen's mood deteriorated further. The ship had been circling Indonesia at the time ready to evacuate Americans as civil unrest escalated across the archipelago following the Asian currency collapse. The carrier had entered Benoa Harbour blocking all other shipping, its impressive array of Harrier jets and Cobra attack helicopters with their 50-caliber machine guns on display, intimidating in every way.

'The Americans support our tourist industry when they're here,' the official attempted to pacify, 'and now that Bali has been approved as an R & R destination for their forces, we have been advised that close to one thousand sailors and marines will be on permanent rotation here.' He challenged the fishermen's spokesman. 'You have a valid complaint and we will have that addressed. However, anti-American demonstrations have the potential of damaging Bali's image as a hospitable destination and the authorities ask that you cease such activities immediately.'

'Good,' the spokesman lifted his forehead measurably, comfortable with the compromise. 'All we want is compensation,' he glanced around confidently, 'after that we don't care how much the Americans spend on the Javanese whores in Kuta.'

Colonel Supadi came to the conclusion that there was no opportunity here. His attendance had been to determine whether the fishermen's complaints could be exploited and directed towards his own interests and, disappointed with the outcome, slipped away unobserved to fill in a few hours in Kuta before his return to Jakarta. Not one to frequent tourist venues he was amazed at the number of Americans with their short-cropped military haircuts packing the bars – miffed when he was initially refused entry to the Sari Club which, he discovered, maintained a policy of no entry for the locals.

Upon his return to Jakarta, Supadi was summoned by General Sumantri. The *Jemaah Islamiyah* operational arm had called its principle players to a high-level meeting in Bangkok, and the General insisted that Supadi meet with Hambali to reassure the *JI* leadership of his ongoing support.

BANGKOK –THAILAND
9th February

The *Jemaah Islamiyah's* senior administrator, Noor Din bin Mohamed Top picked around the cavity in a tooth, wincing as he dislodged the offending gristle.

'We have been sloppy. Before he left for the Middle East, Jabarah told me Khalid was most disappointed.' Noor then tested the gap between his teeth with the tip of his tongue and, satisfied that the problem was resolved, spooned another mouthful of braised lamb into his mouth.

'Jabarah is no longer here,' Dr Azahari Husin sounded pleased. Husin referred to Mohammed Mansour Jabarah, a Kuwaiti-born Canadian who had been ordered by Khalid Sheikh Mohammed, chief of al-Qaeda's military committee and mastermind of the September 11 attacks, to assist in the group's S.E. Asian operations. Jabarah's brief had been to assist and to escalate the *Jemaah Islamiyah's* war against American interests in the region.

Upon his arrival in Singapore four months earlier he had plotted a series of truck bomb attacks against foreign legations in the island republic – the operation failing when Singapore's Internal Security Department discovered their plan. Jabarah had fled to Bangkok and acting upon Hambali's advice, returned to Oman where he acted as Riyadh's financial conduit for sanctioned *JI's* activities.

The others turned to their leader, Hambali, who raised his head. 'I have been in communication with Jabarah and agree with Khalid's suggestions that we change direction in terms of the type of target we select.'

'Such as…?' Husin asked. The Malaysian had earned his PhD in engineering from Reading University in the United Kingdom and in no way considered Jabarah his peer. Husin had also received extensive training in Afghanistan and was considered the *JI's* senior bomb expert, teaching others his deadly art, when he was not lecturing at the Malaysian University of Technology in Johor.

'Azis has an idea that might fit,' Ali Ghufron was keen to have Imam Samudra's suggestions tabled as his close associate had been unable to attend the Bangkok meeting. And, if Ghufron supported the idea and as he was the next in line to replace Hambali as regional commander, he expected that the others present would fall into line. 'Azis raised the suggestion a few weeks back and I believe the plan has merit.'

'What's the proposed target?' Noor asked. He, too, had fled Malaysia for Thailand when Singapore's authorities commenced raiding homes and offices of anyone suspected of having ties with the *Jemaah Islamiyah*. Together with Wan Min bin Wan Mat, Noor was most active in raising funds for the terrorist cells.

'Indonesia's soft underbelly,' Ghufron revealed, 'Bali.'

'Why Bali?' Zulkepli bin Marzuki asked. The wealthy Malay businessman was a close aide of Hambali and had acted as point man for the *JI* whenever Saudis visited Kuala Lumpur. He was also loyal to Abu Bakar Bashir.

'Because the island is full of American tourists,' Ghufron argued, 'and the place is decadent, full of foreign women running around bare-breasted on the beaches, guzzling alcohol and taking drugs.'

'And, being a Hindu community, any collateral damage wouldn't impact too severely on our Muslim brothers and sisters,' Noor added, warming to the idea. 'Besides, Bali and the Christian provinces are like warts on a believer's nose. I, for one, support the idea.'

'When you look at it, Bali makes the perfect target,' Ghufron continued. 'Firstly, the island is wide open; security is almost non existent and we could move materials across from Banjuwangi through Gilimanuk without raising suspicion. Secondly, the tourist destination is known internationally with more than four to five million visitors each year. A successful strike would be rewarded with the world focusing on the attack...and that, in turn, would make the Americans sit up and listen to what we have to say.'

Hambali raised a hand silencing the meeting. Before the Singapore authorities had wrecked their local operations he had planned to bomb visiting U.S. warships, his conversation with General Supadi's envoy, Supadi, coming to mind.

Suddenly, his head was awash with images of drunken American sailors and marines from the U.S. Navy's Seventh Fleet dying in such an attack. 'More importantly, Bali has also become the home for American ships,' he stressed, 'and that makes it a prime target.'

'*Bapak* Bashir would need to be convinced,' Marzuki reminded those present.

Hambali locked eyes with the Malay. Their spiritual leader's position had become decidedly factious following the September 11 attacks, Marzuki conveying Bashir's concerns to the more radical *JI* elements that the West was likely to be more responsive to any new attacks. 'This is an operational matter,' Hambali asserted, 'and as such, the decisions will be made here, today.'

'Then we should vote,' Noor proposed, the group unanimously then agreeing to the target.

'How would such an operation be funded?' Wan Min bin Wan Mat, the *JI's* bagman asked. Wan Mat's appearance belied the man's toughness. He had also received training in Afghanistan and in the Philippines, MILF camp in Mindanao following the foiled *Bojinka* plot.

'I will arrange the funds,' Hambali assured again assuming the leadership role. 'and I propose that Ghufron heads the operation,' and again, they all agreed.

Ali Ghufron aka Mukhlas nodded his assent. His mind raced ahead as to what tasks he would delegate to his brothers, Imron and Amrozi, back in Java. He was ecstatic; his selection to implement and lead the attack on Bali targets would raise his profile as an international leader, and further consolidate his claim to Hambali's position as the *Jemaah Islamiyah* operations commander.

CENTRAL SULAWESI
12th February

In South Sulawesi on the 12th February 2002 after two days of intense negotiations, Jack McBride witnessed Christians, Muslims and the Moluccan government sign an accord, the *Malino II Agreement*, designed to end three years of sectarian violence. The agreement was signed by thirty-five Muslim and thirty-five Christian representatives, along with thirty mediators and observers. The list of mediators included Coordinating Ministers Susilo Bambang Yudhoyono and Yusuf Kalla, Supreme Police Commander Da'i Bahtiar and the Governor of the Moluccas M. Latuconsina.

The agreement was widely hailed as the instrument that would finally bring peace to the people of Sulawesi and the Moluccas.

Among the eleven-point declaration were clauses stipulating that the people of *Maluku* would reject and oppose all kinds of separatist movements including the Republic of South Moluccas (RMS) and that all illegal armed organizations or militias were to be banned and disarmed and expelled from the Moluccan provinces. The *Laskar* groups were specifically named and the agreement also stipulated that all members of these organizations were to surrender their weapons failing which, these would be confiscated and the offenders prosecuted.

Throughout that month and into March both the Muslim and Christian communities endeavored to maintain the peace, striving together to achieve a full reconciliation. When provocateurs attempted to reignite the violence Muslims and Christians marched together in solidarity. By the middle of March, roads had been reopened and harmony appeared to have been restored throughout Indonesia's eastern provinces.

In Jakarta, General Sumantri called an emergency meeting of like-minded, senior officers which resulted in some suggesting that the *Laskar Jihad*, as a force, might have seen its day.

CHECHNYA
19th March

Saudi-born Samir bin Saleh al-Suwailem thanked his trusted fellow-field commander as he accepted the letter. He opened the document and read its contents, glancing up quizzically at his friend as the poison passed through the pours of his skin.

In the following days having endured many months of humiliating losses in Chechnya, the Kremlin claimed a major coup announcing that the Federal Security Service (FSB) had succeeded in killing one of the separatists' top commanders, known by his nom de guerre, "Khattab."

With Khattab's passing the number of parties with knowledge of the Malaysian weapons' repository was reduced to three.

SOLO
20th April

Dulmatin requested a recess to accommodate his weak bladder. Before rejoining the others he checked outside to ensure security remained alert then re-entered his home where the meeting was about to come to a close.

Ali Ghufron, who now insisted on being called Mukhlas by both associates and siblings Amrozi bin Nurhasyim and Ali Imron, had summoned his team to discuss proposed targets for their next operation. The general consensus amongst those present was that the Church bombings carried out over the previous year had been only marginally effective, Imam Samudra pointing to the relatively low body count.

'I have good contacts in Lombok,' Samudra suggested, 'and we could easily hit the Newmont gold mine there.'

'What about the American Consulates in Bali or Surabaya?' Dulmatin asked.

'The number of foreign casualties would be limited.' Annoyed, Mukhlas dismissed the idea. 'We would do better to attack the foreign schools in Jakarta. No, the executive has agreed that Bali will be our target. What we need to do is select a location which will provide the largest collateral effect.'

'Why select just the one target?' Imron asked, keen to be heard.

Mukhlas pondered the question. 'There's no reason why we shouldn't consider multiple locations.'

Imam Samudra butted in. 'This will require a great deal of money.'

'I'll discuss the matter of funding with you later.'

Although Mukhlas' war chest of forty-thousand dollars was significant he was committed to raising even more. Thirty-thousand had been provided by Wan Min on Hambali's instructions and Abu Bakar Bashir had given him envelopes during their most recent meeting; one containing a further six thousand and the other, seventeen thousand Singapore dollars.

'We can source most of the materials locally,' their host assured. Dulmatin, whose real name was Joko Pitono, was considered to be something of a genius in the preparation of explosives. The Javanese car-dealer had been instrumental in designing the bomb used in the attack against the Philippines Ambassador. Trained by the Malaysian bomb-master Dr

Azahari Husin, Dulmatin's deadly expertise had also gained him entree into the Philippines MILF. 'And our brothers in the Philippines will provide detonators if our contacts in *PINDAD* fall short,' he assured, referring to the government-owned army ordnance division in Turen, near Malang in East Java. 'We'll need to identify the targets first in order to determine what our requirements will be.'

'Who'll make the final decision as to the targets?' Samudra asked, rewarded with a sharp look from Mukhlas for exaggerating his authority. The meeting became hushed; there was never any doubt as to who was really in charge here.

Mukhlas moved on, ignoring Imam Samudra's impertinence. 'The executive agrees that October would be an appropriate timing for us to consider.'

The suggestion was greeted with enthusiastic grunts as those present deeply empathized with Afghanistan, and despised the Americans for their missile attack in October, 2001.

'We shall send the United States and its allies a gift to help whilst they celebrate the first anniversary of *Operation Enduring Freedom*.'

AMBON
25th April

Renewed violence on the island of Ambon shattered the uncertain peace when Maluku separatists from the *FKM, Maluku Sovereignty Front* raised the RMS flag, in defiance of new curbs on civil liberties and in a demonstration of their contempt for the Malino accord. The FKM had emerged eighteen months earlier as a revitalized RMS to defend Christians against Muslim attacks.

Alarmed that they might be considered no longer relevant, the *Laskar Jihad* enkindled the conflict by sending a team armed with TNI-issue automatic weapons and grenades, to attack Soya village on Ambon's outskirts.

Shouting '*Allah Akbar*', the men swept into the neighborhood massacring Christians, proceeding from house to house, shooting into those who had been unable to flee. Outraged by bombs being detonated in Ambon's neutral areas mobs burned Governor Saleh Latuconsina's office. As the violence continued to grow, international NGOs and United Nation agencies commenced evacuating most of their foreign staff.

* * * *

'Where are you going?' Rima challenged, aghast at what she saw.

Armed with a deadly *golok* in one hand Johanis Matuanakotta was heading for the door.

'The Muslims are attacking Soya Village.'

Rima had heard when news had swept Ambon. She had wanted desperately to view the action but out of concern for the governor's proclivity to expel foreigners, she had elected to remain at home. The governor had issued an order weeks before banning foreigners from entering the province. Although her documents clearly indicated that she was permitted to reside in Ambon, Rima knew that any activity that might be construed as provocative could result in closure of her NGO. She stood hands on hips, blocking Matuanakotta's exit. 'Johanis, I forbid you to go!'

'I must,' he insisted, the deep resentment he harbored for the militant Muslim *Laskar Jihad* compelling him to join the fray.

'You could be arrested,' she warned, 'or worse!'

He tried to brush her gently aside. 'This is not your war,

Rima.'

She gripped his arm with both hands, Johanis surprised by her strength. 'I won't let you do this!'

He tried to shake her free. 'Let me go!' he shouted angrily, the raised voices bringing Nuci, the housekeeper running into the room.

'Aduh!' she cried out in dismay, confronted by what she saw.

'Listen!' Rima ignored Johanis' mother-in-law, pulling firmly, dragging him away from the door, 'I'll strike a bargain with you if you stay.'

'Listen to her!' Nuci appealed, 'do what she asks, Johanis. Please!'

'Get out of my way, Rima,' he demanded, but not threateningly.

'No!' her grip tightened, 'I'm not letting you go.'

Infuriated with Rima's resolve and accepting that nothing short of a blow would release him from her grip Johanis glared across at Ruci, and shook his head in defeat. Slowly, he extricated himself from Rima's vice-like hands. 'You don't understand,' he protested and, in a demonstration of his exasperation, flung the menacing machete he carried against a near wall.

Rima took Johanis by the wrist and led him to the wicker-cane settee normally reserved for guests. 'Nuci,' bring some of those sago cakes you've been keeping in reserve.' She sat alongside Johanis and held his hand. 'I meant what I said about offering a reward, if you'd stay.'

Still piqued with troubled pride Johanis responded churlishly. 'A cake for an errant student?'

'Be patient and listen to what I have to say,' she chided,

releasing her hold. 'I have decided to write to Amsterdam rec-
ommending you for a training scholarship.'

At first it appeared that Johanis had not heard as he sat
quietly examining her face to see if it were true. Then, 'You're
not just saying that to keep me from joining the other *Cokers*
in the fight?'

'No, Johanis,' she affirmed, 'I intend visiting Jakarta next
month and while I'm there, I'll inform our embassy of our
intention to seek sponsorship for you.'

Johanis' eyes widened with disbelief. 'Is this true?'

Rima nodded, relieved that her news had the desired effect.
'You have my promise.'

'And this is for the… engineering apprenticeship?' he asked,
hopefully.

'That's what the recommendation will be,' she answered.
'However, the sponsoring body will want to know more about
you,' Rima wanted these words to sink in. 'And that will require
a security background check.'

Johanis felt the weight of the words as these spilled from
her lips. 'There may be some problems with that,' he inferred,
recalling his arrest, interrogation and brush with death.

After his near-encounter with death he had kept low for
months, fearful of discovery. When he realized that the *Laskar
Jihad* had not kept records of their prisoners he applied for
replacement identification papers which were issued without
question, upon payment of an appropriate fee.

Rima understood. 'We'll address that problem if it arises.'

In the weeks that followed, *Laksar Jihad* units destroyed village upon village, slaughtering innocents with unabated cruelty.
Moluccan Protestant and Catholic Church leaders appealed to
the U.N Secretary General, Kofi Annan, requesting that the

issue be raised at the United Nations, Rima Passelima amongst the more vociferous critics when a response failed to arrive to address the forgotten war.

Determined to see Johanis out from under the influence of the Christian *Coker* gang and their vengeful reprisals she called Jakarta and made arrangements to visit.

JAKARTA
May

Rima Passelima read the response confirming that Johanis Matuanakotta would soon be on his way to Holland where he would undertake mechanic training, seemingly sponsored by KLM.

Whilst in The Netherlands Johanis would come under the influence of her masters at the *Algemene Inlichtingen en Veiligheidsdienst* (AIVD) which, twenty-four hours before had officially been known as the BVD (*Binnenlandse Veiligheidsdienst*) the Dutch General Intelligence and Security Office. Somewhat out of the intelligence loop due to her deep cover assignment Rima relied on information from AIVD Assistant Director, Volkert van Leeuwen's circuitous communication flow, to maintain contact and keep her up to speed regarding changes within the Dutch intelligence services.

She hailed a Bluebird taxi outside the Royal Netherlands Embassy in Kuningan and returned to her hotel, eagerly anticipating her dinner date with Greg Young.

WASHINGTON

Ian Jefferson mulled over the reports spread across his desk in the ONA's fourth floor office located in the Australian embassy. It would seem that the American intelligence services were about to close ranks, with both the CIA and FBI under media attack for their perceived intelligence failures in relation to September 11. And, for Jefferson, this translated into a further slowing in the exchange of information between the United States and its ally, Australia. He checked the wall clock; his American counterpart was running late; the ONA specialist speculating that the CIA conduit was still rehearsing his explanation for that day. Jefferson expected that whatever information might be made available, the quality of the intelligence would not be of the level enjoyed in the period leading up to the brutal destruction of East Timor by Jakarta-backed militias.

At that time, Australia's intelligence interests were represented by Merv Jenkins, the former head of the elite Australian, highly secret groups of commandos known as 660 Signal Troop which provided communications for ASIS agents overseas and Australian Special Forces operating clandestinely in East Timor. Jenkins, a specialist in covert ops resigned his commission to take up an appointment in Washington as the Australian Defence Intelligence Organisation (DIO) attaché for North America. He was charged with placating the Americans by improving the information flow from the Australian side, at a time when Washington suspected Canberra was withholding sensitive material from its U.S. partners. Jenkins' assignment was complicated by the fact that Australian intelligence agencies resisted releasing any information relating to the country's military operations in East Timor.

Jenkins had come under considerable CIA pressure when they concluded that he was withholding important intelligence relating to the post-Suharto regime. Convinced that he had the authority to pass AUSTEO (Australian Eyes Only) material to the Americans Jenkins did so, and at the time the two countries were negotiating a new agreement over the CIA's joint spy base at Pine Gap near Alice Springs.

In a totally unrelated incident, Jean-Philippe Wispelaere, a former Australian DIO officer was enticed to Washington by undercover agents. He arrived from London carrying more than one thousand high-resolution U.S. satellite photographs he had stolen from the defence offices in Canberra. His arrest deepened the growing rift between the two countries. Jenkins moved to remedy the situation by providing highly sensitive intelligence to the Americans that Canberra would have preferred withheld. As Australia had staked its reputation on the position that the imminent East Timor independence vote would proceed calmly, denying reports that the Indonesian army was supporting the militia violence, the information passed by Jenkins embarrassed Canberra immensely.

When Langley desk officers examined the documents they knew that Australia had been withholding key information relating to Indonesian troop movements in East Timor and, consequently, demanded more from Jenkins. He complied, unaware that he was under surveillance, the investigation resulting in his being interrogated by Australian agents.

Jefferson recalled reading the report when, shortly thereafter, on his forty-eighth birthday Merv Jenkins was found dead, hanging outside his residence on Spy Hill in Arlington, the repercussions of his apparent suicide a lingering legacy that would haunt intelligence organizations for decades.

The phone rang startling the ONA liaison officer.

'Gidday, mate,' the American's attempted Aussie accent caused Jefferson to wince, 'I'm down in the lobby when you're ready.'

* * * *

John Phillips, liaison officer for the U.S. Defense Intelligence Agency (DIA) sat down opposite the ONA attaché and flashed a factitious smile as he pushed a folder across the table. 'A gift from the boys in Langley.'

He watched Jefferson unlock a drawer in his desk and remove a similar file. 'Courtesy of the Office of National Assessments,' the Australian countered, Phillips accepting the documents then casually flipping the cover open to read down the list of contents. 'You guys still don't have anyone on the ground in Ambon?'

'Difficult with the travel restrictions in place,' Jefferson replied, 'most of our information is coming via local assets in Jakarta.'

Phillips roamed the list. 'More on Eluay's murder?'

'Canberra feels that it's significant.'

'Guess so.' Phillips fished for further response relating to the Papuan separatist leader's assassination by Indonesian Special Forces. 'I'll bet there weren't many tears shed by your people Down Under when he went?'

'Quite the contrary, Theys Hiyo Eluay was highly regarded back home.'

'Well, Jakarta couldn't survive with another East Timor on its plate.'

'Aceh is of far more consequence right now.'

'And Ambon,' Phillips added. 'The troubles there just don't seem to want to go away.'

'The conflict doesn't attract much media in Australia.'

'That can only be a positive for Indonesian-Australian relationships.'

'We could do with some level of improvement,' Jefferson suggested, 'we damn near came to blows when our troops arrived in Timor.'

Phillips steered the conversation back to Theys Eluay's death. 'Will the *Kopassus* arrests over Theys' removal impact on your Special Forces in any way?'

'Not really,' Jefferson answered, 'there's not been any real contact between our SAS and *Kopassus* to speak of since '98.'

'Any substance to the claim that the TNI is backing *Laskar Jihad*-style militias in Papua?'

'Unfortunately yes,' Jefferson confirmed, 'the Indonesian army's "Red & White" task force operating around Wamena has been recruiting locals for such a force.'

'You'd better keep your fingers crossed that Jakarta can keep a lid on the secessionists there,' Phillips warned, 'West Papua is a goddamn site richer in natural resources than that backwater, East Timor. If there's any real threat of an uprising you can bet Jakarta will hang onto the province with everything she's got.' He picked the file up as if preparing to leave. 'Can't stay long, I'm afraid,' he said, preparing the ground for the real purpose of his visit. 'Oh, and before I go, Langley asked me to mention that they would appreciate anything you might come across that corroborates linkage between the cleric, Abu Bakar Bashir's *Jemaah Islamiyah* network and Riyadh.'

Jefferson appeared to search his memory. 'Can't say I've come across anything even closely related to…what's his name?'

'Bashir,' Phillips repeated, 'Abu Bakar Bashir. He's reportedly the spiritual leader of this new militant group.' The DIA officer then frowned. 'Your department doesn't have anything at all on the *JI*?'

'Can you be more specific?' Jefferson was now taking notes.

Phillips had the response he wanted 'No, not really,' he lied, 'you know Langley; they see a puff of smoke and start preparing for forest fires.'

'I'll check with Canberra and let you know if they have anything,' the Australian promised.

'Okay, that's fine,' Phillips responded casually, 'there's no real priority. Langley just wants to fill in some missing pieces.' He deliberately glanced at his watch.

'Time for lunch?' Jefferson asked.

Phillips closed the file and locked it inside his briefcase. 'I'll take a rain check on that,' he said without warmth, 'give me a call towards the weekend and we'll see if we can squeeze in a game of golf?'

* * * *

During the drive back to Langley, John Phillips ruminated on the U.S.'s evolving relationship with its ally, Australia, and the impact George W. Bush's determination to engage in a large-scale military operation against Iraq would have on shared-intelligence procedures. Support for any U.S.-led invasion was dwindling with the international community challenging the legality and justification for the President's new doctrine of "pre-emption" leaving the Administration as determined as ever, to do whatever was necessary to build international support for the war against Saddam Hussein.

As a senior analyst, Phillips could articulate a myriad of reasons for such an attack; acts of genocide against the Kurds, the invasion of Kuwait, Saddam's capacity to reacquire weapons of mass destruction and, of course, the question of how to monopolize development of the region's massive oil reserves. However, he admitted silently, although the White House was desperate to prove otherwise, there *was* no evidence that Iraq had been linked in any way whatsoever to the al-Qaeda attacks of September 11. And, with the U.S.'s staunchest allies, Britain and Australia continuing their equivocal stance, the Administration ordered its intelligence agencies to do whatever was necessary to assist President Bush build his case for war.

John Phillips' brief had been to ascertain whether the Australians might have been aware of Mohammed Mansour Jabarah's existence. He was advised not to mention Jabarah's name specifically, the DIA liaison officer now confident that the Australians remained ignorant of Jabarah's arrest in Oman, and his current whereabouts in FBI custody.

Phillips was a member of the limited circle aware of Jabarah's revelations. The al-Qaeda-linked, *Jemaah Islamiyah* financial conduit to Riyadh had been arrested in the Middle East following his meeting with Hambali in Thailand. He had revealed that Hambali had suggested Jabarah abandon his activities in the Asian theatre out of concern that he would be identified and arrested. Then came the bombshell – Hambali had shared a critical piece of information during their farewell meeting hoping that this revelation would result in a substantial cash injection from his Saudi benefactors.

According to Jabarah, Hambali had told him that al-Qaeda, through the *Jemaah Islamiyah* network, had changed its strategy and was now focusing on identifying "nightclubs frequented by Americans" for an unprecedented attack, in Bali.

Under interrogation in Oman, Jabarah also revealed that Hambali had codenamed the operation, "White Meat", John Phillips now deeply conscious of the risks his government had assumed in not immediately disseminating information relating to the threat to those most at risk – nonplussed as to why the White House had ordered that this important intelligence would not be shared.

JAKARTA

When Greg Young's driver opened the BMW's rear door, Rima Passelima covered her nose, assailed by the stench from a nearby bus' exhaust fumes.

'My God, Greg,' she climbed from the sedan and peered up at the two-hundred-year old building. 'I hope they keep the windows closed inside.'

'Ah,' Young followed, steering her to the Café' Batavia's doors, misunderstanding the reason for her comment, 'where would the locals be without Kota's grand canal? His eyes twinkled mischievously. 'But coming from Holland, surely you'd be used to that?'

Rima bristled. 'Our canals don't smell,' she said, defensively, 'but if you'd been there, you'd be aware of that.'

They entered a sprawling lounge-cum-bar, Rima immediately taken by the ambience, the art deco interior transporting the couple back through time into a Dutch East Indies colonial setting. They strolled across the ground floor lounge.

'An oasis,' Rima Passelima exclaimed, then looking up, 'complete with galley and all!' She examined the wall smothered with memorabilia of the rich and famous. 'You're not here?' she teased, Greg taking her elbow and leading his date up an alluring wooden staircase into the Churchill Bar. Rima soaked in the nostalgic atmosphere with its quaint vintage posters and ornate ceiling fans turning sedulously, stirring the humid, tropical air.

'Let's have a drink before we eat?'

'Sure,' Rima moved away from Churchill's censorious glare and across to the crowded cowhide-covered bar where a crisp-uniformed bartender placed a bowl of reheated cashew nuts and took their order.

'Do you enjoy jazz?' Young asked as the band commenced another set.

Rima wrinkled her nose. 'Let's just say that I don't have any in my CD collection back home.'

'Well then, perhaps once you've heard this group play for awhile you might change your mind?'

'I didn't say I disliked jazz,' Rima touched him consolingly on the arm, 'it's just that my preference runs to Duran Duran and Ronan Keating.'

They sat and talked, sipping their cocktails, re-establishing the rapport they had achieved when first introduced at Andrew Graham's residence.

'Are you in Jakarta on NGO business?' Greg inquired.

'Some,' Rima could never reveal the true purpose of her visit. 'Had to renew my visa and permits,' she explained, 'you know, the usual bureaucratic processes one must contend with in this country. When I called your office last week and your secretary placed me on hold, I wasn't sure you'd remember me,' Rima confided

'Hard to accept that it's been two years,' Greg remarked, reminiscently.

'Long time between drinks?' she responded with an innocent air.

'Especially for a thirsty man,' he countered.

Rima pulled a face and challenged, good-naturedly, 'Forgive the analogy but I just can't visualize you not drinking from the trough for more than a few days… let alone two years.'

Greg was enjoying the badinage. 'Metaphorically speak-ing…' he started to respond but Rima slipped from the barstool and took him by the hand.

'Enough…I'm hungry. Let's eat?'

They dined in style, seated by a window overlooking Fata-hillah Square, Greg observing Rima as she gazed out, her mind meandering in other pastures. 'If only it could be like this in Ambon,' she murmured.

'How's the NGO proceeding?' he had expected the subject to arise earlier.

A waiter coasted to their table and topped Rima's glass. She waited for the man to withdraw before responding. 'Well, some of us were foolish enough to believe that the *Malino Accord* might just bring some semblance of peace to the area. For what it's worth, I don't believe anyone in Jakarta really gives a fuck what happens in the province. What sort of message do you think it sends the radicals when even the Vice President offi-ciates at a *Laskar Jihad* meeting and visits their leader, Thalib, while under detention?'

With the unexpected response Greg swallowed, then coughed when his drink went down the wrong way. 'You're… probably right,' he managed, recovering his composure. 'So why did you come here…and then stay?'

Rima became alert, lowering her voice to avoid a couple at the adjacent table overhearing. 'My father is of Ambonese extraction,' she revealed. Then, improvising, she concocted a story to validate her involvement with the NGO. 'I had always wanted to spend time in Indonesia and when the opportunity arose, I jumped.'

'Right into the proverbial,' he joked.

'Well, enough of me for now.' She touched her lips gently with a napkin. 'How's Bimaton faring?'

Greg raised both hands defensively. 'Let's not ruin the evening.'

Curious, Rima persisted. 'Is it something to do with the merger?'

'It wasn't a merger,' he corrected, 'more like a raid by the Malaysians.'

'I sense that you didn't come out of it too well?'

'Bloodied but not devoured,' he raised a smile. 'In the long term it should work out but right now I am not all that enthused with seeing the company I started, in danger of being stripped.'

'And that is likely to happen?' she asked, surprised.

'There is always the possibility when you have predators like Mohamed Aziz Derashid in charge of the roost.'

Rima searched her memory, unable to recall the Malaysian's name. 'And he is...?'

'You've not heard of Derashid before?' he asked, incredulous, 'he's one of Malaysia's wealthiest tycoons. Derashid is young, single...' he paused to signal the waiter for the check, 'and something of an enigma.'

'In what way?'

'Well, he keeps much to himself. You won't find him in Kuala Lumpur social columns and, reportedly, is quite devout.'

'He's Muslim?'

'Yes,' Greg continued, 'although I doubt you would catch him at the mosque.'

'What happened to your partner in Bimaton?'

'Agus Sumarsono would pale if he heard you call him that!' Greg signed the bill then re-gathered his thoughts. 'Originally,

I co-founded a construction group, Young & Budiono. We went public, did well. Then, like everyone else took a major hit with the Asian currency crisis. Agus Sumarsono was one of the largest shareholders. The company remained listed on the Jakarta exchange for a awhile but if the truth be known, Agus controlled most of the shares one way or another, through nominee holdings. Eventually it was de-listed and became part of the Bimaton Corporation.'

'Isn't that unlawful?'

'What?'

'Holding control through nominees without informing the Exchange.'

'Certainly is,' he snorted cynically, 'and everyone does it. Anyway, it doesn't make any difference now.'

'So, Sumarsono has lost control of Bimaton but how does that affect you?'

'Derashid owns Bulan Sabit Holdings in Malaysia which...'

'Bulan Sabit?' she interrupted, bemused, 'what does that mean?'

'Literally, Crescent Moon,' he answered. 'As I was explaining...'

Rima leaned across and touched his hand apologetically. 'Sorry.'

Greg smiled, 'as I was explaining,' he started again, 'Bulan Sabit Holdings now owns control of Bimaton Corporation.'

'And how has this affected you personally?' Rima asked, suddenly flushing when realizing she had overstepped the mark. 'I'm...sorry, Greg, I didn't mean monetarily.'

'That's all right,' he smiled weakly; 'there aren't many secrets in this city.' He selected a breadstick from the basket and broke it in two before the waiter could sweep everything away. 'I'm just one of many waiting for the turnaround to occur.'

'And then…?' she left the question hanging.

'And then,' he stood, 'how about we go back to my place and discuss it there?'

* * * *

Greg Young's driver hit the brakes hard bringing the BMW to a halt. 'Problem, *tuan*,' he pointed up ahead in the direction of Jalan Cendana where the former president remained in residence. Demonstrators had taken advantage of the relaxed, late-evening security and crept into the exclusive Menteng zone to voice their ongoing disapproval at the government's failure to prosecute Suharto.

Rima peered around the headrest blocking her view. 'What's wrong?'

Recognizing the danger he snapped at his driver. 'Turn around and find another way home!' The man obeyed, but before he could turn the wheel a rock shattered the windscreen and he panicked, steering the sedan towards the oncoming protestors.

'For chrissakes, turn the car around!' Greg bellowed, the BMW slowing as the driver struggled to see.

Within seconds the mob was upon them, the students attacking the sedan with rocks and homemade clubs as they screamed their anti-Suharto slogans in the air. A side window imploded under impact leaving the driver exposed, the punishing force of a follow-through-strike rendering the man unconscious. Rima screamed when her side window then came under attack, Greg Young yelling furiously for the students to let them go when the mob commenced rocking the BMW from side to side, leaving the occupants with nowhere to go. Rima cried out when her head cracked savagely against the door, consciousness leaving her as Greg dragged her to the floor. Suddenly, the violence ceased as quickly as it had started leaving the sedan rocking to a standstill, when startled students fled with armed police arriving on the scene.

* * * *

'It's not all that serious,' Rima insisted, touching the dressing gently with her fingertips, 'so I don't need to stay.'

'The doctor thinks otherwise,' Greg stood over the hospital bed. He had accompanied Rima in a police car to the St. Carolus Hospital.

'I'd prefer to go back to my room in the hotel,' she insisted, 'it's only a bruise.'

'It's concussion,' he argued, 'and you should remain under observation.'

'All right; then how about taking me back to your place?'

Greg shook his head. 'Would be smart to remain here for at least the night.'

'Please?'

He threw his hands up in surrender. 'Okay, I'll check with the doctor.'

SURABAYA

Imam Samudra cast Mukhlas and al-Faruq a furtive glance as they slunk alongside the perimeter fence to the east of Kali Mas Harbor reconnoitering the Tanjung Perak Harbor area where the Indonesian Navy moored its ships.

'There!' Samudra whispered, pointing through the early morning light.

Mukhlas stared at the grey silhouettes of four U.S. warships nestled in dock; the *USS Vincennes, USS George H. Philip, USS*

Anchorage and the *USS Morgenthau,* temporary home for the 1,400 marines on board.

'They're just sitting there, the perfect target!' Mukhlas said, momentarily entranced by the opportunity.

'We'll never get close enough with all that security,' al-Faruq cautioned, 'I still think we'd have more likelihood of success by hitting them someplace ashore.'

Unbeknown to the others, although severely tempted to see a repeat of the *USS Cole's* demise, al-Faruq's mission was, in fact, to discourage any such attack.

Mukhlas fell silent considering their options. Details of the U.S. fleet's arrival had been passed to him by Colonel Supadi, the *Kopassus* officer's tardiness in forwarding the information resulting in a hastily conceived plan being prepared to duplicate the October 2000 attack on the *USS Cole* in Yemen.

'Well?' Samudra pressed impatiently, 'do you agree?'

Samudra was a very intelligent man with an extraordinary memory for detail and, apart from his insolent manner, a product of his time spent with the *Mujahideen* in Afghanistan, Mukhlas approved of his protégé and respected his second-in-command's judgment.

'If only Supadi had given us more time,' he remonstrated, disappointment evident in his voice, 'we could have made our mark in history.'

'Supadi claims that these joint exercises are conducted on a regular basis. If that's so, we'll have other opportunities.'

The *Jemaah Islamiyah,* Indonesian Operations Commander turned to Imam Samudra. 'If we abandon this opportunity then I don't believe we should jeopardize *Operation White Meat* by hitting a lesser target.'

Immediately, al-Faruq's ears came alive.

'But the U.S. Consulate would be perfect,' Samudra reasoned, 'we could hit when they have their reception for the fleet's senior officers.'

'No,' Ghufron was adamant. 'Had we been able to mount a successful attack on their ships the outcome would have diminished Bali's importance as a target as we would already have delivered a significant blow. If we attack their Consulate here in Surabaya the casualties wouldn't be all that significant and the Americans might pull their servicemen out of Kuta.' He rose to his feet. 'Come. The Americans are lucky this time. Let's channel all our energy into making Bali the success we might have achieved here today.'

JAKARTA

Greg Young strolled across the marble floor of the master-bedroom to the French sliding doors overlooking the pool and stood admiringly, observing Rima Passelima as she stepped away from the water, her firm breasts, taut at their tips challenging the top of her two-piece costume. He changed, stepped outside then plunged into the lukewarm water and swam effortlessly to the other side.

'Been shopping, I see?' Greg rested his chin on crossed palms, admiring her captivating shape. Droplets caught by the midday sun shimmered against softly-tanned skin as she moved, Greg suppressing a momentary urge to cut to the chase and immediately invite her back inside.

Rima looked down at her bikini. 'Found this in the Taman Anggrek Mall in Slipi.' She executed a slow pirouette. 'What do you think?'

Greg beckoned. 'Coming back in?'

Without hesitation Rima stepped forward and dived back into the pool, coming to rest at his side where she reached up and ran her tongue across his cheek. 'And what brings the *tuan* home this early?' she teased, backstroking away.

Greg lunged, grabbing her by the feet; Rima kicking playfully before surrendering to his powerful arms. They embraced; the touch of her skin and the tantalizing warmth of her mouth driving his arousal, Rima resisting when his hand groped for her thighs. 'Not here, the servants will see us!'

'I'll have their eyes put out,' he offered playfully, relaxing his hold permitting Rima to slip away.

'And just in time,' she cautioned, with the houseboy and another servant appearing on the scene with a number of trays.

Rima turned her head as she climbed out of the pool. 'God, I could get used to this!'

*　*　*　*

Rima woke to the split-unit air conditioner's almost imperceptible click when the compressor kicked in, spilling cool air across their semi-naked bodies. She rose on one arm to discover that Greg, too, had fallen asleep following their last coupling, Rima unexpectedly engulfed with guilt as she watched her lover's chest gently rise and fall with each breath.

A week had passed since her brush with the demonstrators, the days spent recuperating at Greg Young's villa now rhapsodic memories which she would carry throughout her life. With the realization that she had fallen hopelessly in love came the quandary of her commitment to the AIVD and the people of Ambon, and whether she should reveal all to Greg. He had said that he loved her – and Rima was eager to believe, trusting that their interlude would have as much depth in meaning for him, as it did to her.

As the morning advanced Rima came to the conclusion that the perplexity of her situation demanded further consideration. And, deciding it would be in both their interests should she retreat to Ambon and permit nature take its course, Rima contrived a credible story and departed later in that day.

SHOAL BAY – DARWIN
Defence Signals Directorate Station
4th June

When Nick Dennison re-examined the digitally recorded intercept transcripts the senior communications analyst became confident that they had identified a new player connected to General Sumantri's intelligence network. Culled from the high band radio frequency traffic al-Faruq's name would appear in Australian intelligence records for the first time. As the interpretation of his conversation indicated a possible attack on U.S. interests in Indonesia, protocol required that a copy of the report would be flashed to the CIA's Chief of Station at the United States embassy in Canberra.

Alarmed, the CIA immediately activated their exigency plan to remove al-Faruq from the play. The U.S. embassy in Jakarta went into overdrive. *Badan Intelijen Negara* (BIN) officers kidnapped Omar al-Faruq and transported the Kuwaiti to the military airfield, Halim Perdanakusumah. There U.S. agents placed their 'captive' on board the CIA's Gulfstream V jet, registration number N379P, and flew him to Bagram Air Base in Afghanistan and out of harms way.

THE PHILIPPINES
21st June

Colonel William D. Prescott uncrossed his arms and turned away from the prisoner. The U.S. tracking device hidden inside a backpack and monitored by an American spy-plane overhead had resulted in the *Abu Sayyaf's* leader's demise.

'The reward will still be paid,' he addressed the Filipino general who had been waiting anxiously for confirmation that the one-million dollar bounty placed on Abu Sabaya's head, would be forthcoming.

'Thank you Colonel,' the senior officer then moved to complete his side of the arrangement. 'The prisoner is then yours.'

Colonel Prescott wasted no time. Abu Sabaya was bundled into a helicopter and flown to General Santos. Once again, the CIA's Gulfstream appeared as if from nowhere and flew him to Bagram Air Base in Afghanistan. While Sabaya was being held incommunicado, the following Philippines government media release appeared as frontline headlines across the country:

ZAMBOANGA TIMES

Zamboanga: June 22; Abu Sayyaf Group (ASG) spokesman Abu Sabaya (aka Aldam Tilao) was reportedly killed in a firefight with the Navy's Special Warfare Group (SWAG) around 3:30 a.m. on Friday morning according to government sources. The action took place half a mile off the coast of Sibuco in Zamboanga del Norte, site of 'Operation Daybreak' which was launched on June 7 in cooperation with elements of the U.S. 1st Special Forces Group (Airborne). According to Armed Forces Chief Gen. Roy Cimatu, government forces acting on an informant's tip intercepted a pump-boat sailing out of Barangay Parang-Parang, a coastal village of Sibuco. With the aid of night vision equipment the SWAG team detected seven armed persons and when challenged, were fired upon.

Navy officials reported that the government troops rammed the vessel throwing the armed men into the sea. Three were reportedly drowned and four were taken in for tactical interrogation.

According to a Navy spokesman Abu Sabaya was amongst those who were killed. Although earlier radio reports had suggested that Sabaya's body had been recovered government sources have since confirmed that this is not so. However, as the ASG second-in-command's backpack containing his signature black sunglasses, drivers licence, satellite phone and weapons were recovered and other team members claim to have seen their leader die, the Navy has stated it remains confident of recovering his remains.

Today's success comes two weeks after the military rescued American hostage Gracia Burnham who had been held by the Abu Sayyaf for more than one year. Her husband and fellow Christian missionary, Martin Burhham and a Filipina nurse, Ediborah Yap were slain in the attempt. The Burnhams were among a group of tourists captured from a local resort last year. A third American, Peru-born Guillermo Sobero and a dozen other captives were beheaded during that period of captivity.

Abu Sabaya's death will undoubtedly prove to be a major blow to the militant Islamic separatist group who have terrorized the region over the past two years.

American Major Richard Sater, spokesperson for the U.S. military contingent to....

Under interrogation Abu Sabaya revealed all; how funds were channeled from Malaysia; who the important players were and their relationship within the growing al-Qaeda-linked terrorist network; and details of an arrangement that was in place for the *Abu Sayyaf* to transport explosive materials to the *Jemaah Islamiyah* cell in Java, in preparation for the attack codenamed *"Operation White Meat"*. Sabaya would remain the innominate prisoner other inmates could only see from a distance.

Back in the Philippines, in support of their claim that the *Abu Sayyaf* leader was indeed dead the military presented video footage of two of the captured separatists confirming the death of Abu Sabaya. The morale-boosting propaganda was widely broadcast throughout the country and, although some claims of sightings of Sabaya raised speculation that he was still alive, the ruse would remain successful providing growing support for the six-hundred and fifty U.S. Green Berets sweeping through the Philippines' southern jungles.

Information gleaned from Sabaya's interrogation sessions were passed to the CIA's counter-terrorism centre in Langley where the information was dissected and specific names added to the Echelon trigger lists. Amongst these, Abu Umar, who would later achieve worldwide notoriety under his real identity, Imam Samudra for his infamous acts as the "Bali Bomber".

In the following days the Pentagon issued a directive removing Bali from the list of recommended R & R destinations for U.S. troops without informing America's allies.

JAKARTA

General Sumantri finished reading the damming international report and pushed it to one side, pleased with the result from the deliberate information leaks. Classified information had appeared in the international media identifying the *"Barisan Merah Putih" (BMP)* and the *"Yayasan Lembah Baliem"(YLB)* foundation's clandestine relationships between the "Red & White" military faction and their front organizations.

Sumantri cerebrated; the ongoing competition within the TNI's upper ranks had culminated in the creation of a plethora of shadowy agencies under the covert administration of either the "Red & White" modernists or "Green" fundamentalist factions – the General's current concern, how the BMP and YLB had recently overlapped with his own activities blurring the lines of command. Over the past two years control over the country's intelligence apparatus had shifted with the abolishment of the Coordinating Agency for National Stability (*Bakorstanas*) which once held extraordinary powers to maintain security and stability, and the termination of the feared Special Research Agency (Litsus). As BAKIN had been overhauled to become the *Badan Intelijen Negara*, BIN, and other agencies continued their propensity for acting unilaterally, Sumantri was no longer confident that the nation's darkest secrets would remain intact.

He was aware that the BMP was currently active in West Papua and had collaborated with the Mobile Police Brigade in mounting attacks against pro-independence groups in Wayati and Jayawijaya. Sumantri also knew that the Regional Military Commander had established a chapter of the BMP consisting predominantly of Papuan recruits, the overlap occurring with the *Laskar Jihad* forces occasionally working in parallel with the BMP. Then, of even greater concern to the General was the YLB as this 'foundation' had been established under the auspices of the Indonesian National Intelligence Bureau, BIN, the YLB openly supporting the formation of BMP militias in Papua. Sumantri believed that the "Greens" would inevitably be successfully sidelined in the eastern provinces should these two organizations be permitted to grow unchecked, the proposed division of Papua into three new provinces an obvious ploy to facilitate the establishment of more of their command posts throughout the area.

General Sumantri's conundrum was how to restrict the "Red & Whites'" growing influence in the archipelago's east, whilst facilitating the increased presence of the *Laskar Jihad* at the same time. With three thousand *LJ* foot soldiers now present in West Papua supporting the *Kopassus* Special Forces Sumantri hoped that these numbers would prevent the "Red & Whites" from further eroding the "Greens'" predominance within the TNI's leadership.

The national intelligence officer's mind then turned to the report suggesting that the *Jemaah Islamiyah* was currently mobilizing resources again, the General then summoning Colonel Supadi to discuss raising the level of surveillance over all the main players.

*   *   *   *

SOLO – JAVA
July 2002

Amrozi and Ali Imron followed their brother Mukhlas into the meeting where Imam Samudra, Dulmatin, Idris and others were already deep in discussion.

'We were just discussing resurrecting the Newmont mining attack,' Samudra revealed, before surrendering the meeting to Mukhlas.

'No doubt you have all heard that '*kakek*' has given our mission his blessing?' Mukhlas' reference to the *JI* spiritual leader as their grandfather brought smiles to their faces. 'He has agreed that I should lead this operation with Imam here,' he pointed with an open palm at Samudra, 'the operations commander.' He then passed the chair back to his second in command.

Imam Samudra again raised the Newmont matter. 'As I was explaining before your arrival,' he said, speaking directly to Mukhlas, 'a few months back we abandoned the Newmont attack out of concerns that too many of our fellow Muslims would be amongst the casualties. We have some new ideas we wish to discuss with you about specifically targeting their *bule* management which fits in with our Bali operation.'

Mukhlas immediately dismissed the idea of hitting the foreign workers. 'Forget Newmont, we will concentrate on executing the Bali attack only, at this time.'

Samudra deftly disguised his disappointment. 'Agreed,' he complied, removing notes he carried from a plastic folder. 'I have given a great deal of thought regarding the targets,' he commenced, 'and have identified a number of locations in the Legian, Kuta Beach area. I plan on returning sometime next month with Imron, before deciding on the specific targets.'

'What about the American Consulate?' Dulmatin inquired.

'That will remain on our list,' Samudra reassured, 'but not as a primary target.'

Their sense of import lifted in the presence of their brother, Mukhlas, both Amrozi and Imron offered their opinion as to the timing of the proposed attack suggesting that the execution take place on the first anniversary of the September 11, World Trade Centre disaster.

'If we rush this operation then it could fail,' Samudra

pointed out.

Mukhlas came to his aid. 'The precise timing will be determined only when we have everything in place,' he ruled. 'We will follow the original plan set for October.'

Samudra reassumed control over the discussion. 'In that case we should first organize the acquisition of chemicals for the bombs.' He indicated Amrozi. 'Will you be able to source these from your Surabaya contact?'

'Providing we pay him well, as before.' Amrozi had purchased chemicals from the Tidar Kima store at the bequest of Hambali two years before. He had shipped the chemicals to Ambon where Hambali had then manufactured bombs used in the conflict with Christians.

Samudra turned to Idris. 'I'm putting you in charge of reconnaissance and logistics. Okay?'

'Boleh,' Idris agreed.

'Good. Then you will need to make arrangements for accommodation and transport for the bomb team.' Samudra then asked Dulmatin, 'You can have Ghani to help you in the construction of the bombs.'

'We have sufficient funds?' the explosives expert asked.

'Just about,' Samudra smirked, 'courtesy of a Chinese gold store in Serang.' The others laughed; two of their members had robbed the shop of two and a half kilos of gold and jewelry, along with five million rupiah in cash.

The meeting continued until the late afternoon summons to prayer. The group then parted company, their spirits high as the mechanisms clicked into motion for the execution of the Bali attack.

AMBON
29th August

Johanis had reported the outcome even before the local radio station had announced the delay. From Rima's perspective, the Ambon District Court's postponement of the trial of the six members of the pro-independence Maluku Sovereignty Forum (FKM) could not have come at a worse time. The men were all facing subversion charges for raising the South Maluku Republic's flag, Rima deeply troubled that the charge of subversion in this country carried the death penalty.

Johanis Matuanakotta's paperwork was all but completed, the remaining clearance stating that he had not been involved in activities associated with either the FKM or the RMS, imminent. Rima checked the desk calendar and penciled in a number of alternative dates in October to reschedule her trip to Jakarta. She would need to accompany Johanis to the embassy for his visa and ensure that his departure for Holland transpired without incident.

Rima flipped the calendar over to September, reminded of Greg's invitation to accompany him to Canada. He had called and suggested the journey together, promising to make time and show her Banff Springs, once his Calgary discussions with a number of oil-field related interests had been finalized She had listened to her head and declined, Rima no longer at odds with her decision not to go as, in the three months since her return from Jakarta, the local government had continuously raised the possibility that some NGOs may have to close.

Alarmed with the attention the conflict was now receiving internationally and concerned with growing support for the Maluku Sovereignty Front in the wake of losing East Timor,

Jakarta initiated a crackdown on all NGOs in Aceh, Sulawesi, the Moluccas and West Papua. Rima's NGO, the Nusantara Integrated Community Development Organization remained operational due to intervention of Bimaton executives, the AIVD operative agreeing to spend a weekend with Greg Young upon his return from Canada, to demonstrate her appreciation.

TENGGULUN VILLAGE – EAST JAVA
5th September

Having ground the recently acquired Mitsubishi van's chassis and engine numbers down to render them untraceable Amrozi stood back admiring his handiwork, before commencing work on the installation of the false flooring Mukhlas has designed.

'There's someone who wants to inspect the vehicle,' his brother, Imron called, Amrozi surprised when climbing from under the van to discover the bespectacled master bomb builder, Dr Azahari Husin and his fellow Malaysian, Noor Din Top standing, smiling encouragingly.

'Mukhlas tells me that you have done most of the modifications by yourself?' Azahari leaned into the vehicle and gave the Mitsubishi a perfunctory inspection.

Amrozi broke into a nervous giggle and shuffled his feet, intimidated by the British-trained engineer's presence. 'Imron helped,' he managed to say, relieved when the group left him to his own devices and re-entered the dwelling.

* * * *

'We'll have everything in place within the month,' Mukhlas was nearing the end of his briefing.

'After this operation, you may wish to return to Kuala Lumpur for awhile,' Azahari suggested.

Dulmatin looked questioningly at the others. 'Shouldn't we discuss what we're going to do after the attack?'

Mukhlas considered the question. Although none present expected that their involvement would become known he accepted that it would be prudent to have a contingency plan in place. 'We'll put something together, later.'

'Have you arranged an alternative source for the detonators?' Noor asked.

Mukhlas nodded. 'I didn't want to go to the local supplier but in view of what happened in the Philippines there wasn't much choice.'

'Have you decided upon the targets yet?'

'Yes,' Mukhlas confirmed, 'we've identified three or four. Now it's only a matter of determining which will be our primary target.'

'What are these locations?' Azahari's expertise was beyond question as he had considerable experience and success in the past. Hambali had requested that he evaluate the targets before these were set in stone.

'The U.S. Consulate will be one, that's certain,' Mukhlas explained, 'and we have a short list of a number of bars that are popular with American sailors and marines. I asked Imam to...'

'Surely you're not re-considering the consulate as the primary?' Azahari interrupted.

Mukhlas looked puzzled. 'Why?'

'I hope not,' the Malaysian warned, 'as I don't believe the effort even warrant's our consideration.'

Mukhlas' face clouded. 'There was never any suggestion that the consulate would be a major target,' he backtracked, controlling the anger in his voice, 'the intent would be to send them a message that we *could* have done something more significant.'

The following morning Mukhlas accompanied Azahari, Noor, and Dulmatin to Solo where they examined the drawings for the bombs' construction. It was immediately apparent to Azahari that alone, the Indonesians would not be capable of building the weapon required. When further discussion revealed that the team had very little understanding of how to place the bombs to achieve the maximum effect Azahari reported his findings to Hambali, by phone. He also raised the issue over the selection of the U.S. Consulate even as a secondary target, citing security and the lack of any real collateral damage as the basis for his concerns. The former Malaysian University of Technology lecturer then broke established al-Qaeda communication protocols and phoned a number in Yemen, and sought the advice of Syafullah al-Yemeni, believing that the magnitude of the operation required more than his own expertise could offer.

ENGLAND
Echelon Station – Menwith Hill
6th September

In the massive memory banks supporting the intercept spy station's constant, roaming surveillance across most of the U.K. and Europe's communication systems, a solitary trigger activated when the Yemeni's codename, "Syafullah" was mentioned.

The Yemeni's involvement in the 1996 attack on the U.S. Dhahran barracks in Saudi Arabia which had killed nineteen servicemen highlighted the terrorist's trail of terror. He was listed for his involvement in operations against other Western targets including the 1998 kidnapping of sixteen British, American and Australian tourists in Yemen and the 2000 bombing of the British Embassy in the Yemeni capital of Sana'a.

Syafullah al-Yemeni was also known to be one of the principals of the Islamic Army of Aden (IAA), a parallel group to the *Abu Sayyaf* which also engaged in bombings and kidnappings to achieve its goals.

Syafullah was a senior al-Qaeda operative whose file required the director's approval before access could be granted as it was believed that he could lead the duplicitous CIA to bin Laden and, in consequence, the groundwork was being prepared to offer the Yemeni amnesty.

Azahari's conversation with Syafullah al-Yemeni was recorded in detail and, within the hour, a copy of the report had been passed to director of the Counter Terrorist Centre in Langley.

AUSTRALIAN EMBASSY – WASHINGTON
10th September

Ian Jefferson brooded over the *Time* magazine story, underscoring passages with his pen as he read the article for the umpteenth time, deeply annoyed that John Phillips, his liaison contact at the U.S. Defense Intelligence Agency had not forewarned that the story would break. The story quoted White House sources claiming that the U.S. had indisputable evidence of an imminent attack on American interests, naming Kuwaiti-born Omar al-Faruq as the informant.

Jefferson scratched his head, recalling an ONA reference from the Shoal Bay station in the Northern Territory, mentioning al-Faruq's name in relation to a Jakarta communications' intercept. That there had been no interim intelligence cross his desk connected to al-Faruq since that time was now clear, with the *Time* article revealing that the Kuwaiti had been in custody for some months and had broken down only the day before, and revealed everything to his interrogators.

For Jefferson, the article just did not wash. He read between the lines, concluding that the story had to be a CIA worded-release as the detail was fortuitously specific, the article appearing almost one year to the day since the September 11 attack. He knew that Canberra would want to know why Langley had not prepared them in advance, Jefferson's ire with John Phillips rising with the realization that the CIA had been sitting on the information for months. Claims that Omar al-Faruq had been responsible for organizing funding and planning *Jemaah Islamiyah* activities confounded as the ONA had nothing on file with respect to his existence.

He drummed the table deep in thought, the myriad of questions raised by the leaked information certain to cause hemorrhage back in Canberra's intelligence circles.

THE WHITE HOUSE

Excerpt from the September 10, 2002 press conference Question and Answer segment by the U.S. Attorney General Ashcroft and Homeland Security Director Ridge in relation to the Security Threat Level being raised:

"FOR IMMEDIATE RELEASE"
Office of the Press Secretary
September 10, 2002

Director Ridge, Attorney General Ashcroft Discuss Threat Level
Remarks by the Attorney General and Governor Ridge
The Justice Department
1:35 P.M. EDT

ATTORNEY GENERAL ASHCROFT: (In progress)
I want to express my appreciation to Governor Tom
Ridge, who is the Advisor to the President for Home-
land Security, for being here; and to the Director of the
FBI, Bob Mueller, for being here.

The United States government has concluded, based
on analysis and specific intelligence of possible attacks
on U.S. interests overseas, to call government, law
enforcement, and citizens, both at home and overseas, to
a heightened state of alert.

After conferring with the Homeland Security Council, the recommendation has been made to increase the
national threat level, currently classified at Elevated Risk,
to High Risk. The President has accepted this recommendation.

The U.S. intelligence community has received information, based on debriefings of a senior al-Qaeda operative, of possible terrorists attacks timed to coincide with
the anniversary of the September 11th attacks on the
United States. Information indicates that al-Qaeda cells
have been established in several South Asian countries
in order to conduct car-bomb and other attacks on U.S.
facilities. These cells have been accumulating explosives
since approximately January of 2002, this year, in preparation for these attacks.

Q. General, is there any intelligence to suggest that
these -- any attacks are planned domestically, or is the
concern primarily overseas?

ATTORNEY GENERAL ASHCROFT: I would
say that the most recent intelligence which has prompted
us to issue this change in our status has focused prima-

rily overseas. And, frankly, part of our interpretation, or part of the analysis of that is that that's very similar to the circumstances that existed a year ago.

Q. It seems like, with the timing of this announcement, was there new information that you came into knowledge of, or is this based on just an analysis -- continuing analysis of information that's been out there for some time?

ATTORNEY GENERAL ASHCROFT: In a way, the answer is yes. New information has fed into an analytic structure which has made us take very seriously both the new information and the analysis, which leads us to this conclusion. So information has become available very recently, which, together with the analysis of the general circumstances and the situation, leads us to make this change.

Q. Some of the information from senior al-Qaeda operatives which you've operated on in the past and put out alerts have proven to be -- nothing's happened. And so the question has arisen whether or not these al-Qaeda operatives have the opportunity to sort of scare us or jerk our chain. And obviously, you have to consider that in any case. Is there something different this time?

ATTORNEY GENERAL ASHCROFT: Well, we believe this to be credible information. And the analysis that has been undertaken by the intelligence agencies, leads us to conclude that the steps we are taking are appropriate steps in the national interest.

Q. General Ashcroft, you said this was from a senior al-Qaeda operative. Can you discuss who that person is, and give us any indication of where they're being held and what kind of information they've provided?

ATTORNEY GENERAL ASHCROFT: No. Thank you.

GOVERNOR RIDGE: Human instincts as they are, I think most Americans concluded even in their own mind that if you were thinking like a terrorist, then perhaps coming back again over the same date might be something you'd want to do.

Now, we don't believe that they do anything other than operate when they're ready. No particular symbolism -- no particular urgency attached to a symbolic date. But when you attach the symbolic date with the specific information that has been corroborated, coupled with a similar pattern of activity almost a year ago, you put those three things together, and you say, for the time being we've asked to raise the level of emergency in this country.

Q If your concern is mainly U.S. targets overseas, by waiting until the day before the anniversary are you not cutting it kind of close in terms of the preparation that Americans overseas or U.S. corporations or others overseas could be doing for the planning?

ATTORNEY GENERAL ASHCROFT: Well, I think I want you all to be cognizant of what prompted this change, and I hope that we've made it clear that this change is based on an analysis of intelligence that -- some of which very recently became available -- which prompted us to work rapidly to make this change. And we have seen a rather prompt response to this by our own State Department in its activities regarding its embassies in various settings around the world. And we'll do everything we can to give the American people, both at home and abroad, a level of notice which will allow them to maximize their capacity to make the adjustments that are appropriate and necessary.

Q When you say "recent," do you mean hours, do you mean days?

ATTORNEY GENERAL ASHCROFT: Yes. Thank you very much.

Q What? Which one?

ATTORNEY GENERAL ASHCROFT: In the last 24 hours we have had additional information that's been very, very valuable to us, and significant.

Thank you.

END :00 P.M. EDT"

* * * *

Throughout the eve of the first anniversary of the September 11 attacks, having raised the level of terror threats to maintain momentum in the "Global War on Terrorism" the United States wheeled out its propaganda smoke machines to further influence vacillating allies. The information released detailed the account of Omar al-Faruq's interrogation and conveniently provided 'evidence' of connections between al-Qaeda and the *Jemaah Islamiyah*. The anti-Iraq invasion lobby met the announcement with skepticism, considering that the Kuwaiti had, according to the report, finally 'broken down' and revealed everything to his CIA interrogators only two days prior to threat levels being raised.

The CIA then pulled out all the stops and divulged that al-Faruq had confessed to being involved in preparations to attack American and other Western assets around Asia, on September 11, 2002. According to Langley, the targets included embassies, U.S. ships and churches.

There was no mention at all, of *"Operation White Meat"* to the media.

AUSTRALIA
Ward 17 – St. Vincent's Hospital – Sydney
11th September

Energy sapped, Fiona Barnes leaned back against the pillows struggling to maintain consciousness, willing her eyes open to catch the CNN report another patient had tuned in to view.

'Is it loud enough?' someone asked, the former stringer journalist uncertain whether the question was aimed at her. 'I'll turn it down if you like?' she heard the voice again, Fiona gesturing with a faint wave of the hand to the patient fiddling with the remote from the end of her bed. She lay quietly listening to the U.S. State Department's worldwide travel caution announcement, her level of attention heightened with the mention of Indonesia, her thoughts immediately distracted as still-framed pictures of places and events suddenly invaded her mind.

In the months following her deportation from Indonesia Fiona had developed a chest infection, the incident, almost terminal; subsequent tests revealing that she was HIV positive and may have been so for some time, the journalist unable to identify who had passed the disease to her as many of her past sexual partners had been casual, at best.

Outraged by her treatment at the hands of the Indonesian authorities and what she perceived to be a cover-up of events across the country's eastern, Christian provinces Fiona had made the issue her own *cause celebre*, determined to use her writing skills to expose those responsible for the unrest. Within eighteen months she had developed fully-blown Aids, Fiona's current diagnosis incontrovertible that she would imminently die. Bedridden, she still occupied her mind reading as much material as she could find relating to what was happening in the Moluccas, occasionally submitting her own editorial comments to the press, delighted whenever a piece was published.

'Do you mind if I change the channel?' a distant voice inquired, Fiona unresponsive as soft orange hues of a fading Balinese sunset over Kuta touched her mind.

Her breathing became shallow. She closed her eyes, the soft gentle breeze from an oscillating bedside fan caressed her face as she surrendered, and the world finally passed her by.

SYDNEY – LAKEMBA

Amir Subroto listened intently as the visiting Indonesian cleric alluded to another historic moment in the making, praising the ten-member cell for its efforts in expanding the *Pan Asia Islamic* presence across Australia and encouraging all to study the manual he provided, *Studies In Jihad Against the Tyrants*.

Amir looked across enviously at the two new faces who had been introduced following prayers at the mosque, the pair dispatched to Sydney to lead the organization.

'Today we celebrate the anniversary of our fellow-believers' attack on America's citadel, New York. Soon you shall have news of another auspicious event.' The cleric smiled knowingly. 'And when that time arrives you must prepare yourselves for the new face of Islam for we shall take our *Jihad* to the Australian people for their support of the United States against our comrades in Afghanistan.'

'When will this great event take place?' Amir was eager to know.

'Soon, Amir… soon.'

'Will *kakek* show us how this is done?' the young Javanese asked.

'No,' he said knowingly, 'but I will send the one who will instruct you.'

'What is his name, *kakek?*' asked another.

'You will know that when the time has come.'

'We welcome his visit and assure you we shall work tirelessly to further the *Jemaah Islamiyah's* aims.'

'*Insha Allah,*' the cleric replied.

* * * *

JAKARTA
16th September

Fred Burks, the U.S. State Department interpreter selected for the task translated Washington's request for Jakarta to arrest Abu Bakar Bashir and surrender him to the Americans. For a moment there was an uneasy silence in President Megawati's living room as the secret U.S. delegation waited for her response. The President's family had a deep distrust of the Americans, reaching back to the 1950s and 1960s when the CIA's covert activities in Indonesia orchestrated all five assassination attempts on the founding President, Sukarno.

As leader of the world's most populous Muslim nation Megawati knew she had to accommodate the rising anti-American mood resulting from the U.S. attacks on Afghanistan. Then there was the issue of al-Faruq's convenient confession. She had been convinced by presidential advisers that the CIA had leaked the concocted evidence to *Time* magazine specifically to blacken Indonesia's reputation. Nevertheless, as a gesture of goodwill she had agreed to receive the Americans in her home, the group including a woman introduced as a 'special assistant to the American President', Megawati taken aback by the underlying threat in the envoy's tone. Unbeknown to Megawati, the woman was, in fact, a senior CIA officer who, immediately following the meeting, would fly to the U.S. detention centre for al-Qaeda terrorists, in Bagram, Afghanistan where al-Faruq was reportedly held.

'If I were to hand an Indonesian citizen over to you this would create an impossible situation for me,' Megawati explained.

'Madam President,' the CIA envoy persisted, 'I cannot see how you would not want to have Bashir out of your hair. There is clear evidence that he was the mastermind behind the 2000 Christmas Eve bombings. Also, we are able to provide evidence that Bashir was involved in at least two assassination attempts on your life. Surely having him in our custody would be in Indonesia's interests?'

'The only way I could do as you request would be if public opinion somehow turned against Bashir.'

'We understand that you have legitimate concerns,' the special envoy persisted, 'but this comes as a direct request from the White House.'

Megawati looked at her visitors, took a breath, smiled weakly and said, 'Even so. I'm sorry. I cannot fulfill the request of the U.S. President.'

'President Bush has instructed me to relay that if Bashir is not turned over to the U.S. government before the APEC meeting next month, then the situation will become very difficult for us all.'

U.S. Ambassador Ralph Boyce and the U.S. National

Security Council official, Karen Brooks waited for Megawati to bend. Brooks, a former Fulbright scholar had been selected to accompany the others as she was considered to have the Indonesian President's ear.

President Megawati Sukarnoputri did not waver. She needed to retain the support of the Muslim political parties to remain in power. 'I regret that I cannot agree to your request,' her words were translated, 'however, on behalf of the Indonesian people I hope that my decision in no way will affect ties between our countries.'

Disappointed, the U.S. delegation departed, returning to the embassy empty-handed, the Pentagon then lifting the stakes with a carrot and stick approach, offering to reinstate the supply of material equipment and spare parts should Jakarta fulfill Washington's request to surrender Abu Bakar Bashir to American authorities.

Again, Megawati declined.

JAVA
Tenggulun & Surabaya
25th September

'You don't think the shipments are too heavy?' Imam Samudra asked, inspecting the fifty-kilogram bundles Amrozi and Idris had prepared.

'That will work in our favor,' Idris assured. 'Larger shipments are less likely to be misplaced.'

'Why not transport the chemicals ourselves?' Amrozi asked, 'we could put it all in the van.'

Samudra shook his head. 'No, we'll keep to Mukhlas' original plan.'

'By bus?'

'Yes,' Samudra confirmed. 'Mukhlas wants us to break the shipments into separate consignments to avoid suspicion. We can start by sending the first bundles in a couple of days.' He turned to Idris. 'You will have to leave tomorrow so you can collect each of the shipments as they arrive at the bus terminal in Den Pasar.'

The foot-soldiers obeyed; the first fifty-kilogram package being placed on board a Bali-bound bus on the evening of the 27th September, the remaining stockpile broken down into individual consignments and dispatched throughout the following week.

WESTERN AUSTRALIA
Kojarena Electronic Intercept Station
Tuesday, 1st October

Thirty kilometres from the Western Australian town of Geraldton, American analysts discussed a satellite telephone intercept triggered by the codename "Syafullah". The Kojarena Station was nearing its tenth year of operation and, although on Australian soil and outwardly under the supervision of the Australian Defence Signals Directorate (DSD), in reality, the facility belonged to and was managed by the United States as an integral part of the worldwide, Echelon System. With more than one hundred employees at the station, which was situated on a thirty-five hectare base and surrounded by a four-hundred hectare buffer zone, the facility could not be entered without U.S. approval.

Less than twenty percent of all facsimile, email, data and telephone traffic captured via the four satellite antennae off

Intelsat satellites over the Indian and Pacific Oceans was made available to Australian intelligence agencies; the rest, siphoned off and communicated directly to the CIA and National Security Agency.

'Best guess is that the call originated from the Roghani Camp area in Chaman,' the U.S. analyst decided, having correlated all the relevant information.

'Sounds about right,' his associate agreed, 'he *would* pick something on the Afghanistan-Pakistan border.'

The senior analyst read the text of the brief and enigmatic conversation intercepted shortly before the call had been terminated.

'Langley will want to see this a.s.a.p,' he said, looking in the direction of an adjoining facility. 'This will be a 'no-share', Dave,' he added, winking conspiratorially as he left to forward the intercept to the CIA.

Syafullah al-Yemeni was on the move – and it was an Osama bin Laden lieutenant that had given the game away.

WASHINGTON
Australian Embassy
Friday, 4th October

Ian Jefferson read the CIA's updated security warning received only moments before the embassy closed for the weekend. The advice differed from earlier alerts insomuch as there was now a strong suggestion that the United States and its allies could expect an al-Qaeda related attack on the anniversary of the first day of the war in Afghanistan, October 7, and explicitly identified Indonesia as the target area with the *Jemaah Islamiyah* as the perpetrators. Jefferson glanced at the desk calendar, noting that this would fall on Monday. He added his comments by way of a hand-written, covering memorandum and delivered the documents to the embassy's Counselor.

Details of the raised level of threat were communicated immediately to Canberra from where the information was disseminated to all Australian diplomatic and consular posts. However, the Australian Embassy in Jakarta and the Consulate in Bali's most recent travel advices revised at 1200 hours on 11th September 2002 which quoted as follows remained unchanged:

"AUSTRALIAN EMBASSY JAKARTA"

Bulletin to Australian Citizens Living in Indonesia Revised 1200 hrs (Western Indonesia Time) Friday 13th September 2002 EST.

This advice has been reviewed. It contains new information or advice *but the overall level of advice has not been changed.*

In view of the ongoing risk of terrorist activity in the region, Australians in Indonesia should maintain a high level of personal security awareness. Australians should avoid travel to west Timor (outside of Kupang), Maluku and North Maluku, and Aceh. Australians in Papua (Irian Jaya) and North Sulawesi should exercise caution and seek current information from the Australian Embassy prior to travel. The recent attack on foreigners in the Freeport Mine area underlines the need for Australians in Papua to monitor developments that might affect their safety. Australians in Poso, the middle of Central Sulawesi, should avoid inter-provincial and inter-city bus travel and exercise caution following recent attacks on passenger buses. Tourist services elsewhere in Indonesia are operating normally, *including Bali.* "

DEN PASAR – BALI
Monday, 7th October

Mukhlas mentally checked the names of those present, the list a veritable 'who's who' of the *Jemaah Islamiyah* command, the meeting arranged in premises at Jalan Manjangan 18, rented by Imam Samudra and Imron, the month before. Dulmatin, Amrozi and Ali Imron looked the worse for wear as they had arrived late the previous evening; Samudra having met them at the Hotel Harum and whisked them away for the remainder of the night.

Sitting in the corner of the room with eyes cast to the floor were the only two non-*JI* members present, Arnasan and Feri, members of the underground, *Darul Islam* movement. Mukhlas paused momentarily when his eyes fell upon Arnasan recalling when the young man had come to him with a dream in which he had been asked by Osama bin Laden to offer his life for the cause.

Mukhlas opened the meeting, nominating Samudra to take the floor. 'Let's bring everyone up to date on how the preparations are proceeding,'

'Mixing the chemicals took much longer than we expected as Imron, Sawad and Ghani had to do this by hand.'

'But you've finished?' Azahari asked.

'All done,' Samudra reassured.

'And the van?'

Amrozi came alert with a nudge from his brother.

'Is the Mitsubishi ready?' Mukhlas repeated the question.

Amrozi suppressed a yawn. 'It's ready.'

'Where are we at with the filing cabinets?'

'We'll bolt them into place tomorrow,' Amrozi was now awake. He and Dulmatin had purchased the twelve plastic filing cabinets on their way through Java. Their plan was to bolt the cabinets to the L300's false floor, arranged three wide and four deep, as casing for the chemicals.'

'*Pak* Azahari?' Mukhlas then addressed the Malaysian bomb expert.

'I will have the booster charge ready once the other cabinets are in place. I'm going to fill one of the drawers with TNT to ignite the bomb.'

'Then it would appear that we are almost there,' Mukhlas smiled confidently.

The meeting continued with the men breaking into smaller discussion groups leaving Arnasan and Feri to themselves, the two suicide bombers' impending death paramount in their minds as they considered their fate. Arnasan waited until Mukhlas moved away from the others before approaching with his request.

'*Pak* Mukhlas, I would like to ask your help to write some letters for my family and friends.'

'That would be the correct thing to do.'

'What should I say?' Arnasan had asked.

Mukhlas placed his hand on the younger man's shoulder. 'Whatever is in your heart.'

'Would it be okay if I ask for my family to forgive me for what I will do?'

Mukhlas did not hesitate, 'Of course.' He then sat beside the near-illiterate peasant's son and helped him compose his final testament.

In the document, "Jimi", as he was known by his associates in the underground Darus Islam movement, wrote encouraging his friends in the village of Malingping to follow in his footsteps as martyrs, and sacrifice their lives for Islam. Then, in a second letter addressed to his family, Jimi asked that his clothes be given to the poor and pleaded for his parents and siblings to understand why he had given his life in the defence of Islam.

Wednesday, 9th October

'Careful!' Imron shouted angrily, milliseconds too late.

Amrozi haphazardly dragged one of the filing cabinets across the tiles covered with residual chemical ingredients, the resultant explosion rocked the building sending neighbors running into the street.

'What was that?' the family living immediately alongside knocked on the door and confronted those inside.

'Sounded like a car tire bursting,' Mukhlas lied.

'Are you sure it didn't come from inside?' the Balinese woman tried to peek into the building.

'No, it's nothing,' Mukhlas moved quickly to pacify, 'it was probably one of the big balloons they use for advertising.'

Suspicious, the woman remained outside on the street gossiping with others. Sentiment ran high in this neighborhood against the Javanese.

'That was close!' Amrozi giggled nervously when Imron bunched his fist threateningly.

'Don't drag the cabinets,' Imron wiped the sweat from his brow, 'wait and we'll lift them together.'

Filled with apprehension as a result of the near call Mukhlas left Bali with Dr Azahari and Dulmatin, leaving Samudra in charge of Amrozi, Idris, Imron and the two suicide bombers.

Mukhlas returned to Java to prepare for Syafullah al-Yemeni's arrival.

SUKARNO HATTA INTERNATIONAL AIRPORT – JAKARTA

Jakarta-based U.S. agents closely monitored the passengers as they disembarked from the Malaysian Airlines flight, the team leader deciding that two Middle Eastern men lining up at the immigration counter deserved a closer look. Surveillance had been dramatically heightened at all ports of entry across Indonesia ready to ensnare Syafullah al-Yemeni as he arrived.

Syafullah closed his wheeled, carry-on case, smiling politely when the customs officer returned the forged U.S. passport permitting the now cleanly-shaven Yemeni dressed in Levi's and T-shirt to pass into the exit hall. The agent's ten years of field experience told him that there was something unusual about the new arrival and, as Syafullah al-Yemeni completed the customs formalities the American signaled his partner of his intentions to take a closer look at the man.

He followed the passenger through the exit area, stopping then turning on his heel when an attractive woman broke through the waiting crowd and publicly embraced his quarry. The agent wheeled quickly and retraced his steps, rejoining his partner who, by the shake of his head indicated that the second possibility was also a washout. Syafullah al-Yemeni's general description had been widely circulated across the region. However, as there were no recent photographs of the Yemeni on file he had easily slipped through immigration on the doctored U.S. passport, provided by Hambali as he passed through Malaysia.

Colonel Supadi spotted Angelina Panjaitan clinging to Syafullah's arm and eased the Mercedes forward, remaining at the wheel until the luggage was loaded and his party inside. He drove into the city, dropping Angelina along the way before proceeding to Semarang. Having fulfilled his obligation to Hambali the Colonel then reported to General Sumantri by phone who, in turn, warned those who may be affected by the fallout of the *Jemaah Islamiyah* operation, to lay low.

* * * *

JAVA & BALI
Thursday, 10th October

Syafullah al-Yemeni examined the plans and concurred with Dr Azahari. 'I need to visit the targets and most probably modify the bomb.'

Fatigue had crept into Mukhlas' voice. 'I'll check for seats on Garuda.' He phoned Yogyakarta and was advised that only two seats were available.

'There is no point in my being there when you have Syafullah,' Dr Azahari pointed out.

Mukhlas agreed, and they were driven from Semarang to Yogyakarta where they boarded a Garuda flight for Den Pasar, arriving at the Ngurah Rai domestic terminal in Bali four hours later. They drove past the proposed targets in Legian on their way from the airport then went directly to inspect the bombs.

Amrozi, Imron and Imam Samudra were summoned and sworn to secrecy, all undertaking never to reveal any knowledge of Syafullah al-Yemeni's visit. In awe, Amrozi listened as the Yemeni explained why the targets had to be reversed and how this would achieve the maximum effect from the explosions. An argument developed when the visitor condemned the selection of the U.S. Consulate as a target, Mukhlas then instructing a disappointed Imam Samudra to reduce the size of the designated bomb.

* * * *

Miffed that he had not been consulted in changes to the overall plan Imam Samudra paced the third-level dwelling, having dispatched Imron on the Yamaha motorcycle purchased just hours before.

The bombs, originally prepared by Dr Azahari and then altered to accommodate Syafullah al-Yemeni's experienced hand, were all but ready. The plastic filing cabinets had been filled with a mixture of potassium chlorate, aluminum powder and sulphur with TNT kicker-charges, and bolted together inside the Mitsubishi van, the RDX electric detonators then fitted to the TNT. The van was rigged with a number of backup detonation systems including an automatic detonator, rigged as an anti-handling device that would trigger the bomb, should one of the filing cabinet lids be tampered with.

In all, the huge bomb weighed more than a tonne.

* * * *

Imron rode over to meet with the suicide bombers to discuss the change in plan. After explaining to Jimi that he was to explode the car bomb outside the Sari Club once Iqbal had entered Paddy's Pub, and detonated the bomb inside his vest, Imron escorted the two young men on a familiarization tour of the target area.

Pestered by throngs of persistent street hawkers hustling their wares, tourists strolled along crammed, narrow and congested lanes where magic mushrooms and marijuana could be bought on the cheap, the holidaymakers oblivious to Imron, Jimi and Iqbal as they passed amongst them, reconnoitering the scene. When the team passed a bar where a number of unruly, half-naked men were arguing with the staff over the bill, Iqbal paused to gape, unaccustomed to seeing drunk or heavily stoned foreigners before – Imron tugging at his shirt to draw him away before security arrived.

They crossed the street to avoid a group of rubber-thonged New Zealanders negotiating with a young peddler holding a T-shirt up for all to see, the inscription "No, I Don't want A fucking Bemo, Massage, Postcard or Jiggy Jig" entirely lost on the three; Imron bringing the group to a halt outside the Sari Club with its sign prohibiting locals from entering.

Friday, 11th October

'Well, we finally made it!' Greg Young wrapped an arm around Rima Passelima's waist and led her out to the terrace overlooking Jimbaran Bay.

Distant lanterns blinked on the ocean swell, the brightly painted fishing boats now faint silhouettes under the enchanting sky, Rima nestling her head on her lover's shoulders as she watched the moon, the tranquil scene causing her to sigh.

'Hard to believe that so peaceful a place could exist so close to all the violence.' A *tokek* sounded above, Rima glancing up in time to catch the gecko disappearing, upside down into the villa's overhanging *alang-alang* thatched roof.

'Are you hungry?' Greg asked, having forgone the snack offered on the early evening flight from Jakarta.

'A little,' she raised her head and nibbled him gently on the ear. 'I might just have this for starters.'

Greg laughed, 'Suggest you save that for later. Come on, let's head down to Kuta and I'll show you the sights.'

The villa came with a company car and driver; the couple

drove through Kuta Square, along the beachfront then around and back into Jalan Legian, their passage temporarily blocked by a stalled Mitsubishi van.

* * * *

'I thought you could drive?' Imron was appalled by the discovery. He had taken Jimi into Legian with the van to carry out a number of test runs in preparation for the following night.

'No one told me I was expected to drive!' Jimi panicked, again stalling the van in gear. Immediately, the air filled with cacophonous horns and curses with motorcycles dangerously weaving their way around the Mitsubishi.

Fearing discovery, Imron shouted at Jimi to change places then yelled, 'Let's get the hell out of here!'

WASHINGTON
Friday, 11th October

John Phillips, liaison officer for the U.S. Defense Intelligence Agency (DIA) read the announcement deeply concerned that his government had not alerted America's allies that one of the most senior, known terrorists associated with al-Qaeda was known to be in Indonesia somewhere, his presence obviously connected to the intelligence forewarning that Bali would come under attack.

"WORLDWIDE CAUTION PUBLIC ANNOUNCEMENT

**U.S. Department Of State – Office of the Spokesman
Posted October 11, 2002**
This Worldwide Caution Public Announcement supersedes the Worldwide Caution Public Announcement

285

dated September 9, 2002. In light of the recent audio tape attributed to Usama bin Laden and other reports of threats to American interests, this Worldwide Caution is being issued to alert Americans to the need to remain vigilant and to remind them of the continuing threat of terrorist actions that may target civilians. This Worldwide Caution expires on April 8, 2003.

The U.S. Government continues to receive credible indications that extremist groups and individuals are planning additional terrorist actions against U.S. interests. Such actions may include, but are not limited to, suicide operations. Because security and security awareness have been elevated within the U.S, the terrorists may target U.S. interests overseas. We remind American citizens to remain vigilant with regard to their personal security and to exercise caution.

Terrorist groups do not distinguish between official and civilian targets. Attacks on places of worship and schools, and the murders of private American citizens, demonstrate that as security is increased at official U.S. facilities, terrorists and their sympathizers will seek softer targets. These may include facilities where Americans are generally known to congregate or visit, such as clubs, restaurants, places of worship, schools or outdoor recreation events. Americans should increase their security awareness when they are at such locations, avoid them, or switch to other locations where Americans in large numbers generally do not congregate. American citizens may be targeted for kidnapping or assassination.

U.S. Government facilities worldwide remain at a heightened state of alert. These facilities may temporarily close or suspend public services from time to time to review their security posture and ensure its adequacy. In those instances, U.S. Embassies and Consulates will make every effort to provide emergency services to American citizens. Americans are urged to monitor the local news and maintain contact with the nearest American Embassy or Consulate.

As the Department continues to develop information on any potential security threats to Americans overseas, it shares credible threat information through its Consular Information Program documents, available on the Internet at http://travel.state.gov. In addition to information on the Internet, U.S. travelers can hear recorded information by calling the Department of State in Washington, D.C. at 202-647-5225 from their touch-tone telephone, or receive information by automated telefax by dialing 202-647-3000 from their fax machine.

See http://travel.state.gov/travel_warnings.html for State Department Travel Warnings."

Phillips placed the circular inside the loose-leaf file, deeply troubled that information relating to *"Operation White Meat"* had been deliberately withheld for a more sinister purpose, to further his country's war against terror. He checked the time, noting that it was already early morning on the following day in Canberra, the liaison officer unaware that although copies of the announcement were disseminated to all U.S. allies, Australia's Travel Warning issued by the Department of Foreign Affairs had remain unchanged.

CHAPTER TWELVE

U.S. INTERROGATION CENTRE – BAGRAM
AIRFIELD – AFGHANISTAN
Saturday, 12th October
1135 Hours

Colonel Raharjo joined his BIN colleague in the VIP room, the *Badan Intelijen Negara* officers guests of the CIA's interrogation centre at the Bagram air base north of Kabul, in Afghanistan.

'Well, that about wraps it up,' their escort officer announced, glancing at his watch in an obvious manner, indicating to the Indonesians that they had run out of time. 'Is there anything else that I can assist you with before we call it a day?'

The visitors were unanimous. They had their envelopes and wished only to be on their way.

Following the release of the *Time* magazine article revealing al-Faruq's admissions, Washington still refused to give up on Megawati, hoping that the Indonesian BIN agency officials would return to Jakarta and substantiate the CIA's claims relating to Abu Bakar Bashir. The U.S. Embassy in Jakarta had arranged for the team to be flown to Afghanistan where they were given the opportunity to question the thirty-one year old Kuwaiti.

On location, the Indonesian agents were introduced to a

convincing environment of barbed-wire pens erected inside a large hangar, under high-powered lights. Colonel Raharjo was permitted only to communicate with the Kuwaiti via closed-circuit television, the detainee immediately pleading for their assistance to reveal his situation to the media, complaining that he had been regularly stripped naked and beaten by Afghan Special Forces' interrogators.

It all seemed so real.

Airborne, Raharjo unbuckled the seat belt and asked of his friend, 'After bringing us all this way, why didn't they let us meet him in person?'

His fellow officer shrugged. 'They did permit one of our Foreign Office people in to witness him signing his statement.'

'Yes,' Raharjo agreed with reservation, 'but how could we be sure it really was al-Faruq?'

'I'm afraid we'll have to take their word for it.'

'Knowing something of their interrogation techniques I still don't understand why it took three months for him to break.' He peered down at the barren landscape below wondering how anyone could possible survive. 'Did *you* believe what he said?'

'Doesn't really matter now, does it?' The BIN officer patted his top pocket, also highly skeptical of al-Faruq's fortuitous admissions the day prior to the first anniversary of the September 11 attacks in New York.

'No, I guess it doesn't,' the Colonel agreed, then lay back and drifted into sleep.

BALI
1200 Hours

'Here, Iqbal, I'll show you again,' Imron offered, patiently, taking the vest and showing how to use the switch that would activate the suicide bomb. He had brought the pair to Jalan Manjangan where the bombs had been prepared and stored.

They practiced a number of times and when Imron was satisfied that Iqbal had mastered the procedure, he then turned his attention to Jimi and instructed him how to use the firing mechanism that would detonate the massive charge, strapped inside the Mitsubishi L300.

The suicide bombers then spent the afternoon in meditation then bathed in readiness for the *Magrib* sunset prayers.

JAVA –*Laskar Jihad* HEADQUARTERS
1625 Hours

When the announcement was broadcast few paid any attention to the media release. The vicious, militant group supported by Indonesia's *Kopassus* Special Forces went to the airwaves and declared that they were disbanding and would withdraw all fighters from the strife-torn Moluccan Islands.

Jafar Umar Thalib, who was on trial for inciting hatred declared that the *Laskar Jihad* leadership had made the decision to disband, for "purely ideological reasons."

MENADO – SULAWESI
1930 Hours

Aware of the imminent attack in Bali, fifteen hundred kilometers to the South, elements of the *Abu Sayyaf*-linked, *Laskar Jundullah* hastily prepared a bomb and were in the process of placing this at the Philippines Consulate in Menado when the explosives detonated prematurely.

Injured, the perpetrators fled the scene.

Upon learning of the unauthorized attack, General Sumantri dispatched Colonel Supadi to muddy the investigation, his successful intervention prompting rumors that the attack had been the work of the pro-Suharto, 'Red & White' generals, eager for a return to power.

BALI
2000 – 2100 Hours

Imron stood facing Iqbal and Jimi. 'It's time,' he said, 'make your final preparations.'

They obeyed, Iqbal moving around the rented accommodations as his agitation grew, Jimi assuaging his accomplice's fears with reassurances that they would be greeted upon death, as heroes of the Islamic revolution.

'I will be back in thirty minutes,' Imron told them and proceeded to Jalan Pinang where Imam Samudra had rented separate premises. Imron reported that everything was ready then returned to Jalan Majanga. He placed the bomb planned for the U.S. Consulate inside a plastic bag and connected the explosives to a remote hand phone before sealing the deadly package. He then climbed on the Yamaha and rode to the target in Renon District where the consulate was situated.

Approaching the consulate he throttled back and checked for pedestrian flow. Satisfied that he would not be observed Imron flicked one of the three switches he had installed the evening before, and the engine died, faking a breakdown. He bent down pretending to investigate the cause of the problem and placed the bomb.

Cautiously, he restarted the Yamaha then departed the scene.

BALI
2230 Hours

Imron led Iqbal and Jimi downstairs to the white Mitsubishi van.

'Don't squeeze that too hard,' he warned Iqbal who clasped the vest tightly to his chest. 'Jimi, you sit next to me.'

They climbed in and Imron started the vehicle, the van sluggish under the weight of the one tonne of explosives as they drove towards Kuta and Legian.

* * * *

BALI – KUTA SQUARE
2245 Hours

At the top of the steps leading from the beach Rima stopped, held Greg Young's hand for balance and brushed sand from her feet.

'Care for a nightcap?' he asked, indicating the Hard Rock Hotel & Café across the beachfront.

'Sure, why not?'

They strolled across the esplanade into the grounds past the artificially-created, sand- island-swimming pool and now-deserted cabanas, into the Centerstage lobby bar.

'Looks like they're gearing up for quite a night,' Greg commented, the popular venue filling with tourists.

'What?' Rima had to lean closer to hear.

'I said it looks like it's going to be some night!' he raised his voice, rocking to the music's beat as he fell into mood.

'Just don't ask me to dance,' Rima warned, 'I'm not...'

'Say again?'

Rima surrendered and mouthed the words, 'Forget it,' as the band was greeted with wild cheering and applause.

* * * *

BALI – JALAN LEGIAN
2308 Hours

Imron flashed the indicators and pulled over to the side of road before reaching the T-intersection with Jalan Legian. He turned to Iqbal. 'You should put the vest on now.' He watched closely as Iqbal did as he asked. 'Jimi, join the detonator cable to the switch.'

When this was done Imron pulled back out into the traffic and turned into Jalan Legian where he stopped four hundred metres short of their target and opened the driver's door. 'Okay, Jimi, it's all yours now.'

Jimi slipped behind the wheel and waited for Imron to climb behind Idris who had been following on the Yamaha. As Idris now had custody of Imron's cell phone he dialed a number stored under the codename "little house", triggering the consulate bomb, unaware that the blast would prove to be ineffective, completely missing the U.S. mission, destroying a solitary tree in a vacant lot and the footpath where the package had been placed.

Jimi drove to the Sari Club and stopped on the right hand side of the busy thoroughfare permitting Iqbal to alight. Jimi's hands were now perspiring profusely and he hurriedly locked all the doors from inside, the sound of his heart pounding in his ears as he locked the steering wheel into position effectively blocking the road to those vehicles moving slowly up Legian from behind.

Wearing the vest fitted with eight pipe bombs Iqbal slipped into Paddy's Pub and made his way through the crowded bar towards the disc jockey's podium. He tensed, uttered *'Allahu Akbar'* and flicked the switch, the diversionary bombing driving survivors out of the bar and into Legian Street where the Mitsubishi van was waiting.

Seconds later Jimi closed his eyes and pressed the Nokia hand phone button, the devastating explosion resulting in an incredible release of energy in the form of gas, heat and light that ruptured the earth as it destroyed everything in its path.

For one very brief moment even the Gods were stunned. And then, amidst the carnage and human misery the cell phones started to ring.

* * * *

Seismic equipment at the Den Pasar geophysics station confirmed that the earth had undoubtedly quaked, the tremor which registered 0.2 on the Richter lasted five seconds and was felt over a radius of twenty kilometers.

Australia would suffer the greatest number of casualties with eighty-eight losing their lives. Four Dutch, six Germans, Nine Swedes, twenty-six Britons and at least thirty-eight Indonesians—most of whom were Balinese—also lost their lives.

Only seven Americans would be listed amongst the dead.

As Rima Passelima and Greg Young joined others who had poured into Legian's streets and run to the scene of the double explosion Syafullah al-Yemeni, the expert who had rearranged the structure of the bomb in order that it might achieve maximum effect, sat patiently at Ngurah Rai International Airport, awaiting his flight.

* * * *

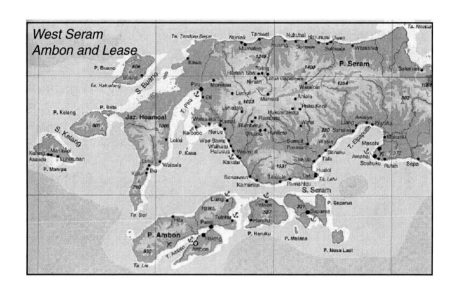

BOOK THREE

THE PRESENT

CHAPTER THIRTEEN

When trading closed on the New York Stock Exchange with the bench price for spot crude eclipsing market expectations, surprisingly, the corresponding announcement of the Raja Seram Gas discovery in Indonesia's eastern province in no way dampened speculators' spirits. The futures' buying frenzy had been driven by China's voracious appetite for fossil fuels, alarming governments around the globe.

Then, with the news that a consortium had made a significant oil discovery off Ambon's adjacent Seram Islands, it would seem that Indonesia's rapidly dwindling oil and gas reserves would no longer be an issue. BP, Shell, Total and ExxonMobil's executives poured into Jakarta to take up previously unwanted concession areas only to find themselves queuing behind China's Sinopec and its domestic rival, the China National Petroleum Corp – the rush to acquire resource property testing time-forged commercial and political relationships across the region. Ambon, the Moluccan capital suddenly touted as becoming the world's largest gas producing field finally achieved a position on the international map, this attention reigniting the sectarian conflict that had smouldered in the presence of an uneasy peace.

The war against terrorism continued and, although the list of senior al-Qaeda, *Abu Sayyaf* and *Jemaah Islamiyah* captured or killed had thinned terrorist leadership ranks measurably, the United States remained embroiled in military action on seventeen fronts, maintaining troops in one hundred and thirty six countries. Militant separatist groups mushroomed across S.E. Asia; some, unable to establish international support for their individual causes amalgamated with others, their collective voice a force contributing to regional instability.

In Southern Thailand's Muslim-dominated provinces the shadowy insurgency continued, the death toll resulting from clashes with government troops now well into the thousands. In Malaysia, militant cells had increased spreading along shared borders, whilst in the Philippines a number of new and well-armed separatist organizations had appeared in the Mindanao region, challenging the presence of U.S. Special Forces.

Across Indonesia, undeterred by the central government's increased military presence, secessionist groups continued to gain momentum in the country's northern and eastern provinces. In Aceh, the GAM, Free Aceh Movement had laid down its weapons and signed an accord with the central government following the disastrous tsunami which struck as 2004 came to a close.

With the failure of the *Malino III* accord remnants of the South Maluku Republik and Maluku Sovereignty Front separatists united, their organization metamorphosing into a well organized, cohesive and hardened core of dedicated members known as the *Maluku Brigade*.

Spurred by what appeared to be unlimited opportunity with the huge oil and gas discoveries, Indonesia's generals obtruded and within months, fueled by TNI vested interests, sectarian violence again exploded. With the loss of East Timor indelibly stamped in their minds and fearing outside intervention

Jakarta responded, positioning an additional fifty thousand troops across the eastern provinces, the ensuing confrontation attracting the wrath of the U.N. community.

As a result of international condemnation the era of rapprochement that had seen the restoration of Australian-Indonesian relations during President Susilo Bambang Yudhoyono's term in office soured, transporting both back in time, jeopardizing Australian commercial interests across the volatile archipelago. With Indonesian-Australian ties at their lowest since East Timor gained independence, China moved swiftly to fill the political void to ensure its supply of oil. Concerned by Beijing's aggressive bid to influence control over international shipping lanes lacing Indonesia, the United States increased its presence in Northern Australia by positioning elements of the Seventh Fleet in Darwin Harbour – the move interpreted as provocative by the majority of S.E. Asian states.

Amidst the political instability, Asian-based multinationals such as Bulan Sabit Holdings Sdn Bhd continued to compound wealth and power, the Malaysian conglomerate poised to dominate the oil and gas construction arena, with its subsidiary Bimaton winning the first contracts to develop the Raja Seram Gas field.

JAKARTA

The press room was packed with media, Greg Young continuing with the announcement as digital cameras and recorders captured the moment.

'The Raja Seram project will be the largest capital development in the eastern provinces ever undertaken and represents Bimaton's ability to bring world-class engineering, construction and project management skills on such a scale. The consortium has within its expertise, both executives and technicians who are recognized as amongst the finest in their field, all with excellent records of achievement in bringing on line other LNG projects. The scope of the project includes the construction of a three-train LNG processing plant and associated support facilities. Each of these trains will have a capacity of five million tonnes per annum. Raja Seram will include extensive infrastructure development both on the immediate site and in related areas. The project will bring direct benefits to the local communities by way of employment and the creation of a new community to service the operations. We expect to be in full production within three years with initial product shipments to North America, Japan, South Korea and China.' He paused to recognize the other consortium representatives. 'I am honored to announce that Mr. Agus Sumarsono will chair the group's new entity, P.T. Raja Seram Resources and advise that I have accepted the position of CEO to bring the project to fruition.'

'Didn't someone suggest you were going to retire?' a familiar face quipped from the back of the room, 'and what in God's name are you going to do with all that extra money?' The gathering relaxed with the injection of humor.

Greg Young's euphoric mood was evident when he responded with light-hearted banter. 'Well, as you can see, I'm not going anywhere Steve,' he beamed, 'and yes, my own fortunes will certainly improve.' He winked at the journalist. 'Who knows, this time around I might even manage to keep some of it.'

'Mr. Young,' an Indonesian reporter sitting in the second row waved his notepad in the air, 'would you like to comment on rumors that the consortium has allocated shares in the venture to the President's family and the TNI?'

In the momentary silence Young's face turned to stone. 'I don't respond to rumors.'

'But, wouldn't it be reasonable to assume that with a contract valued at more than eleven billion dollars you would have had to accommodate some of the local interests along the way?' The room fell hushed. 'After all,' the reporter continued, 'the investment is in an area where separatists continue to challenge the central government's authority. My question is, how does Bimaton intend to secure the area unless there are assurances from the TNI and, if that is so, has Bimaton allocated any shareholding to the military or its foundations in exchange for that commitment?'

Young attempted to deflect the question. 'Bimaton *is* the only local interest. Our partnership is with Taiwan's Petroleum Corporation and Japan's...'

'That's not what I meant, Mr. Young,' the reporter persisted, 'having lived and worked in this environment for so many years you, of all people, would appreciate that some understanding must have been arrived at with local interests in securing such an important contract...and to provide for the necessary security to ensure the realization of the project?'

Young glanced over at the Agus Sumarsono whose expression signaled that he would have to go it alone. With arms crossed indicating his displeasure at the impertinence of the suggestion Young addressed the room.

'The consortium's shareholders are a matter of public record and that's all I intend saying on the matter.' Young then fielded another question then raised both hands. 'I'll take two more questions and then we'll adjourn for refreshments.'

'Greg, would you mind elaborating on the relationship between the partners involved in the Raja Seram project?'

'Sure, Des,' Young had anticipated the request. 'As outlined in our press release, the consortium consists of P.T. Bimaton which, as you know, is now a wholly owned subsidiary of Bulan Sabit Holdings from Malaysia. As for the other shareholders...'

*   *   *   *

Agus Sumarsono nestled into the leather upholstery and rubbed tired eyes, loosening his tie as the Mercedes made its way through Jakarta's congested, afternoon traffic. He extracted a pulsing hand phone from a breast pocket, read the SMS then looked over at Greg Young. 'Don't lose any sleep over it. Eventually, they'll find out one way or another.'

The consortium's CEO nodded slowly in agreement as he stared through partially misted glass, the view ahead befogged images of metal and a fusion of light. 'Yes, I guess they will.' He rubbed the side window with the palm of his hand. 'But it will complicate things.'

Agus sighed. 'We would never have won the tender without their backing.'

Again Young nodded. 'I know that.' The Mercedes slowed to a crawl and he partially closed the air-conditioning vent on his side. 'I just hope that we can keep a lid on it until all the funding is in place...that's all.'

'They're not about to go public,' Agus's voice lacked conviction.

'Well, if they do before the bankers set everything in place then we'll pay dearly in terms of refinancing delays, not to mention the political fallout.'

They continued in silence until Agus suddenly leaned forward and rapped a knuckle against the window isolating them from the driver's compartment.

'Drop *Tuan* Greg off first,' he ordered then punched the button re-closing the partition. 'On second thoughts it might be an idea if I go and speak to them again tonight.'

Young was relieved. 'Someone's talked. And the General needs to know how damaging it would be for the backers to discover that we're holding a substantial stake in the project on the Palace's behalf.'

Agus did not respond, considering instead and with some annoyance the value of the ten percent of the shares in the Raja Seram project they had been obliged to surrender, to ensure their winning bid and the project's ongoing security.

KUALA LUMPUR

Mohamed Aziz Derashid peered anxiously through the miasma of forest fire smoke that had drifted across the Malacca Straits from Sumatra obscuring the city's skyline. The helicopter landed heavily, leaving the Bulan Sabit Chairman with a grateful sigh. The Malaysian billionaire's personal assistant hurried across the helipad and escorted his employer into the skyscraper's well guarded, surround-view penthouse, which dominated the three upper levels of the building.

Derashid went directly to his suite where he bathed in preparation for the *Mahgrib* prayers then dressed into a floor-length robe before dropping to his knees' customary position, in the dedicated room with its ceiling-to-floor armor-plate glass windows facing the West.

He prayed; the sun disappeared leaving the city lights wreathed in illuminated haze, Derashid then content to sit alone in the palatial setting pondering his empire and Bulan Sabit's most recent commercial gain.

More than a year of lobbying Indonesian government interests had borne fruit delivering the Raja Seram concessions to his conglomerate via Bimaton Holdings. The undertaking was not without risk, the Malaysian now heavily overcommitted financially to the venture. Derashid's links to Riyadh remained intact; his Saudi associates responsible for influencing his nervous bankers when they hesitated in providing funding for the multi-billion dollar project, due to rising security issues.

Although the al-Qaeda power base had diminished significantly across S.E. Asia it had been slowly superseded by similarly inspired Muslim extremist groups, the *Maluku Brigade* currently of most concern to investors in the area associated with the Raja Seram oil and gas concessions. Derashid's thoughts turned to the *Jemaah Islamiyah* with its leadership in total disarray following Hambali's arrest in Thailand and more recently, the end to Azahari Husin and Noordin bin Top's reign of terror. *JI* was now a spent force and merely a historical shadow to the powerful Pan-Asia Islamic (PAI) movement which had evolved to take the lead in radicalizing the region's two hundred million Muslims.

Publicly supported by Islamic elite Derashid had emerged from the shadows as chairman of the PAI to announce that the organization would establish a political arm to contest future elections in all S.E. Asian states.

In Indonesia the PAI achieved an understanding with both the major Muslim parties, the Nahdlatul Ulama and Muhammadiyah securing their collective voice of seventy million members. In Malaysia, where the *Barisan National* had dominated the political scene for decades Derashid's PAI absorbed the *Parti Islam Semalaysia* and attracted many followers from the United Malays National Organization. Malaysia's Indian and

Chinese communities which represented less than half of the nation's overall population were destined to be marginalized with Derashid determined to shift wealth back into indigenous hands.

Derashid believed that the Pan-Asia Islamic movement's real challenge would come from China's rapidly growing influence across the region; Beijing's march only preventable by exploiting the nation's Achilles Heel. He understood that China was desperate to protect the shipping lines through which eighty percent of its imported oil and other raw materials had, until recently, passed unhindered. The level of piracy had increased dramatically raising Beijing's ire, the country's navy now charged with protecting these sea lanes to the south, in Indonesian waters. Also, Beijing's 2nd Artillery Corps had deployed close to one thousand short-range ballistic missiles in Fujian and Jiangxi provinces, the intimidating tactic pointedly designed to demonstrate the Mainland's intentions with respect to Taiwan, whilst maintaining trouble-free passage for shipping through the straits.

He had studied China's energy supply conundrum, and the delicate balancing act that was underway ensuring interrupted supply of oil while construction raced ahead for the completion of another forty, one-thousand-megawatt capacity nuclear power stations.

As China had become desperately deficient in energy production, global research endeavors for energy supply solutions were of paramount, strategic interest. Beijing was now leading the way in the development of an International Thermonuclear Experimental Reactor (ITER), having first commenced developing a fusion operation torus forty years earlier in the isolated mountains southwest of Sichuan Province. By successfully developing a prototype version of the ITER, an Experimental Advanced Superconducting Tokamak, China had demonstrated that its aim to build a thermonuclear reactor to supply its populous country with sustained electricity was achievable. However, Derashid believed that as realization of such an ambitious project would not be feasible for at least another ten years China's thirst for fossil fuels would still need to be quenched and this would drive the nation's military growth even further to guarantee the necessary lines of supply.

Derashid understood that China's transformed military now tilted the regional balance of power in its favor. With soldiers skilled in the use of high-technology weapons the country's intensive modernization program was rapidly drawing the nation to the brink of reaching one of its principal goals, to field enough sophisticated weaponry to prevent the United States from interfering in the annexation of Taiwan. Armed with cruise and other anti-ship missiles capable of piercing U.S. vessels' electronic defenses, China had now completed its acquisition of Russian-built Sovremenny-class guided missile destroyers and Kilo-class submarines. The Mainland's arsenal now included two thousand multi-role fighter aircraft, Julang-2 missiles capable of carrying independently targeted warheads ten thousand kilometers, and an impressive inventory of Dongfeng-41 ICBMs capable of striking North America and Australia.

China's signing of a new generation Strategic Alliance agreement with Indonesia in support of Beijing's "String of Pearls" strategy, was of immediate interest to Derashid.

He believed that the door was now wide open for S.E. Asia's giant neighbor to dominate the archipelago's natural resources and channel these to meet China's edacious energy needs. With the expansion of Beijing's interests across the region Derashid anticipated a parallel increase in the country's military excursions, having already secured the disputed islands in the South and East China Seas. Burma had surrendered control over the Coco Islands in the Bay of Bengal permitting China to establish signals-monitoring facilities there to complement installations recently constructed in Pakistan. These were close to the Iranian border at Gwandar, overlooking tankers sailing through the Persian Gulf adding to the ambitious "String of Pearls" methodology which required a line of military-related agreements linking China through Cambodia, Bangladesh, Thailand, Burma and Pakistan.

Derashid remained thoughtful as he stared blankly into the evening sky considering his strategy to block China's aggressive pursuit of oil and gas resources across S.E. Asia. The Pan-Asia Movement would be his instrument in achieving this aim, with profits from the Raja Seram project to fund the realization of his dream for an Asian Islamic State.

SUKARNO-HATTA INTERNATIONAL AIRPORT

Anwar Suprapto stood admiring the new Citation Sovereign jet's interior.

'You certainly lucked out, Imam,' he said, turning to his twin. 'What's Pak Agus paying you to fly his pretty lady?'

The former military pilot grinned from ear to ear. 'Two thousand dollars a month, a pickup and a generous housing allowance.'

Anwar whistled. 'Sure beats the hell out of flying for a government carrier.'

'Come on,' Imam joshed, 'you've nothing to complain about.

Garuda 777-300 captains seem to be doing nicely, thank you!'

Anwar snorted. 'We would…if our salaries were on parity with our international counterparts.' He coughed heavily, recovered, dismissing Imam's concerned look as he entered the cockpit. 'What's its range?'

'Just over two and a half thousand miles, carrying eight passengers and fully fueled.'

Anwar was impressed. 'Speed?'

'Around five hundred.'

Anwar remained thoughtful for a moment before returning to the lavishly appointed executive cabin. 'Let me know if Agus ever needs another pilot.'

Imam laughed and slapped his brother on the back. 'If you're serious I'll see what I can do.'

Anwar left Imam with the fifteen-million-dollar Cessna and strolled across to the main building to prepare for his flight to Bali which would take him onto Sydney and Melbourne. As he approached the security entrance Anwar buckled under another coughing attack, tempted to call in that he was too sick to fly.

PORTMAN RITZ-CARLTON HOTEL – SHANGHAI

The lift's lights blinked ominously then failed. Andrew Graham felt the elevator shudder then lock into position with the power outage, the claustrophobic setting stenched with fear when the lift lurched then dropped another few inches. Someone behind whimpered then cried out, Andrew wincing with pain when struck in the knee by a flailing boot. He leaned his heavy frame into the corner and elbowed the panicked passenger in the stomach, the man then collapsing breathless to the floor as the lights blinked back to life, the whir of motors washing the occupants with relief as airflow was reinstated.

'Good grief!' a London-based visitor exclaimed stepping away from the prostrate form, 'did he faint?'

Andrew shrugged, shuffling behind the others. 'Looks like it.' He hit the lobby button and stepped outside onto the fourth floor.

Exiting the lift Andrew joined the stream of guests gathered in the pre-function lobby area where pre-dinner cocktails were being served to the symposium delegates. Armed with a flute of Moet & Chandon, the American mingled until the guests were invited to move into the adjacent Marble Hall Ballroom for the opening dinner event. Andrew gravitated to his designated table – disappointed that he had not been placed closer to the Indonesian delegates.

'Ah, Mister Graham,' the Chairman of the Shanghai Regional Development Committee acknowledged Andrew when he joined the influential group, 'do you know everyone here?'

Amidst the rising clamor as five hundred guests took their positions, Graham followed the sweeping gesture and nodded at the others seated around the table and smiled. 'I don't believe so.'

'We are honored to have representation from the prestigious Washington Strategic Policy group at our table,' the chairman gestured for Graham to sit. 'As you all know, our American guest is considered an expert on Asian affairs.'

Seated, Graham raised open palms in response. 'Not quite, Mister Chairman,' he offered good-humouredly, 'just an observer keen to learn more about China and its people.'

'Have you visited China before?' the woman on his right asked politely.

Graham replied with measured courtesy. 'Only briefly, I'm sad to say.'

'Then you should make this visit longer,' she countered leaning closer.

Graham reeled back as a snapshot image of her foul breath was unfortunately recorded in time.

'That is my plan,' he managed, as subdued applause at the front of the hall closest to the dais drew a thousand eyes to a tall, elegant beauty crossing the platform. The sleeveless golden rose cheongsam clinging to her resplendent form, hushing the assembly as she stepped up to the podium and addressed the gathering.

'Deputy Premier,' the woman paused respectfully and bowed slightly before welcoming the other VIPs, 'Chairman of Shanghai Economy Commission, Vice Chairman Shanghai Foreign Investment Commission, representatives of the…'

Thunderous applause greeted the symposium's chairman when he moved to the lectern and delivered his opening speech, Andrew Graham's mind wandering as chatter around his table at the back of the ballroom rose to a level that made it impossible to hear.

The symposium had taken place amidst growing concerns that China's current great leap forward would drive oil prices to levels that could only jeopardize world economies. Low on fuel, the great engine driving China was desperate for new supply lines to satisfy the esurient giant. SINOPEC service stations across the Mainland now operated on a roster basis as pumps all too frequently ran dry and electricity blackouts across the nation's southeast grid continued to cripple commercial endeavours throughout the industrial corridors.

Strategic alliances forged in recent years with Indonesia,

India and Malaysia had not alleviated the problem, China now aggressively pursuing acquisitions in the oil and gas sector across the globe. Western analysts blamed Beijing for setting the prices for fuel and electricity too low with China's Communist rulers forever in conflict with its increasingly capitalist present, providing its consumers with the cheapest petrol and diesel anywhere in the world.

What commenced as a ripple was now a wave washing Western market shores as disruptions in Asia's markets for fuel oil products polarized resource-dependent nations in their concerns over China – now the world's second largest oil importer.

'And China is now directing its energies in resolving many of these issues associated with lines of supply. We are confident that…'

Andrew cranked his head and caught the eye of the retired Indonesian general who now headed the restructured Pertamina group, which had fallen precariously close to bankruptcy through mismanagement and corrupt practices, bequeathed from the Suharto years. Andrew had prearranged to meet with the general – an old acquaintance – and would do so later in the session.

'You don't seem particularly interested in what the speaker has to say?' the woman on Andrew's left interrupted his thoughts as the chairman's opening speech dragged on, the delivery painfully slowed by the continuous interpretation breaks. 'Not at all,' he responded, 'I have difficulty understanding what is being said with the PA system the way it is.'

'Never mind,' she leaned closer, 'you'll be able to read the speech in its entirety when the handouts come around.'

Andrew turned. 'And you would know this how?'

She looked back in surprise. 'It's mentioned on the back of the program.'

* * * *

Approaching midnight the more resilient amongst the guests had broken into groups and moved on to other venues. Following dinner Andrew had met briefly with the Indonesian general in the mezzanine bar, the American treating his old friend to a Cuban Montecristo from the walk-in humidor before settling down over coffee together.

'We miss you back in Jakarta,' the general leaned back and affectionately rolled the cigar between his fingers.

'More like you miss taking me to the cleaners at golf,' Andrew scoffed. 'Will you have time for a game while we're here?'

The general looked directly at the American. 'Not this time. I'm only here to show my face then I'm off to Kuala Lumpur.'

Andrew found the opening he needed. 'Will you be catching up with Malaysia's new star?'

'Derashid?' the Indonesian broke into a grin. 'Now how on earth would you know that?'

The American laughed softly. 'Word is, everyone who's anyone is beating a path to his door.'

'And, not just those involved in the oil and gas sector.' The general sat upright and stretched. 'He has become quite an influential force since you moved back to the States.'

'Have you met him before?"

'Yes, but only briefly.'

'I hear that he is sailing dangerously close to the wind, financially?'

'No, not any more,' the general confided, 'he has raised more than what's required through that Islamic bond issue last month.'

Andrew probed. 'Who's holding the paper?'

The general pulled a face. 'The Arabs' coffers are over-flowing.' He placed the cigar back in its tube and tilted his head thoughtfully. 'Seems that Islamic banks have provided the back-to-back guarantees he needed.' The Indonesian rose slowly to his feet and extended a hand. 'Why don't you swing back via Jakarta and catch up on the local gossip before return-ing home?'

'I plan on doing just that.'

'Okay, if you decide to drop in, give me a call. I'll be back in Jakarta by the weekend.'

Alone in the mezzanine bar Andrew ordered a nightcap and sat listening to the jazz group as he weighed the import of the Malaysian entrepreneur, Mohamed Aziz Derashid's recent emergence as a powerful player on the Asian stage. Andrew was not surprised to learn that it had been Middle East inter-ests that had come to his aid when financing of the Raja Seram project faltered. Andrew had studied the increase in Islamic bond sales as the Malaysian government eased restrictions. Sales of Islamic bonds or debt that complied with the Koran's ban on paying and receiving interests had hit record levels after Kuala Lumpur lifted restrictions on foreign purchases. Bulan Sabit Holdings had used their Saudi connections to tap into the oil-rich nation's petrodollars to finance their Indonesian venture. He understood that the mechanism often required that bonds be backed by assets sold to a company established specifically by the borrower who then rents back these assets, the 'rent' or lease payments then circumventing the need to pay interest and therefore complied with the Islamic code.

The band ceased playing and Andrew took advantage of the lull, speed-dialing a number in Kuala Lumpur. It rang twice before his party responded, Andrew Graham then informing the U.S. Embassy contact in Malaysia of the general's imminent visit to meet with Derashid.

TENTENA – CENTRAL SULAWESI

Jack McBride had been deep in thought seriously considering the recent communication offering him a transfer to another post when he heard the first explosion.

'It came from the direction of the town market,' Netty followed the American outside to survey the scene.

'Probably another gas cylinder,' he moved off the road as to avoid being hit by a passing motorbike. 'There's no smoke so I don't think it's anything serious.'

Drawn deeper into the Tentena market area, curious town residents stepped through pulped watermelon and scattered buffalo flesh as baffled vendors moved to salvage produce from the disarray – the market gardeners taking the brunt of the second and much greater detonation when this ripped through the early morning scene scattering shards of metal in every direction and shattering windows across the street.

Police arrived at the scene to discover two of their own lying dead amongst the carnage. When Mobile Police discovered a satchel containing a timer discarded by the market bombers nearby to where the mission clinic fronted the main road, Netty and two assistants were arrested. McBride's clinic came under attack, Jack consumed with anger with the return of radical Islamic warriors into the area. Screaming anti-American and Chinese slogans the well-armed *Laskar PAI* streamed through coastal Christian villages destroying seven hundred homes and killing two hundred within the week.

* * * *

Jack McBride fought to remain patient as he sat cooling his heels at the police chief's office waiting to negotiate the release of his staff. Tentena was again surrounded by AK-47-wielding militants, McBride learning in the early hours that another church had been razed to the ground.

'The Colonel will see you now,' an unsmiling Mobile Brigade lieutenant led the American down the corridor, McBride's fears for Netty growing when he heard screams through the walls as he passed an interrogation room.

'Ah, Mister McBride,' the police chief remained seated when the American was ushered into the room, 'no doubt you wish to discuss the detention of your staff?'

'Why have they been arrested?'

'Sit down Mister McBride,' the chief suggested, 'you might be here for some time.'

'Are you detaining me also?' McBride remained on his feet.

'Just sit down and listen to what I have to say.'

McBride bristled, swallowed his tongue then flopped angrily into a chair. He had no authority here and knew that challenging the chief would only exacerbate the situation.

'We had a report that your staff were seen carrying weapons.'

Incredulous, McBride jumped to his feet at the accusation. 'That's a damn lie and you know it!'

'Sit down!' the chief shouted, also rising from his seat, 'or I will have you placed under arrest.'

'Do that and you'll have the U.S. Embassy all over your back within hours,' McBride threatened.

'Sit down!' the officer yelled, McBride trembling with rage as an armed aide flung the door open and pointed his weapon at the American's chest.

'*Duduk!*' the aide demanded, and McBride obeyed, lowering himself slowly into the chair.

Tense moments passed before the chief appeared satisfied that he maintained control. He dismissed the aide and returned to his desk. '*You* of all people should not have to be reminded that you are a guest in my country. I could have your bags packed and you on a flight with one call to Jakarta.'

'Then do it!' McBride challenged.

The chief's face paled. 'You'd leave your girlfriend…what's her name, Netty, behind?'

McBride felt the knot growing in his stomach. His jaw tightened, mocked by the officer's sneer when he fell silent. 'That's more like it, *Mister* McBride…or shall I call you Jack?'

'Call me whatever you want. Just release my staff.'

'I'm afraid that won't be possible,' he was told.

'Have they been charged?'

'This is not the United States, Jack.'

'And…?'

'They're being interrogated.'

'On the grounds that someone claimed they were carrying weapons?'

'Because two of my men were killed in the market attack and evidence connected to the bombing was found at your clinic.'

'That's preposterous and you know it,' McBride's voice fell to a steeled whisper. 'Our mission has never taken sides in the conflict. We provide care for Christians and Muslims, alike.'

'Lip service only,' the chief replied. 'You collect funds from Christians overseas solely to propagate your own faith.'

'That's not entirely true…'

'Have you ever given funds to our mosques for their social support groups?'

McBride frowned. 'Of course not, but we…'

'Why,' the chief stood and leaned across his desk, 'when the greater majority of people in need are Muslim?'

'We provide assistance to any who come to our clinic regardless of their faith.'

'Do you deny that you or your staff or others associated with your Church have tried to convert Muslims when they have come to you in need?'

'That never happens!'

The police chief leaned back and slipped both hands into his trouser pockets then smiled, his ensuing comment dripping with honeyed sarcasm. 'That's not what one of your staff has admitted.'

McBride wanted to leap across the room and slap the arrogant smirk from the other man's face. With fingers locked to the underside of his chair he breathed slowly, deeply, avoiding direct eye contact as adrenalin flowed, the missionary drawing upon inner reserves, struggling for self control. To strike the chief might bring gratification but he knew to do so would also seal Netty and his other staff's fate.

Moments dragged by and McBride knew he had no choice but to try another path. He looked up at the chief and nodded. 'What do I have to do to secure their release?'

The Mobile Police officer crossed his arms and leaned against the teak desk. 'Why don't you go back to your clinic and consider what you might have to offer?'

McBride was caught by surprise. 'You will release them all?' he asked hopefully.

'No,' we'll detain the men for a few more days but Netty might be able to go…' he left the offer hanging.

The officer accompanied Jack McBride back to the clinic where the American went directly to his quarters. There he emptied a locked drawer of its contents, wrapping the bundle of Rupiah in a brown manila envelope and surrendering the equivalent of five hundred dollars to the chief. An hour later Netty was released into McBride's custody, the incident resulting in the missionary to seriously consider the offer to accept another post, and relocate to an Australian Outback centre administered by his Church.

*   *   *   *

CHAPTER FOURTEEN

BOGOR – WEST JAVA

Predictably, as Bogor's pre-dawn skies filled with a brilliance only lightning can deliver revealing the dominating, three thousand metre volcano *Gunung Gede* the hill-station's surrounding mountain air exploded with unremitting claps of thunder. It was as if the Gods were determined that *"The City of Rain"*, indexed in the *Guinness Book of Records* for having recorded three hundred and twenty two thunderstorms in one year, should live up to its intimidating reputation.

Lightning arced, a bolt finding earth at a nearby PLN state-owned electricity substation. Across the park, high in the mosque's towering minaret a muezzin, preparing to call the faithful to prayer abandoned his dangerous position, scrambling down the column's precarious steps to the safety of the near empty main hall, where he decided to activate the prerecorded *Fajar* prayer summons.

Confronted by the blackout he muttered complainingly to himself while hurriedly lighting candles, anxious to complete his duty before sunrise officially passed, as his faith strictly forbade prayer whilst the sun was in the ascent – even when inclement weather eclipsed the event.

Then, having located his *tikar* prayer mat he bent on both

knees in the direction of Mecca and commenced to worship with the pronouncement, *"Allahu Akbar"*.

* * * *

Ten minutes by jeep along the twisting, Sukabumi road and not twenty kilometres from Bogor, a series of thunderous claps drove a rain-drenched Major General Sutrisno into near muscle spasm whilst clearing perimeter security. Unsmiling Special Forces guards peered into the vehicle, saluted and waved the National Intelligence Chief through – the torrential downpour blurring the landscape as he drove slowly along the unsealed path leading to the clandestine army barracks.

Craaack! Another blinding flash obscured his vision. Instinctively, he released the wheel clasping impotent hands protectively across his face anticipating the inevitable strike. The jeep stalled – millions of volts discharged to ground alarmingly close to the covert base and again the Javanese officer tensed, preparing for the ear-shattering roar that would inevitably follow.

Sutrisno remained hunched over the wheel once the thunder had passed regaining his composure, cursing his decision to journey out in such inclement weather without his usual driver. When Lt. General Sungkono had called and suggested he attend the closed meeting, the recently appointed *Badan Intelijen Negara* chief had not hesitated, the invitation confirming his suspicions that Sungkono, the *KOSTRAD*, Army's Strategic Operations Commander was laying the foundation for his challenge to assume the Presidency. Sungkono, supported by hardliners within the *'Green"* military faction had emerged from obscurity following the *'Greens"* usurpation upon the power of the remaining fiercely nationalist "Red & Whites" associated with the defunct New Order. The thought appealed to Sutrisno.

With the old guard now replaced with a more sophisticated leadership team the TNI had managed to rebuild its support base and return power to the generals; Sutrisno, a major player in the revitalized, fundamentalist "Greens" team.

The General rolled a jacket sleeve back to check the time. He was late for his meeting. He re-started the engine and drove the remaining two hundred metres to what had been the *Laskar Jihad's* field training headquarters where he was met and immediately escorted inside.

'Ah,' General Sungkono looked up and frowned as Sutrisno entered, 'now we are all here, we can start.'

Sutrisno ignored the mild rebuke. He brushed at his dampened uniform then dropped into the remaining chair opposite the Special Forces commander, General Supadi, accepted coffee and settled back as Sungkono opened the meeting.

'You all know why we're here,' the Strategic Forces general commenced 'and what we must do to ensure the ongoing integrity of the unitary state of the Republic,' he scanned the faces of the other three officers who each, in turn, nodded in agreement. 'And restore the TNI's authority to where we were before the so-called democratinization processes were introduced.'

Sutrisno caught General Supadi's eye; both understood where the conversation was heading. The erosion of TNI's power had commenced during the post-Suharto vacuum when politicians had orchestrated the removal of the TNI block of allocated seats in Parliament. Within ten years the military had been stripped of all commercial enterprises leaving cupboards bare at all levels. Sutrisno and Supadi were conscious of General Sungkono's presidential aspirations. As Commander of the Strategic Forces he wielded considerable power. It was not lost on the two subordinate officers that the former president,

Suharto, had launched his own coup against Sukarno from that very position.

'Our country's resources are being delivered to the Chinese, concession by concession and I believe it is not in the Republic's interests to continue to do so.'

'They're ensconced through internationally binding agreements,' Sutrisno reminded.

'Agreements can be revoked,' Supadi stepped in. 'The government could simply demand to renegotiate the terms of all existing contracts.'

'The President would never agree,' Sutrisno insisted.

'Then, other than assuming the Presidency what else can we do?'

'Nationalize all oil and gas operations,' Sungkono suggested with a wave of a hand, 'and place these natural resources under TNI control.'

'And this could be achieved, how?' Sutrisno leaned forward.

'By introducing martial law,' Sungkono replied.

'The *rakyat* would never agree,' Sutrisno challenged referring to the Indonesian people; his, the voice of reason. 'Unless, of course, we effected a coup?'

'No,' the Strategic Forces commander held a palm in the air, 'the West would reintroduce embargoes. We have to be more subtle than before.' The General rose and moved to the wall map to the rear of the room where he stood with his back to the others. 'Our answer lays here, gentlemen,' he turned and pointed to the group of islands in the country's east, 'in Sulawesi and Maluku. With the recent Raja Seram Field discoveries any escalation in violence would be perceived as a threat to national security...' the General turned to face his co-conspirators.

'And should the unrest spread as far as the capital, this would deliver to us the opportunity to declare martial law and return the Republic to its rightful leadership.' He engaged Sutrisno directly. 'and with the restoration of the 'Agency', you, *Mas* 'Trisno, will play a leading role.'

General Sutrisno had expected as much as he also chaired the powerful Coordinating Agency for National Stability, or BAKORSTANAS, undoubtedly the most feared organization to evolve under Suharto's military dictatorship. Abolished in the post-New Order years the agency had now been restored.

The Agency operated outside the legal code and had wide discretion to detain and interrogate persons considered a threat to national security. Following Suharto's rise to power between 600,000 and 750,000 government opponents were detained in a vast number of prisons, hastily prepared detention centers and work camps. The Armed Forces, ABRI had hastily established the intelligence body, KOPKAMTIB, to administer the arrest, interrogation and trials of these political prisoners. When ABRI was reorganized in 1985 KOPKAMTIB was abolished and its widespread powers passed to BAKORSTANAS. The two intelligence agencies, the National Intelligence Agency (BIN) and the Armed Forces Strategic Intelligence Agency (BAIS) were integral components of the new agency.

Sutrisno understood that what Sungkono was suggesting was, in fact, a return to the past. Camps would have to be prepared to contain the tens of thousands of dissidents and other prisoners and special squads would be required to ensure that the more high profile agitators simply disappeared. He looked solemnly over at General Supadi. As Commander of the Special Forces the provision of such units would fall into his domain. Quietly he considered the repercussions should their intentions be discovered and remained confident that even should they be challenged by the incumbent President, the positions all three enjoyed simply carried far too much power for them not to succeed. However the question that disquieted remained: whether the TNI had sufficient resources to reign in the *Maluku Brigade* should they be permitted to grow much further in strength.

The meeting continued throughout the night, the generals returning to their respective commands the following morning to initiate General Sungkono's praetorian plan, one which would evoke a paroxysm of international rage hitherto unseen since the New Order, 'communist cleansing' of 1965.

* * * *

HALMAHERA SEA

The chest pain caught the captain of the *M.V. Rager* by surprise. He staggered into the wheelhouse with the Nikon binoculars gripped firmly in one hand, the other searching his pockets for antacid tablets. Burning pain struck from behind his sternum, the severity of the attack freezing Bartlett in his tracks. Agonizing moments passed and, with an economy of movement he slowly stripped the covering foil from two tablets and managed these into his mouth, remaining deathly still waiting for the chalky compound to work. As the pain subsided the mercenary leaned back against a row of waist high timber lockers and belched, then returned to his watch.

Suddenly Bartlett tensed with the reflection of sun on glass in the distance. He squinted at the horizon and raised the powerful 8 x 30DIF glasses, grunting when he became satisfied that the vessel was another inter-island trader. He stepped back into the wheelhouse to monitor the Global Positioning Satellite receiver and waited for his client's ship to call.

Bartlett had sailed from Basilan across the northern tip of Sulawesi, down the eastern coastline of the Halmahera Islands aware that the Indonesian Navy only occasionally patrolled these waters. Within hours he would rendezvous with another vessel off Pulau Tobalai and transfer his final shipment of NATO-issue weapons to members of the *Maluku Brigade*. Not one to surrender to superstition Bartlett did, however, experience a sense of foreboding in relation to this mission as not only was this to be his last shipment, he was venturing much deeper into Indonesian waters than initially contracted.

Although he had been introduced to the client through a reliable contact, Bartlett initiated his own background check on the Belgium weapons' supplier via a Manila-based, CIA source. Even when the report had come back clean Bartlett had still hesitated in accepting the contract, his gut telling him to beware. Having arbitrarily tripled his usual rate he was amazed when the client had unquestioningly accepted. Then, when the cargo was delivered to his ship at anchor in Mindanao he reasoned that he was dealing with a government-backed supplier as the weapons were the most recent NATO issue, U.S.-manufactured XM8 lightweight assault rifles – all produced in parasniper configuration, new to Bartlett as he had never held one in his grip before. Aware that the XM8 could fire close to eight hundred rounds per minute he appreciated the significance of such a weapon in the hands of separatist rebels.

The first eleven runs had been completed without incident, Bartlett delivering the shipments with relative ease as the transfer points were offshore Menado in Sulawesi's north. With heightened surveillance off Indonesia's common sea borders due to an ongoing dispute over demarcation lines defining ownership of oil and gas deposits, his client had requested a change in the delivery procedures. Having considered the added risk Bartlett renegotiated his rate, agreeing to undertake a further three deliveries. Tempted by the bonus payments he had then completed a fourth, adamant that the current incursion would be his last.

The mercenary scratched at a scarred indentation faded with time under a thinning, grey head, the imposition of a ghost from his past troubling as it reminded the former ASIS agent that in his line of work treachery was a constant companion.

Bartlett recognized that it was time for him to move on, sell the *M.V. Rager* and find a more suitable place to live under the sun. The southern Philippines, his operational base and home for the past twenty years was on the brink of becoming the next Afghanistan with Mindanao stamped as the new Mecca for terrorism. The influx of Islamic militants had bolstered the twenty-thousand strong Moro Islamic Liberation Front to a point where U.S.-backed government forces continued to lose ground to the rebels – Bartlett deciding that after this final run he would call it a day.

The radio squawked. Bartlett listened attentively, mentally deciphering the coded Indonesian message which signaled the imminent approach of his target vessel. Again he raised the Nikon binoculars and scanned the sea ahead, comforted when he identified the motorized *perahu* as it appeared around the lower tip of Tobalai Island and steamed in his direction.

Having exchanged its shipment of assault rifles for fuel the *M.V. Rager*'s hold was now filled with drums of diesel. Bartlett set a course which would take him to his new haven, the small island nation of Palau, five hundred kilometers east of the Philippines. He opened a foot locker and removed a bottle of

Bacardi 8, stepped out onto the deck and, as he stood watching the *Maluku Brigade* vessel disappear from sight he twisted the cap and lifted the neck to his mouth, savoring his first moments of retirement.

*   *   *   *

The covert Dutch-sponsored weapons' shipment was unloaded at a coastal village along the Seram Strait and then transported upriver into the hills and stashed in the *Maluku Brigade* arsenal. Upon receiving confirmation that the assault rifles and accompanying ammunition had arrived safely, Rima Passelima sent a simple message via her NGO through to the embassy in Jakarta, the content of which was then relayed to the AIVD in Holland.

*   *   *   *

CANBERRA
Office of National Assessments

Having read the submission earlier Peter Rigby grew impatient, eager for the senior analyst to complete his report.

'And, as political Islam and regional terrorist organizations continue to consolidate in tandem across S.E. Asia we should expect to see a substantial increase in support for the more radical groups in Indonesia, Malaysia, Southern Thailand and the Philippines. Pan-Asia-Islamic-backed commercial interests' influence over ASEAN has become more transparent and we should anticipate greater opposition to Australia's inclusion in the newly created trading zones.' The analyst paused, canvassed the room over rimless bifocals and, satisfied he had not lost anyone along the way, continued with his presentation. 'As to the impact of higher oil and gas prices on China and the ASEAN economies, we...'

Deputy Director Rigby accepted that experts had been predicting an oil supply crisis for thirty years. With demand outstripping supply he understood that the looming energy crunch was as important an issue as regional defence – the price of petrol at the pump of more concern to the general public than any potential threat that might arise from growing separatist issues immediately to the nation's north. Rigby believed that the unitary state of Indonesia would be unable to contain the separatist threat, and was of the opinion that Australia needed to consider new alliances in order to survive. He had argued volumes citing the Indonesian military's incapacity to settle sectarian conflicts in Sulawesi and the Moluccas, his prognostications supported by few.

'It is widely recognized that as Australia is capable of producing some eighty-five percent of its domestic fuel needs. However, from a strategic viewpoint there could be some risk to our production capacity as two-thirds of Australian oil is produced in the north and north-west which would make these facilities more vulnerable to attack by radical elements operating across the Indonesian archipelago.'

Rigby resisted glancing at his wristwatch as the analyst droned on presenting data pertaining to China's burgeoning relationship with Indonesia, the product of strategic bilateral agreements reached under the Yudhoyono Presidency when Beijing's state-owned petroleum companies were scouring the globe for new supplies to keep the economy growing. As a consequence China's investment in Indonesia's energy sector provided a closer source of supply than the distant and politically volatile Middle Eastern states. At the time Rigby identified Beijing's move imperative to its long term interests as Indonesia straddled the Southeast Asian waterways through which seventy-five percent of China's oil imports passed. It was clear to the Deputy Director that Beijing wished to ensure unhindered passage of its commercial and naval shipping between the Pacific and Indian oceans, the separatist issues along those lanes obviously of growing concern.

However, China's attempt to monopolize energy resources also greatly troubled Rigby.

Australian-American oil-and-mining lobby interests were growing increasingly rattled by China's entreaties with Jakarta to reconsider existing lease arrangements with Western resource giants – particular at this time when Houston's Japanese partners had abandoned the U.S. for joint production in the disputed East China Sea, the rich gas deposits now being developed under a new arrangement between Japan and China leaving the Americans out in the cold.

The East China Sea was believed to contain more than one hundred billion barrels of oil making it one of the last unexplored high-potential resource areas with close proximity to established markets. Decades of boundary disputes had hindered development until the recent joint development agreement had been reached, the move galvanizing Malaysia and Indonesia, Vietnam and the Philippines into action, contesting boundaries claimed as far south by Australia in the East Timor Sea.

Rigby was aware that Australia's current discord with China had its origins back in time when Australia and East Timor agreed on the development of gas fields along redefined borders. China had entered into agreements with the Indonesian state-owned oil giant, Pertamina, for lease areas that were in dispute. Australian interests had forged ahead, subsequently constructing facilities in Darwin to implement the agreements.

Indonesia cried foul and China threatened to revoke its Free Trade Agreement with Canberra which amounted to more than thirty billion dollars in benefits to the Australian economy.

As East Timor had defined its territory to incorporate the lease areas under the laws relating to territorial sea rights, the area ripped from the Indonesian claim was substantially rich in oil and gas deposits. Frequent incursions by Chinese naval ships had raised political tensions between Canberra and Beijing, the United States then increasing its already significant presence in northern Australia at Darwin defence installations.

'Our trade agreement with China which has delivered a twenty-five billion dollar bonanza to our economy over the past five years would therefore come into question should Beijing's pursuit of strategic alliances with Indonesia and other S.E. Asian nations result in Australia being sidelined in future, regional trade pacts.'

When the analyst's delivery concluded the attendees returned to their respective domains to consider the import of the intelligence brief's recommendations; Rigby was amongst those convinced that Australia had reached a watershed in its relationships with its near neighbors – one which would challenge the nation's long term survival.

AMBON – SERAM

Whilst most of the Indonesian archipelago had undergone significant change, Seram, the second largest island in the Moluccas had remained virtually untouched—until the Raja Seram Field oil and gas discoveries—because of its wild, rugged interior – the primary consideration for the *Maluku Brigade* leadership basing their operations there.

Led by a secretive cabal of Protestant Christian conspirators the *Maluku Brigade,* supported by pro-independence groups within Holland's Ambonese commnity, had grown into a formidable force.

On the 9th November the Brigade concluded a series of secret meetings with the *Organisesi Papua Merdeka,* (Free West Papua Movement) leadership resulting in both separatist groups issuing declarations severing ties with Indonesia.

That night a heavily-armed *Maluku Brigade* paramilitary force moved unhindered under cover of darkness through the coastal port town of Amahai towards the Bimaton construction site. Local security forces abandoned any pretence of resistance permitting the four-hundred-strong separatist group to assume control over the refinery and communications centers, sending shockwaves reverberating throughout the region.

In the weeks that followed the Indonesian military managed to balance its campaign against the separatists, the media playing into General Sungkono's hands suggesting that martial law should be seriously considered across the archipelago's restive eastern provinces. Then, without warning, thousands of *Laskar PAI* militants from the Southern Philippines and Malaysia flooded into the Halmaheras. The fighting escalated further, the bloody toll resulting in a groundswell of support for U.N. intervention and the TNI leadership suddenly became gravely concerned.

* * * *

CHAPTER FIFTEEN

DARWIN

Greg Young remained in a black mood as he was driven from the Bimaton holding compound in the harbor past rows of idle equipment, mobilized months earlier for shipment from the northern harbor to the Raja Seram project. With construction having fallen behind schedule, Bimaton was facing heavy non-performance penalties, the consortium's backers urging Mohamed Aziz Derashid to explore the possibility of declaring a *force majeure* in view of the Indonesian military's apparent inability to bring about a cessation of hostilities in the country's eastern provinces.

'The men will want to know if there's going to be any layoffs,' the local manager slowed the Toyota land cruiser as they left the bonded area to avoid a group of American sailors returning to their ships. Since Darwin had become home to elements of the Seventh Fleet the number of U.S. military personnel permanently based in the Northern Territory had increased by five thousand.

'Not at this time,' Young replied wearily, 'but if we aren't able to improve our performance we'll all be looking for new employment.'

'You'll give me fair warning if there's going to be any retrenchment?'

'You have my word.'

The manager shook his head in dismay. 'I don't understand how the separatists have managed to keep the Indonesian army at bay.'

Young gazed out across the harbor to where the *USS Kitty Hawk* dominated the skyline, the ageing aircraft carrier dwarfing the guided missile frigate and destroyer alongside. With Washington and Canberra's growing concern that the escalation in the conflict to Australia's near north had seen an increase in Chinese naval activity throughout the archipelago's east, the United States had countered accordingly. As an additional security measure Canberra declared a one-thousand nautical mile security zone which required all ships sailing through the zone to provide details on their journey and cargo. Beijing ignored Australia's 'extension of geography' and continued to sail to within the recognized two-hundred mile limit, unchallenged.

Speculation that Indonesia's eastern provinces would follow East Timor had ASEAN nations nervous, the naval build up in Darwin raising concerns in Jakarta that Australia, with the blessing of the United States was preparing to support the separatists declaration of independence from the Republic of Indonesia.

Again Beijing took the lead demanding that Canberra review its half-century-old military pact with the U.S. warning that the ANZUS alliance threatened regional stability and that the naval buildup in Darwin would have negative consequences on existing economic and political relationships.

KUALA LUMPUR

Mohamed Aziz Derashid was enraged at the prospect of losing the Raja Seram projects, and how this would impact on his personal fortune and position at the helm of the Pan-Asia Islamic movement. He believed that with time Jakarta would be successful in dealing with the separatists as they had in Aceh. However, with the threat of an Australian-led, American-backed peace keeping force on the horizon, Derashid had no illusions as to what the future would hold should Bulan Sabit Holdings' subsidiary, Bimaton, lose this core asset.

Determined to discourage the Australians and punish the United States the Malaysian entrepreneur sent a coded request via his Saudi associates for assistance to prepare what he referred to as the *Sword of Allah* and, within the week, Syafullah al-Yemeni, the explosives expert who prepared the 2002 Kuta bombings arrived in Thailand, where he was met by Derashid and driven south across the border.

Although Derashid's telephone communication was recorded by the Echelon system with Syafullah's name triggering the intercept, the Malaysian was not identified due to his disciplined use of prepaid SIM cards. Syafullah al-Yemeni was tracked into Bangkok where he disappeared, the level of alert immediately being raised by Langley, the code *'Sword of Allah'* immediately being registered as another trigger for further intercepts.

* * * *

AMBON

With the imagery of traumatized children fresh in her mind Rima Passelima's driving skills were severely tested when she rounded the corner and was faced with an armed personnel carrier lying on its side. She slammed her foot on the brake and swerved, narrowly avoiding the smoldering APC, the Daihatsu pickup's uncontrolled slide sending *Maluku Brigade* freedom fighters leaping for safety as she slid past and slammed into a tree. Bruised and badly shaken Rima climbed groggily from the vehicle to survey the scene.

'Are you hurt?' several of the separatists had run to her side.

Rima steadied herself against the pickup. 'Give me a minute,' she said, gently rubbing her forehead. She checked her fingers for blood, surprised that she had escaped without any serious injury.

'You shouldn't stay here too long,' the group's commander held a cell phone to his ear listening to reports of enemy troop movement. 'They have choppers coming our way.'

Rima squinted into the sky then back at the Brigade soldiers who, armed with the latest American XM8 lightweight assault rifles stripped the bodies of Indonesian army regulars and dumped them alongside the British-supplied APC. The commander barked an order directing his men to push Rima's vehicle back onto the road and within minutes, having driven less than a kilometer she was stopped at a hastily prepared *Kopassus* checkpoint, and ordered out of her vehicle. The Daihatsu was searched, her papers checked and Rima was questioned as to the purpose of her journey, her roadside interrogation interrupted when helicopter gunships passed low overhead searching for the missing APC – moments later, the distinct sounds of an engagement, then silence, Rima silently praying that the separatists had managed to flee.

Once cleared Rima drove more cautiously as she headed back to her NGO office in Ambon, the increased presence of military hardware strung alongside the road a reminder of Jakarta's determination to enforce its will.

Six thousand more had died in the Sulawesi-Moluccan

conflict since Jakarta had declared martial law in the province and launched an offensive to crush elements of the *Maluku Brigade*. Another fifteen hundred had been arrested and interned at the notorious *"Camp Ambon"*, where access had been denied to all including the Red Cross.

Although the TNI had mobilized a significant force to address the separatist movements in the Moluccas, Sulawesi and West Papua, Jakarta had failed to prevent the growing number of well-armed, foreign *Laskar PAI* militants arriving, their presence evolving into the most serious military confrontation the central government had faced in fifty years. Military hardware purchased from the United States, France and Britain had been transported from Java in support of the offensive, Rima now accustomed to seeing British Scorpion tanks with their heavy machine guns and armed personnel carriers tearing through the countryside in breach of Jakarta's assurances that British equipment would not be used for offensive or counter-insurgency purposes. Hawk jets streaked across the skies whilst updated versions of the American Broncos, duplicating the methodology applied during the occupation of East Timor, scoured the countryside bringing terror as they randomly strafed villages across the terrain.

Rima entered a section of the now clearly demarcated city where churches and mosques once stood in pride; their burned out shells the new legacy of these turbulent times. Makeshift dwellings pockmarked the desolation, Rima proceeding slowly, tapping the horn to warn a group of early teenage children squatting precariously close to the road. As she eased past, Rima could see from their hollow expressions and emaciated bodies that these youngsters were but a small part of the huge refugee population that had exploded across the province, their overwhelming need driving the children into the city in search of food and clothing.

Rima arrived at her office to find an army vehicle parked outside. Drumming the steering wheel impatiently as her security struggled to slide the steel-plated gate out of her path she mentally prepared herself for the inevitable confrontation. She parked the pickup inside the heavily fortified complex, climbed out of the vehicle and dusted down her clothes, startled when a familiar voice greeted her from the door.

'I thought I'd missed you.' Johanis Matuanakotta followed Rima through the office and into the accommodations at the rear. 'I can't stay long,' he explained, 'my plane leaves in less than an hour.'

'I wasn't expecting you until next week.'

'The company is looking at beefing up its local facilities. I've been here since early morning with a team from the Raja Seram group. They chartered an aircraft to fly us over from Bali.'

'That explains the jeep,' Rima was relieved having avoided another visit from the local military commander's office. 'When will you be back?'

'I still plan on returning as originally scheduled.' Johanis held her by the hand, his eyes searching her face. 'You look tired.'

Rima smiled thinly. 'Thanks for the compliment.' She tilted her head at the connecting door which led to her quarters. 'Have you spoken to Anna?'

'Briefly,' he replied, 'we'll have more time next week.' He became solemn. 'You know I'm grateful for your taking her under your wing.'

'Nuci is the one who takes care of your daughter, not me.'

Abruptly, he turned on his heel. 'I should leave.'

Rima walked him to the door. 'Be careful, Johanis,' she warned, 'you know that they'll be watching.'

Johanis glanced over her shoulder where others on the NGO staff were working. 'Jakarta accepts me as one of them, now,' he lowered his voice, 'it's *you* who must be careful!'

*　*　*　*

Following Johanis' departure Rima treated herself to a long bath to wash the mental residue of the day's experiences from her mind. As she lay quietly soaking in the tub Rima considered Johanis' passing warning. Her work undercover with the AIVD had been demanding and dangerous, but understanding how the local people had benefited from her presence she accepted those shortcomings, proud that she had contributed in such a substantial way. The NGO continued to provide support for the needy and the *Maluku Brigade* had grown into a formidable force with the covert support of her masters.

Greg Young's image floated into her thoughts and she closed her eyes saddened that she was still unable to recall his face without the scene of the devastating Bali bombing aftermath filling her brain. Rima in no way doubted that she continued to hold deep feelings for the British entrepreneur. However, with Bimaton Holdings' association with the TNI coming to light she retained mixed feelings as to whether she could ever enjoy a meaningful relationship with someone who remained in bed with the enemy – not that she could ever reveal her own status quo in relation to her involvement with the AIVD.

Electing to maintain a distance relationship with Greg Young had been less than satisfactory, their communications now far less frequent than before. Rima understood that the Bimaton executive was now under extreme pressure faced with the threat of losing the Raja Seram Field operations. And, examining her own contribution in the creation of Young's misfortune by assisting arm the *Maluku Brigade* she fell into disconsolate mood and remained dispirited throughout the day.

* * * *

Johanis idled the time staring down at the necklace of islands strung along the sea between Ambon and Bali, his thoughts preoccupied with the task ahead and how he had arrived at this point in his life.

Johanis acknowledged that he owed everything to Rima Passelima; the scholarship she had sponsored, his time studying in Holland, the practical training that followed and his return to Indonesia where Rima had arranged for his employment as a ground engineer under a joint KLM-Garuda program. She had encouraged his mother-in-law, Nuci to bring Anna into her household, Johanis a stranger to his daughter when he finally returned to Ambon upon completion of his training overseas.

During his first weeks in Amsterdam he had gravitated towards others within the Dutch-Ambonese community which, inevitably, led Johanis into the fellowship of the self-exiled separatists, the RMS. Unwittingly, Johanis Matuanakotta did precisely everything that was expected of him which, ultimately, led to his indirect recruitment by the AIVD. He had returned to Indonesia and excelled, his diligence being rewarded with a permanent position on Garuda Airlines technical ground staff stationed at the Bali hub, the appointment also orchestrated by the AIVD's long-reaching tentacles into Indonesia.

Johanis Matuanakotta's deeply-ingrained hate for everything Javanese for what their soldiers had done to him and his family had not diminished with time.

He played an integral role in providing the *Maluku Brigade* with intelligence relating to the movement of troops from Bali under the *Udayana Command,* responsible for the province of Maluku. Although his involvement was directly operational he did, nevertheless, attend the Brigade's leadership meetings whenever the opportunity arose. Having access to the airline enabled Johanis to travel back to Ambon regularly, his most recent visit in the company of Raja Seram Field executives to inspect the damage incurred with the recent Brigade attacks on the construction sites which had resulted in all work on the project grinding to a halt.

Johanis strongly supported the Brigade's position in forcing work to cease on the sites. They had argued that the Moluccans would not, apart from the creation of a few hundred local employment opportunities, benefit from the massive investment. If Oil and gas were to flow from the fields whilst under Jakarta's control then the people of Moluccu would be unlikely to enjoy any share in the enormous revenues that would be generated by these extensive resource developments. And, in consequence, the Bimaton sites had been attacked, the Brigade determined not to permit the further exploitation of their resources by the Javanese as they had elsewhere, across the archipelago.

*   *   *   *

CANBERRA

The Prime Minister's emphatic response drowned the meeting into silence. The Attorney General leaned gently forward to catch Peter Rigby's eye, the almost unnoticeable shake of the AG's head signaling the recently appointed intelligence chief not to reply. Rigby then crossed his arms and stared across the table at a Russell Drysdale canvas on the far wall, the moment interrupted when the PM cleared his throat to continue.

'We will *not* engage in any public debate in support of the separatist movements. Our position must appear clear to Jakarta on this matter.'

'Might be too late for that,' the Foreign Affairs Minister suggested. 'The Indonesian tabloids are already suggesting that we might go down the same path as we did with East Timor.'

The PM's eyes narrowed at the Queenslander. 'Then it might be an appropriate time for you to revisit Jakarta and put an end to the speculation.' Then he looked directly at his intelligence chief. 'Can you substantiate this claim that the separatists are receiving support from the Dutch government?'

Peter Rigby returned the PM's stare. 'No, but that is the conclusion we have drawn.'

'How do we know this isn't simply a group of exiles sympathetic to their cause?'

'The *Maluku Brigade's* armory contains some of the latest NATO issue.'

'Could it have been stolen or purchased on the black market?'

'Possibly...' Rigby hesitated. '...but we don't believe so.'

'Why?' the PM challenged.

'Shoal Bay intercepts suggest that the Dutch General Intelligence and Security Service, the AIVD have an agent on the ground in Ambon.'

'Wouldn't we expect that?'

'The communications we have indicates close liaison between the AIVD and the separatist groups.'

'Why?'

'The West Papuans are receiving growing support amongst Pacific Island nations to seek a U.N. resolution to revisit the so-called Act of Free Choice.'

'The U.N. would never agree,' the PM scoffed.

'They might if the groundswell was supported by both Holland and China.'

'How would the Dutch benefit?'

'If West Papua was successful in achieving independence from Jakarta there would be a rush to sign up resources. The Royal Dutch Shell group would have the historic advantage and China's spiraling demand for oil would make them an obvious partner.'

'Do we have any evidence of Chinese support for the Moluccan separatists?'

'Only the rhetoric in their media…we have not received any information that the Chinese have actually attempted to establish dialogue with the *Maluku Brigade* leadership but our best guess is that contact has been made. After all, the Raja Seram Field would be quite a prize for whoever ends up in control of the area. Our analysts also feel that collectively, the Ambonese and the West Papuans *do* stand a chance of succeeding as the TNI is stretched, engaged across the entire eastern sector.'

'But surely Jakarta has more than enough resources to deal with the situation?' the PM directed his question to the Chief of the Armed Forces.

'Yes, they could send in another fifty to seventy-five thousand troops but that would make them vulnerable elsewhere. If we go back in time we would see that Jakarta has never deployed more than half of its resources outside Java over concerns that any local insurrection would be unmanageable.'

The PM turned to his intelligence chief. 'Then the threat of the separatists achieving their goals is much greater than we have believed until now?'

'Yes,' Rigby's eyes roamed those present. 'And that raises

the probability of our being dragged into direct confrontation with Jakarta.'

'Shit!' the PM muttered surprising the room. He looked up, then down the length of the table and warned, 'I don't want to see anything in the media that there is any suggestion the government is considering a call-up. We're coming into an election year and under no circumstances do I want the voters being spooked by the imagery of conscripts fighting Indonesians.'

* * * *

Chapter Sixteen

Malaysia

Mohamed Aziz Derashid sat in the secrecy of the isolated villa contemplating the simplicity of his iniquitous plan and what would be required to develop his radiological weapon, or 'dirty bomb'.

The Radio Thermal Generator's outer casing had long been discarded, leaving the RTG's core safely encased in an impervious, protective layer of lead designed to absorb radiation. With his engineering skills and Syafullah al-Yemeni's expertise it had not been overly difficult to produce the bomb as no special assembly was required, his plan demanding only that the explosion would disperse the radioactive material upon detonation.

With his engineering skills and Syafullah al-Yemeni's expertise it would not be overly difficult to produce the bomb as no special assembly would be required, his plan requiring only that the explosion would disperse the radioactive material upon detonation. Derashid smiled with the thought that although the potential weapon he possessed might not be classified as a Weapon of Mass Destruction, it most certainly could be classified as a Weapon of Mass Disruption.

Derashid had utilized conventional explosives to widely scatter the strontium 90 when the bomb exploded. Dynamite had been easily acquired through his construction activities, the container packed with the deadly contents and shipped initially, to the bonded area in Darwin. He was confident that the container would not be subjected to customs inspection as the shipment was to be held in the bonded area pending transshipment, ostensibly, to the Raja Seram Field. Even had he considered sending the container directly to its final destination in Australia, the likelihood of discovery would have been minimal with less than two percent of all containers being inspected at the country's harbours.

Ingeniously, he had rigged a Palm Pilot device to trigger the detonators, the signal to be transmitted to a disguised antenna running along the outside of the container.

He understood that the initial death toll would be limited to those in the blast's immediate impact zone and others who would succumb to radiation contamination. As the explosion would be far less than that of a nuclear device, Derashid knew that his target would be susceptible to the deadly impact contamination it would leave...possibly paralysing the area for years with radioactive fallout.

The Sword of Allah was raised, ready to strike.

JAKARTA

General Sungkono brooded in quiet introspection, staring into space considering his options in the wake of the most recent intelligence reports supporting the conclusion that his duplicitous associates, Generals Sutrisno and Supadi had seriously underestimated the *Maluku Brigade*. Having created the very scenario that now threatened the nation's existence Sungkono recognized that expeditious action was required to remedy the situation – action that would destroy the separatists once and for all and in so doing restore the military to power, taking out the pestilent *Laskar PAI* along the way.

Sungkono accepted that the real challenge was the imminent threat of outside intervention, and mulled how best to discourage the growing Australian sentiment supporting the Moluccan and West Papuan independence movements.

The General accepted that it would be foolhardy to directly engage any proposed international force recalling the brinkmanship displayed by both the TNI and the Australian-led U.N. INTERFET forces following the East Timor independence referendum. Indonesian submarines and fighter aircraft had initiated aggressive probing tactics by shadowing ships carrying Australian and New Zealand troops, resulting in escorting warships going on to full battle stations.

Having later learned that Australia had been on the brink of sending its F/A-18s and F-111s in to engage Indonesian fighters, General Sungkono remained resentful of the arrogant posture taken at that time. Determined to send a clear signal to the Australian public that Jakarta would no longer tolerate their interference in Indonesia's domestic affairs, the would-be President summoned General Supadi to discuss how best this might be achieved.

* * * *

BANDUNG

Anwar Suprapto sat quietly with his head between his knees slowly sucking air into his lungs when he was again beset by a coughing attack which left his mouth filled with blood. In the solitude of the mountain cottage the minutes passed slowly, the Garuda captain inspecting the handkerchief clenched in his right hand, no longer alarmed with what lay there.

He peered out through the latticed window, splinters of diffracted light distorting the image of terraced rice fields surrounding the bungalow setting, Anwar aware that it was time to prepare for his return to Jakarta or risk missing his scheduled flight. He rose, showered, examining his now gaunt features as he shaved, no longer surprised at the reflection mocking him in the mirror. Anwar had gone to extraordinary lengths and cost to ensure that his medical records did not reflect his dire condition. Disguising his illness had not been easy. His frequent physicals as required by the airline had been the most difficult, Anwar manipulating his way through the examinations and tests to hide his secret. He knew that over the past year his tardiness had resulted in some criticism, and he would not be able to continue much longer, cursing whoever had been responsible for his demise.

Leaving the idyllic setting he had chosen for its solitude and pollution-free air Anwar decided to take the new highway back to the capital and onto the international airport, Sukarno-Hatta where he joined his crew in preparation for the long haul to Melbourne and Sydney.

The Boeing 777-300 departed on schedule, passengers and crew none the wiser that at best, the pilot at the helm had less than a year to live.

* * * *

JAKARTA

Greg Young was of two minds with the announcement that Agus Sumarsono had accepted the President's invitation to join his Cabinet, the move requiring Agus to relinquish his position as chairman of the Bimaton Board.

'I have informed Derashid,' Agus stood with hands clasped behind his back, Greg Young sitting cross-legged, his face wrapped with a deep frown. 'He will advise as to whom he will fill the position with by the end of the week.'

'Coordinating Minister for the Economy?' Young understood the implications this could have for Agus' future business activities, 'that really places you right up there!'

Agus smiled at the recognition. 'Well, I've always believed that no one knows the economy better than those who've been responsible for building it.' He dropped into a leather armchair facing Young. 'And the President has asked that I visit Australia and do whatever I can within the business community to convince them that it's in their interests for Indonesia to resolve the separatist opposition without foreign interference.'

'When are you leaving?'

'At the end of the week…why not join me?'

Young considered the offer. 'Which cities will you visit?'

'Sydney… Canberra of course… Melbourne.'

'How long do you plan on being away?'

'No more than a week. I have asked our Ambassador to get the ball rolling.'

'Are you taking the Cessna Citation?'

Agus raised an eyebrow. 'Of course…and we'll overnight at my villa in Bali on the way.'

With the mention of Bali, Young suddenly had a thought. 'Would you mind if I invited Rima along?'

Agus shrugged. 'There's more than enough room.'

'Great,' Young was already calling up the number on his cell phone, 'I'll give her a call and see if she can meet us in Bali.'

'Good,' Agus was genuinely pleased. Then, jokingly, 'ask her to bring a friend.'

* * * *

AMBON

'Greg, there's nothing I would enjoy more right now than to go with you but I just can't abandon everything, especially with the current situation.'

'It's only a week, Rima,' he insisted, sensing his attempts to cajole her into accepting were working in his favor. 'Besides, everyone knows you deserve a break.'

'I don't know, Greg…it just doesn't seem appropriate. The hospitals are full of injured and…'

'And if you don't take some time off you could easily end up as a patient yourself,' he argued.

'When do I have to decide?'

'Anytime, up to when we leave Bali on Sunday.'

'You're arriving on Saturday?'

'Yes. We can stay at Agus' villa or somewhere else if you're not comfortable with that.'

'Let me have a couple of days to see if I can get things together here first?'

'Sure,' Greg was now confident Rima would come, 'but I will be very disappointed if you don't make it.'

'Okay, okay,' she unconsciously waved a hand in the air, 'call me again on Friday.'

'Done,' he promised before the line dropped out as it frequently did.

Rima placed the receiver back on its cradle then leaned forward with her elbows on the desk. She closed her eyes with chin on open palms, fingers gently massaging temples as the image of her distant lover drifted into her mind. Rima acknowledged that Greg's invitation was indeed tempting, but to leave Ambon at such a crucial moment would be irresponsible.

The conflict had taken on another dimension with the *Maluku Brigade's* declaration, the toll on both sides from what now amounted to civil war placing even greater demands on her NGO with other agencies having already fled. The AIVD has placed even greater demands on her limited resources with the *Laskar PAI* growing in strength, her reporting of the situation to Holland via the embassy network becoming increasingly difficult with communications frequently down.

Resigned to remain in her self-proclaimed prison Rima was in no way bitter with the choices she had made, yearning for the day that she could return to Amsterdam and her parents and witness their expressions when they learned of her contribution to the old RMS cause.

* * * *

SYDNEY – LAKEMBA

Amir peered cautiously along the street to determine if he had been followed. Since the Kuta bombings he knew that Indonesians and Malays resident in Australia were regularly scrutinized, many falling under ASIO's surveillance, some arrested as a result of raids. He strolled casually out into the open again, stopped, lit a cigarette, cast a final glance around then entered the designated building to meet with the Saudi from the embassy in Canberra.

'You are late,' Amir was reprimanded, 'did you take the usual precautions?'

'Yes, as you instructed,' he replied, intimidated by the visitor whose family, he knew, was related to the King.

'You will be responsible for providing whatever local support is required for the placement of the consignment when it arrives. Is that clear?'

'I will do whatever is asked of me.'

'You are not to disclose any of this to the others in the group.'

Amir was surprised by this demand. 'But how will I convince them to do what is required when the time arrives?'

The Saudi's brow wrinkled. 'That is for you to devise.'

'When am I to be told more about the shipment?'

'When it is appropriate.' The Saudi would not reveal more than an important shipment would be delivered and that the local representatives would be responsible for its delivery to the designated destination. Derashid had discussed their options, at length, the final target not yet defined.

'Take this,' the Saudi presented Amir with a prepaid cell phone. 'I will call you next time. Meeting in person is becoming far too risky.'

A week later when Amir received his instructions via the dedicated number he was standing in the lounge of his one-bedroom apartment in the Sydney suburb of Lakemba, home to a diversified cultural mix from around the world.

'The *Sword's* arrival is imminent,' the Saudi's voice advised, 'and you shall soon receive further instructions.'

'I am ready now,' he replied.

'Good,' the embassy official appeared pleased, 'then keep this number by your side. I shall call you again soon.'

Amir placed the hand phone back inside his jacket then headed out for the day. The Saudi's efforts to remove the possibility of detection had been compromised by the very fact that Amir had taken the call whilst in his apartment, one of many that had been bugged by Australia's domestic security service, ASIO. The information gleaned from this and other conversations resulted in the level of surveillance over the apartment being raised, the analysts responsible for interpreting the conversation deciding that the *"Sword of Allah"* was either an emissary from the Middle East or, at worst, a suicide bomber who was due to arrive.

In an environment where intelligence information is jealously guarded and reluctantly shared, the information remained within the confines of ASIO's own intelligence walls.

DEN PASAR – BALI

Being scheduled as the duty ground engineer, Johanis Matuanakotta learned of the Cessna Citation's flight schedule when he turned up at Ngurah Rai airport for his shift on Saturday. Throughout the day, Johanis could hardly contain his excitement at having been delivered the opportunity to punish the wealthy Bimaton Holdings entrepreneur, his appetite for revenge sweetened further with the knowledge that his actions would demonstrate to Jakarta that the *Maluku Brigade* was preparing to take the fight to their door.

During the course of the morning Johanis contacted a number of Brigade-linked associates then jumped on his motorbike during the lunch break to discuss his requirements with his fellow conspirators. Assured that his demands could be prepared by Sunday morning Johanis waited eagerly for the twin-engine aircraft to arrive.

When the executive jet landed Johanis identified himself

to the pilot, Imam Suprapto, and was immediately given access to the VIP aircraft. Upon completion of his shift the Dutch-trained Ambonese engineer met with his colleagues and worked through the night preparing the device he would place on board Agus Sumarsono's plane.

* * * *

AMBON

'I'm sorry, Greg, but I just can't get away.' Rima could hear her words echo down the line to Bali, fifteen hundred kilometers to the west.

'There'll be other opportunities,' she heard him say.

'When things improve...' the words became distorted with weather setting in along their path.

'Say...again?'

'I said... when conditions here... permit, I'll...' Rima glared at the cell phone, redialed Young's number but without success. She tried again later on Saturday night, failed again then went to bed. No sooner had she slipped into a deep sleep when she was awakened by a call from Johanis on her cell phone.

'I have exciting news,' Johanis announced.

Rima rubbed her eyes awake and squinted at the bedside clock. It was eleven o'clock. She had not been asleep more than fifteen minutes. 'It's late, Johanis,' she fought back a yawn, 'can't this wait until the morning?'

'No, I have to tell you now...'

'Why...what's happened?' Rima became alert sensing the urgency in his voice. Then, 'Johanis, what have you done?'

'It's what I *will* do... tomorrow... that will make the news,' he responded enigmatically.

'What is it?' Rima asked annoyance creeping into her voice.

'Remember those we agreed... who would benefit most from the... exploitation of our oil and gas... deposits?'

Rima frowned. *What was Johanis trying to tell her?*

'The big boys... from Jakarta,' Johanis implied, Rima then understanding.

'What about them?'

'Well... after tomorrow... one of them won't be with us... anymore.' The line started to break up as it had earlier.

Rima paled. 'What... are you planning to do?'

'He's going... south, tomorrow,' she thought she heard him giggle, 'and I mean that in more... ways than one!'

What started as a small knock became a hammering in her brain, the worrying thought sweeping through her mind with the realization that Johanis was referring to Agus Sumarsono she shouted into the cell phone, 'No, Johanis, you can't!' Rima heard her voice reverberate down the line...then, silence, followed by static interference and finally, nothing.

Rima bounced out of bed and ran to the landline. She grabbed the handset and listened, stabbing furiously at the cradle but there was no dial tone. She yelled for Nuci, bringing the woman running from her quarters and instructed her to stand by the phone and in the event her son-in-law called, Nuci should tell him not to do anything until Rima had spoken to him again. Then, dressing hurriedly she ran outside and jumped onto the security guard's motorbike and went to the Brigade's underground headquarters to access their communications. Upon arriving at the covert operation Rima began to panic when she discovered the building had come under siege by the Indonesian Special Forces.

* * * *

WASHINGTON

Miles Gardner listened, gob smacked as the U.S. NSA liaison officer apologized for his department's tardiness in forwarding the alert update on the Yemeni, Syafullah al-Yemeni's movements into S. E. Asia.

'You've had this for how long?' the Australian ASIS attaché searched the heading for a timing, 'my God, this intelligence is months out of date!'

'It was overlooked because it did not appear relevant to Australian interests.'

'But now you believe it does?' Gardner pressed, forever suspicious of the NSA for its history of misleading America's allies.

'Syafullah al-Yemeni was tracked into Thailand and we had no reason to believe that he was heading down your way.'

'But now you think you might have got it wrong?' he challenged. 'and this codename, 'Sword of Allah', what's the significance of that?'

'Again, at the time we interpreted this to mean an individual.'

'And now?' Gardner's eyes narrowed in anger. Something of urgency had prompted the Americans into revealing this intelligence, out of the blue.

The NSA officer squirmed considerably. 'I have been instructed to inform you that we now believe that the "Sword of Allah" could refer to a weapon.'

Gardner felt his insides roll. 'What type of weapon?'

The American avoided the Australian's eyes, 'Could be a nuke-sized suitcase bomb.'

The room went silent at the enormity of the statement, the

NSA officer leaving Miles Gardner speechless with the revelation that a nuclear weapon might have fallen into the hands of Islamic extremists, and could be heading for Australia's shores.

* * * *

DARWIN

'Don't cry, Johnny,' the child's father lifted him onto his shoulders, 'see if you can see the ships now.'

'I can't see anything!' the boy wailed, the father then carrying him to the rear of the pickup where he climbed up into the vehicle.

He sat Johnny on his shoulder and pointed out towards the horizon. 'They're they are, son, way out there!'

'I still can't see them,' the boy scanned the sea off Darwin Harbor, the aircraft carrier barely visible as the ships of the Seventh Fleet sailed away from the city to reposition twenty miles off the coast.

'Never mind, mate,' the youngster's father let Johnny slide down his side, 'I promise to bring you back again when they return.'

When the signal had arrived hours before, the ships had immediately pulled ropes, all leaving some of their complement behind. The message from the Commander-in-Chief, Pacific Fleet had been alarmingly concise, the Fleet's senior officers moving swiftly to protect the navy's assets from any potential strike.

BALI
Ngurah Rai Airport

Greg Young held his hand in the air momentarily to hold the

cabin steward in limbo then finished his call and turned off his cell phone, the Cessna Citation then taxi-ing out to the runway with Johanis Matuanakotta waving to Imam Suprapto as the pilot passed his line of sight.

Five minutes passed before Agus Sumarsono unbuckled and moved forward to see what was causing the delay.

'Minor electrical problem, Pak Agus,' Imam Suprapto informed, 'shouldn't take more than a few more minutes to rectify. Have an instrument playing up... nothing to worry about... can happen even to new aircraft from time to time. The tower has asked that we taxi back onto the apron so I'll move us over there and attend to the problem.'

Agus took it in typical stride and returned to his seat.

A further ten minutes dragged by when the passengers heard the telltale sounds of engines closing down, Agus then infuriated that this could happen to his new fifteen-million-dollar Citation.

'Pak Agus,' the pilot advised, 'that Cathay Pacific flight is leaving shortly,' he said, pointing across the tarmac, 'Do you want me to check if they have seats available?'

Agus scowled. 'So, you can't fix the problem?'

Imam Suprapto shook his head. 'I have called the ground engineer to check it out. We might be here for minutes but there again, it could be hours.'

'Sialan!' Agus cursed then gave the go ahead for the pilot to check with the airline.

Receiving confirmation that seats were available Agus' entourage boarded the Cathay Pacific flight leaving their baggage aboard the Cessna. Thirty minutes later they were in the air en route to Sydney.

Johanis boarded the aircraft infuriated with the change in

events, tinkered with the offending instrument light which, by chance, had gone on the blink as a result of his earlier tampering. The Cessna then departed for Sydney, forty-five minutes behind the Cathay flight.

AMBON

Not normally one to panic Rima found herself helpless with communications into Bali remaining down until mid morning. She was still unable to contact Johanis, Rima shocked to discover from the airport authorities that the aircraft had already departed.

Rima elected not to inform the Indonesian authorities. As a last resort she decided to contact the AIVD attaché to the Dutch Embassy at his home, guardedly informing him of the dilemma.

The attaché knew it would not be appropriate for him to phone the local or Australian authorities. Instead, he went into the embassy and dispatched an urgent communiqué to his superiors in Holland.

The information relating to the possibility that the Cessna may have been sabotaged was immediately buried by the AIVD as the agency's Director, when awakened in the early hours of Sunday morning, could see no benefit from alerting the Australian or Indonesian authorities.

DARWIN
Shoal Bay Intercept Station

Nick Dennison agreed with his subordinate's interpretation of the digitally recorded intercept transcripts between Ambon and Jakarta, the senior communications analyst immediately advising Defence in Canberra of the contents culled from the high-band radio frequency traffic between Ambon's warring factions and their respective contacts.

A copy of the prioritized signal was passed to the Prime Minister as he was about to enter Church for the late morning service, the contents turning the PM on his heels causing him to be whisked away for a hastily convened emergency meeting of the National Security Committee.

When the Prime Minister arrived at the meeting he was thunderstruck when briefed regarding the Washington attaché's revelations, those present unanimously agreeing that Agus Sumarsono's Cessna Citation was most likely carrying a lethal weapon destined for an Australian capital city.

The question was, *did Agus Sumarsono know?*

* * * *

The Jindalee Operational Radar Network (JORN) consists of two Over The Horizon Radar (OTHR) systems, one near Longreach in outback Queensland and the other near the Western Australia gold mining town of Laverton.

Capable of all weather detection of air and surface targets inside an arc of three-thousand kilometers in range extending from Geraldton on the West Australian coast across to Cairns in the far north-east, the network's Coordination Centre at South Australia's RAAF Base Edinburgh was jacked into high gear upon command.

Unlike conventional radar systems which work on the principle of line-of-sight, the OTHR system looks 'over the horizon', detecting objects that would otherwise be invisible.

As the system could detect low flying aircraft thousands of kilometers away by painting 'signatures' of its targets, Agus

Sumarsono's executive jet was identified within minutes and tracked as it crossed the Indian Ocean and headed for Broome.

CANBERRA

'Hasn't there been any radio contact with the pilot?' the Prime Minister wanted to know.

'Air traffic control centers have been in communication,' replied the Minister for Defence.

'Why don't we just turn the aircraft around?'

'What reason would we give? The flight has been cleared in advance.'

'Where is the aircraft now?'

'Approximately thirty minutes from the West Australian coast.'

'Does he carry enough fuel to make it to Sydney?'

'Yes,' the air force spokesman confirmed, 'but it would be tight. The flight plan submitted in Bali indicates that the aircraft will land and refuel in Broome.'

'Why not initiate a customs search there. If there is something nasty on board and it detonates then the collateral damage would be limited?'

'I agree,' the Attorney General concurred.

'Well I bloody well don't!' the Deputy PM snapped, immediately concerned he was in jeopardy of losing his constituents, 'there are twenty-thousand Australians living in the area.'

'What if the aircraft doesn't land there and heads directly for Sydney?' the PM continued, ignoring the leader of the minority in his coalition.

'We would know that within the next minutes.'

'Does the RAAF have any aircraft in the area?'

'Yes Prime Minister, two F18 Hornets were dispatched from Learmonth where they were participating in an exercise. They have refueled and are now in the air.'

'We need your decision as action is required now, Prime Minister,' the Chief of the Armed Forces insisted.

'What if we're wrong? Shooting down a civilian aircraft would have far reaching ramifications!'

'What if we're right and we permit the aircraft to enter Australian airspace?' the Minister for Defence argued.

'Destroying an Indonesian aircraft with one of their most influential citizens on board would be tantamount to more than just poking that sleeping tiger along our northern shores,' the Foreign Affairs minister warned, 'and we should expect retaliation.'

An aide entered the room and passed a folder to the Defence chief who cleared his throat then passed the contents to the Prime Minister.

'Gentlemen,' he watched the PM's expression change to one of puzzlement as he made the announcement, 'it would seem that Agus Sumarsono is not on the plane.'

'Will someone please explain what in the hell is going on?' The PM's voice filled the room.

'This doesn't reduce the risk in any way, Prime Minister,' the Defence chief asserted. 'If anything, his absence raises the probability that the aircraft is, indeed, carrying something sinister.' The general turned to the others present. 'Considering Sumarsono is not on board my recommendation is that we shoot the aircraft out of the sky and worry about recriminations later.'

'Is there any way we could keep this from the Indonesians?' the PM asked, hopefully.

'We could have the Hornets remove the target without the public learning of the action,' the officer responded.

The Prime Minister searched his colleagues' faces and knew that they concurred. 'Okay, General,' he dropped the Cathay Pacific passenger list onto the table, 'but let's have it done while the aircraft is still over the sea.' He paused then, 'and pray that this is the end of it all.'

INDIAN OCEAN – NORTH WESTERN AUSTRALIA

Upon receiving their instructions both RAAF F18 Hornets turned in the direction of their nominated target. Capable of speeds approaching 2,000 kilometres per hour and armed with AIM -7 and Sidewinder heat-seeking missiles the executive jet had no chance. In those last minutes as the Australian pilots roared towards the Cessna Johanis Matuanakotta's handiwork took control of the play.

Imam Suprapto's co-pilot was in communication with the Broome air traffic controller when the cockpit erupted into a ball of flame, the Cessna Citation disappearing from the radar screen, leaving bewildered Australian airmen to report that the aircraft had gone down without having been engaged.

* * *

Agus Sumarsono learned of the loss less than four hours later when, upon arriving in Sydney, he and Greg Young were met by cautious Australian officials and advised of the incident – the possibility that his aircraft had been carrying a nuclear device was never raised.

Agus stared at the Australian official in disbelief. 'Do you have any other information?' he asked.

'I'm sorry, Mister Sumarsono,' the Foreign Affairs representative offered, 'at this time all we are able to ascertain is that the aircraft malfunctioned in some manner and fell into the sea.'

'Were there any survivors?'

'We're still looking,' the official responded without conviction. 'Coast Watch and Search and Air Rescue have already commenced operations combing the area where we believe the Cessna went down.'

'You'll keep me posted?'

'If we learn anything you'll be the first to be notified.'

Greg Young glanced over at the man who had become his friend over the years and could see that the powerful figure was considerably shaken by the news.

'All I can say, Agus, is that we were both very, very lucky not to have been on board.'

Agus turned to Young. 'That thought has been foremost in my mind from the moment we were informed.' He flopped back into the limousine's seat as the approaching city skyline filled their view. 'If it hadn't been for that technical hitch back in Bali we would most likely both be dead.'

Young felt an involuntary shiver tremble its way down his spine. 'It might be that the two incidents are connected.'

Agus fell silent momentarily. Then, 'Do you think the aircraft might have been deliberately sabotaged?'

Young tilted his head to the side. 'Do you?'

Agus shook his head slowly. 'One makes many enemies along life's journey.' He peered outside as the vehicle left the freeway and headed into the central business district then down into the 'Rocks' area and the Hyatt Hotel, harbor side. 'Guess we'll find out more once they have the wreckage.'

MALAYSIA – KELANTAN

Derashid was taken by surprise when the call came through from Yemen; the Bulan Sabit chairman deeply concerned with the break in protocol as no communication had been prearranged.

'We wish to know what progress you have made,' Syafullah al-Yemeni inquired, 'and when the delivery will be completed?'

'This is an open line. I will call you back,' Derashid disconnected quickly then changed SIM cards before dialing the number in Yemen.

'Please don't do that again,' he warned.

'I won't, I assure you,' Syafullah apologized, 'it's just that we have associates who have family and friends in the proposed destination who are becoming anxious. We need to give them sufficient advance warning to ensure they remain safe.'

'It won't be long now,' Derashid promised, 'final arrangements will be in place very soon.'

'Then the Sword will strike!'

'Allah willing,' Derashid replied, and hung up.

MENWITH HILL – ENGLAND

'We've got him!' The U.S. intelligence analyst beamed, hurrying to report the Echelon intercept findings to his superiors.

Within minutes the information was relayed to Washington where details of the conversation were disseminated to the White House and the relevant intelligence agencies. Another hour passed before the decision was made for the Secretary of Defense to place his call to his opposite number in Thailand.

Meanwhile, on the other side of the globe U.S. Rangers were already airborne and within striking distance of their target near the Yemeni border.

MALAYSIA – KELANTAN

Derashid had been updating data on the Palm Pilot when the call came.

'They have captured Syafullah al-Yemeni!' the Saudi's shrill voice announced with alarm. 'You might not be safe!'

'They took him alive?' Derashid shuddered at the consequences should this be so. He had learned what had happened to Hambali once the former *Jemaah Islamiyah* operations commander had been taken to Diego Garcia for interrogation. The joint British-American facility operated as one of many CIA 'ghost prisons' and had become home to U.S. prisoners who, subsequent to their capture, had simply disappeared from sight.

'We don't have enough information but it would appear so.'

'If they have him in custody then we shall all fall!'

'What will you do?'

Derashid felt the chill envelop his body. 'It is something I have yet to consider.'

'May Allah be upon us all,' his old school friend wailed, Derashid disconnecting when he heard a commotion outside.

The ten-man "Night Stalkers" team, elements of the U.S. 160th Special Operations Aviation Regiment had crossed the Thai-Malaysian border aboard a MH-47 Chinook. Using night vision devices the air crew could operate at low altitudes with pinpoint navigation during the full darkness of night, the helicopter hovering above the rice fields two hundred metres from their target. Aided by the aircraft's fast-rope rappelling system the team had surrounded Derashid's villa within minutes.

Alsatian guard dogs alerted the Malaysian household to the presence of intruders. Derashid heard his security sound the alarm, his guards opening fire as they retreated into the villa under the onslaught. The "Night Stalkers" team had instructions to take Derashid alive, the siege ending with his death shattering the dream of a Pan Asian Islamic empire.

*　*　*　*

Chapter Seventeen

Jakarta

Anwar Suprapto's loss of his twin brother, Imam coupled with the illness that had beset the Garuda pilot was more than he could possibly bear. When he learned that some parts of the wreckage had been identified and the search for survivors had been terminated on the fourth day, Anwar had requested and was granted compassionate leave from work.

When, after a week following Imam's demise, an aide from General Supadi's Special Forces visited his accommodations and suggested that they take a ride, he obeyed but greeted the invitation with deep reservation. However, the suggestion that the General had important information relating to Imam's accident piqued his curiosity and he set his concerns aside. He was escorted to the General's residence, Anwar somewhat bewildered by the warm reception he received upon meeting with the Special Forces commander.

'My condolences at the loss of your brother,' the General shook Anwar's hand considerately, 'his, was a tragic death.'

'Thank you *Pak* Supadi. I still can't believe that he's gone.'

'He left family?' the General asked, even though he already knew.

'Yes, a wife and two children.'

'That will be hard for them.'

'Imam was no longer entitled to an air force pension.' Anwar's eyes swept the room. A *Kopassus* regimental flag hung listlessly in one corner, the walls covered with a black and white ménage of photographs reflecting highlights in the Special Forces commander's career.

'His life would have been covered by company insurance.'

'I spoke to the personnel officer at Bimaton. It appears that there is some dispute.'

'Dispute?' the General feigned surprise.

'Yes,' Anwar elaborated. 'There is some suggestion that the insurance company might deny the claim on the grounds that Imam should not have flown the aircraft out of Bali until he was certain that the technical problem that occurred, had been resolved.'

'That shouldn't affect his life insurance. What about Jamsostek?' Supadi inquired, referring to Indonesia's mandatory, massive superannuation fund with its fifty million members.

'That won't provide enough. We'll manage somehow,' Anwar's attention was drawn to a fading photograph intentionally positioned at eye level next to where he had been invited to sit. He leaned closer to the wall to examine the face then turned to the General with surprise written across his face. 'Is that my father?'

'Yes.'

'How...?'

'I knew your father,' Supadi revealed.

'May I?' he rose without waiting for the General's response.

Supadi watched the Garuda pilot closely as he held the framed picture in both hands. 'We bumped into each other from time to time.'

'Here, in Jakarta?'

'Yes,' the General raised his eyes to the ceiling in reflection, 'when he was at AURI headquarters in Gatot Subroto.'

'That was well before he was killed in Bangkok.'

'Yes, that was most unfortunate.' The General referred to the Garuda Indonesian Airlines DC-9 aircraft "Woyla", designated Flight 206, that had been 'hijacked' by five members of the *Komando Jihad* when en route from Jakarta to Palembang – and flown to Bangkok. Anwar's father had been the undercover air force officer killed when the Special Forces had attempted their rescue mission.

Anwar's face clouded. 'We never did receive a satisfactory explanation as to what he was doing on that flight.'

'And we most likely never will.' The General flicked a hand in the air relegating the past to diminished history. Nearby, the amplified call to afternoon prayers wafted in their direction.

Anwar replaced the photograph then returned to his seat. 'I was told that you wished to discuss my brother's accident,' Anwar reminded, not impolitely.

General Supadi's mouth firmed. 'It wasn't an accident.'

Anwar stared at the General in disbelief. 'I don't understand.'

'We have evidence that the Australians shot his aircraft down.'

Anwar shook his head vehemently. 'How could that be?'

'It's true,' the General's face a mask covering his mendacious side. 'RAAF fighters, we believe F-18s, were scrambled for whatever reason and were responsible for the aircraft going down.'

'How do you know?' Anwar struggled to understand.

'From our own intelligence sources both here and abroad.'

'Why would the Australians want to shoot down a civilian aircraft?'

'We don't know. There was a military exercise under way at the time so we can only assume that the Cessna strayed and was shot down in error.'

Anwar lifted his head with a jolt. 'The aircraft *did* have a malfunction before departing Bali.' He stared at Supadi. 'Do you think that the insurance people are right... that there's some connection?'

'The question remains, *was* it an accident or did the Australians deliberately destroy the aircraft believing Agus Sumarsono was on board?'

'What would *that* have achieved?' the Garuda captain asked, heatedly.

'There's been some conjecture but, to be honest, we don't really know.'

General Supadi observed the younger man closely gauging his response, cautiously manipulating the conversation through the confusing grey line separating supposition from fact. 'It has become apparent that the Australians are supportive of the separatist movements in Ambon and West Papua. Some of our analysts have suggested that the downing of the aircraft is part of a greater agenda to ensure the collapse of the Indonesian unitary state.'

Anwar coughed then rose angrily to his feet. 'And there'll be justice for my brother?'

'*Insha Allah* – God willing,' the General replied, the meeting ending soon thereafter with an invitation for Anwar to return.

* * * *

Upon Anwar Suprapto's departure General Supadi sat quietly considering what had transpired, confident that the toxic seed he had planted would germinate and grow in preparation for their next meeting. He unlocked the top drawer to a polished teak desk and removed the confidential folder containing Captain Anwar Suprapto's records.

These indicated that the Garuda pilot's flying career had been less than exemplary, and was imminently facing retrenchment.

General Supadi then made a call to the Garuda offices to ensure that this would not be so.

*   *   *   *

Shocked by the report of Mohammed Aziz Derashid's murder, Greg and Agus returned immediately to Jakarta. Agus Sumarsono's visit to Australia had been disastrous with the business community shunning invitations to attend discussions with the former Bimaton chairman, the mood soured by Agus' undiplomatic and vitriolic attack against BHP Billiton. On the day Agus was to speak at the Canberra Press Club the Sydney Morning Herald reported that the company had initiated discussions with separatist leaders in both the Moluccas and West Papua with respect to future resource acquisitions.

Greg Young was obliged to immediately examine his options considering the devastating collapse in fortunes for all associated with the Bimaton Holdings Group. When news broke of Derashid's death during what was described as a botched kidnapping attempt close to the Thai border, the Malaysian's untimely demise had naturally panicked bankers – Bimaton's accounts then temporarily frozen.

Across the Straits in Malaysia the Bulan Sabit conglomerate's administrators moved expeditiously to offload the Raja Seram Field investments, the financial albatross immediately optioned by the Japanese. Tokyo had offered to recognize the *Maluku Brigade* officially raising the stakes with Beijing in the race for the extensive oil and gas deposits.

CANBERRA

With the threat of a nuclear attack having been averted by the Bimaton executive jet's fortuitous loss, the nation's intelligence leaders pressed for stronger legislation. As the government controlled both the Lower House and the Senate, amendments to the *Security Legislation Amendment (Terrorism) Bill* and the *ASIO Legislation Amendment (Terrorism) Bill* were passed, ignoring strong opposition from Civil Libertarians.

A succession of ASIO raids were conducted across the continent resulting in a substantial number of arrests. However, the Lakemba, Saudi-linked cell was already abandoned when the troops arrived, a copy of Amir Subroto's *Studies In Jihad Against the Tyrants* the only evidence that an extremist group had operated there.

AMBON

Rima Passelima returned from Seram Island where the tide had turned against the Indonesian troops with the *Maluku Brigade* claiming control over the greater part of the province. Ambon remained a hostile environment with Jakarta's forces heavily entrenched, the number of casualties from both sides now having reached twenty-five thousand over the past month. Rima's NGO continued to play an integral role in providing support to the local population, her activities rewarded with an occasional drive-by attack on her offices by Jakarta-backed militia and *Laskar PAI* thugs.

She had been highly critical of Johanis' actions, deeply

relieved that Greg Young had not become another victim of the Moluccan separatist movement. Rima and Greg had talked briefly upon his return to Jakarta, Rima burdened with guilt when learning of his financial demise with the collapse of the Bimaton Group, conscious from their conversations that his spirit had been broken by the turn in events.

* * * *

JAKARTA

Anwar Suprapto stared through the rear window of General Supadi's Mercedes as Jalan Sudirman's buildings with their exaggerated portals passed slowly by – Anwar mentally bidding the city he had grown to love, farewell.

Having considered his doctor's prognosis Anwar decided that there was only one way he could escape his predicament. In consequence, he accepted the General's proposition; Imam's wife and children would be adequately cared for, the ten-thousand dollars to be paid to the family of Anwar's late-brother upon completion of the proposed mission. Philosophical with respect to ending his own life Anwar felt that at least he would have the satisfaction of knowing he would be punishing those responsible for Imam's death – whilst sending a clear warning to the Australian public as to what they might expect should their government continue to support the disintegration of the Indonesian republic.

He was scheduled to fly to Melbourne and Sydney the following week – the Boeing 777-300 with its three-hundred-and-seventy-passenger configuration most likely to be fully laden when, having refueled in Sydney, he would drive the aircraft into the city's centre.

TENTENA – CENTRAL SULAWESI

Jack McBride's chest swelled with pride as he lifted Netty's veil, the assembly erupting with applause when he gently kissed his bride.

'I will always love and care for you, Net,' he promised, lifting his voice so all present could bear witness, 'and with God's grace, our children.'

The couple turned with arms entwined and walked slowly along the aisle, smiling broadly as they exited the church, the sound of bells ringing surreal amidst the sectarian-torn environment.

Jack looked across Tentena's surrounding hills, the memory of all that had transpired leaving him with mixed emotions. He placed his arm around Netty and held her reassuringly. 'We will build a new life in Australia.' Jack and Netty McBride had accepted the offer to work at an Outback mission in Queensland's west, Jack proposing to Netty the month before.

Stepping outside they posed for the traditional photographs, an hour later the couple were whisked away by car to Poso where they caught the feeder flight to Menado, connecting to Bali, en route to Australia.

*　*　*　*

CHAPTER EIGHTEEN

BALI

Johanis Matuanakotta snorted abruptly, dragged the thick, sticky lump from deep in his respiratory tract and spat the phlegm in the direction of the catering crew slowly loading the aircraft. 'Lazy bastards,' he muttered to himself then impatiently checked his wristwatch, aware that the passengers were already boarding. 'Come on guys, let's get a move on!' he called, his demand falling on deaf ears as a British Airways flight landed, the scream of engines dominating the scene.

Johanis adjusted his sunglasses and moved closer to the loading vehicle anxious to see the back of this flight and an end to his day.

* * * *

'Would passengers leaving on Garuda GA953 to Melbourne and Sydney please proceed to Gate Fourteen as your aircraft is ready for boarding. Passengers…'

Andrew Graham emptied the Chivas with one swallow, gathered his briefcase and jacket then left the lounge, strolling with the casual gait expatriates acquire after years of living in tropical environments. He passed a row of eager shop assistants ignoring their entreaties as he wandered by, stopping at the Java Books' store to briefly examine the dust cover of a new Wilbur Smith release. Reminded that he would have little time for reading, as he had yet to put the final touches to his presentation for the Melbourne conference the following day, he handed the novel back to a disappointed assistant and continued on his way.

* * * *

'Are you Mister McBride?' the Garuda station manager asked as Netty and Jack were about to enter the aircraft.

'Yes,' the missionary replied, Netty with a worried look on her face.

'Ah, Mister McBride,' the affable manager flashed a broad smile. 'You and your wife have been upgraded.'

'Business?'

'No, first class,' the airline officer replied.

Netty's brow creased with surprise and she tugged her husband's sleeve in excitement. 'Oh, Jack, she did it!' A member of their Tentana parish had promised to call her brother who worked with Garuda.

'Thank you,' was all McBride could muster whilst accepting the new boarding passes.

The couple entered the Boeing 777-300 where they were ushered forward to their adjacent seats on the window and aisle.

* * * *

Anwar Suprapto ceased coughing, holding the handkerchief firmly at his mouth as he offered a muffled response to his co-pilot. 'I'm okay… just swallowed the wrong way.' He climbed out of the left hand seat and stumbled towards the toilet, locking himself inside where he convulsed with pain then threw up.

Long minutes passed before he managed to steady himself. Slowly, he washed splattered blood from around the basin then stood facing the gaunt, hollow-eyed image staring back from the mirror. Suddenly he lurched forward and vomited again partially filling the washbasin with blood.

It was then that Anwar knew he would not make it to Australia. And, if even if were able to sustain another attack there was the chance of his being declared unfit to fly whilst there, a risk he would not contemplate.

Anwar reached into a pocket for pain killers and spilled half of the prescription tablets into the palm of his hand then pushed these down his throat and waited. When he was satisfied that his appearance would not raise the crew's curiosity he returned to the flight deck and assumed the captain's seat, unlocking his briefcase he had stashed alongside.

* * * *

Johnny Matuanakotta had not bothered waiting for the Boeing to taxi out to the runway. His shift finished, the Ambonese engineer hurried away, tearing along Jalan Raya Tuban on his motorbike to make his appointment at a coffee shop on Kuta Square.

* * * *

Andrew Graham smiled at the passenger taking his seat directly ahead, the man's stony-faced response causing the American to drop his eyes and look away. Andrew accepted champagne from the stewardess, waited for her to pass then turned to the passenger sitting directly across the aisle.

'Couldn't help overhearing…where are you from in the States?' he asked.

Jack McBride emptied his glass of juice. 'Tennessee… and you?'

'Rochester.'

'New York?'

'Yep.' Andrew leaned forward indicating Netty. 'Wife?'

'Just married,' McBride winked, 'we're taking up a position with an Outback mission Down Under.'

Andrew smiled courteously and raised his near-empty flute. 'Congratulations...on the marriage and the new undertaking.'

Both then ceased talking when the intercom came alive with the chief purser's welcoming announcement. *'Selamat siang, para penumpang dan selamat datang dipesawat flight nomor GA953 tujuan Melbourne dan Sydney.Anda...'*

* * * *

Forward on the flight deck Captain Anwar Suprapto completed the final departure checks, his mind filled with a determination to complete his suicide mission and take his passengers to their death. 'Cabin crew please take your positions for take-off,' he heard the co-pilot's voice say, the three-hundred ton aircraft then slowly moving forward gathering speed as the huge, twin General Electric GE90-115B turbofan engines thrust the Boeing into life.

The aircraft shook as it raced down the runway, the terrifying thump as the plane took to the air unsettling passengers, many grasping armrests in fear.

Airborne, and to the surprise of the co-pilot Captain Suprapto turned the aircraft sharply from its designated course.

'What are you doing?' the co-pilot challenged, paling when Suprapto reached down with his left hand and produced the handgun he had secreted there.

'Pak Anwar?' the co-pilot's next words failing when he took a bullet to the chest and slumped dead.

The man sitting directly ahead of the two Americans heard the shot, the flight marshal immediately drawing his weapon and leaping towards the flight deck, falling off balance across the aisle when the pilot suddenly banked the aircraft hard. Jack McBride unbuckled and leapt forward – Andrew Graham searching behind trying to determine what was happening here.

Scrambling to his feet the air marshal banged at the cockpit door, McBride powering from behind raised his foot, the crushing kick revealing the co-pilot's expressionless eyes as he lay crumpled on the floor.

Anwar Suprapto did not hesitate. He fired at the air marshal hitting the man in the head, McBride lunging at the captain attempting to grapple the weapon from Suprapto's hand, the missionary hearing the shot then slowly back-peddling with hands to his stomach, a disbelieving look spreading across his face as he fell to his knees.

KUTA

Bali's Kuta seaside ambience ruptured with cacophonous roar when the aircraft barely cleared the coconut palms, the Boeing's engines screaming passage across the tropical, midday setting startling tourists from somnolent mood.

'Goddamn cowboy pilot!' someone yelled, the statement lost in the thunderous aftermath as spectators cranked necks skywards gaping, incredulously, at the low-flying, wide-bodied jet struggling to regain altitude.

In the time taken to address the intruders Suprapto had lost his opportunity, over flying his target. He tossed the huge aircraft dangerously from side to side as he set a new course, deciding to circle back from over the sea, unconcerned that pandemonium had erupted throughout the aircraft with passengers screaming, believing they were about to die.

Along Kuta's coastline tourists and vendors alike observed silently when the aircraft wavered then appeared to recover, banking towards the sea and away from the congested seaside community, those on the beach offering a compound sigh of relief as the Garuda flight disappeared on the Northern horizon.

On board Flight GA953 the pilot, Captain Suprapto, reassured by the sight of McBride and the flight marshal's prostrate bodies, turned the Boeing back towards the island, determined to take his three-hundred and eighty passengers to meet their destiny.

* * * *

McBride felt the cold deck against his cheek as he peered through half-closed lids. He could see the pilot divided his attention between the cockpit door and the course ahead. The aircraft bumped in low turbulence and he winced with pain, and he prayed silently, *God, just this one more time,* before summoning all his strength. He climbed to his feet, Anwar Suprapto succeeding in firing another shot hitting the American missionary in the shoulder, failing to prevent the American's huge hands from grasping his chin and near snapping Anwar's head from its torso.

The aircraft plunged, McBride ignoring the terrified, rolling screams from the rear. He pulled the dead captain from his seat and with excruciating pain tearing at his gut and shoulder, slowly lowered his own frame into place. Waves of darkness threatened consciousness as he searched the rows of instruments, his hands firmly on the controls.

In the distance of his mind he could hear a voice, McBride suddenly aware that he was hearing the Bali tower, air traffic controller's anxious calls and immediately grabbed for the dead pilot's headset. He looked up, recognized that the aircraft was dangerously low as it left the ocean and crossed Jalan By Pass, McBride slipping into unconsciousness with Netty's screams from the cabin behind pounding in his ears.

*　*　*　*

Johnny Matuanakotta looked up as he crossed the road in front of Café Dulang and earned a clipped elbow from a passing motorbike's wing mirrors for his trouble. He froze as the sight of the Boeing's four-story tail appeared barely seconds before the entire aircraft filled his view over the Matahari Store end of Kuta Square.

Then his world disappeared in a maelstrom of devastating proportions when the fuel-laden behemoth struck the market building then nose-dived, exploding into the tourist-filled square, the ensuing fireball cremating all who were there.

*　*　*　*

CHAPTER NINETEEN

Following the disastrous event in Kuta the Balinese tourist industry all but collapsed. Unemployment levels exceeded those recorded following the October 2002 bombings, foreign tourists abandoning the destination altogether as Indonesia moved closer to civil war.

The Australian government anxiously monitored the situation to the country's immediate north as support for the *Maluku Brigade* and the West Papuan OPM continued to gain momentum – Canberra now in secret discussion with the leadership of both separatist movements offering aid and defence cooperation packages should the birth of their nations become a reality. Washington increased its naval presence in Darwin, the port rapidly becoming the Seventh Fleet's Asian base of operations.

Rima Passelima's NGO received a substantial increase in Dutch government funding via one of its many, covert fronts operating out of Belgium, Rima's role even more significant with Ambon now under the Brigade's control. Weapons continued to flow into separatists' hands through obscure and nefarious channels, fuelling the rising tide of secessionism amongst the neglected ethnic minorities in Kalimantan, Sulawesi and to a lesser extent, North Sumatra.

Faced with rising dissent throughout the archipelago, the Javanese-dominated, Jakarta-based Indonesian government acquiesced and offered to revisit the concept of the unitary state being replaced with a more equitable commonwealth philosophy. Oil, gas, mining, timber and other resource-generating revenues would be more fairly split, the people of Bali immediately demanding a reversal in the policy which had seen ninety-five percent of the islands' income siphoned off into Jakarta's coffers.

With the increased probability that the secessionist movements in the Moluccas and West Papua might succeed, China substantially increased its naval presence in the area, precipitating the collapse of negotiations between Bulan Sabit Holdings and the Japanese over the acquisition of the Raja Seram Fields. Mohammed Aziz Derashid's empire was seized by the banks and sold off, scattering the assets amongst financial carrions throughout the region.

The Pan-Asia Islamic movement elected a new leader whose bellicose rhetoric resounded across ASEAN, sending shockwaves through Indonesia's two major Muslim parties, the *Nahdlatul Ulama* and *Muhammadiyah*, resulting in these more conservative organizations to withdraw their support for the militant PAI and its military arm, the *Laskar PAI*.

Al-Qaeda cells continued to grow in number across the southern Philippines, Malaysia and southern Thailand, whilst clandestine operational groups within Indonesia's military, the TNI continued to prosper with the *Laskar Jihad* reinventing itself – now operating as a more covert force in support of the once-marginalized generals.

Agus Sumarsono regained control over Indonesia's Bimaton Group through a leveraged buy-back and appointed Greg

Young as President Director. A condition precedent required by the group's bankers was that Bimaton divest itself of its holdings in the Raja Seram Fields operations. Young personally oversaw the liquidation of these interests which resulted in the corporation's substantial equipment inventory held in Darwin being liquidated and dispersed widely.

This action included the container housing the *Sword of Allah* which the Saudi network were obliged to abandon with both Derashid and Syafullah al-Yemeni both out of action.

Purchased as part of a 'job lot' based on Bimaton's general inventory holding lists, the container was given the most cursory of inspections before being stacked on board a rail freighter along with a myriad of other equipment, and shipped to Adelaide from where the deadly cargo was forwarded to a freight holding yard in Victoria.

*   *   *   *

EPILOGUE

KELANTAN – MALAYSIA

The village child sat idly drawing some abstract form with his toe in the soil. Bored, he decided to enter the partially-demolished villa to ask his father if he could return to the *kampong*. Inside, Samad bin Ahmad was rummaging through the rubble that had once been Mohammed Aziz Derashid's country retreat, the entire property declared off limits by the authorities subsequent to the raid.

'Boleh ikut Pak?' the child asked, seeking permission to help.

The farmer cast a furtive look outside concerned their presence might be detected by passing security patrols.

'Best you remain outside and call me if you see anyone coming.'

The child's face fell; the farmer reaching into his pocket and passing what he believed to be a play station, to his son. *'Here, keep yourself occupied.'*

The boy snapped the Palm Pilot from his father's hand and ran outside in glee.

The enhanced power source remained on standby waiting for a signal, blinking to life immediately upon command. An hour passed before the youngster could make any sense of how the instrument operated, annoyed and frustrated that he had been unable to determine how to access the games once he had turned the Palm Pilot on.

Stubbornly, he continued manipulating the buttons with his tiny thumb, the display screen suddenly coming alive with the comic face of a round cartoon character from Smiley Central. The boy's innocent eyes opened wide with surprise. He worked the controls with renewed vigor until inadvertently opening yet another file, the sword-carrying pixilated cartoon character that appeared with this action warning that the operator had but ten seconds to rescind the command.

The child sat mesmerized by the numbers as they appeared, rolling back from ten until reaching zero, the boy deeply disappointed when he blinked, and the program appeared to freeze then close down.

Thirty-six thousand kilometers above the equator, an earth-synchronous, geo-stationary communication satellite received the signal via uplink and sent the command on its way. Eight thousand kilometers to the south-east an interfacing-Palm Pilot sprang to life, first arming, then triggering the *Sword of Allah* as an unsuspecting driver shunted the container aside, in a Melbourne, inner-city freight yard.

*   *   *   *

Author's Notes

The Bali Bombings

That one of the world's most treasured tourist destinations came under terrorist attack on Saturday 12th October 2002 is an unfortunate historical fact. Almost half of the number of victims who perished were Australians, the single most devastating attack on Aussie civilians since the Japanese bombed Darwin during the Second World War. There can be no doubt that had our intelligence agencies understood the importance of the contents contained in the white Toshiba laptop discovered in the Dona Josef apartment fire in Manila in 1995, Hambali would have been arrested and the Malaysian terrorist cells would have been closed down.

Then the devastating September 11 attacks and the Bali bombings might have been prevented.

Bali was an obvious target as it represented Indonesia's soft-underbelly. There were overt warnings that demonstrated Bali had been identified for such an attack. There was obvious intelligence sadly overlooked by the Australian agencies. Headlines of articles posted to my current affairs site and a copy of the Department of Foreign Affairs Travel Advice issued primarily to Australian residents in Indonesia, are copied at the end of these notes. The Australian Consul in Bali also issued copies of the Jakarta embassy warnings to Australians living on the island. However, the original was altered at that time to suggest that Bali remained a safe destination *when it was obviously not.*

EXCERPT FROM 'ANTARA'-
INDONESIA'S NEWS AGENCY

Filipino Bomber Arrested in Bali.
Tuesday 19th September Sept 2000
Filipino arrested (Bali) over explosives

DENPASAR (IO) – Philippine national Hernandes Oscar Mercado was yesterday arrested by police officials at Ngurah Rai International Airport, Denpasar, after police discovered explosive material in his luggage. The arrest began when the x-ray detector at the airport found material in his bag. At first, police thought it was narcotics. But after they opened the bag, they discovered 10 kilograms of carbon, 10 kilograms of sulfur, and 0.5 kilogram of lime.
"If these were mixed in a certain proportion, they could explode," said an official with the airport. Mercado was then arrested. The Bali Police Office is now launching an investigation into the case. Bali Police Chief Brig. Gen. Wayan Arjana said his staff will launch an intensive probe.

*Author's Note: They never did.

*　*　*　*

Many continue to speculate as to the motivation and the identities of all those responsible for this tragic event and whether the United States had prior intelligence identifying the targets in Bali. It is significant to note, however, that in the period preceding the Kuta attacks the six-hundred strong American marine R & R rotation ceased without warning. The *U.S.S. Bellawood* was but one of the many American ships that had visited Bali in previous years with most of its three thousand complement frequenting Kuta's bars during their stay. Elements of the U.S. Seventh Fleet frequently sailed through Indonesia's waters. Ships from the *U.S.S. Kitty Hawk* battle group, the *U.S.S. Gary*, *U.S.S. Curtis Wilbur* and the *U.S.S. Kitty Hawk* aircraft carrier all involved in an incident relating to an Indonesian fishing vessel being swamped on Saturday 13th of October 2001, almost precisely one year to the day before the Bali attack. Analysts maintain that Paddy's Bar and the Sari Club were regularly crowded with marines on R & R from this battle group. Then, suddenly, American military presence on the island disappeared. There can be no doubt that sentiment regarding Australia's position with respect to supporting the Bush Family's determination to wage war with Saddam Hussein swung favorably in their direction following the Bali tragedy.

The real irony is that our participation in the Coalition of the Willing has delivered a gift of epic proportions to the Islamic extremist fringe and will most likely result in Australia suffering an attack of disastrous proportions.

* * * *

With the Kuta bombing, international intelligence services immediately laid the blame on al-Qaeda without first examining other, and less obvious terrorist groups such as the *Jemaah Islamiyah* and the *Laskar Jihad*.

ABU BAKAR BASHIR & JEMAAH ISLAMIYAH

In 1971, Abu Bakar Bashir an Indonesian citizen of Yemeni descent co-founded a puritanical Islamic boarding school near Solo in Central Java. That school still exists today. Suharto had Abu Bakar jailed from 1978 to 1982 for attempting to form an Islamic militia called *Komando Jihad*. Within months of his release from prison he was again convicted of subversive activities and, consequently, fled to Malaysia where he quietly went about gathering other Indonesians, Malays, Filipinos and Singaporeans who shared his vision for a Pan-Islamic state which would incorporate Indonesia, Malaysia and the Philippines. This was, in effect, the birth of the *Jemaah Islamiyah*, or Islamic Community group.

RIDUAN ISAMUDDIN (aka HAMBALI)

'Hambali', the nom de guerre of Riduan Isamuddin is a 39 year old Indonesian cleric who, prior to his capture was al-Qaeda's mastermind in South East Asia and the one who authorized the bombing of the Bali targets.

Hambali was born in Sukamanah, a village in west Java, in 1966. With Abu Bakar Bashir Hambali fled to Malaysia in 1985, fearing President Suharto's repression of hard line radical Islamic groups. From there, he traveled to Afghanistan and joined in the fight against Soviet Russian forces.

By 1990 Hambali and Bashir moved to Malaysia to recruit supporters from the predominantly Muslim country. Their intention, to build a network that would work towards the creation of a Pan Islamic State incorporating Indonesia, Malaysia and the Philippines.

It was Hambali, not Bashir, who first led the movement towards violence. By 1998 nearly 20 Malaysians had been to al-Qaeda's training camps in Afghanistan. Split into two cells for security, they began to look for possible targets. Eventually the group decided to attack a bus service for US servicemen in Singapore. In mid-1999 a 'presentational' video was made in the hope of convincing al-Qaeda to fund the operation.

Interrogations of *Jemaah Islamiyah* members arrested in Singapore have revealed that the al-Qaeda leadership used a Saudi Arabian charity to transfer substantial funds to Hambali. The Indonesian then used a Malaysian recruit who ran a clinical pathology company to purchase four tons of ammonium nitrate.

Hambali's cache has never been found and investigators believe only part of the explosives may have been used in the Bali bomb.

It was Hambali who arranged accommodation in an activist's flat in the Malaysian capital of Kuala Lumpur for two of the September 11 hijackers, Khalid al-Mihdhar and Nawaq Alhazmi. Hambali was arrested near the Thai-Cambodian border and surrendered to the United States. Currently he is being held on a joint American-British air base on the remote Indian Ocean island of Diego Garcia. The Indonesian authorities were not given access resulting in Jakarta's case against Abu Bakar Bashir with respect to his involvement in the Bali bombings being significantly weakened, resulting in a number of charges being dropped and a relatively light sentence being handed down on the guilty verdict.

Hambali's (*Jemaah Islamiyah*) forces, participated in the combined three-year killing spree in the Moluccas and Sulawesi obviously supported by the TNI's Special Forces, *Kopassus* who had the capacity to prevent the ongoing slaughter of unarmed Christians but ignored the atrocities, under instructions from Jakarta.

THE *Laskar Jihad* & JAFAR UMAR THALIB

Jafar Umar Thalib, a veteran of the Afghan-Soviet war has close links to former President Suharto's family, friends and cronies. He is known to have met with Osama bin Laden in Pakistan in 1987 and founded the fundamentalist Muslim *Laskar Jihad* (Allah's Holy Warriors) in 1998. The *Laskar Jihad* grew into a 12,000 strong, paramilitary force across the archipelago whose followers flooded eastern Indonesian provinces killing an estimated ten thousand Christians in the Moluccas (Ambon) areas.

Since Suharto stepped down in 1998, Jakarta's elite and powerful TNI leadership, who had enjoyed substantial material benefits during the dictator's reign, suddenly found themselves facing the prospect of being marginalized. Within months of the creation of the *Laskar Jihad*, there was a steady stream of powerful visitors to Jafar Umar's door including General Prabowo and Amien Rais. Jafar Umar preached his own brand of fundamentalist Islam, imbued with Indonesian nationalism, opposed to any break-up of the Republic making it a natural ally of the TNI. That the sectarian violence continued unabated, observed by the Special Forces, is a clear indictment of the TNI's role in supporting the sectarian violence as an end to maintain instability throughout the nation, with the purpose of encouraging the people to support a return to military rule.

On 9th May 2002, the day following the *Laskar Jihad's*

leader's arrest for inciting a massacre of Christian villagers in the Maluku Islands, Indonesia's Vice President of that time, Hamzah Haz visited the detained Thalib.

And yes, a charter plane carrying more than one hundred and thirty hardened, Mujahideen, Afghani troops *were* flown into Ambon and Sulawesi to support the Muslim militants in their fight against the Christians. A welcome desk at the Ambon airport did exist. One would have to question as to how a charter flight carrying foreign troops into the country was not prevented by Madame Megawati at that time.

THE LASKAR JIHAD LINK

Hambali returned to Indonesia after Suharto stepped down and immediately began recruiting local operatives. That Christmas, 20 bombs exploded almost simultaneously in nine Indonesian cities, killing 18 people, many of them in churches. Dozens more were defused or failed to explode. A series of suspects identified Hambali as the mastermind. In 2000 Hambali urged his followers to travel to the Moluccu islands in eastern Indonesia to join a brutal, long-running conflict between Muslim and Christian villagers, waged by the Laskar Jihad which, co-incidentally, closed down its website just hours before the Bali bombings, and disbanded.

According to Indonesian intelligence officials, more than 300 Indonesians were trained in al-Qaeda's camps in Afghanistan. Some have joined movements such as *Laskar Jihad* or *Jemaah Islamiyah*, but many more have simply gone to ground, meeting occasionally in small groups, staying in touch with more senior men.

The local muscle for the Bali bombs included several of these people.

Acts of violence perpetrated against religions and religious symbols are a fact of life in Indonesia today. Since the founding of the republic in 1945 up to the end of 2004, a total of 920 Christian churches had either been destroyed or extensively damaged by acts of violence, or prohibited or closed by authorities. This figure does not include parish rooms and houses, schools, kindergartens, convents, orphanages and other Church institutions destroyed during the same period. The rate of increase in the destruction is particularly alarming. Whereas just two churches were destroyed in the 21 years the first president, Soekarno, was in office, 456 churches were destroyed in the 32 years under his successor, Soeharto, 158 in the 17 months under B.J. Habibie, 232 in the 21 months under Abdurrahman Wahid and 68 in the first 29 months under incumbent President Megawati Soekarnoputri. These figures include the 192 churches destroyed or damaged since the beginning of 1999 along with 28 mosques in clashes in the Moluccan Islands and the Poso region of Central Sulawesi.

Sectarian violence and 'ethnic cleansing' continues throughout Indonesia's eastern provinces. It is estimated that approximately ten thousand have been killed over the past five years.

*　*　*　*

Others mentioned in Crescent Moon Rising

SYAFULLAH AL-YEMENI

The Yemeni national entered Indonesia by using a fake U.S. passport a few days before the explosions in Kuta, supervised the fine-tuning of the chemical mixture of the main Bali bomb to achieve maximum impact, leaving Indonesia just hours before the bombs were detonated. Syafullah is a senior al-Qaeda operative whose trail of terror goes back to involvement in the 1996 bombings of a U.S. military barracks in Dhahran, Saudi Arabia, which killed 19 servicemen. The United States government has been able to track and record Syafullah's movements raising the question as to why the Americans have never arrested this terrorist. *Could it be that Syafullah, not unlike Omar Al-Faruq, is not what he appears to be?*

OMAR AL-FARUQ

This is one of the most bizarre aspects of CIA operations in Indonesia. Indonesia's former BAKIN (State Intelligence Coordinating Board) chief, A.C. Manulang revealed that Al-Faruq is a CIA-recruited agent and if this is correct, the U.S. government funded the growth of the *Jemaah Islamiyah.*

Al-Faruq was 'arrested' in West Java on 5th June 2002 and flown out of the country in the CIA's now infamous Gulf Jet-stream. Al-Faruq was assigned to infiltrate Indonesia's Islamic radical groups. He entered the country as a refugee and married locally. He holds Kuwaiti citizenship and travels on a Pakistani passport. Al-Faruq testified that he had masterminded the plan to murder President Megawati and a number of bombings in Indonesia. He was whisked away on the CIA's Gulfstream V, aircraft number N379P, a covert operations referred to as *'Torture Air'* by those in the know. The aircraft is registered to Premier Executive Transport Services Inc, a CIA-owned shelf company.

The United States claims that they currently hold Al-Faruq in Guantanomo Bay.

MERV JENKINS

Merv Jenkins was a graduate from the Royal Military College in Duntroon. Two years after graduation he assumed command of an elite and highly secret group of commandos known as 660 Signal Troop which was responsible for providing communications for Australia's Secret Service ASIS agents overseas. Jenkins also served as the Commanding Officer of 72 Electronic Warfare Squadron in Queensland.

In 1996 he was posted to the USA as the DIO Attaché for North America.

His position required that he work to improve the information flow to the Americans who were, at that time, complaining that Australia was less than supportive. He liaised with the CIA and the U.S. Defense Intelligence Agency. The CIA believed that Australia had been holding back information on intelligence surrounding Suharto's regime and events in East Timor. They applied pressure. Coincidentally, at that time both governments were renegotiating the US-Australian joint spy base in Central Australia at Pine Gap. It was at this time that a young Australian DIO officer, Jean-Philippe Wispelaere flew into Washington from London carrying more than 1,000 high-resolution U.S. spy satellite photographs which he intended to sell. He had stolen these from the DIO offices in Canberra and had already offered the photographs to Asian interests. He had been lured to Washington by the FBI; his arrest of deep embarrassment to Canberra. It was at this time also that the militias in East Timor were on the rampage. The Americans pressured Jenkins for more information which in part, he delivered. When the CIA examined the intelligence they realized that Australia had, in fact, been holding back. Part of these revelations was a highly sensitive top secret report indicating that the Australian Army deliberately ignored intelligence reports about the impending massacre of East Timorese by Indonesian-backed militias. The Americans wanted to know why Canberra had been withholding information relating to Indonesian troop movements. The CIA applied pressure and former Colonel, Merv Jenkins was discovered dead on his 48th birthday, hanging from a rope in his garage in Washington. Later, one Captain Andrew Plunkett, a 3rd Battalion RAF intelligence officer revealed that Australian intelligence agencies had instructed his and other units to conceal evidence of war crimes by elements of the Indonesian Armed Forces and their militias.

FRED BURKS

Fred Burks is the U.S. State Department interpreter who was selected for the task as interpreter when Washington sent a delegation with a request for Jakarta to arrest Abu Bakar Bashir and surrender him to the United States. President Megawati received the Americans in her home. The meeting as reported in this story is basically accurate.

OMAR IBN AL KHATTAB

Omar Ibn al Khattab aka Khattab was born in Jordan to a tribe living near the border with Saudi Arabia. He fought in mainly Muslim parts of the former Soviet Union such as Tajikistan and Azerbaijan But it was in Chechnya that he made his name to the wider world, moving there in 1995 to fight Moscow's attempts to reclaim the separatist region, first in the 1994-1996 war and then after Russian troops returned in force in 1999.

Moscow says Khattab played a key role that summer in

leading a rebellion by Islamic militants in Chechnya's neighboring region of Dagestan. He founded a training camp for Islamic fighters along the lines of camps in Afghanistan.

He was killed by a poisoned letter slipped him by Russia's Federal Security Service (FSB).

RAMZI YOUSEF & KHALID SHAIKH MOHAMMED

Ramzi Yousef was instrumental in the bombing of the World Trade Centre. Khalid Shaikh Mohammed was the mastermind of the *Bojinka* operation who had been appointed by Osama bin Laden to command al-Qaeda's worldwide military operations and was number three in the terrorist hierarchy. They operated in the Philippines through the Malaysian front company, Konsojaya Sdn Bhd which, incredibly, failed to be spotted on either Kuala Lumpur's or the West's intelligence screen. These men plotted, successfully, attacks across the globe and were substantial supporters of the militant Islamic group, the *Abu Sayyaf.*

ALDAM TILDAO aka ABU SAPARA

Tildao inherited leadership of the Abu Sayyaf in the Southern Philippines. It is widely believed that his brief interrogation before being covertly executed yielded significant intelligence to the United States identifying Kuta bars as targets.

AUSTRALIA'S SPY STATIONS

The following list is the best unclassified shot at describing the locations of the ground-based "ears" of *Puzzle Palace* (The NSA) locations in Australia. It does not include the substantial number of listening units on vessels and aircraft or those operating from U.S. embassies, consulates, and other representative missions.

KEY:

1) Joint facility operated with a SIGINT partner. SIGINT = Signals Intelligence.
2) Joint facility partially operated with a SIGINT partner.
3) Contractor-operated facility.
4) Remoted facility.
5) NSA liaison is present.
6) Joint NSA-CIA site.
7) Foreign-operated "accommodation site" that provides occasional SIGINT product to the US.

Bamaga	6, 7
Cabarlah	7
Canberra (Defense Signals Directorate Headquarters)	5
Harman	7
Kojarena, Geraldton	1
Nurunggar	1
Pearce	1
Pine Gap, Alice Springs	1
Riverina	7
Shoal Bay, Darwin	1
Watsonia	1

ECHELON

Echelon runs a matrix of spy satellites, satellite and radio listening facilities, undersea listening devices and eavesdropping spy planes to monitor the world's phone, radio, telex, fax and internet traffic. Australia's contribution is a ring of powerful satellite and radio intercept ground stations. The main ones are at Pine Gap in Central Australia, Cabarlah in Queensland, Kojarena near Geraldton in Western Australia, Shoal Bay in the Northern Territory, and the newest, the DSD Riverina station near Wagga Wagga in NSW.

The Echelon worldwide network of powerful computers searches through masses of messages for pre-programmed addresses and key words. The intelligence services of each of the UKUSA countries pass these addresses and key words on to each other in the form of "dictionaries" reflecting concerns of the day. A telephone conversation, fax or email need only contain such words and names as "Hambali", "assassinate", "guerrillas", or names like "Syafullah", for the communication to be identified, recorded and analyzed. These listening stations are located at low latitudes to pick up every beam from the Intelsat satellites.

RADIO THERMAL GENERATORS AND SUITCASE BOMBS

In Georgia a search is underway for at least two of the devices, called radio thermal generators, or RTGs, believed to have been abandoned and then stolen after the closing of a Soviet military base. A few years ago woodcutters in northwestern Georgia suffered massive injuries after stumbling upon a similar device in the middle of a forest. The RTGs, used by the Soviets to power navigational beacons and communications equipment in remote areas, each contain up to 40,000 curies of highly radio-active strontium or cesium.

RTGs are self-contained power sources that convert radioactive energy into electricity. Compact and relatively small—Soviet models are between two and four feet in length and weigh between 400 and 1,200 kilograms—they are ideal for remote areas with little access to traditional fuels. The Soviets are known to have built more than 300 of the devices, most of them to power navigational beacons along arctic shipping lanes.

In Soviet-made RTGs, the device's core typically is a flashlight-size capsule of strontium 90, surrounded by thick lead to absorb the radiation. When the lead cladding is intact, the generator is essentially harmless. But if the shielding were missing or cracked, someone standing nearby would receive a fatal dose of radiation within hours.

Extract from the Jerusalem Report: October 25th, 1999 "Master terrorist Osama Bin Laden has acquired portable nuclear devices, a U.S.-based expert on non-conventional terror believes. The only real question now is whether Bin Laden has "a few," as Russian intelligence seems to think, or "over 20," a figure cited by Western intelligence services. Bin Laden's associates acquired the devices through Chechnya, paying the Chechens $30 million in cash and two tons of Afghan heroin, worth about $70 million in Afghanistan and about 10 times that on the street in Western cities." 1998 testimony by former Russian security chief Alexander Lebed to the U.S. House of Representatives. Lebed said: "that 43 nuclear suitcases from the former Soviet arsenal, developed for the KGB in the 1970s, have vanished since the collapse of the former Soviet Union a decade ago. One person could detonate such a bomb by himself and kill 100,000 people."

INDONESIA'S SPY AGENCIES

BAKIN

(Badan Koordinasi Intelijen), the Indonesian State Intelligence Coordinating Agency was created by President Suharto in 1967 subsequent to seizing power from Sukarno. Staffed at the most senior levels by serving or retired officers it was feared for its brutal and malicious political intervention against political opponents. BAKIN regularly mounted both domestic and international operations in support of the presidency. Amongst these, the successful penetration by the agency's agent provocateurs of the *Komando Jihad,* (Holy War Command), eventually taking charge of that organization and turning it, ironically, into a militant band of thugs and murderers. The philosophy behind the operation was to create widespread publicity to the re-emergence of radical Islam in the belief that Indonesians would be reluctant to identify with any form of political Islam. The security forces then used the *Komando Jihad* scare to haul in suspected critics of the government.

BIA

(Badan Intelijen Strategis, Strategic Intelligence Agency), on the other hand, reports to TNI Headquarters (Mabes TNI), especially to the Commander-in-Chief (Pang TNI). It is left to him which intelligence he passes on to the President.

BIN

Badan Intelijen Nasional – Replaced BAKIN

INDONESIA'S SPECIAL FORCES

KOPASSUS units were involved in 1981 in freeing the hostages from the "Woyla," the Garuda Airline plane hijacked by followers of Imran, leader of an Islamic splinter movement in West Java. Imran forced the plane to land at the Don Muang Airport in Thailand. These Special Forces are trained in intelligence gathering, a variety of special operations techniques, sabotage, and airborne and seaborne landings. KOPASSUS soldiers are easily identified by their distinctive red berets.

Former strong man President Suharto's son-in-law Colonel Prabowo Subianto was appointed command of the 6,000-strong force in December 1995.

In 1997 the three top positions at the Indonesian Armed Forces headquarters were held by KOPASSUS Special Forces officers. This "domination" of the upper ranks at ABRI Headquarters had never happened in preceding periods. KOPASSUS is associated with human rights abuses and "disappearances" which have been documented by respected human rights organizations and the Indonesian government.

Beginning in early 1999 a campaign of systematic liquidation of the resistance was under way in East Timor, forcing thousands of people to flee into the jungles. The operations were backed by at least a section of the Indonesian armed forces and intelligence service, notably KOPASSUS. In the countryside, village chiefs in favor of independence were systematically liquidated, and even villages considered not enthusiastic enough for autonomy, were destroyed.

Chronological List of Selected Headlines from Indonesian Articles Posted to the Author's Current Affairs Site leading up to the Bali Bombings

YEAR 2000

Sunday	18th June
	"Bali – 2 Dead, 3 Shot by Police"
Sunday	23rd July
	"Bali – 1,000 Police Guard Fuel Stations"
Monday	21st August
	"Bali – 13 Europeans Arrested in Bali for Drugs"
Tuesday	29th August
	"Bali – Police Open Fire – 1 Dead, 6 Hurt"
Wednesday	13th September
	"Jakarta's Stock Exchange Bombed kills 15"
Tuesday	19th September
	"Bali – Filipino Arrested over explosives"
Tuesday	19th September
	"Article stating that Bali is Indonesia's 'soft underbelly' and would be a likely terror target"
Thursday	21st September
	"Bali Island & Aussie Embassy listed as targets"
Tuesday	24th October
	"Nuclear Materials stolen in Indonesia"
Sunday	29th October
	"Muslims Order Hotels to bar Americans"

Monday	30th October
	"Indon Military sweep hotels in Java demanding American guests leave the country"
Thursday	9th November
	"Bali Mob Attacks Worldwide Fund for Nature"
Tuesday	12th December
	"1 Killed, 2 wounded in Bali clash"
Saturday	16th December
	"Investor Killed in Bali"
Sunday	24th December
	"14 Arabs Detained at Bali airport heading for Australia"
Monday	25th December
	"Explosions Rock Indonesia at Xmas"
Thursday	28th December
	"U.S. Warns its citizens NOT to visit Indonesia"

YEAR 2001

Friday	5th January
	"9 Massacred in Lombok next to Bali"
Monday	8th January
	"Lombok – Bomb Explodes"
Sunday	14th January
	"British Government Warns citizens in Indonesia"
Tuesday	16th January
	"Pres. Wahid accuses Gen. Prabowo of bombings"
Thursday	15th February
	"Bali Student Demonstrations"
Wednesday	18th April

"Suicide Squads Flood Jakarta"

Thursday   24th May

"Australian Artist murdered in Bali Burglary"

Tuesday   2nd June

"Japanese woman Murdered in Bali"

Thursday   2nd August

"Indonesian Police find explosives cache"

Saturday   18th August

"Australia urges its citizens to 'take care' in Indonesia"

Friday   21st September

"U.S. Warns on travel to Indonesia after Sept 11 attacks"

Sunday   16th September

"Osama bin Laden now operating in Indonesia"

Tuesday   18th September

"Osama linked to Laskar Jihad in Indonesia"

Friday   21st September

"Canberra upgrades Indonesian Travel Alert"

Friday   28th September

"U.S. Warden Notice urges citizens to leave Indonesia including Bali" – *"All U.S. Govt personnel in non-emergency positions urged to leave Indonesia"*

Friday   28th September

"Australian Govt refuses to follow U.S. in urging its citizens to leave Indonesia"

Monday   8th October

"Australian Embassy in Jakarta Special Bulletin to citizens living in Indonesia". It should be noted that this bulletin does not specifically

mention Bali as being safe whereas the
Australian Consulate version has amended
this original to allude to the fact that they
considered Bali as being safe.

Monday   8th October
*"Australian Consulate-General in Bali Travel
Advice stating that 'All Australians should
consider deferring all holiday and normal
business travel to Indonesia, **excluding Bali**'.*

Sunday   14th October
"Britain warns against travel to Indonesia"

Tuesday   16th October
*"Australian Govt issues renewed travel warnings
for Indonesia with the exception of Bali"*

Thursday   18th October
*"Laskar Jihad calls for Holy War against U.S.A
& Allies"*

Wednesday   7th November
"Grenade Blast rocks Aussie School in Jakarta"

Wednesday   21st November
"Al-Qaeda terrorists trained in Indonesia"

Tuesday   27th November
"Fifty Indonesians captured in Afghanistan"

Saturday   15th December
"Laskar Jihad militias Sweep Indonesia's east"

Wednesday   19th December
"Garuda Bomb Threat on flight to Bali"

YEAR 2002

Tuesday | 13th August
"Brussels-based Think Tank warns of TNI backing for JI"

Saturday | 17th August
"Australian Govt issues renewed travel warnings for Indonesia with the exception of Bali"

Sunday | 8th September
"Militant Muslims launch Sweeps against Foreigners"

Wednesday | 11th September
"U.S. Closes Jakarta Embassy due to threats"

Friday | 13th September
"Muslims attack in Lombok next to Bali"

Friday | 13th September
Australian Consulate-General in Bali circulates updated travel advice amongst Australian citizens living in Bali. Copies are not disseminated to the general public in Australia nor to travel or tour groups. Bali is specifically mentioned as being safe in this release.

Thursday | 19th September
"Australian Consulate-General in Bali issues warnings on terrorist activity throughout Indonesia but specifically nominates Bali as safe"

Thursday | 19th September
On the same day the Consulate updated its travel advice the following appeared in the morning papers in Indonesia. "Al-Qaeda

network in Indonesia – Philippines' arrest reveal Hambali has acquired more than 1.2 tonnes of explosives for use in attacks on Jemaah Islamiyah targets."

Saturday 21st September
"U.S. Embassy in Jakarta issues Bali travel warning and possibility of Laskar Jihad attacks"

Tuesday 24th September
"Indonesians deny presence of Al-Qaeda terrorists"

Thursday 26th September
"1000s of militant Muslims declare Holy War in Java rally"

Friday 27th September
"Indonesian Military, TNI admits terrorist network is operating in Indonesia"

Tuesday 1st October
"Mob burns mosque in Lombok next to Bali"

Monday 7th October
"Radical Muslims arrested in Jakarta over bombings"

Tuesday 8th October
"Muslims attacked in Lombok adjacent to Bali"

Saturday` 12th October
Bali Bombings

COPY OF THE AUSTRALIAN EMBASSY TRAVEL ADVICE FOUR WEEKS PRIOR TO THE BALI BOMBINGS
(Circulated to Australians living in Indonesia but not the General Public in Australia)

TRAVEL ADVICE: INDONESIA

The Advice was issued on Friday 13 September 2002 EST
This advice has been reviewed. It contains new information or advice but the overall level of advice has not been changed.

In view of the ongoing risk of terrorist activity in the region, Australians in Indonesia should maintain a high level of personal security awareness. Australians should avoid travel to west Timor (outside of Kupang), Maluku and North Maluku, and Aceh. Australians in Papua (Irian Jaya) and North Sulawesi should exercise caution and seek current information from the Australian Embassy prior to travel. The recent attack on foreigners in the Freeport Mine area underlines the need for Australians in Papua to monitor developments that might affect their safety. Australians in Poso, the middle of Central Sulawesi, should avoid inter-provincial and inter-city bus travel and exercise caution following recent attacks on passenger buses. Tourist services elsewhere in Indonesia are operating normally, including Bali.

SAFETY AND SECURITY

Australians in Indonesia should monitor carefully developments that might affect their safety. Demonstrations occur from time to time, particularly in Jakarta. Australians should avoid large public gatherings and be alert to their surroundings.

Bombs have been exploded periodically in Jakarta and elsewhere in the past, including areas frequented by tourists. Further explosions may be attempted. In view of the ongoing risk of terrorist activity, Australians should maintain a high level of personal security awareness at all times.

All travel to west Timor (outside of Kupang), Maluku and North Maluku should be avoided until further notice. In particular, a high level of security alert remains for west Timor, following attacks on United Nations personnel there. Foreign nationals are prevented from entering Maluku (especially Ambon) under civil emergency law. The situation in North Maluku is unsettled. Violent incidents continue in Aceh and Australians should avoid travel to the province.

In light of a recent attack on foreigners in the area of the Freeport Mine in Papua (Irian Jaya), Australians in Papua should exercise caution and monitor local developments that might affect their safety. Prior to travel, Australians should seek current information from the Australian Embassy. Police permits are required for travel to Papua (except Jayapura and Biak)and should be sought well in advance of travel.

The security situation in Central Sulawesi has deteriorated and sporadic clashes continue. Australians in Poso, the middle of Central Sulawesi, should avoid inter-provincial and inter-city bus travel and exercise caution following recent attacks on passenger buses.

Following recent combat operations in the Southern Philippines, Australians are reminded of the Abu Sayyaf terrorist group's practice of kidnapping foreigners in South Western Philippines, near Indonesia. This practice poses a potential risk to foreigners in areas close to the Philippines, such as North Sulawesi and in particular the outlying islands. Australians should exercise caution and seek current information from the

Embassy prior to travel.

Tourists traveling to Mt Rinjani, in Lombok, have been the target of criminal activity. Australians should get advice from the local authorities and only use a registered guide.

Tourist services elsewhere in Indonesia are operating normally, *including Bali*. Further information on developments within Indonesia may be obtained from the Australian Embassy in Jakarta.

GENERAL

Australians in Indonesia are required to register with the local Rukun Tertangga (RT) Office, the local police and if staying more than 90 days, the local immigration office. Australians are also required to carry proper identification [Australian Passport or Kartu Ijin Tinggal Sementara (KITAS) or Residents Stay Permit] and ensure their visa remains current at all times.

There have been a number of incidents where Australians in and around Jakarta have been robbed after having their car tyre deliberately punctured. In these situations it is best to remain in the vehicle, with all doors locked, while the tyre is being changed. Australians should consider hiring taxis from reputable firms, either by phone or from stands at major hotels, following threat and assaults being committed in taxis.

HEALTH ISSUES

For information on prevalent diseases and inoculations, travellers should consult their doctor or a travel clinic. Contact details for travel clinics can be found in our 'Travelling Well' brochure available on the department's website.

TRAVEL AND HEALTH INSURANCE

Travel and medical insurance is strongly recommended for all overseas travel. Travellers should check with their insurer to make sure that their policy meets their needs. In particular, travellers should be aware that some insurance companies will not pay claims which arise when travellers have disregarded the Government's travel advice.

CONSULAR ASSISTANCE AND REGISTRATION

Australians should register and may obtain consular assistance from:

Australian Embassy
Jalan H R Rasuna Said Kav
C 15-16 Jakarta Selatan 12940 Indonesia
Telephone (62 21) 25505555 Facsimile (62 21) 5261690
Website http://www.austembjak.or.id/news

Australian Consulate General
Jalan Prof Moh Yamin 4 RenonDenpasar Bali Indonesia
Telephone (62 361) 235092 Facsimile (62 361) 231990

Limited consular assistance, which does not include the issue of Australian passports, may be obtained from:

Australian Consulate
Jalan R A Kartini
32 Medan 20152 North Sumatra Indonesia
Telephone (62 61) 4157810Facsimile (62 61) 4156820

The Department of Foreign Affairs and Trade also offers an on-line registration service, accessible via the internet, at http://www.orao.dfat.gov.au

The Department of Foreign Affairs and Trade in Canberra may be contacted on: (02) 62613305.

Australian Consulate General Bali
tel - (62-361)235092
fax - (62-361)231990

Copy Of Declaration Of
Independence For The Moluccan Republic

Republik Maluku
(Republic of the Moluccas)

An Independent Moluccan State By Virtue Of The
Right Of Self-determination?

translated 10.06.93
Secretary homeland mission 1950
P.O. Box 53
6980 AB Doesburg, The Netherlands
Telephone/Telefax 08334-7 53 88

On April 25th 1992, a new Government, The Government of
the Republic of the Moluccas in Exile has been formed, with
Mr. J. Sounauwe as President.

This new Moluccan government in exile is formed on the
initiative of the of the Moluccan political organisation "Homeland Mission 1950". The main aim is to obtain the independence of the Republic of the Moluccas.

After the transfer of sovereignty from the netherlands-
indies to the united states of indonesia in december 1949,
an internal strive between the unitarian group and the
federalists began. The unitarian group was aimed at a
unitarian state while the federalists stood by the decision
made during the round table conference (r.T.C. - Treaty)
august 3rd - november 2nd 1949; determining that
indonesia will become a federate state. Several federate

states joined the republic of indonesia, which had the disposal of the strongest military troops. Only the federate state east-indonesia left over, of which the moluccas made a part.

On april 25th 1950, the republic of the south moluccas was proclaimed in ambon, capital city of the republic of the south moluccas.

* * * *

Kerry B. Collison
Melbourne
October 2005